Published by Jelly Bean Press
PO Box 548
Osawatomie, Kansas 66064

Copyright ©2016 by Nichole Giles
Edited by Heather Justesen
Cover design by Melissa Williams Design
Cover photograph by Fresh Stock via Shutterstock
Author photo by Erin Summerill

ISBN: 978-1-63034-020-9

Nichole Giles's author website is http://nicholegiles.blogspot.com

LEGACY

NICHOLE GILES

JELLY BEAN PRESS

LEGACY

NICHOLE GILES

JELLY BEAN PRESS

For Madison, who is wise beyond her years.
And for Mckay, who is braver
than he knows.

No matter where life takes you, home will
always be found in the arms
of your family.

The New Generation Has Risen.

ONE

Runaways

ABBY

The air in Houston is muggy and hot. With the absence of the sea breeze to which I've grown accustomed, sweat drips between my shoulder blades and glues the back of my T-shirt to my skin. Even my eyes feel sticky as I follow Kye to baggage claim.

I slept for most of the drive through the Mexico jungle, and again on the plane, but it's been restless sleep at best, and nothing like the Healer's sleep that usually incapacitates me after a major healing ordeal.

We've actually done it. We've run away. The first time I considered running away with Kye was in New York—after we'd already left our homes and families so suddenly. Back then I thought this experience would be as easy as that trip, when we were able to keep in touch with our families, visit people we knew, and expect that our travels would eventually bring us home. I was unquestionably in love with Kye, and he with me. We were stupid enough to believe that running away together would make us happy, despite the curse that would eventually kill us, and a demon army on our heels.

Now ...

We've hardly exchanged more than five sentences since we left our parents behind in Mexico.

Ironically, as I boarded the plane—and pretty much ever since—all I can think of is how Gabe will react when he wakes up and finds out that I'm gone. No goodbye or explanation. I couldn't even leave him a note. Just gone. Maybe forever. My chest throbs with an ache that's different from any other I've experienced, and is wrapped in anxious confusion—which doesn't help anything.

The commuter foot traffic is in full swing as we loop toward the turnstile. Frowning, Kye glances back and offers me his hand. He hasn't touched me once since we left. Another thing I never expected would happen. The last time we traveled together, he held my hand—held me—through everything. Now it's like there's a wall between us. One we're both holding up from our respective sides.

His brows knit together as if he's experiencing a similar variety of panic, but he keeps hold of my hand and tows me forward. After we've claimed our luggage, we get in line to go through customs, exchanging awkward glances. "Now what?" I finally ask, because the silence only makes me feel more lost.

His jaw tenses in the familiar way I've seen so many times as he snaps out of lost-puppy mode and back into himself. "Rental car, I guess. Unless you want to fly somewhere else?"

"We can't afford Ireland, can we?"

"Not ..." he hesitates. "Probably not a last minute ticket. Not without using the platinum card. Overseas travel is crazy expensive when you plan it in advance. You don't want to know what it costs to get a same-day fare. It would cost more money than we have, and might not get us home."

Disappointment balls inside me. Kye's college fund is limited, and it's our only source of funds. It won't last long. It's wrong of me to ask about Ireland as if it's a possibility. But I stick my hand in my pocket and crinkle the slip of paper on which my father's address is written, and the only thing I can think is that if I can find him, everything else will be better. He'll know the answers to my questions. He'll be able to fix everything wrong in my life, including my relationship with Kye.

LEGACY

Out of necessity, I set aside my longing to immediately follow this lead, and remove my hand from Kye's to check my new travel documents—the ones that claim I'm twenty-two and share a last name with him. "We should drive then. Any thoughts about where?"

"South." He runs his hand through his hair, and I'm relieved by the familiarity of the gesture, the spark of home it hits inside me. "I know someone down the coast. She's not connected to the Dragons anymore, and might be able to help us."

She doesn't sound like someone I want to meet. Especially not now, when I'm feeling insecure and vulnerable. "How can she help us? What do we need help with? What are we doing, Kye?"

His sigh is one of supreme annoyance. "Surviving, Abby. Okay? The most important thing right now is for us to have a single destination where we can get our crap together and work out what's next." Frustration rolls off of him like waves over a beach.

Outside, the purple sky dazzles with the sparkle of early evening stars. I'm careful to keep my voice even. "Why don't we find somewhere nearby for the night? We can rest. Get some dinner. No one's following us yet, and we'll both do better after sleeping."

He leads me past a sign that directs travelers to the rental car counters. "Yeah. Okay."

Without a reservation, we're forced to take what's available, and the man at the counter assures us that the convertible he offers is the *only* car he has. I highly doubt that, and I tell Kye as much, but after a debate, Kye accepts the convertible and signs the papers.

"It's too expensive," I insist. "Let's try another company."

He squeezes his eyes shut and hands them his platinum card. The one we shouldn't be using.

"Kye," I say louder. "That's the wrong one. They'll find us."

He replies with a curt shake of his head as if trying to be discreet, and then asks the attendant. "If I pay for today using cash, will you not charge this until tomorrow?"

"I'm sorry sir," she says. "I have to run it before you take the car, and we don't accept cash without a credit card."

He hands it over. "Sorry babe. You can sleep while I drive."

And just like that, it hits me that we're still running. Until whenever *he* decides it's safe to stop. We *can't* use the card to go to Ireland, but we *can* take a chance using it on a rental car. We have nowhere to go, no plan, except that Kye has a friend in a town somewhere near here, and he seems dead-set on seeing her.

Joy.

We find the car—a metallic green mustang convertible—and load our suitcases in. Kye closes the trunk and turns to me with a bleak, vulnerable look. "Are you sure you want to do this Abby? Keep running with me? I can take you home if you want. To Jackson."

I don't know how to answer him. I do want to go home, and I also want to be with him, but I'm so confused. I've never been so confused in my life. "We need to stick together."

"I know." He edges me back against the passenger side of the car, with him inches-that-feel-like-miles away. "But that's not what I'm asking. Do you want to be here? With me? It's not our ideal situation. Believe me, this is not how I envisioned us starting a life together, but I'm here *for you*. Because *of you*. I admit, I'm angry. And hurt, and—yes, crazy jealous about Gabe—but everything else aside, I love you. I'll do anything and everything I can to protect you. Whatever else has changed, that hasn't. Not even a little bit."

"Kye, I ..."

He moves closer and his body—a fraction of an inch away— brings mine to life from sheer proximity. "I want you to know ... even if you don't want this, want me—in that way—it's okay. I'll protect you to the death, regardless of where we go or what happens."

My whole body shakes with need, but I can't move, can't scale the invisible wall between us.

"And if you want—if you really want—I'll take you home."

"I don't want to go home."

"But you don't want to be with me either, do you?"

4

"I don't know, Kye, okay? I haven't had time to think since ... since our fight. Since the cenote. Since anything. Given that I Healed Gabe less than a full day ago, it's a miracle I'm awake right now, let alone upright and semi-functioning." He swallows, and the movement of his throat reminds me that he's hurting too. I soften my voice. "I do love you. That hasn't changed because I'm upset. I need to rest, to chill. We both do."

He takes a long, drawn-out breath. "You're right. I'm sorry. I have a terrible habit of pushing you at the worst possible times." He opens my door. "We can't stay in Houston or they might find us, but there are small towns everywhere in this state. The Dragons will have no way of knowing which way we've gone until we use that card again—which we're not going to do."

"Are you sure they won't look for you at this person's house? If they know you have a friend in Texas, it would make sense. We just left evidence that we rented a car here. Won't her house be the first place they look?"

"They don't know we're friends." His attention falls to our feet. "And I'm pretty sure she's off the radar. For now."

Uncertain how to take his comment or the hidden nuances woven into his response, I slide into the seat, appreciating the comfort of butter-soft leather. I dig out an elastic from my purse so I can tie back my hair while he figures out how to work the car's gadgets. "Where are we going, exactly?"

He adjusts the rearview without looking at me. "Toward San Antonio. We don't have to stop at Kiersten's, but it would save money, and she might be able to help us find information about your dad."

"Who is she?"

"I told you. An old friend." He puts the car in reverse and backs out of the stall. "Haven't seen her in years, but she'll be discreet. I know she'll help us."

Because of how he says it, and the guilty look in his eyes, I'm pretty sure *good friend* has a different meaning than I want to consider, but I'm too exhausted to fight about it. "Fine."

We grab fast food on our way out of town, exchanging only the most necessary words. When I can no longer take the silence, I turn on the stereo, searching desperately for something to fill the awkward space that has never before existed between Kye and me. I lean my head back, eyes closed, and breathe in the sticky air as it rushes past. This, at least, I can appreciate.

After two hours of driving, the car slows and I open my eyes as we pull into a hotel parking lot. It's not the Marriott in Times Square, or any of the hotels in Las Vegas. Just a small-town version of a bigger chain, and a small one at that, but the sight of it almost brings tears of relief to my eyes.

"This is far enough for tonight," Kye says, parking near the door.

I swallow a lump in my throat. "Thank you."

Since our IDs claim we're married, and since we're now relying solely on Kye's savings for an indefinite amount of time, there's no point in getting two rooms, though I'd love some space to myself so I can take a breath. Think.

Once we're checked in, I follow Kye to our room, dragging my suitcase behind me. He opens the door and waves me ahead of him. I stumble to the bed and fall backward onto it to stare at the ceiling. Kye's face appears above mine. "You okay?"

I nod. "Exhausted, but I'll live."

His smile eases some of the tension between us. "I hope so. If you didn't, I couldn't." He sits next to me and runs his fingers down my jaw, across my cheek. "I thought it would be good to have some time alone. We should talk before we get to Kiersten's."

We've been alone since we left. My gut twists with anxiety, and I can't prevent the catch in my voice. "More confessions?"

His fingers continue to trace my collar bone and shoulder. "No. We need to make a plan, decide where we're going—what comes next. Sleeping arrangements." He glances meaningfully at the pillows. "Didn't occur to me until now that maybe I should ask for a double. We've been sharing for long enough that I assumed."

I close my eyes, too exhausted, too confused to seriously think about anything right now. The truth is that more than anything else, I need to be held. Our lives have been turned upside down and inside out. We've left behind everything and everyone we've ever loved except each other—and we have no idea when we'll see any of them again—if ever. He's all I have, and I'm all he has. Regardless of past hurts and mistakes and issues, we're going to have to learn how to let go and depend on each other, regardless of whether we want to be together the way I once thought we would.

My lack of response has him sighing as he stands. "I'm going to take a shower. Do you need to get in the bathroom first?"

"No, go ahead." I don't move except to turn my head and watch him go. Everything about him screams misery—frustration. The cure for his frustration could come from me, but I don't know how to give it to him. Not in my current state of mind.

When he comes out twenty minutes later with wet hair, wearing his flannel pajama bottoms and a T-shirt, I'm still lying in the same spot. He pauses next to me, a bemused expression lighting his eyes. "It's all yours. If you want it."

Sighing wearily, I stand, expecting him to move, but he doesn't, and his position leaves us close. "Abby. Talk to me. Tell me what you're thinking. Please."

I shake my head, not because I don't want to talk to him—I know, *know*, I need to. But I'm exhausted, and overwhelmed, and my brain is so full, I don't know where to start. His palm cups my cheek, and I lean into it, eyes closed. His relief is nearly palpable as we stand there, close enough to touch, and yet miles apart, because the contact of his skin on mine—even palm to cheek—still makes me quiver, heats my blood. And Kye feels it.

Eventually, I cover his hand with mine and hold onto it as I step around him, keeping our fingers connected until I step into the already-steamy bathroom and close the door.

7

There's no therapy quite like a hot bath—even one without bubbles—and I soak in it for a long time, lathering and deep conditioning my hair and vigorously scrubbing any remaining cenote water off my skin, while being extra careful of the still-bloody gash on the inside of my arm. I don't have many herbs on hand, but make a poultice for the cut with what's available in my Healing kit, and bandage it as best I can. By the time I emerge, smelling of herbal lotion and wearing my soft cotton pajamas—the ones Kye has seen a number of times—I'm coherent enough to know two things.

First, no matter what happens, Kye and I have to be extremely mindful of the risks involved with us sharing more than sleep in that bed. Second, though I'm not sure I trust the current state of our relationship, when I strip away all the layers, his arms are still home—regardless of where we are—and we both need that reminder today.

"Feeling better?" He's propped the pillows against the headboard and is reclined against them, channel surfing.

I melt onto the bed next to him. "So much better."

He turns his head, eyes searching mine. "I can sleep on the floor if you'd rather."

Hurt curls in my belly. "Is that what you want?"

He shifts to prop himself up on his elbow. "You know I don't. Babe, how many times do I have to apologize? What else do you want me to say?"

I squeeze my eyes closed and pull the covers to my chin. "Don't say anything. Just hold me, okay? I need you to hold me."

And the amazing thing about him is that though he's hurt too, and every bit as conflicted and confused as me, though I see in his energy that his personal threads are about to snap, because I ask, because he knows I need it, Kye turns off the TV and slides under the covers. Then he slips his arms around me and pulls me into his chest.

He keeps me there all night long.

TWO

Broken Rose

ROSE

I wake in a dark hotel room in Mexico with the worst headache of my life. Every heartbeat throbs like a drum in my head, pulsing and pounding without end, unrelenting. I sit up, gripping the comforter to my cramping stomach as I fight the urge to hurl.

It's been forever since the last time I threw up. The third grade, probably. Yet, in the hours since I learned of Alejandro's death, I've lost track of my stomach's convulsions. There's nothing left in me, so when I think about him, about the pain he must have suffered in his last moments as he ping-ponged down the sides of the cenote and crashed into the water, I'm reduced to dry-heaving over the garbage can at my bedside.

It's both humiliating and exhausting to be so wrecked. I'm pretty sure they drugged me, and I don't react well to downers, even if they're of the all-natural plant variety that Abby mixes. I have a vague memory of yelling at her, screaming about her inability to help Alex, to save him. There's a part of me, however small, that understands her explanation about why. I know she's right. That once he was dead, there was nothing she could do. But another part of me is still angry, so angry, at her for not trying. I'm angry because she's my best friend, and I expect more from her.

She's a Healer. Not just any Healer, either, but the chosen one. The only living direct descendant of Raina and Theron, and if anyone in this world has the ability to bring someone back from the dead, it's her. I was falling in love with Alex, and she didn't *try* to save him.

She's been so caught up in herself, stringing along Gabe while walking the tightrope with Kye, that she didn't notice the impact Alex had on me. Abby has two men in her life, and I only barely found one—and now he's gone.

Alejandro's gone.

Aunt Christine stays with me through the night, stroking my head when I wake up on a pillow soaked in tears, and offering me water when I can't breathe for sobbing so hard. I'm crushed. So broken. I need my best friend right now, but again, she's caught up in her own issues—leaving me to grieve alone.

Christine has taken Abby's bed, leaving me wondering where Abby is sleeping. I've covered for her and Kye for nearly two weeks, and she can't be bothered to show up on the one night when I really need her? "Can I get you anything?" Christine hands me my half-full water bottle. "Something more to help you sleep?"

I sip slowly, hesitating because I know that whatever I put in my mouth has a good chance of coming right back up again. "No, thank you." My voice scratches against my raw throat, coming out barely audible.

She indicates the bottle, encouraging me to keep drinking. I ignore her advice, twisting the cap on and setting my water on the nightstand so I can pull the comforter tight around me once again. As if she can read my mind, Aunt Chris says, "Abby's just sick that she can't be here with you right now."

"Why isn't she?" I croak, unable to carve the anguish from my voice. "I need her tonight."

Her intake of breath is the first indication that I'm not going to like her answer. "She left. With Kye."

I wouldn't have believed I could feel more devastated, more betrayed than I do in this moment. "To where?"

"I'm not sure, but wherever they end up will be far from here."

"Now? They had to run away *now*?"

"It's complicated, but yes. It was time. They had to go before the Dragons dragged them in for a de-briefing."

Suspicion rears up, sparking flames in my chest. "What are they afraid of? Did they do something wrong?" What I'm really asking: did they do something wrong to Alex? Did they find him alive and let him die anyway? I know their secrets—all of them. Except what happened in that cenote when Alex was killed. What if that's the reason they left? What if they couldn't face me with the truth?

Christine shakes her head. "No, sweetie. They haven't done anything wrong. There are reasons beyond their control, and they had to go immediately."

"Without saying goodbye?" My entire friendship with Abby is unravelling. How could she? I was her only friend when she moved to Jackson. I introduced her to ... everyone, including Kye. I've covered for her every time she snuck off to be with him, and every time she needed help with anything, I was the one who showed up. For weeks I've tolerated being the third wheel for the sake of keeping the peace while they played house.

I even lied to Gabe. That night at the club, when Abby was drunk and Gabe accused her of being pregnant, I told Gabe that I didn't believe she was meant to be with Kye. I told him that Raina could as easily have ended up with her guard—we all know she could have gotten away with it. I gave him false hope so he would pursue her and help her move on.

Gabe lit up like I'd given him the greatest gift. He was so obviously smitten, and she so devastated by my stupid cousin. I made sure the two of them were alone when walking back to the villa that night, and then, when I woke up in the morning, somehow Kye was magically there.

Bam.

I wonder if she said goodbye to Gabe. I wonder if he means more to her than I do. Clearly, I don't mean much, since she didn't even have the decency to say goodbye. "Did she leave a note?"

"Oh, sweetie, she *wanted* to be with you. So badly."

"Sure she did," I mumble, unable to smear sugar over the blackness bubbling inside me.

"She was worried about you," Chris continues, "but Eoin and I felt like they needed to leave immediately, so we rushed them to the car with their bags half-packed, and sent them on their way."

I bury my head under the pillow and close my eyes to hide the tears as they flood in again. I will never forgive my best friend.

THREE

Unhinged

ABBY

In my dreams I see demon battles; Endless waves of shadows teeming with red-eyed creatures that grow and writhe as they pursue everyone I love in search of Kye and me. I see my mother's tears, Rose's desperate attempts to get over her loss, her anger at me for leaving. And Alejandro's face. Over and over again, his distorted face flashes as a still shot on the screen of my dreams.

My arm throbs as the wound from the dagger burns with liquid fire. I wake screaming and fly into a sitting position, panting for breath. Kye sits up too, squeezing me tight to calm my violent thrashing. "Shh. Babe. It's okay. Just a dream. It's over now. You're safe. We're both safe."

Still trembling, I let Kye pull me back and wrap the blanket around me, and then hold on until my shaking calms. Eventually, I loosen my grip and wipe hot tears off my cheeks before drifting into a fitful, restless slumber. I've never felt so unhinged.

The next morning, Kye waits until we're loading our things in the car to bring it up. "Do you want to talk about your nightmare?"

I hand over my suitcase with a shake of my head, still traumatized by the bits and pieces I remember. "No."

"You sure?"

"Yes," I insist. "Let's find some breakfast and get on the road."

"Might help you feel better." He opens my car door, the way he hasn't done since before we started getting sick.

There's a lump in my throat that feels as big as a golf ball. "You don't know how I feel, so how would you know what will make it better?"

All emotion drains from his face until it's a blank mask. Once I'm inside he closes my door with a quiet click, then comes around to the driver's side. He buckles in and starts the engine in silence. Breathing is the only sound we make for the duration of the drive.

It is the loudest breathing ever.

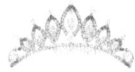

A few hours later, we arrive in a coastal town and roll to a stop at a large house situated on a deep blue bay. The red brick has mostly faded to orange, and appears to be coated in a film of white salt that sparkles in the sunlight. It's flanked by lush, green lawn with blades wider and thicker than the grass in Jackson, and when I step on it, it feels spongy. The walk is lined with fern-like palm trees, different from the ones I loved in Mexico, but beautiful in their way, and near the bright blue door, thriving shrubs of red, yellow, and pink hibiscus.

I accept Kye's offered hand, wondering again what we're doing here and why I consented to come.

The woman who answers is young—so much younger than I imagined the woman of the house would be. She can't be more than two or three years older than me, and crazy beautiful with black hair and long dark lashes that frame startlingly blue eyes. Her full pink lips move from a pout to a smile when she sees Kye, and jealousy tugs on my already-exhausted emotions. She's wearing a filmy gauze dress over the top of what I can only hope is a bikini.

"Kye Murphy," she murmurs. "Never thought I'd see you here again."

Kye flushes pink. "Hi, Kiersten."

She notices me belatedly, drawing her eyebrows together, puzzled. "Hi."

"Kiersten," Kye says, "This is Abby."

"Nice to meet you, Abby." She extends a hand, which I accept for a shake, insulted when she drops it quickly and returns her full attention on Kye. "What brings you to Texas?"

"You know me," he hedges, "always on the go." He turns his heart-stopping grin on full wattage, effectively cementing my unfounded hatred for the half-dressed Kiersten, whose returning smile does nothing to soothe my building anger.

"Well. I'm glad your travels brought you back to my door. It's been way too long." She grabs hold of his shoulders and plants a kiss full on his mouth.

Kiersten has become my enemy as surely as the demons.

Kye squirms out of her embrace, darting an uncomfortably panicked glance at me. It takes everything I have to not storm back to the car. As if he can read my mind, Kye squeezes my hand—the one he's still holding—with a death-grip to keep me from doing exactly that, and drags me with him into the house. We follow my newest enemy inside the spacious living room and out back, where three young children splash in the shallow end of a pool. She takes her place on a lawn chair perched at the pool's edge and invites us to sit as well. "I'd invite you inside, but I'm supposed to be out here with the children. Shouldn't have left them to answer the door."

"I'm glad you did." Kye drops into the chair next to Kiersten's. I try to remain standing, but Kye pulls my arm, hard, until I sit next to him on the chair.

Kiersten eyes our joined hands, then turns and sips from a soda can, swallowing deliberately before asking, "If you're not going to tell me what brings you here, are you going to tell me what you want? Pretty sure you didn't come here for me."

Kye takes a deep breath, extricating his fingers from mine, and leans toward Kiersten. "Abby and I ..." he trails off and clears his throat. "We need to stay under the Dragons' radar for a while."

Kiersten's raised brows indicate that this surprises her. "Then why are you here? For all you know I could be surrounded by them."

He licks his lips. "We have a lot of stuff happening. Demons chasing us, a curse that's coming to a head, and to make that worse, Abby's been wounded by the Arawn Dagger—and that injury is not getting better. Not even a little bit." He reaches back and takes my hand again, preventing me from rubbing my bandaged arm. "I was hoping we could crash here for a couple of days? Give us a chance to catch our breath and make a plan. Maybe figure out how to treat Abby."

Kiersten yells at one of the children to not dive in the shallow end, then turns back to Kye, her eyes avoiding contact with mine. "Of course. You're welcome to my guest room." Her eyes flick to me. "But I only have one, with that same full-size bed."

Kye throws me a weak smile and then turns back to Kiersten. "That's all we need." When Kiersten doesn't respond, he finally—finally—says, "I ... uh, wanted to tell you in person. I have some news. Abby and I are getting married."

She sits back like he's slapped her. Dumbfounded. "Married?"

He nods, jaw clenching and his eyes narrowing like a trapped animal. Feeling the need to leave them alone for this discussion, I withdraw my hand from Kye's. "Kiersten, would it be okay if I use your restroom?"

She gives me directions, then goes back to staring at Kye with wide, devastated eyes. "You're getting married?" Her low voice carries behind me as I slip inside the house and down the hall. Once inside the bathroom, I stare in the mirror, anger seething from every pore because Kye should have warned me about Kiersten. He should have warned me about a lot of things. But instead of being honest, he brought me into a lioness's den, and plans to keep me here for several days.

Again, I wonder how much I don't know about Kye, and if I'll ever be okay with those things. Then I wonder how much he's lied about. And who. And when. Jealousy climbs up my toes and slides across the backs of my legs. It crawls across my back and trails through to burn in my chest, shoving a lump of heat into my throat. The list is so long.

I sit on the closed toilet seat for several minutes, head in hands, trying hard to breathe. Just breathe.

I wonder what Gabe's doing. How did he react when he realized I left without him—without saying goodbye? I wonder if he would have tried to stop me had he been given the chance. If he would have cornered me and tried to kiss me again.

Lips, running across my cheek, gentle, firm, demanding.

I wonder how Rose is handling Alejandro's death now that she's had a couple of days to process it. I wonder how angry she is that I didn't come find her to say goodbye.

Mom and Landon were left shouldering the responsibility for everything we left behind—for saying our goodbyes, cleaning up our messes, and for somehow explaining to the Dragons that we've left—to where, they don't know—and aren't planning to come back anytime soon. I wonder how that went over—or how it's going over. Pretty sure Val and Zane are two unhappy Dragons. Very. Unhappy.

I don't know how long I've been in the bathroom, but eventually, I hear voices and know I need to come out—show my face. I smooth my hair and apply lip gloss while I gather my courage, and then open the door slowly. I've only taken a few steps into the hall when I hear hushed voices. I pause, not trying to eavesdrop, but unable to resist.

"... sorry. I should have warned you we were coming." It's Kye. Obviously trying to keep the conversation mum, but I can hear every word bouncing across the marble floors.

"Yes, you should have," Kiersten says. "It's not that hard to use the phone. Pretty sure you have my number."

"I don't have a phone right now. Abby and I both had to leave them behind when we left Mexico."

"Ever heard of a Go-phone? Might come in handy."

"Look. I'm sorry," he says, and I detect a hint of tenderness in his voice. One more reason to hate Kiersten. "I'm sorry if this is hard for you, but K, none of this has been easy for me or Abby, either. Three days ago, we were trapped in underground tunnels of water—with a dead friend and no scuba gear. We fought demons, freed a mermaid, and faced down the new leader of the Dark Elen. Then, to top it off, Abby—who was already practically unconscious herself—Healed one of our friends in order to save his life. We then returned to a base-camp, only to discover that our own people—people we love, and who I have trusted my whole life—have a seedy agenda to keep the two of us apart. An agenda that makes no sense, but that involves a great deal of suffering from both of us. I can't live without her, Kiersten. Even if I didn't love her—which I do—I *physically* can't live without her. We're exhausted. Abby's sick. Everyone and everything from our past—good and bad—is now looking for us. I was hoping we could crash here for a couple of days."

"Kye, I ..."

"I can't lose her, K." His voice holds a desperate edge that softens my anger a fraction of a degree. "I'm sorry. I'm really sorry for how I left, for not saying goodbye, for not being able to love you the way you needed me to. I am. And I'm so, so sorry for asking this of you, but there are very few people in this world who we can trust to help us without blowing the whistle."

"You don't look sick," she says, sounding reluctant. "But you do look exhausted."

Kye's reacting sigh says a lot more about his state of mind than his words. "The only reason I'm holding it together right now is because have to be strong for *her*. Please, K."

She sighs, loudly. "You know I could never tell you no. That's been one of my life's biggest challenges."

"Thanks." Footsteps, clothes rustling. "I owe you."

Her voice is muffled. "You already owed me. A lot. What is this, like seventeen?"

He laughs, and I decide it's time to make my presence known. I peer around the corner. The sight of Kye holding Kiersten in his arms shouldn't bother me—not after what I've heard, but it brings to mind Crystal, and graduation, and everything I've so recently discovered about what happened in the days that followed, and I can't stop my gasp—can't blink fast enough to keep my eyes from filling. Kye lets go of Kiersten like he's been burned and steps toward me. "Abby, wait. Don't leave. It's not what you think. My relationship with Kiersten isn't like that."

I shake my head. I want to tell him I know. That I understand, but for some reason, I can't speak. Thick mucus clogs my throat, holding hostage the words that want to spring forth—the words that would make this moment, and everyone in it, so much less awkward.

"Abby," Kiersten says. "He's not lying."

I nod my understanding, but still can't move. My head is spinning in crazy circles, and my eyes burn with hot tears. One breaks free and runs down my cheek. Though I slept last night, exhaustion from the last several days takes its toll and pounds across my shoulders and along the backs of my knees. Kye comes to me, arms open as if waiting to see if I'll step into them, but I can't move.

I squeeze my eyes closed allowing more tears to fall, and gasping for air.

"Babe. Please. Please don't cry. It breaks my heart." He gathers me in his arms, and upon feeling his touch, my frozen muscles collapse into him. He swallows hard and asks Kiersten, "Where can I take her?"

Kye picks me up—something he hasn't done for a long time— and Kiersten leads us out the back door and across the patio. She opens another door, revealing a small, yet strangely cozy pool house which has been set up for guests. There's a thick layer of dust covering the dresser, nightstands, and the TV on the wall, and the double bed in the corner has been stripped of bedding. "Didn't think you'd be back," Kiersten says. "If you'd warned me, I'd have had it ready for you."

Kye shakes his head, the movement causing the skin in his neck to rub against my cheek. "It's perfect. Thank you." There's a loveseat situated under a large window that overlooks the pool, and Kye sets me on my feet next to it.

"I'll bring you some linens." Kiersten turns away from us. "I can get the housekeeper to dust everything later this afternoon. Is there anything else you need?"

Kye looks at me, eyebrow raised, but I shake my head. "Are there still water bottles in the mini-fridge?" he asks.

"Probably," she says. "You were the last person to stay here. You might want to double check, in case the kids have been pilfering the stash."

His laugh is brittle as he strides to the little black box tucked into a corner on the other side of the room and opens it. "Yep, there's plenty. This is great."

Kiersten stands in the doorway, hesitating with a hand on the knob and her dress fluttering in the slight breeze. "I ... uh—I can kick one of the kids out of their room if you need separate ones?"

I don't have the energy to blush, and Kye must not doesn't either. "No. We'll share. Thanks."

Finally, I look up, take in Kiersten's sharp cheek bones and smooth porcelain skin. She's so well put together, her beauty appearing effortless. But there's pain written in her eyes, the set of her mouth, and the way she stands, two fingers still stuck to the silver doorknob, like the connection will somehow change the thing she doesn't want to accept. In this moment, for a split fraction of a second, I feel sorry for her. I know how it feels to love Kye, and to believe that love isn't returned. I have felt the ache that is etched in the creases near her eyes, the droop of her false smile. I understand that pain.

"Kiersten," I croak. "Thank you for taking us in."

Kiersten nods, blinking rapidly. "I'll send one of the kids to bring you bedding and towels in a little while. I'm about to make lunch, if you're interested."

"Thanks." Kye sits next to me and tips up my chin. "Did you want anything? Need anything?" I shake my head.

Nodding slowly, as if to allow reality to set in, Kiersten pulls the door closed. "Have a nice rest."

When she's finally gone, Kye relaxes against the loveseat and pulls me down so my head is resting on his knees. "I'm sorry," he rasps, pain evident in the way he strokes my hair, and then allows his fingers to trail along my skin. "So sorry to put you through this. I promise I have nothing going on with Kiersten. Promise. I've never felt a spark with her. That looked bad, but ..."

"Stop apologizing," I mumble. "I know. Okay? I know you don't want her. Not right now. If you do, you're crazy good at hiding it."

"I'm not hiding anything," he says, exasperated. "I promised to never lie to you again, and I intend to keep that promise."

"It would have helped if you had warned me," I point out. "But this isn't about Kiersten. I've left my mom behind again. And Rose, who needs me." And Gabe. I can't tell Kye, but after the months spent with Gabe as a constant fixture in every hour of my life, he is whose absence aches the most. "I don't know what comes next."

Kye's fingers pause in the act of stroking my neck. "I don't either. There's a whole lot of uncertainty in our future right now, but I promise that no matter what happens, no matter where we end up or what comes next, I'll be here, protecting you, standing next to you, loving you with everything I have in me. As long as you want me, I'm yours. We'll be together, and I'll do everything I can to make our life special."

"Will they look for us here?" I take his hand and bring his palm to my lips so I can kiss it. His eyes flutter closed and relief blankets his face.

"They might. The only person who knows I'm friends with Kiersten is Landon. Even if he told them immediately—which he won't do—it would take them days to track her down."

Though my head is throbbing, I sit up slowly. "How do you know her?"

"We lived in the same neighborhood when I was eight."

My eyebrows raise in amusement. "And she's still carrying a torch for you?"

"Well. No. I moved away—as I always did. Then I ran into her again as I was travelling a few years back, and she recognized me. We've kept in touch."

"You've come here and stayed."

He nods, slowly. "Again, not romantically. I've never stayed in her room, Abby."

"But the invitation was there."

He runs a hand through his hair, clearly uncomfortable. "In the interest of being honest, it's still there. Always will be, I'm afraid."

Annoyance ripples over my skin. "Isn't she married?" I glance around the guest house, consider the expansive bigger house, the kids in the pool.

Kye lets out a long, slow breath. "No, Kiersten's single, as far as I know. Those kids aren't hers. She works for a trainer—sort of like Val, only less intense—who takes in Gifted children and teaches them how to hone and use their Gifts. A lot of parents don't understand the importance of these Gifts, nor do they know how to help their children control their abilities, so Jonathan runs a live-in training facility."

"So it's like a boarding school?"

"More like a camp. They don't stay long term. A month at a time, then they go home to their families. Sometimes they come back when they're older for more refined training, but it's always short-term. Anyway, Kiersten helps train the kids, but more than anything, she's a caretaker. She feeds them, makes sure they take baths and brush teeth, and complete their school work, or practice whatever lessons they've been working on with Jonathan."

Suddenly, I'm feeling horribly inadequate. Kiersten's helping to raise the next generation of Gifted, to prepare them for battles with demons, and here I am, doing my absolute best to avoid having to ever fight one of those battles again. "What are we doing here again?"

Kye takes my hands in his, rubbing his fingers over my knuckles. "Hiding out. This guest suite is as workable as any hotel room, only free, and safer because if we ask, she'll keep us hidden back here and never tell a soul she saw us."

"And you know this because of her feelings for you."

He lets go of my hand and pinches the bridge of his nose. "I know it because that's the kind of friend Kiersten is. She'd do it for you too, even if I wasn't here."

"Even though it's painful for her to know that we're staying here together?"

He nods slowly. "Yes."

I take a shaky breath. "Do you want to stay in here with me? Or …"

"Of course I do. I want to be where you are, even if it's painful for my friend Kiersten." He lowers his voice. "Because the thing is, I still intend to marry you. Whether you're ready for that now, or if I end up having to wait another year or two. Or five. Or even ten or more." He fingers the ring I still haven't taken off. "No matter what's happened while we've been apart, you said yes once. I know you love me. I know it. Kiersten—and everyone else on the planet—is going to have to get used to the fact that I'm taken. Committed. Consumed. Obsessed, body and soul. I'm yours. I will always choose you. Always."

I don't know when Kye turned into a poet, but his words melt my insides like chocolate until I want to absorb all of him and let his flowing energy roll over my skin. When did I become a sucker for pretty words?

A soft rap on the door is followed by the entry of a little girl with curly blonde hair and striking blue eyes. She can't be more than seven, but her arms are loaded with sheets. "Brooke has your towels," she says. "But she won't come in. We're not allowed in here most days, and she doesn't want to break the rules."

I accept the sheets, offering the girl a gentle smile. "Thank you. I'm Abby."

Her grin could light up a city, if power like that could be harnessed. "I'm Kinsey. I'm supposed to tell you that there are blankets in the closet, and Kiersten will bring you a clean cover when she gets it out of the drier.

"Thank you, Kinsey." I accept a stack of towels from another little girl, who seems to be mute, but who I suspect is merely shy. When the girls are gone, Kye helps me make the bed. We find a down comforter in the closet near the bathroom, along with a stack of clean white pillows, and pile the bed high the way a hotel maid would.

Kye goes to the car to retrieve our luggage, and I flop onto the soft bed and take a calming breath. It's ironic how, even knowing Kye as well as I do, I'm experiencing such similar emotions to the ones I experienced the first time I ran away with him. Back then, I had no idea what I was getting into. All I knew was that I was in love and hopeful, and the situation was more exciting than frightening. This time my emotions are similar, only about ten times more conflicted.

And there are so many more people I miss. Knowing this, missing them, makes everything we're doing feel that much bigger, and every mile we cross that much longer.

"You okay?" Kye shoves open the door and wheels our suitcases inside.

I sit up and smooth down my hair. "Yes. Just thinking."

He leaves our suitcases near the closet and sits next to me. "What're you thinking about?"

I swallow, trying to find the right words. "I was remembering Las Vegas and New York. I'm wondering what comes next, and what's happening to the people we left behind. Mostly, I'm wondering about my dad. If he's still alive, why haven't I heard from him for so many years?"

Kye rubs my shoulders. "I'm sure he has a good reason. There's no way he left you voluntarily. If he did, why would your mom know how to get a hold of him?"

"That's the other thing," I murmur. "If my mom knew he's still alive—all this time—why didn't she tell me? Why let me believe he's dead?"

"Maybe she's been protecting you," he says. "The way she always has."

"By lying?"

"By hiding painful truths."

I want to tell him that I'd rather know the painful truths than have the people I most love trying to protect me with lies—but then I consider Gabe. My feelings for him, and my confusion, and I look at Kye and see his devotion, believe he has given himself to me fully, and I realize that if a tiny piece of his heart still belongs to Crystal, or to Kiersten, or whoever else is in his past, maybe now isn't the best time for me to know that. Maybe it's not my business. Maybe I should learn to accept the part of Kye that belongs solely to me, and be happy with that portion of him. Maybe it's unrealistic for me to want every bit of him. Maybe that's an unhealthy expectation for anyone. Because somewhere, deep down, there's a tiny part of me that will probably always belong to Gabe. No matter how much I love Kye, how badly I want to work things out and be with him for the rest of our lives, I have a fierce instinct to guard Gabe's piece of my heart, to wrap it in bubble wrap and tape it in a box marked fragile. Maybe Kye doesn't need to know every detail of that part of me either. Maybe it's okay to give him his own piece— it's such a large portion anyway—and put the rest in storage.

"Look, Babe," Kye murmurs. "I understand it's bothering you that your father is still alive, and your mom is seeing Akers—but you have to give her credit. She's been alone for a lot of years. No one should have to be alone for that long. She deserves to be happy too."

I close my eyes. "I agree." But I hate that he's pointed out the thing that's been chipping away at the back of my mind, festering like a wound. "I don't know if my parents are still married. There are so many things I don't know about my own family. Why does no one ever tell the truth? Why can't they tell me what's happening? Tell me about my Gifts and my dad and whatever other secrets they're keeping, because now we don't know who to trust, and I'm wondering if I can trust my own mother!"

"Shh." Kye pulls me close. "Maybe—"

"Don't. I don't want you to make excuses for her, Kye. Don't try to make me feel better. I want you to let me be angry, and agree that I have a right to the truth. Be indignant. Be angry with me. And if you can't, be quiet, because I don't want soothing right now. What I want—"

"I am angry, Abby. You have no idea how angry I am for you. No one has the right to hurt you like this. Not your parents, not your friends, and especially not me. But I need you to tell me how I can help you. What do I do to make this better for you?"

I pull out of his arms enough so I can drag his face to mine and kiss him. There is nothing gentle or soft about this kiss. My lips and teeth demand; my tongue coaxes until our breathing is labored. I angle my body and shove Kye back until he's lying on the bed, and I'm crushing him, tugging on his shirt with one hand while the other clutches a handful of his hair. I drag his shirt over his head, and reach down to do the same to mine, when his arm clamps around me and he rolls me under him. "Don't do that. Babe, you have to leave your clothes on. I'm not a monk. I can only take so much before I snap."

"So snap," I mumble. "I don't care anymore."

A rogue tear sneaks out the corner of my eye and rolls into my hair. Kye wipes it away, swearing. "I do. I care. I want you so bad I almost can't breathe. But not like this. Not because you're angry, or have a twisted need to get back at your parents, or because you're desperate to forget everything else. I want everything from you, Abby. Except regret. That's the one thing I can't live with, and I'm afraid if we do this now, in this moment, you will regret it."

"I won't."

He nods. "You will, a ghrá. I know you. And I love you." He sits up, muscles shaking. "Believe me, if I didn't love you as much as I do, I would never, ever be able to say no to you right now. You have no idea the self-restraint this requires." He leans in to kiss me again, backing away at the last second and squeezing his eyes shut as he presses his lips together. "Your hair is spread across the comforter, and your clothes are twisted, and you're looking up at me with eyes loaded with devastation and desire and your lips are swollen from kissing me and—goddesses, I want you right now worse than I have ever wanted anything. Ever."

"You have me," I tell him, resting my hands on his biceps and trying to pull him toward me.

Abruptly, he stands, brushing my hands away, and storms into the bathroom. I sit up, straightening my clothes while I stare at the bathroom door. When the shower turns on, I give up on the idea of him coming out and changing his mind, and will my blood to settle, my brain to calm. He's right to hesitate, but in my recent moments of utter devastation, I've decided that I'm tired of putting off my own happiness. I want what I want, now. There's no point in waiting. Life isn't that long, especially for people in our situation. If we died tomorrow, I don't want waiting to be something I regret.

But he's right about our need to be cautious. So as I open my suitcase and arrange my belongings on a shelf in the closet, I make a mental note to pick up some cautionary supplies. Triple birth control it is.

FOUR

Nothing Left

ROSE

"Let me help you with that." Gabe grasps the handle of the suitcase I've zipped closed, and hauls it off the bed, setting it near the door. "Is this all of it?"

I wander through the room, double and triple checking—drawers, under the bed, in the closet—and finding nothing, but feeling like I am about to leave something huge and important behind. "I think so."

He raises his brows in surprise. "Seriously? One suitcase? I'm shocked and amazed."

He's trying to get a rise out of me, trying to make me snap at him for insinuating that all girls fit within a stereotypical pop-culture category, and I wish I had the energy to be my snarky self, but I don't. I'm dead inside. "Swimsuits don't take up much space. I came here expecting to spend a week on the beach, working on my tan, not a month in the jungle fighting demons."

"I came here expecting to go everywhere with Abby, to help protect her from the demons that almost killed us." Something flickers in Gabe's eyes before he shutters them, his face smoothing until it's carefully devoid of emotion. "No one could have planned for this, let alone packed for it."

I wonder what will happen to Gabe now that Abby has left. He's probably out of a job, and in a lot of trouble from Zane. It's clear that he developed strong feelings for Abby along the way. He's hurting too. "Well at least you remembered your dancing shoes. Priorities."

"I don't own dancing shoes." His eyes narrow in confusion.

"It's a metaphor."

"For what?"

I shake my head, wishing I could think the way I did three days ago, before the demon army attacked, and Abby and Alex and I were dancing our cares away at the cantina. "I meant—you went dancing anyway. It was supposed to be a compliment."

He raises a brow. "Um, thanks?"

"Don't mention it." I pick up Alejandro's pillow, flooded by memories of his hand on my waist as we turned and shuffled across the dance floor. The ache in my chest punches, hard. I wonder how long it will take before I'm not reminded of my loss by every single thing. "Seriously, don't." I clutch the pillow to my chest, inhaling the remnants of exotic cologne.

Gabe picks up my suitcase. "Are you ready to go?"

I bury my face in the pillowcase, unwilling to leave this scent behind. "I have nothing left here but memories."

Gabe's eyes fall on the couch where he last sat with Abby, lingering there in what can only be the equivalent of him squeezing her pillow. He takes a deep breath and opens the door. "Me either."

While I've been out of it, the council has been in an uproar. Val and Zane arrived last night, furious with Eoin and Landon and, well, pretty much all of us. I'm told I've missed a number of angry exchanges, which is fine with me. I wasn't part of the planning. I wasn't part of the fight. I wasn't important or instrumental in anything except keeping Abby happy, so it's easy for me to skip meetings and keep to the outskirts of yelling matches. No one cares about my opinion on what we should do next.

Only days ago, it frustrated me to be treated like I'm insignificant, but now I'm grateful for the mercy of it. I have nothing to offer, nothing to contribute, nothing to say. I want to go home.

I follow Gabe to the parking lot, my every movement jerky and wooden, wondering what's next. Will we go straight to the nearest airport to chase after Kye and Abby? Will the Dragons put me on a flight back to Jackson? And if I do go home, what then? Everything before this past three weeks feels so far distant that it could be someone else's life. Maybe it is. Maybe I am someone else.

I'm inexorably changed. My life will never be what it was before I came to Mexico.

Gabe stalls behind Christine's SUV, pinning me with a steady gaze. "Landon and Marian rented a car, but I suspect they'll want to ride with Christine and Eoin to catch up on details of what's happened. I expect Kye and Abby will be the main topic of conversation for the next year—at least—or until they're found, whichever comes first. Since I'd prefer not to be part of *that* conversation, I'm driving the rental. You're welcome to come with me."

When I don't respond immediately, Gabe frowns, opening the back of Christine's SUV. "It's cool. You probably need to be near your aunt and uncle right now, for support. Of course. They're family."

He starts to lift my suitcase into the car, but I stop him with a hand on his arm, ignoring how warm his skin feels, and how tightly it stretches over his muscles. "Are you sure you don't mind driving me? We haven't been the best of friends."

"We're not the worst of enemies either." Gabe's eyes linger on the place where I'm clutching his forearm. "And we could both use a break from …" his gaze shifts to the resort, then moves on to the forest beyond. "All of this."

The Dragons will likely be transporting Alejandro's body back to Playa Del Carmen today. I swallow the lump that forms in my throat when I realize that if I stick around, I'll have the torture of watching. "Can we leave soon? I don't want to be here anymore."

LEGACY

Gabe slams the hatch of the SUV and pops the trunk on the car. "Can't imagine why we should stay. The others are finishing up the business of moving headquarters and checking out." He tosses my suitcase into the trunk and closes it. When he turns back to face me, I recognize misery in the wideness of his glossy eyes, the tense set of his shoulders, and tightness in his stance. This is likely the first and last time Gabe and I will ever have so much in common.

"I need to return Christine's keys and get my suitcase." He hesitates, deliberately avoiding looking into the jungle a second time. "After everything that's happened, I'm not comfortable leaving you alone in the parking lot, but I understand if you'd rather wait here than go inside and face the Dragons."

I take one last, long look at the resort, clutching Alejandro's pillow tighter. "There's nothing left for me here." His eyes roam my face as if searching for something, but I'm not fragile and needy like Abby. "I can take care of myself."

He nods—he already knows this about me—and hands me the keys.

31

FIVE

Traumatic Childhoods

ABBY

The first time I meet Jonathan, he's standing at the edge of the deep end of the pool with a child hanging off of each arm, and one clinging to his neck. The kids squeal as Jonathan roars the playful gnashing roar of a pretend sea monster and jumps off the edge, taking all three children into the water with him.

I burst out laughing. "I thought he was training them? It looks more like they're playing."

Kiersten leans back in her chair, sliding on a pair of designer sunglasses. "The games make the training fun. Plus, the kids can't help but respect a man who loves them and plays with them as if they were his own. It's the best way to learn."

Her statement bothers me. Kye has always considered Val his father figure, but from my perspective, he was closer to, and spent more time with Landon. It was Landon who loved him in a fatherly role, and in the end, it was Landon who came to his rescue, who loved him enough to help him hide, and then help him run. But Val was Kye's guardian, and I can't figure out why, especially when Kye's own parents were clearly capable of raising their son, even after his Gifts manifested.

A little girl paddles to the edge, wispy blonde hair sticking to her face, and large dark eyes wide with glee. "Sea monster! There's a sea monster on the loose."

Jonathan grabs her ankle and drags her across the pool. She shrieks in delight as he holds her aloft long enough to catch a breath, and then dunks her under. A boy—probably about eight—growls. "Let her go," he bangs on Jonathan's bicep, trying to free her. "You can't eat my sister, sea monster."

"Come on, Colby," Jonathan urges. "You can do better. You're trying to save her. How else can you do that?"

A buzz crackles above the water, and Jonathan flinches. "Good. Not strong enough, but good." He lets the girl up, and she gasps for breath. "Don't do that anymore. I can't breathe underwater."

"Sorry, Kinsey," Jonathan says. "One more time. Big breath." He drags her under once more, urging Colby to try again. "Remember, only get me, not your sister, and especially not the pool. You'll electrocute us all."

Colby squeezes his eyes closed. The energy shifts as he pulls it out of the air and snaps Jonathan with a current that sends sparks into the ground near my feet. The jolt forces Jonathan to free Kinsey, and the girl paddles to the ladder, gasping, while Johnathan slides into the water, unconscious. Colby screams, "Sorry! I'm sorry! I didn't mean it. Kiersten!"

Kiersten rips her cover-up over her head and lobs it over her shoulder as she dives in, gliding down to haul Johnathan to the surface. I reach over the edge and grab his arm to help Kiersten pull him out, but he's a big guy—solid muscle—and this isn't an easy task. Kye comes running out of our room and helps us drag Jonathan onto the cement.

He's not breathing.

I have a momentary flashback of Alejandro; my throat tightens painfully and a scream builds inside me. Kiersten begins CPR, while Kye pumps hard on Johnathan's chest, counting each compression. "Abby, don't panic. He's going to be fine."

But he might not. Alejandro's mangled face flashes, flashes, flashes. I can't let another person die, but since I was stabbed, my Healing power has drained to the point where I can scarcely see an aura anymore. Any attempts I make to Heal another will likely result in epic failure, but if Jonathan needs to be saved, I have to try. Terror rocks me on my heels, threatens to knock me to the floor.

"Babe, please calm down. You're scaring the kids." Kye continues compressing, and Kiersten's diligent with mouth to mouth, but Kinsey and Colby clutch the edge of the cement pool deck, tears streaming from wide eyes.

Before my anxiety can spill over, I draw the children out of the water and wrap each in a towel. "I didn't mean to kill him," Colby wails. "I was doing what he said. He told me to zap harder, so I did, and that's why I'm not supposed to zap anyone ever, because people die when I do. I told him. I told him."

Memories of my own troubled childhood parade across my mind as I sit, tugging Colby onto my lap. "Jonathan isn't going to die. We won't let him."

"But he looks dead," Colby cries. "Like that mean bully Rod."

Gram lies on the floor in a pool of blood, surrounded by shards of broken energy I couldn't gather.

"He's not going to die," I repeat. "Know why? If Kye and Kiersten can't wake him up, I'll take care of him. I'm a Healer."

As Colby squeezes me tight, Kye mutters, "Oh, no you won't," which leaves me bristling all over again, but before I can respond, Jonathan gasps, spits, coughs, and then his arms flail. When his breathing regulates, he mumbles unintelligible words. Kye offers the kids with a weak grin. "Jonathan says to tell you good job."

Later, I find Jonathan lounging in the sitting room off the kitchen. He's pale, but seems to be recovering from his near electrocution. He offers his hand. "Hello, Abby. Nice to officially meet you."

When my palm meets his, a familiar electric current—that of Gifted energy—zings between us. A laugh bubbles between my lips. "Likewise. How are you feeling?"

He sips from a tea cup, his eyes frank in a way I appreciate. "Grateful. That boy will be an asset to us someday." Children's voices echo from the playroom, and his head tilts as he hones in. "He's eight. I can only speculate, but ten years from now, his abilities will be remarkable."

"I'm glad you're happy about Colby, and I agree that he'll do great things, but I was asking about you."

He continues to sip from the concoction—which smells of aloe, calendula, and elm. "I'll be fine, thank you. No need to break out the crystals and risk yourself for me."

The electricity that sparked in my palm rises into my face. Johnathan can't know how conflicted I've been about Healing since Mexico. "I would have if it was necessary."

"Thank you. It means a lot that you would risk yourself, but please don't. You're a guest here, and Kye has brought you to rest. Your energy is dangerously low." He waves toward my bandaged arm. "If we had a Healer available—aside from you—you would certainly take precedence over me."

"I wasn't nearly electrocuted, and I wouldn't allow—"

He interrupts. "One look at you would adjust her priorities. Even I can see how weak you are. So tell me, Healer, If you were asked to treat someone suffering from a comparable wound, who's dark under-eye circles drooped to her cheekbones, and whose skin matched the white in her dress, someone whose normally blue-green irises could pass for gray—what would you do to help her?"

I try to channel Gram as I scroll through the files in my brain. "I'd have her wear bloodstone and amber, and make her a detoxifying tea, similar to what you're drinking now. But I'd add marshmallow and Echinacea to the mix. Maybe honey. Then I'd research ways to drain the poison from her system without taking it into mine."

Jonathan drains his cup and sets it on the end table, pressing his lips together in a way that makes him appear to be rather pleased with himself. "Great. Sounds like a plan. Let's go ahead and do that then."

Before I can blink, he's dragged me into the kitchen pantry to dig through jars of dried herbs and spices. "Use whatever you need. I assume you're already wearing whatever crystals you have available, so while you conjure your potion, I'll see if any of my crystals come close to what you need." He mumbles on about research and books as he exits, leaving me gripping a cast iron teapot and wondering what just happened.

By the time I've crushed an ample amount of roots and leaves and crammed them into the steeper, Jonathan returns, juggling crystals that are too large to be worn on a chain or strapped to my wrist. "Sorry," he says. "These will have to do."

The smoky-gray bloodstone pulses with energy when I pick it up. This one will be a tremendous help. The chunk of amber is also highly charged, to the point where it nearly glows gold in the dim of twilight. Though touching them goes against acceptable crystal handling behavior, I pick up the amber as well, cradling both in my palms. "I'm surprised and impressed by your knowledge of crystals. These are nice pieces."

He perches on a stool near the counter. "When you've been training Gifted children for as long as I have, you learn to collect important items." He nods at the jars of herbs still on the counter. "Struggling with your recipe?"

I swallow, not wanting to admit that all my Healing knowledge is fuzzy and dull. I can think of the specific recipe, but not focus on the ingredients so I can mix the right combination. I'm embarrassed that I can't remember a simple detoxifying mixture. As if sensing he's hit a sore spot, Jonathan opens a container and holds it to my nose. "Smell."

I take a whiff and come away coughing. "Not that one."

"Good." He covers the first and opens another, repeating the action. "Now this."

Again, I cough, sputtering, "Definitely not."

We repeat this process until we find one that doesn't make me cough, one that helps open my nasal passages and my tight throat. "That. Set that one aside." He does as I say, and then continues opening the herbs and urging me to smell.

"This isn't a technique I've ever learned," I admit, sniffing. "What made you think to try it?"

"Common sense. You've been cut by the dagger," he says in a no-nonsense voice. "Which means your Gifts are draining with every second that passes. It's imperative that we find a way to stop— or at least slow—the drain. I've never worked with a Healer before," he says. "But you have the ability to Heal yourself. It's about figuring out which of your senses continue to function at full capacity, and where your weaknesses currently lie. Next, we need to determine how extensive the damage is, and then how to replenish your energy."

He holds another herb to my nose, and I nod it into the yes stack. "How long do you think all this will take?" I ask. "Because I'm not sure how long we'll be here."

"Hopefully only a few days." Jonathan hands the last container to me and clears away the discards. "But possibly longer. You'll be comfortable in the pool house, though."

"Yes, it's very nice." I add pinches of the last herbs to my tea. "Thank you for having us."

"And safe," he adds. "Might be as good a place as any to hide out for a while."

Except for the awkward moments between me and Kiersten. I don't know how long I can stay here, however unreasonable my feelings, so I reply with, "Might," and squish the herbs into the steeper harder and faster.

Kye stumbles in, his arms loaded with books. "Sorry, babe. It looks like a lot of reading material, but Jonathan and Kiersten and I will help you."

"Help me what?"

He sets the books down and approaches me from behind as I plop the steeper into the kettle of heating water. "Research. We need to know how to restore your energy."

I groan. "I thought we were done with homework when we graduated."

Kye presses a kiss to my hair. "You thought wrong."

Jonathan finishes his tea and stands, approval evident in his gaze as he skims the titles Kye has brought in. "Now that the two of you have somewhere to start, I'll be in with the little ones, explaining why we won't be working with Colby in the pool anymore."

When the teapot whistles, Kye watches me pour some into a teacup and bends to sniff it.

"Do you want some?" I offer.

He crinkles his nose in disgust. "I don't know. What's in it?"

"Detoxifying ingredients. You could use some too. That cenote was crazy toxic."

"All right," he says. "I'll try it." For the life of me, I can't decide if he actually wants the tea or if he's trying to keep me happy, but I pour a second cup, grateful to have him sitting with me, rather than off with Kiersten. Our conversation is light, but stilted, and there's an added element of tension. It makes me nervous, because I'm not sure what it means.

As I'm finishing the bitter tea, sunlight sparkles off my rings—both of them. "Do you ... should I give you back your ring? I mean, until ... we decide?"

His head snaps up as if I've hit him. "Do you *want* to give it back?"

"Only if you want me to."

He sighs, annoyed. "If I wanted it back, I would have asked for it long before now. If I wanted it back, we wouldn't be here. If I didn't still want to marry you, we wouldn't have had to run." His eyes find mine, searching. "Do you feel like you *should* give it back? Or maybe that you want to?"

I set my cup aside. "I don't know what I want, Kye, but giving back your ring—I don't want to do that. I had to ask—make sure."

His fingers graze my cheek, and he laces them into my hair, drawing me toward him so he can brush his lips over mine. "I wouldn't take it back. You're going to have to wear it."

I sigh, relieved, and lean into him, prepared to release what's left of my resentment and anger, when someone clears her voice.

Kiersten hovers in the doorway a few feet away, her face a carefully blank mask. "Um. Hi." She sets more books on top of the ones Kye brought in. "Sorry to interrupt. I need to get started on dinner. You're welcome to help if you'd like, but you might want to get started on your workload—given the size of some of those volumes, this project could take weeks."

Guilt flows over me. As hard as this situation is for me, it must be worse for Kiersten. "I'm happy to help. Since we're going to be staying here, I insist on helping wherever I can."

Kiersten turns away without looking me in the eyes. "Great." She opens a cupboard and pulls out a cutting board, then hands me a knife and an onion. "You can start with this."

Kye brings our teacups to the sink and plants a kiss on the back of my neck. "I'm going to take the books to our room and then find Jonathan to see how else we can help while we're here."

Kiersten's knife thwacks onto her board.

"Good idea." I'm desperate to keep Kye close, but understand why he's uncomfortable in the current situation. I feel the distance growing, feel his absence as he walks out, leaving me alone with Kiersten.

We work in strained silence. When my onions are chopped, I glance at her board and see that she has deftly chopped a small garden of greens, and has moved onto a red pepper. I pick up a green one, eyebrow raised in question. She nods, and I chop that too. When I can stand the silence no more, I say, "I'm sorry if my presence here makes you uncomfortable. Believe me, I would never impose if we weren't desperate."

Kiersten sweeps the greens into a bowl, and then brushes the peppers onto a plate. "I know. I'm sorry for making you feel unwelcome. You've been through a lot, and everything else aside, I'm grateful for what you've done. Please understand, any aversion you feel coming from me has nothing at all to do with you personally. I'm sure that if I knew you—if I were to get to know you well—I'd adore you. I'm sure I'd see why he seems to love you the way he claims. Problem is I *don't* know you. I do know Kye, though. I've had these feelings for him since we met—years ago. I've always thought—hoped, maybe—that someday he'd come back, after he finished all the things he was put here to do, and then maybe he'd be ready for me."

"Kiersten ..."

"It's not your fault," she opens the fridge, rummaging. "He never loved me. I knew it then like I know it now. Still hurts, though. He's a great guy—a one in a million catch—and I'm glad he's happy. I want that for him. I always hoped that someday *I* could be the one to light his eyes the way they shine when he looks at you."

She turns to face me, letting the fridge close without having retrieved anything from it. "It's obvious that he loves you to the moon and back. Just ..." She pushes stray hair out of her eyes with her wrist. "Don't break his heart."

I nod, blinking away tears, and feeling the wound in my own heart fester. How many women across the world are in love with Kye? How many Crystals might there be in our future? How will I ever find that place where I can fully trust him again? Where I don't spend our time apart wondering if he's with one of them?

The knife grows heavy as my wounded arm screams in protest, so I set it aside, fighting a wave of dizziness, and hear the metal clatter to the floor. Spots swim in my vision as I stumble to a chair. Kiersten is talking, but I block out her words—unable to deal with imagined threats or admissions of love in my current state. My chest tightens—a familiar sign, typical of energy drain.

I close my eyes, waiting for the vision to come, but it doesn't. It pushes, shoves against the edges of my consciousness like ripples in the air—but never quite reaches me.

Kiersten hollers for Kye and Jonathan, and then Kye's hands are on my cheeks. "Abby? Babe—look at me. Snap out of it and look at me. I need you to push through this and come back." I blink, wondering how long my eyes have been closed. What I've missed. When I laid my head on the table. "That's it," Kye says. "Come back. Remember what you Saw?"

My fingers twitch. "Nothing."

"Okay." He turns his head. "I'm going to take her to our room to lie down. So sorry ..." He urges me to stand, and I lean heavily on him as we cross the patio into our room. The bed now has a fluffy comforter atop what was already there, and I climb on and lie in the nest of pillows. "Now," Kye says. "Tell me what you Saw."

My eyes fall closed. "Nothing."

"Nothing? What do you mean, nothing?"

"I mean nothing. As in no vision. No energy. No aura. Just a whole lot of blurry nothing. It never took shape."

"That's new." The bed creaks as he kneels on it to lean over me. "Never happened before?"

I shake my head. "Either the curse or the cut—not sure which one to be afraid of at the moment."

Kye takes my arm and shoves aside the flowing silk of my blouse to peek under the bandage. His gasp of alarm tells me everything I need to know. "This. Healing this wound is our number one priority."

"I can't Heal it, Kye. Remember? I already tried."

He lies next to me, propping himself up on his elbows. "I know, babe, but we have to come up with something. It's not a normal wound. It's festering green and it looks horrible."

He's right. It's not normal. It's a wound left by the Arawn Dagger, and my energy—my life force—will continue to leak out until I find a way to close it permanently. Kye doesn't know this, and now doesn't feel like the proper time to tell him. The truth is it's entirely possible that this wound can't be Healed. That battle in the cenote might kill me yet, more slowly and painfully than Alex. The thought has me burrowing into Kye's neck and drawing him closer. Suddenly, all the reasons I've held back, stayed angry at Kye, seem like small and stupid things. He holds me tight as if I'm everything he'll ever need, and I squeeze back, because in this moment, it's true.

I don't need a nap. The energy drain leaves me weak and out of shape, but compared to how the curse sickened me before I left Jackson, this seems a small thing. Ironically, I feel better physically, which leaves me more nervous about what's happening inside.

Kye's restless, and gets up to pace after only a few minutes of cuddling. When I can no longer take his brooding, I suggest he go help Kiersten in the kitchen, assuring him that I'm fine, and will continue to remain so. He throws a last skeptical glance at me as he closes the door, but I'm relieved to have him gone.

Once he's inside the main house, I pull off my blouse and unwrap my bandage to check my arm myself. My own surprised gasp startles me. The wound oozes bright green, red lines stretching out in every direction, spanning my entire elbow and climbing up my arm. My hands shake as I dig into my suitcase for my Healing kit.

I dribble herbal oil onto the open sore, massaging it until my skin absorbs it all, and then I apply more. When my arm is stained brown, I wrap a silver Healing stone in gauze and tape it in place. This is not something I can let anyone else see.

After drinking tablespoons of liquid herbs, chased with copious amounts of water, I dress again, arranging my sleeve to cover the bandage, and then venture outside to lounge in the sunshine and soak in some vitamin D.

Kye brought me here to rest—it's time I did that.

SIX

Shards of Glass

ROSE

I arrive home with little fanfare. My parents welcome me with open arms and teary eyes, but neither of them asks about all that's happened. Either the Dragons or my aunt and uncle must have updated them. It doesn't matter who told who what, though. None of them will ever know how much I've lost in these last days.

Nothing feels right anymore. Everything that was once good about this place where I grew up is hidden beneath a fog, yet so many new things about the world have become crystal clear.

My father tries to joke with me as he loads my suitcase into the car at the airport, but his punchline falls flat because I can't laugh. I might never laugh again. I'm still clutching the pillow that was Alejandro's, having taken it from the hotel, and I bury my face in it again, worried what I'll do when the smell that still lingers begins to fade. I cannot let his memory fade too. "Sorry Dad," I mumble. "I'm not up to talking right now."

My dad wraps his arm around me and squeezes. "That's okay, pumpkin. It's been a bad few days, but you'll get your smile back eventually."

I want to scream. *No. No, I won't. I don't want to ever smile again!* But instead, I bury my face in my daddy's shoulder and sigh, wishing I could find more tears, and wondering what it means that my eyes are dry and my heart is flat.

Flat. I climb into the back seat of my parents' SUV, gazing up at the jagged Tetons that spear the sky like broken shards of glass. We drove for hours in Mexico, through jungle so thick you could scarcely stick a pencil through the vegetation, but there were no mountains, and nothing nearby to pierce the enormous sky except trees, trees, and more trees.

Such different landscapes. Such different lives. Minutes ago, as our commuter plane landed, we flew over an erupting geyser and a large prismatic spring—such color, and interest—and then the wheels touched down and we taxied toward the miniscule terminal, dodging a moose that had wandered through the fence and onto the runway. "We're not in Mexico anymore," I'd said to Gabe.

He didn't even pretend to crack a smile. At least we have that in common.

We exited the plane together, neither of us having spoken more than two or three sentences since we left the others behind to clean up the details. I'm not sure how Gabe got out of debriefing with the rest of the Dragons—maybe he told them he was protecting me. I'm okay with that this time, because ever since Abby showed up last year, they've been so focused on her that no one has bothered to worry about me. No one remembered that I matter too. Except Alex.

Alex saw me. I didn't have to *try* to get his attention. I had it from minute one. That's why I liked him.

"Baggage claim is this way," Gabe had said, nudging me from where I'd stopped in the boarding area. "Your parents are picking you up."

I nodded, my throat still raw and clogged, and my voice rusty from sobbing for so many days, and followed him like a lost pup. He'd been right, of course. My parents were waiting for me near the baggage distribution belt, ready to whisk me away to the safety of home.

As we leave the parking lot and head toward town, I stare out the window at the overly bright colors that seem muted at the edges. In the distance, a herd of bison grazes on grass that is drying to yellow as the weather cools. This is familiar, and same. It is all the things I've known for as long as I can remember.

No, it's not Jackson that has changed since I left last month. It's me.

After nine days of hibernating in my bedroom with an endless list of old movies, my mother knocks on my door to tell me, "Baby? Gabe's here to see you."

"Tell him to go away." The automatic response formed in my brain long ago—back when I disliked Gabe. When I believed we had nothing in common except that we both loved Abby, and before our shattered hearts became another common bond. My mother remains, awaiting a more polite response. I pull Alex's pillow tighter against my chest and sit up to straighten my T-shirt. "I'll be down in a minute."

The ghost of a smile flutters over her lips. She's uncertain how to handle this sad version of her once overly-animated daughter. "Okay."

I haven't showered for days, but to be nice, I stop in the bathroom to brush my teeth. Gabe can deal with my greasy, unwashed self, wearing the same sweatpants I've worn all week and a T-shirt Alex left in my hotel room, but I won't subject him to halitosis. Grief is no excuse for poor dental hygiene. Even the most depressed girl should have *some* standards.

I find Gabe relaxing in my father's recliner while my mom serves him bottled water and store-bought cookies. Mom sees me walk in and grins like she believes I'm still alive. "And here she is," she says. "Miss Suzy Sunshine."

"Don't do that." I drape sideways across a second old, brown recliner. "Don't pretend or make jokes about me being cheerful or happy. I'm not. We all know I have depression issues—which, I should add, are totally justified."

"I agree," Gabe says. He doesn't look much better than me. "You have every excuse, and it's completely reasonable for you to hole up in your room, un-showered, and let rats build a nest in your hair while you watch TV dramas."

The truth in his words ignites a spark of anger—the first I've felt in weeks. It's a sign that I'm still capable of feeling something. "No one asked you."

"Rose," my mother chides. "Be nice. Gabe came to visit you. He brought you flowers." She indicates the prickly plant on the side table.

I snort. "That's not flowers. That's a cactus with a bloom on it."

Gabe nods, his brows rising. "Prickly pear. Thought it might remind you who you are."

"Who I am? How is a cactus supposed to remind me who I am, when even *I* don't know anymore? You know nothing about me, Gabe, which is increasingly apparent with every moment we spend together. If you knew me at all, you'd understand that I don't like cactus. Never have. They're ugly and pointy, and serve no purpose other than to store water for people who are stupid enough to get themselves stranded in the desert."

"Rose!" My mother jumps to attention, her deep frown insisting that I'm out of line.

I stand and whirl on her. "It's true! And if Gabe brought me a cactus to remind me who I am, it's because *he* thinks I'm prickly and spiny, and full of flavorless water."

Gabe stands, his jeans bagging at the waist as if he's lost a significant amount of weight. "That's not—"

"Oh no? Then what is it? Did you hope I'd prick my fingers on it and get the needles stuck in my skin?"

Fire burns in Gabe's eyes—the kind that flamed to life when we used to argue about Abby. "Maybe I did. Maybe I hoped you'd pick the thing up with your bare hand. Maybe I wanted you to get stuck so you'd experience pain, bleed, force you to remember that you're still alive—even though Alex isn't."

"Don't you say his name," I hiss. "Don't you ever say his name again. I don't want you to talk to me about Alex. I don't want you to talk to me about Abby. I don't want to talk to you at all. I can't believe I came downstairs so you could taunt me with my heartache."

His fierce expression fades, but before he can close the shutters, I glimpse misery that seems similar to my own. "Obviously. Of course I did. Because I'm a truly horrible, deplorable person. I'm sorry I bothered you."

My mother's still holding the plate of cookies, and trips over the rug to follow him as he storms toward the door. "I'm so sorry, Gabe. She's usually not like this. Give her a few days, maybe she'll have had time to process her grief ..."

He pauses in the doorway, but doesn't turn to look at me again. "Don't apologize for your daughter, Mrs. Westover. She's hated me since we met. She's always like this, with or without the grief." He slides his arms into the leather jacket that was so popular in the halls of the high school where he guarded Abby. "Thanks for the water."

"Have a nice day." Mom's voice fades as Gabe snaps the door closed. Then she whirls, anger burning, but rather than chew me out as she would normally do, she presses her lips together and glides into the kitchen.

In one fell swoop, I've alienated two of the three people who know I'm back in Jackson.

It's fine though. I don't want to see anyone anyway.

SEVEN
Tangible Desperation

ABBY

We spend the evening pouring over the books Kye found in Jonathan's library. There's such a wealth of fascinating information. I could lose hours reading the history and techniques of the ancient Gifted, but we don't have time for that. For now, we're after one important piece of information. Some way to Heal a wound caused by the Arawn Dagger.

Unfortunately, after hours of skimming the enormous tomes, the only thing we've found is records of people who died from wounds like mine, their powers draining slowly away, and taking their life force with it.

Kye doesn't say anything, but his desperation has nearly become tangible.

In the wee hours of morning, I slap my book closed and stand. "This is giving me a headache. I'm going to bed. We can start again in the morning."

He waves a hand in the direction of the bed. "Go ahead. You should rest. I'll finish up and join you soon."

But after my face is washed and my teeth brushed, and I've changed into sleepwear, Kye continues reading. When I snuggle into bed, he flicks off the overhead light and turns on a dim lamp. "I'll be right there," he mumbles. "I want to finish this section."

And though I need nothing more than to be held, I close my eyes and fall asleep, alone.

The next morning I sit up and rub my eyes. Kye's asleep with his head on the desk. I croak, "Kye?"

He doesn't move, so I swing my legs over the side of the bed and stand, fighting vertigo as I move carefully toward Kye. His face is pressed against the antique pages, and black ink stains his forehead. I shake him. "Kye. Come to bed."

He has three books open, and a notepad with pages covered in sloppy, incoherent scribbles that make no sense to me. I pick out random words and phrases that can actually be read: enemy, friends, curse, men who are gods and gods who are men, empath, resurrection of the soul, sacrifice.

His skin is warm, and his upper body rises and falls with slow, even breaths. He doesn't stir when I brush my fingers over his stubbly cheek, so I brush my lips across his. He jerks, eyes popping open in disoriented surprise. "What's the matter? Are you okay?"

I blink, trying not to laugh at the way his hair spikes in one direction, or the hot pink dot near his temple that originated from a highlighting pen. "Come to bed."

He rubs his eyes, sniffling as his brain struggles to function. "Can't. Gotta find something."

"Kye, it's a waste of time to read when you're too tired to comprehend what you're seeing. You need to rest." He opens his mouth as if to say no, but I cut him off. "Besides, I need you to hold me so I can sleep."

He blinks again, squinting at the window, where the first rays of sunlight send pink streaks across the blue-gray sky. "Okay."

He climbs in, pulls me into the cocoon of his arms, and drops to sleep almost immediately. My mind roils, and my arm burns with the ache of fire. I'm supposed to know how to fix the things that ail people. I should know how to fix this. I feel like I do, that somewhere deep down in the box of secret knowledge that belonged to Raina, I have the answer.

Maybe I need to find a way to unlock it.

EIGHT

Maybe

ROSE

Eventually, I take a shower to appease my parents, who have grown increasingly disgusted with my stench. I can't smell anything, but they vow that they feel otherwise. This morning, my mother invaded my room at eleven o'clock and kicked me out, insisting it's laundry day and that my sheets are top priority.

It's a lie. My mother has been making me wash my own sheets since I was tall enough to reach the shelf where she keeps the laundry soap. Every Saturday, without fail, I have faithfully followed my mother's instructions to wash, dry, iron, fold. My bedding. My clothes. In our house, Saturday means all things dirty are made clean again.

Saturday.

Today is Tuesday, and I haven't done laundry since Mexico. My mother has done it all for me—except my sheets, because I've refused to leave my bed.

I take Alejandro's pillow with me into the bathroom, protecting it fiercely, lest she attempt to wash his smell out—it's already fading far too fast. I turn the water to scalding, and dig through my cabinet for an old bottle of store-bought body wash and shampoo. For the last several months, Abby supplied me with homemade toiletries infused with her experimental blends of herbs—and I've loved everything she mixed for me. Now the bottles remind me of Abby, which reminds me of Alex, and so I sweep every last container into the trash and replace them with long unused bottles of the cheap crap I used *before*.

After stripping off my clothes and throwing them into the hall for my mother, I catch a glimpse of myself in the mirror. My usually olive skin is nearly as pale as Abby's, which is telling, since Abby is the whitest girl I know. My eyes are dull, and my cheeks plumped with the extra pounds I've gained from inactivity and comfort eating. And dammit, Gabe was right. It does look like rats have built a nest in my hair. I pick up a brush and attempt to tame some of the tangles, but after five full minutes, decide it's pointless and give up in favor of stepping into the shower to deep condition instead.

Wrapped in a towel, I return to my room to find it dusted and cleaned. My dirty clothes, dishes, and trash can of empty water bottles have magically disappeared as if cleaning faeries have been here. The floor is striped with vacuum marks, and the carpet reeks of air freshener. My blinds are open, allowing afternoon sunlight to stream over the flowering cactus from Gabe. I frown and stalk to it. "I swear I threw this thing away." I dump it upside down into the trash can, still insulted by its presence.

My bed is as naked as me. Either my mother is coming back, or she expects me to make it myself with the spare sheets in the linen closet. If it's the latter, I may go without bedding.

I drop my towel and search for my cut-off sweat pants to wear with another of Alex's T-shirts. Maybe it was wrong, but we spent a lot of time together in Mexico. He left five shirts in my room— preferring to go without one in the heat and humidity—and when I left, I took them all. Maybe his family is angry. Maybe the Dragons wish they had his clothes for evidence. Maybe karma considers it stealing. But I don't care. It's destiny. Like he left them there on purpose so I would have a piece of him when he was gone. Like maybe he knew he wasn't coming back. I won't forget. Upon arriving home, I hung all the shirts on my closet door so I can see them from my bed and remember how he never wore one for long.

"Don't you feel better now?" My mother strides in, arms loaded with freshly laundered bedding, which she sets on the mattress, oblivious to the fact that I'm standing here in my underwear. "Isn't it nice to have your hair clean?"

I glare in response as she picks up Alex's pillow from where I dropped it on the bare mattress when I returned from showering. "This boy must have been really special," she says softly, "That you brought so much of him back with you. I wish you'd tell me about him so I could get to know him too." She unfolds the fitted sheet and spreads it over my bed, tucking the corners with deft fingers, while I pull the T-shirt over my still-dripping hair, and then drag on my shorts.

"Yes," I tell her, rubbing my hair with my towel. "He *was* really special. Really, really special."

She glances at me as she unfolds the top sheet. "He would have to be. I've been telling your father since the day you were born that only the most exceptional of all extraordinary men will be good enough to win your heart."

The tears come, so swift and sudden, that I don't feel it coming before I'm crumpled on the floor, sobbing hysterically. And then my mother's there. She pulls me into her lap—even though I'm taller than her—and holds me, her motherly voice and familiar embrace the strongest form of comfort a girl could need.

She dries my tears with the corners of the sheet and then surrounds us in it as we lean against the closet wall. And then she does the most comforting thing she could ever do—something I never would have expected. She cries with me.

Eventually, we get my bed made, and my mom talks me into joining her in the kitchen while she makes dinner so I can tell her about

Alex. About how we met on the beach, and the way he comforted me when the wave came and I thought we were all going to die, and again in the car, after Abby pulled her trick of going back into the house for Murtagh. I tell Mom about how Alex stuck close while we were learning to scuba dive, and how he was instrumental in helping me learn to further develop my Gift of Communication, how we trained together to go into the cenote. I tell her about the bar where he taught me to Salsa dance, and how it was him who knew Abby was in trouble on the night of her birthday, and he who single-handedly kept us both safe while we fled from the Dark Elen.

I talk and talk, and before I notice how much time has passed, my mother sets a meatloaf on the table next to herbed red potatoes, green beans, and gravy. She hands me plates and glasses, and I automatically set the table, not realizing what I'm doing until it's already done.

There's something infinitely comforting about returning to a routine that is so ingrained that the actions are automatic.

My father joins us for dinner, and I've eaten half my meal when it occurs to me what's happened. I've set the table and had a conversation. I'm showered and wearing clean underwear. My heart hasn't unbroken, but with my mother's help, I took a tiny step forward. She dragged me out of the cave I'd crawled into and decided to remain indefinitely. I'm not sure I want to be out. Not long term. Not yet. But it feels good to talk—to share stories of Alex with my parents rather than keeping them locked inside me.

I may go back to hiding later tonight, but when my father turns on the TV and rents a movie I wanted to see before Mexico, I snuggle into his arms, feeling for the first time in months like I'm not—don't have to be—completely alone.

NINE

The Weight of Memory

ABBY

We stay with Johnathan and Kiersten for three weeks. Me and Kye. Once again in the same room, sharing a bed, and this time, Rose isn't here to keep us in check. We're all each other has, and sometimes that overwhelming realization tangles us together in sleep. Other times the memories of all we've given up, everything and everyone we've left behind, divides the bed in half, leaving us each to scoot as far as possible toward the edges.

Part of this division is due to my reluctance to let Kye see my wound should we get carried away, and another part due to Kye's reluctance to ... well, to get carried away. I'm not in any condition to push, however I want to, and Kye seems ultra-aware of that fact, and uses it as a shield.

But in front of people—specifically Kiersten—Kye is as dedicated and devoted as ever, which alleviates some of my jealousy for this person who owns a piece of Kye's past. It does not, however, help Kiersten's jealousy, which is nearing the point of open hostility by the time Kye decides we've been stationary as long as he dares and it's time to move on.

One morning, I wake to rain. Not the slow, steady curtains that fell in the jungles of Mexico, but a downpour so intense it's like the sky is a water bucket that has broken open from the bottom, accompanied by thunder that shakes the whole world and rattles the windows in their panes.

A glance outside earns me a view of the grassy area beyond the pool, where a new pond has formed, continuing to grow with each minute that passes, each figurative bucket that falls. Kye comes out of the bathroom rubbing his wet hair with a towel. "It's all yours," he says, indicating the bathroom. "But be quick, if you can. We should get on the road as soon as possible."

I swing my legs over the side of the bed, taking a moment to steady myself, and grip the headboard for balance. The vertigo worsens daily. "We can't drive in this. It'll be impossible to see the road."

Kye glances outside too, seeming less concerned. "Don't worry, the worst of it should pass soon. It's a gulf storm. Downpour one minute, sunshine and blue skies the next. I suspect it'll let up by the time we eat breakfast and load the car." He watches me make my way to the bathroom, slower than a snail as I pause to lean against the wall after every step. "I wish you would let me help you."

I lack the energy to fight, and Kye knows it. "You just want to see me naked."

"Obviously," he says, the heat in his eyes leaving no question. Kye's not joking, even if I am. "But that's not why. Abby, you're struggling. With everything. You won't let me help Heal you, and you barely let me touch you unless Kiersten's watching. You could at least let me help steady you when you can't do it on your own. Or hell, I can run your bath if that's what you need. Let me do *something*."

"Okay." It's not so much me giving in as not wanting to fight, and having Kye's help will get us out of here faster. While I love being isolated from the rest of our problems, and enjoy playing with the children, I agree that it's time to go. I won't miss feeling Kiersten's gaze bore into me every time we're in the same room.

Kye helps me to the bathroom, and I lean against the counter while he runs the water. I direct him to bottles of liquid herbs and instruct him to add drops of each. When the tub is full and frothy with bubbles, he turns off the tap and stands, bracing his hands on either side of me, and leaning in so our noses touch. "I love you. No matter what happens. Regardless of our past or our future. Forever. Remember that, okay?"

"I do," I breathe.

He shakes his head. "You don't. But it's all right. I'm going to do everything I can to help that happen. I'm not going to give up on us. I promise." He kisses the tip of my nose and leaves me alone. I strip off my clothes and slide into the tub until I'm submerged to my neck in foamy, fragrant bubbles.

Even I don't understand why I vacillate between love and anger at Kye. He has apologized more times than I can count, sincere apologies that come from a place deep inside him that I'm fully aware belongs to me, and me alone. I'm not perfect either. Maybe I didn't chase after Gabe actively, but I did allow myself to develop feelings for him—and I kissed him.

Oh boy, did I kiss Gabe. And he absolutely kissed me back. If I'm honest with myself—and every once in a while I can be—I remember that night, that kiss, and how it was Gabe who didn't push, and Gabe who did the honorable thing, and Gabe who walked away when I might have given into other temptations.

And I will never know what would have happened between me and Gabe if I hadn't opened that door and found Kye on the other side.

No. I'm not innocent. Not even a little bit.

I'm angry with Kye, but not for the reasons he thinks. Yes, I'm hurt over the thing with Crystal, and because he kept secrets from me, and because of the way he tried to push me into getting married before his secrets came out, but I can get past those things. I can. In a lot of ways, I already have. The thing I can't get over is the part where Kye knew Gabe was still alive and didn't have enough faith in my Healing ability, enough faith in me, to let me choose whether or not to help him. To Heal him.

And I'm harboring resentment that I was forced to leave Mexico so fast that I couldn't explain to Gabe how or why or that I was going. Or to Rose. Rose needed me more than ever, and I disappeared. Though I recognize, logically, that it's not Kye's fault, part of me blames him for our current circumstances. Because the part of me that loves those two has developed a festering tumor of guilt that won't heal until I find a way to talk to them. To see them and hug them and show them how sorry I truly am. I feel as though my choices have been taken from me all over again, and though it makes no sense, that part of me is searching for a way to make this Kye's fault too.

Even though it's not. Not really.

I emerge from the tub with clean skin and clean hair and soothed nerves, realizing that I'll never truly be able to focus on Kye until I find a way to talk to the two people who were most affected by my leaving. It's the most basic, fundamental stage of Healing a wound. First purge the infection, then apply the salve. I don't know what the salve is in this case, but purging the infection—that's going to mean talking to them. Both of them. Saying things that were left unsaid.

Kye knocks on the door. "Abby, I'm going to the main house for a few minutes. Will you be okay? Do you need anything?"

"No thank you," I tell him. "I'm fine. Go ahead."

"Should I bring you some juice or something?"

"No," I tell him, wrapping my hair in a towel and pulling on my robe. "I'll be over for breakfast soon."

Once again I carefully dress the festering, green wound, caking on my strongest concoctions. As I'm repacking my herbs, my fingers brush the bottle of an experimental mixture meant to help me See visions more clearly.

Freezing in the caves under the cenote, alone and terrified.

When I tried my hardest, even though I was searching for Kye, I channeled in on Gabe. I've never figured out why—maybe because he was in the most trouble—but I wonder if I could do that again now.

Still wrapped in my robe, I crack the door and peer into the bedroom to make sure the coast is clear. When I glance out the window and find Kye in the main house talking to Jonathan, I dress in shorts and a tank top, adding a lightweight sweatshirt to protect against the humidity. I rub a liberal amount of the psychic blend on my forehead and behind my ears, then gather amethyst, emerald, and quartz crystals and lie on the bed, placing them along my body as I close my eyes.

Focus. My mind spins with everything that's happened, leaving it impossible for me to focus on one event. Alejandro's death, Rose's tears, Gabe floating unconscious and lifeless as Kye hauled him to the surface. Saying goodbye to my mother—again, and the scrap of paper she secretly handed me as I was leaving.

A window of light opens in my mind, fixated on that scrap of paper. I blink, and the light goes away. "No, I want to see Gabe," I tell myself. I need to know that he doesn't hate me. That he's still doing okay. That I truly Healed him. I close my eyes again, intent on Gabe's face. Focus, focus, focus. But the light never comes. My mind wanders until I'm drifting in a dream-like state.

I blink again. Kye's waiting. He asked me to hurry. I can't fall asleep. I rub more oil on my forehead, humming to clear my mind, and trying again to focus, and again, land on that scrap of paper. It bothers me. My father—after all these years—could still be alive. If that's the case, where has he been all this time and why hasn't he come to find me? And if my mother knew about this, why is she now dating? None of this makes sense.

The light comes slowly, a tiny flicker that wavers like a flame that's trying to decide whether or not to ignite. I catch a glimmer of familiar eyes, and then the light dies with all the finality of a flame being snuffed out.

I blink, discouraged and confused. This is not what I hoped for. I haven't had a vision since Mexico, nor have I felt any Healing power since Gabe. I even struggle to see auras. "What's wrong with me?" I wonder aloud. The only reply is the rain tap-tap-tapping on the window, pounding on the roof.

I sit up, swamped with dizziness, and fighting tears of frustration. I can't help anyone until I pull myself together.

"Babe, you okay?" Kye's standing in the doorway, concern evident in the wrinkle that forms between his eyes.

I press my fists into the bed to steady myself. "Yes. Light-headed. It's like being drunk all the time. Not fun."

He gently pulls me to standing. "You should eat. It'll help."

He leads me through the rain and into the kitchen, where I'm greeted by the warmth of cooking breakfast meats and the happy voices of the children, who are lined up on barstools at the counter.

"Miss Abby!" Kinsey says. "I saved you a seat, and I got you a plate with bacon on it, because bacon is good for you."

"Thank you, Kinsey." I claim the stool, shrugging at Kye, who seems unconcerned about sitting.

"I already ate," he informs me, nodding at the plate. "Fill up now. Not sure how long it will be before we get another homemade breakfast. I'm going to go map us a route. Whenever you're ready, I'll load the car."

The reminder casts an air of sadness over the room, and causes the ever silent little Brooke to ask, "Miss Abby where are you going?"

Needing something to do with my hands, I fill my glass with orange juice. "It's time for us to move on, sweetheart."

She slides off her stool and sidles up to me. "You going to find more children to teach?"

"I hope so," I tell her sincerely. I've developed a hint of envy for Kiersten, not because she's beautiful or talented—though she is both of those things—but because she has the freedom to choose her future, her job. She's here looking after these children because this is what she wants to do, and where she wants to be. Ever since I found out what my Gifts mean, I've felt my own freedom draining away as the burden of responsibility grew. I was never given a choice, but if I was, I could fit here, with these young people who seem so happy and loving. I can tell they adore Kiersten and Jonathan. Maybe I wouldn't stay here, in this exact place, but this seems like a profession I would enjoy, something I could live with, wherever I ended up.

"I want you to stay here," Brooke says. This is the most she has talked since we arrived, and I'm hit by a twinge of regret.

I pull the girl onto my lap and offer her a slice of my bacon. "I want to stay here too. You're such good kids. I wish I could watch you grow up, but Mr. Kye and I have other things to do."

"Will you come back to visit?" She swings her legs so her heels bang into my calf.

"I'll certainly try."

"Will you bring your baby next time?"

"What baby?" As I ask, wisps of memory flutter through my brain, the angelic face of the little girl in my visions.

"The one you used to have when I was a grownup."

The blood drains from my face as I glance at Kiersten, who has joined us. "Brooke, do you remember being a grownup before?"

"I remember lots of things." She helps herself to my toast. "I was a grownup lots of times, and then a baby again, and then I grew. Sometimes I had a different mommy and daddy, but one time my parents died in a fire, and then I was all alone."

Kiersten watches with a raised brow, and interjects, "Brooke's Gift is that of memory. She remembers all the lives she's lived, which, from what we can tell so far, has been close to five, and she remembers the people who were directly involved or important in those lives. It's interesting, because she's very much a child in intellect and behaviors, but her memories tend to be chillingly adult. There's not a lot we can do to help develop her Gift—it is what it is. So instead of training her to use it, we're teaching her how to function with the weight of her memories. She's only five, but has already helped us fill in lots of holes in our recorded history."

If she remembers, if she was there, I wonder if she knows what happened to Theron and Raina. I wonder if she knows how to break the curse. I wonder if she knows what happened to the lost city.

"Brooke," I ask, trying hard to keep my voice steady. "Do you know what happened to the baby?"

"The grandma-lady took her away, and I never saw her again."

"Do you know who the grandma-lady was?"

She shakes her head. "I can't remember her name. She had gray hair and a long dress, and she must have lived far away, because after the king and queen died, the lady took the special baby and left, and they never came back again." She finishes off her toast, and scoots off my lap. "I'm all done. May I be excused?"

I nod, trying to remember that this girl is only five, and can't know the importance of what she's told me before running out to play. When she's gone, along with the other children, Kiersten scoops fluffy scrambled eggs onto my plate, urging me to eat. "Don't worry. Jonathan keeps it written down—as told from Brooke's point of view—in the library, and Kye made copies of everything we've gleaned from her."

I focus on the eggs and pancakes on my plate. I'm starving, but struggle to find an appetite, so I'm slow about it, pausing to sip my juice after each bite to make sure that what's going down stays there.

Kiersten takes the seat next to me. "I haven't been the nicest person to you, and I'm sorry. Please don't take this the wrong way, but I don't think you should be leaving in your condition."

"My condition?" I raise my brows, wondering if she's about to accuse me of being pregnant too. Won't be the first time. Although, having Kiersten worry about me and a non-existent baby is far more amusing, and perhaps slightly more satisfying, than when Gabe did.

But Kiersten indicates the sleeve covering my bandage. "Your wound. It's not healing, is it?"

It's not healing. In fact, it is growing steadily worse, and I don't know what to do about it. "I'll be fine. I can take care of myself. I'm a Healer, remember?"

"And yet," she plows on, "You haven't Healed this particularly dangerous, perhaps life-threatening injury. You've been here for three weeks, and I've seen Jonathan offer to help you a whole bunch of times, all of which you refused for a plethora of lame reasons that were really excuses. To me, this can only mean that either you don't want to be Healed, or your attempts have been unsuccessful."

Kiersten is smarter than she lets on. "Why would I not want to be Healed?"

She raises her eyebrows. "Exactly. Why not? You have the guy, the life, the chance to change the world. Why would you want to die? That leaves us with you having tried to Heal yourself, and your attempts not working." I start to respond, but Kiersten silences me with a look. "This is the Arawn Dagger we're talking about. The weapon designed to drain a Gifted person's power by spilling their blood. The most powerful Healer in the world might not be able to reverse the effects of this."

"Doesn't mean I won't try." I push my chair away from the table and stand, wobbling on my feet. "I have a lot to do before I die."

She purses her lips. "Like bear the next golden child and restore a fallen culture? Heal the rift that broke Dryden in the first place?"

"Yep." I lift my plate and start for the sink, but she takes it from me, shooing me away from any possibility of work.

Her eyes flicker toward the ground. "Look. Kye isn't mine. He'll never be mine. Believe it or not, I've accepted that. But I worry about him. I care about his well-being and what happens to him. Before you go traipsing across the country in your condition, you should consider going home. He's in over his head, and I don't want to see him sink."

Just what I needed to hear. The knot of aggravation in my gut tightens. How could she intimate that I would intentionally endanger Kye? "If we were in over our heads, we wouldn't be here. This wasn't a decision we made lightly."

The ghost of a smirk flits across her face. "Well, then never mind. I'm sure you're right. I'm sure he'd tell you if he felt that way. He would never keep anything that important from you."

The ugly head of the anger I've kept buried rears up inside me, and it takes everything I have to not let it loose. "Kye loves me. We don't keep secrets from each other."

Her eyebrows rise, and this time, the smirk blooms as she indicates the sleeves covering my injured arm. "Don't you?"

I'm saved from having to answer when Kye walks in. "Hey, babe, are you ready to get packed? Jonathan's going to return our rental and let us take one of his cars. We should get on the road soon."

I nod and follow him back to the pool house, leaving Kiersten, and her smirk, behind.

When our newly-acquired car is packed, we say our goodbyes in the foyer, swarmed with hugs and kisses from the children. Jonathan offers advice on which direction we should go, and signs to watch for that might indicate we're being followed. Then he pulls me aside, claiming he has a gift for me.

He folds a velvet pouch of crystals into my palm. "I'm sorry I don't have an ancient crystal on hand. That could be the one thing that would be powerful enough to get this wound on the mend. I've never sent someone away in worse condition than when she arrived."

I have such a crystal. The pink diamond given to me by the goddesses Morrigana. Using it could mean the end of my life on Earth—and any potential future lives—and yet ... if this wound is to be the end of everything anyway, I may have no choice.

I squeeze the pouch in my fist and hold it against my heart. "Thanks for these. They'll get me through for a while."

A few feet away, Kiersten throws herself into Kye's arms, sniffling, and he hugs her back, his eyes finding mine and holding, as if to reassure me that he still loves *only* me. Eventually, he pushes her away, and because I'm truly grateful for her hospitality, I hug Kiersten too. "Thank you. We owe you big."

Her returning smile is watery, but genuine. "Yes, you do. Take care of him, and consider the debt repaid."

Flushing, Kye ushers me outside and to the car. As he puts the car in gear and pulls away from the house, he says, "I've been thinking. How would you feel about visiting the last place you lived with your family intact? Dad and Grandma and you and your mom?"

Nerves buzz along my skin, though I don't know why. "I'd love it. Why there, specifically?"

"We need to find out what happened to your father." He turns onto a main road. "Maybe there are still clues. Or maybe the echo of memories will spark a vision. Also, you need to find lost memories of your grandmother. She's the one person I can think of who would know how to Heal your wound."

He's thought it through, and I appreciate that he knows me so well. "That's a good idea. I guess we're heading for Phoenix?"

"Unless you object." His lips turn up in a smile.

Thoughts of Phoenix bring to mind my friend Tanya, who I haven't seen in over two years. "I have a friend there I'd like to look up. Maybe she'll let us crash at her place for a night, save some money."

"Do you think she'll have room?" His tone exposes his obvious reluctance.

"Probably not," I admit, tamping down the urge to insist that it's *my* turn to look in on *my* past, the way he did while we stayed at Kiersten's. Only Tanya is female, which is a planet of a different variety. "But she'll make room if we need it. She's good like that." When he doesn't reply, I stand my ground. "I'll call her next time we stop."

"Okay." He reaches over and takes my hand, lacing our fingers together. I don't want to believe that Kye feels like he's drowning— but I'm not sure how to tell. There's a desperation to our every move, but then, Kye's been moving like he's desperate since the day we met. There's no reason for me to believe he would rather be anywhere else, so I dislodge Kiersten's words from my head and attempt to trust that Kye will truly keep his word and never lie to me again.

TEN

Prickly and Resilient

ROSE

That damn cactus is back again. I keep throwing it away, and then find it sitting upright and undamaged on my nightstand, or my desk, or the table in the corner where I pile all the crap I don't want to put away. I can't get rid of it!

This is my mother's way of showing me how resilient a cactus can be, and if it can survive a beating, so can I. But seriously.

"You're determined to live, aren't you, stupid thing? Who gives someone a prickly, ugly cactus anyway? It's not like we live in a desert where nothing else can survive." I pick the bizarre plant off my night stand, determined to take it outside and toss it away once and for all, but then change my mind. For whatever reason, my mother thinks I should keep it, and she's tried so hard to help me move on. I can't throw it away again, for her sake. So I move it to the windowsill and crack the blinds so that sunlight falls over the bloom that should have long-since broken off or wilted. It *has* proven surprisingly hearty.

Outside, our ginormous maple tree ruffles in the breeze, some of its leaves beginning to yellow. Higher in the mountains, shades of orange, brown, and red signal the return of another glorious fall. Alex would have loved this season in Jackson. He once explained to me that they don't have different seasons in his part of Mexico.

Further north, he claimed, some cities could get quite chilly, but in Playa Del Carmen, it's pretty much the same climate, year round, give or take a few tropical storms.

Once, as we walked hand-in-hand through the jungle, he said, "I would like to come visit you. I would like to see your American mountains, and your geysers and mud pots and wildlife. I would like to see where you come from and how you came to be who you are."

No one has ever taken such an interest in my life that he would travel thousands of miles to learn more—especially not a boy. Alex was not only interested in my appearance, or my ability to party. He was interested in my history, my daily life. What a remarkable gift I found in him. "I would have brought you back with me," I whisper, hoping that wherever he is, he can hear me.

On the street below, a car passes, and for a second, the driver looks like Gabe. Maybe I should apologize to him for being so rude the other day, for trying to throw away his gift. My gaze dips toward the cactus, and then back to the car as it turns the corner. It's not Gabe.

Guilt settles in. I've been opposed to Gabe's existence since the day Abby and I met him. In so many ways, he stood for everything I believe is wrong with the way the Dragons do things. But at a time when he's also devastated, he brought me this plant. I'm not sure why he chose a cactus, or what it's supposed to mean, but it was a thoughtful thing to do, no matter how I look at it.

In a moment of weakness, I find my phone—on the floor under my bed—and send a text before I can change my mind.

Thanks for the gift. It was a sweet gesture, and I appreciate it.

Then I toss the phone on the bed, sighing. Gabe doesn't need my thanks. He's like the lone wolf, content to offer a portion of his kill before he slinks back into the shadows of the forest, but it feels good to offer my thanks anyway. It stings that he never cared about me before Mexico, but he's been nothing but kind since we got home. It's time I offered him an olive branch.

I'm curled on my bed, halfway through another episode of my favorite TV drama, and nearing the end of a bag of salt and vinegar potato chips when my text chime sounds. I pick it up, hopeful that maybe Jen has found some time and wants to come over. I texted her the other day, but she hasn't replied. She knows I'm here, but hasn't made the effort to communicate with me at all. Probably doesn't know what to say—like all the rest of the people in my life.

I'm surprised. The response isn't Jen pulling her head out long enough to care about her best friend. It's Gabe. Who I never thought gave a crap. Responding to my text only minutes after I sent it.

You're welcome. <smiley face> I thought for sure you would throw it away.

I swallow a laugh. He knows me well.

I did. Six or seven times. My mom keeps rescuing the damn thing.

It takes him a minute to reply. Long enough that I wonder if I've offended him. Then my phone chimes again.

It's made to survive, like you. And me.

For a moment, I allow self-pity to creep in, but then I remember that though Abby isn't dead, to Gabe, she might as well be. Since Alex died, I've wondered if there's anything in the world worse than the deathly ache of losing someone I loved to an untimely tragedy. How would I have felt if Alex had run off with someone else? No explanations or goodbyes. Just gone.

Abby was more than a job to Gabe, but she *was* also his job. So I suspect he got in huge trouble with Zane—maybe lost his position with the Dragons, which would explain his sudden abundance of free time.

"Misery loves company," I tell myself, and respond:

Do you want to hang out sometime?

I regret clicking send the instant I do, hoping he doesn't think I'm going to fall into his arms for a rebound. I only want company from someone who knows what miserable feels like. His response is strangely comforting:

Only if you promise to get dressed.

Gabe shows up at my door an hour later, ultra-casual in faded jeans and a T-shirt that barely stretches over the muscles in his biceps. One look at me and he rips off his aviator glasses in annoyance. "You're supposed to be dressed."

Eyebrows raised, I glance down at my cutoff sweatpants—the ones I have now worn for three days in a row. "Do I look naked to you?"

"You know what I mean."

"No, I don't." I shake my head, indignant. Maybe this was a bad idea. What was I thinking inviting Gabe to hang out? I don't want to hang out; I want to be alone. I want to hole up in my room and be a hermit until this ginormous ache in my chest shrinks.

It would be hard to miss the way he rolls his eyes and buttons up his irritation. "We'll be leaving your house for a bit. I'll wait while you change into suitable attire for being seen in public. Or at least for being outside."

I glance down again. "Why is this not suitable? Where are we going?"

He gestures at one of the opalescent disks the Dragons sometimes use for transportation. "For a ride, to start. You could use some sun."

I step onto the cold porch with him, barefooted. "This is fine for going for a ride. Besides, who are we going to see?" To be honest, I wouldn't care. I'm not out to impress anyone. Least of all Gabe.

"Rose," he starts, and I can feel a lecture building inside him. I can also tell he's being super careful not to let it out.

"What?" I ask after an extended pause.

He points at my feet. "Put some shoes on."

I can't argue with that. If the disk runs low on solar power, we'd end up walking for whatever distance we flew. I go inside to retrieve my shoes, and while the door is still open, he says, "Grab a jacket too. The temperature drops in the shade."

I'm used to the cold. Been living in Jackson for most of my life, so climate changes are normal and expected. I doubt I'll need a jacket, but Gabe's watching, and I don't have the energy to argue, so I grab a sweatshirt out of the coat closet. "Happy?"

With a snort, he shakes his head, "Sure. Whatever." He directs me to the disk, and I climb on, holding tight to his waist, grateful to know that when we make a concerted effort to avoid fighting, we can actually get along. Temporarily.

ELEVEN

A Narrow Escape

ABBY

I'm running from a foe I can't see. It's a shadow that takes shape whenever I look back, and each time I do, it becomes a different form. It's my father, my grandmother, Rose. Then it's Gabe. It becomes people from my past, children I went to school with, bullies who pushed me around, bookworms who were kind. There's one small child who isn't old enough to walk, let alone chase, and I suspect this might be the child Brooke mentioned—the one who is in my future. Or my past. When I turn back again, the shadow becomes Alejandro. Not the live Alejandro, but the one I last saw, with his mutilated body and already decaying face.

A scream builds in my throat, escaping beyond my control.

I'm running from everything in life, moving toward some unseen conclusion that may or may not come to pass, and I'm scared. What if I fail? Alejandro is proof that I can't save everyone, maybe not even myself.

When my throat is raw and sore, the shadow lifts, overwhelmed by light. Three bodies stand before me, and I'm finally able to stop running and catch my breath. The women smile, and I recognize the goddesses of the Morrigana.

"Abigail Johnson, you are exactly where you are supposed to be," one says.

I jerk awake, sweat beading on my forehead, as Kye clutches my hand in one of his, while the other cups my cheek. "There you are. Come on back to me, babe."

My eyes sting every time I blink. Sunlight streams through the car windows, warming my skin, and bringing me back to reality. "Where are we?"

He shakes his head, looking up as if it's the first time he's paid attention. "I don't know. Middle-of-nowhere Texas."

"Why are we stopped?"

He raises a brow. "About the time you started screaming bloody murder in your sleep, I figured maybe it would be a good idea to pull over."

"Sorry." I close my eyes against the burning sun. "How long was I out?"

"About an hour. We still have a long way to go, but we should find a gas station or restaurant and take a break. You could use some air. "

"It's okay. I'm fine."

"You're clammy, and warmer than I like. What happened?"

He sits back, allowing me to straighten in my seat, at which point the vertigo hits me hard. I roll down the window and gulp the thick, salty air. "Might have been a dream."

"Are you sure?"

"Of course not. There's always the chance that it's a vision, but it didn't seem like one." And I haven't had any visions since I Healed Gabe. This would be the first.

"Do you remember any important details?"

I tell him about being chased, about the Morrigana. "It's probably a dream, the kind people have when they sleep."

Kye's chuckle is rich and relieving because it's genuine. "Babe, we both know you don't do normal. When it comes to you, everything—every thought, experience, and yes, dream—means *something*."

A glance at the stress lines in the corners of his eyes and the tightness in his shoulders reminds me that Kye has as much on his mind as I do—maybe more. He knows I'm in bad shape, without seeing my wound. "You're right. We should stop for a break. I'd like to stretch, maybe grab a cold drink and a snack."

"On it."

Basking in the sunshine as we have lunch at the outdoor café does a lot to revive me. We've thrown away our trash and are on our way to the car when my eyes catch on an unnatural line of black clouds, heading straight for us.

"Uh oh," I murmur. "That's not good."

Kye's head whips around, his jaw tightening with concern. "Nope. Not at all. How did the demons find us faster than the Dragons?"

I grab his hand and pull him toward the car, desperate to deny what's right in front of us. "We don't know that it's demons. It could be a real storm that looks like demons."

Kye fumbles in his pocket for the keys. "There's no such thing."

"We can hope."

"And sit here waiting to find out? No way." He hits the lock button, but before I can get in, a gust of wind shoves me against the car, pounding hard on my back.

I'm trapped against the warm metal, unable to catch my breath, so rather than fight it, I rest against it, hoping to soak up the warmth left behind by the sun so I can channel it. I've fought demons like these before, in Mexico, Jackson, Las Vegas, and every time, I've had the ability to fight back. But this time I have no energy, no warmth. I have no fight left in me. I'm running again because I don't want to fight anymore. Part of me wants to give up and let them take me, but they would take Kye too, and I can't let that happen.

I especially don't want to find out what will happen if they do take me. Maybe they'll turn me dark. Maybe I'll become as evil as the demons. Or become a demon. That's not what I want for the rest of forever. I'm tired of being good, but I definitely could never deliberately choose to be evil.

I lie against the car on the verge of surrender. Kye throw his arms up to protect his face and makes his way around the car, where he lays his body against mine—protection from the battering wind. He squeezes his arm between the car and my body to grasp the door handle. "I'm going to open this," he says. "Let's lean back so it can happen, and then you jump in and pull it closed as hard as you can."

I try to nod, but can't move my head. The wind is too strong. "What about you?"

"Once you're in the car, I'll go to the other side and do the same thing."

"Okay." He counts, and we lean, but the wind buffets hard, making it nearly impossible to open the door more than a few inches. Kye holds tight, working it open until I can squeeze my body through. When he's sure I'm in, he lets go. I try to yank it closed, as promised, but the wind tries to rip the door off the hinges, so Kye throws his body against the metal until the latch catches.

Inside the car, I can breathe. Kye clings to the bumper as he fights his way around the trunk to attempt the feat again. I sense a disaster in the making. He tries to open his door, but it doesn't budge. I shove at it from the inside, pounding with my feet, but with no success, so I crawl into the back and try the driver's side passenger door. The latch releases and with effort, the door flies open on a huge gust of wind.

I grab Kye's shirt and pull him in. He dives gratefully to the floor, and together we heave the door closed.

Breathing heavily, we climb into our seats and buckle up—because driving away is the only escape at this point. A dark presence creeps under the seats, sending a chill across my shoulders. It swirls our heads, fogging the windows and dropping the temperature to icy cold. I've been this cold before—in Mexico, on the pyramid. I don't remember for sure what made the demons go away, but I suspect it had something to do with Murtagh and his sprite friends. This time Murtagh isn't here.

Neither is Gabe or Christine, both of whom came to my rescue back then. It's just Kye and me, now, and because of who we are, the demons won't get tired or bored and leave us. They won't stop until we're frozen in ice or dead in a smashed car in the middle of nowhere. This is not a time when I can lie down and wait it out. I have to find the power to act, whether I have it or not.

It helps that I've been outside and my skin is warm with sunshine and dewy with coastal Texas humidity. I don't have to reach too far before the light hovering under my skin flares to life, burning the demon to smoke. It fills the car with damp stickiness until the air is heavy and thick.

Across the parking lot, a mini-van stops at a gas pump, and three children hop out, followed by a young mother, all squealing about the wind as they hurry into the store. There are three other cars, with various occupants, also affected by the shadows. We can't drive away and leave the innocents to the demons.

Kye's expression tells me that he's having similar thoughts. We need to draw the shadows away from the public and deal with them where we don't have an audience. He squeezes my hand and turns off the car. One squeeze, two. On the third, we let go, each diving out of the car.

The black wind pummels me as I bolt for the cornfield across the street, trying hard not to scream and attract attention. I'm so concerned about the children behind me that I miss seeing a hole in the ground and step right in it. Next thing I know, I'm rolling in the dirt, clutching my throbbing ankle while pain shoots toward my knee.

The shadows pound, swirling dirt and grass and other loose debris from the field so that I can't see anything. I don't know where Kye is, and that worries me almost as much as the fact that the demons have found us. I don't know how we thought we could escape by leaving Mexico.

I've closed two tombs, but Christine claims there are lots more. All over the world. This is not something I can contain on my own, and I'll never understand how the Dragons believed that I could begin to solve this problem. As I lie on the ground, walloped by wind and debris, I wonder how modern leaders protect all the people and make all the choices and sacrifice all the happy things in their lives for people who don't know they're being protected. For people who will never appreciate the sacrifices made for them.

I don't know how, but as I think back on my life and the people I've loved, I do know why. Because humanity, even at its worst, can be inherently good. People, human beings, make choices to do good things and treat others with kindness and respect, or not. It's not the results of those choices I'm defending and protecting, but the ability to choose at all.

Maybe running away wasn't the best choice for Kye and me. Maybe it was. But we did it—we made that choice, and we'll pay the consequences with our lives if it comes to that. But not today. Not right now. We won't risk innocents.

And so I reach toward the sky, searching for fingers—or any other form—of Light, and call them toward me. I don't have much left, but I've learned how to use my surroundings, and the Texas sunshine is my new best friend.

I call my Light, and though it takes ages longer than it should, eventually the sunlight answers, racing toward me, burning swaths through the clouds of shadows holding me hostage. The Light approaches, nearly reaching my fingertips, and then ...

Stops. Completely. As if a barrier blocks it from linking with my skin. Panic builds in my chest and works up my throat, but a hand catches mine, and strong arms surround me, lifting me off the ground. With Kye's touch, the Light connects. I immediately turn it on the shadows, shattering them to bits and then dissolving those bits until there's nothing left but wisps of smoke.

Kye exhales. "Are you okay?"

I nod, trying to catch my breath over the raw ache in my throat. "I think so."

"We should get out of here before they come back." He lifts me to my feet. "Last thing we need is to deal with more innocuous shadows."

Pain shoots in my ankle when I put weight on it. "Those *innocuous shadows* have almost killed me on more than one occasion."

"True. But they feed on fear. If you don't feed them, they can't hurt you."

"Easy for you to say." I gingerly rotate my ankle to stretch it. "You've never been the one to wake up on a sacrificial altar with no recollection of how you got there, and no idea why the shadows disappeared before you were dead."

He takes a deep breath. "We should still go."

I don't understand how he can be so blasé about the dangers we're facing, especially considering what just happened, but I'm annoyed beyond reason that he isn't more shaken. Gabe would be in full panic mode right now, but I'm not with Gabe anymore, and that is painfully clear in the moment.

"I agree. Let's go."

TWELVE

Hungry

ROSE

My afternoon with Gabe is not the worst day I've had in recent weeks. He takes me to a nearby park, where Abby and I used to go during lunch on warm-weather days. The memory makes me infinitely sad. I miss Abby, even though I'm angry with her. She was my best friend, and that's not a bond easily broken.

Gabe's Jeep is parked in the lot, and we pass close to it as he slows the disk to a stop. I hop off and stride to the swing set. "Why are we here?"

"I assumed you liked this place?" He steps onto the grass, following my lead.

"I mean, it's *okay*. Mostly we came because Abby needed the sunlight." I claim my usual swing and rock my feet to set it swaying.

"It's peaceful." He occupies the swing next to mine and pushes off. It's amusing to watch—a big guy with bulging, rippling muscles, playing on a child's swing set.

"I've never seen this side of you," I comment without thinking. "Relaxed. Calm. In the moment."

"I was always working when you saw me before."

I wanted to avoid talking about Abby, but here with Gabe, it feels natural. "I guess you're out of a job now?"

He skids his feet on the dirt below the swing until he spins from side to side. "No, I'm sure they'll find something for me to do eventually. When they're done being mad that Kye and Abby left."

He took the blame. Gabe was one of their top guys. Has been for years. Must be humbling to not have an assignment. "So in the meantime, you're hanging out?"

He shrugs. "Thought about going back to my Ranger gig, but it's nice having space to breathe. I can't remember the last time I wasn't constantly on guard, watching out for danger to other people."

I'm thunderstruck. It never occurred to me that Gabe could get tired of doing what he did for Abby, but of course he could. Any normal person would. "When's the last time you had more than a day or an hour off?"

He stops the motion of his swing to raise his eyebrows at me, then grins as he twists the chain and spins again. "So long I didn't remember what freedom felt like. I was recruited at ten, and I've been in training or on assignment since then."

"And you've never taken a vacation from it? At all?"

He shakes his head. "No one else can do what I do—which, in Abby's case, didn't turn out to be much. Felt more like I was along for the ride. Still. Our people need protection. I was given this Gift to provide that. Bad things don't cease to happen so the protectors can take vacations. They continue. Day in and day out. Hour after hour. Someone has to protect the sheep from wolves."

"But it doesn't always have to be *you* doing the protecting. I mean, yes, you're good at it—no one could argue that—but at some point, we should all be able to protect ourselves, whether you're there or not. The fact that you have a useful Gift doesn't mean you don't deserve to have a life. Aren't the other Dragons capable of protecting people, too?"

"They are, and they do, but I've never seen any Dragon take time off unless they were deathly ill." His feet stir up a cloud of dust as he grinds his motion to a halt. "Truth is, I never asked for a vacation. I like doing what I do. Gives me purpose."

I kick dirt in his direction. "It's no wonder you're so uptight. Gabe, you can't live your entire life for other people. Every once in a while someone has to think about what *you* need, even if that person is you." He looks about to object, so I plow over him. "It's not selfish. It's healthy. If you don't take care of yourself, who will?"

"I take care of myself, Rose. I have honestly never had so much stress that I needed time off. Until now. So whether the Dragons like it or not, I'm taking all the time I want. I can't forget everything about this last summer, and I'm not sure I want to. I'm not in any position to jump back into work again. Not this time." He stops the motion of his swing and stretches his arms toward the sky, still clinging to the chains. "I'm not focused anymore. Not well enough to be effective, anyway. Don't think I'll be comfortable going back to it until I'm in a better place, mentally and emotionally."

"Well look at us being all broken." Now it's my turn to take off swinging. The cool air whips my hair across my face and stings my eyes. It's glorious and exhilarating. "You'd think we experienced a trauma or something."

Grinning, he kicks a dirt clod at me while I swing, and misses by half a mile. "Wanna race?"

I don't answer, choosing instead to pump my feet until they look as if they can spear the sky. "Here you go," I shout. "Beat this!"

And to my surprise and delight, Gabe takes off and starts pumping too. We only stop when the metal part of the swing-set groans a complaint, and I can see Gabe visually checking the concrete where the poles are to make sure it won't come loose.

By then we're both breathless and grinning. Gabe's cheeks are pink from the cool, dry air, but his eyes shine with freedom. "Do you wanna get something to eat? I was going to bring a picnic, but I don't know what your appetite is like these days, so I figured I should wait to see what you can stomach."

I'm breathing so heavily my chest hurts, but only in the way of gaining some much-needed exercise. "This is the part where I remind you that I'm not miss Abby-throwing-up-everything-in-sight. I can eat anything and everything. Like pizza. I can inhale almost a whole one by myself when I'm hungry. And burgers. And French fries. I like my food."

His raised brow leads me to believe that he is skeptical of this fact.

"Have you not seen me eat?"

"Of course I have, but you've lost, what, ten pounds in the weeks since Mexico? You were thin to begin with, so that can't be healthy."

The fact that he thinks I've lost weight—when I have actually gained at least that much—makes me grin like a loon, though I don't want to try to guess why. I stand from my swing, gaining my balance swiftly, as I always have, and start toward the car. "Well. I'm not into healthy these days. I vote pizza. And ice cream. And cookies too, maybe."

He laughs, deep and rich, the sound of which starts my heart thrumming and warms my skin. "Okay," he says. "Any particular place and kind?"

"Mama's Pizza on Main Street," I tell him as he unlocks the car and joins me. Clouds drift across the sun as we talk, causing shadows to creep along the ground. I shiver. "And then the Creamery after."

"You're serious about that?" He frowns at me. The temperature has dropped drastically, so I pull on my sweatshirt, not wanting him to know I wish I'd brought a jacket like he told me to. It's a relief to climb in the Jeep, because while it's not warm, being inside cuts the chill of the wind from outside.

Gabe stands near the hood, frowning at something behind us in the forest. I start to open the door so I can join him, but Gabe puts his hand out to stop me, then meets my eyes and shakes his head. Seconds later, he takes his place in the driver's seat and starts the engine.

"What was that about?" I ask.

He shifts into reverse and backs out. "Maybe nothing. Probably nothing."

My brows raise, because there is no maybe-probably for Gabe. He's not that guy. "What's the alternative to nothing?" Anxiety spikes my heartrate.

"Shadows." He hits the gas. Our tires squeal as we pull out of the parking lot. "But Abby got rid of the shadows. It must be a storm."

Somehow, I have a hard time believing that.

THIRTEEN

Baby Love

ABBY

We arrive at Tanya's house in Phoenix the next evening, having stopped for the previous night—without further incident—before we reached the New Mexico border. Against Kye's wishes, I called Tanya and warned her that we were coming. As much as I don't want to tip off the Dragons, or the demons, about our location, I couldn't show up unannounced.

Tanya meets us at the door, holding a screaming baby. "I can't believe you're here." She talks over the earsplitting wails as tears gather in her eyes. "I never thought I'd see you again. You left so suddenly, like ..." Her smile falters, but then she pastes it back on as she hugs me with her one free arm. "I'm so happy to see you."

I squeeze her, careful of the little one between us. "I'm sorry I deserted you." The baby tugs on a lock of my hair, and I run my finger along his perfect cheek. "I can't believe I missed this. His birth. The story. Senior year."

Tanya shakes her head as if setting aside a nightmare. "Hey. We all have our stuff. You couldn't control whatever Marian and Isabelle were running from, and you were too young to choose to stay behind. I get it. They're your family."

And just like that, I'm forgiven for leaving my best friend in the middle of the night, with no warning, no explanation, and no further contact. This is a wound I didn't realize needed to be Healed, but standing in Tanya's doorway, I recognize that part of moving into my future involves examining the important moments and people of my past. Tanya was one of the most important. I don't know how I didn't get that until now.

Kye clears his throat.

"Is this your new flame?" She appraises Kye with raised brows. "I approve."

"Tanya, meet Kye, and yes, I guess you could call him a flame."

Kye shakes Tanya's outstretched hand. "I prefer the term fiancé."

Tanya snatches my hand, gasping at my rings, and then fixes her piercing eyes on Kye. "Did you give her this?"

He answers with a curt nod, fidgeting with discomfort as he casts a hesitant glance at me. We have neither discussed nor decided on anything to do with the future past today, so Tanya's questions hit sore spots for us both.

"He did," I finally say, desperate to break the awkwardness. Even if I inherited the one from Gram, Theron had the ring created for Raina, which is how it eventually came to me. Apples and oranges. And Kye did give me the band.

Tanya lets out a high-pitched squeal that startles the baby, who wails along with her. "Wow." Clearly impressed, she urges us inside and closes the door. "Now tell me he has a great job with a future." Her eyes drift to my belly, then back to my face. "You're not pregnant, are you?"

I've forgotten how fast Tanya speaks, how fast she moves from subject to subject with barely a breath, a lot like Rose. "No," I assure her. "I'm not pregnant, and yes, Kye has a wonderful potential future." I can't bring myself to lie about the job part. If I want to get technical, we're both supposed to have jobs. Val and the Dragons have assured us that we will draw a more than comfortable salary if we accept the responsibility that's been handed down to (read: dumped on) us. But that was before we ran away. Now, I'm sure things have changed. We essentially turned the jobs down.

At this point, we'll end up working fast food under fake names.

The baby continues to cry as Tanya ushers us into her tiny living space. I catch a whiff of lingering disinfectant. "You didn't have to clean for us. You've got your hands full already."

She shakes it off as if it's nothing, gesturing for us to sit. "Had to be done anyway; you gave me the motivation. Besides, I wanted to have my time free so we can catch up." But she looks about to fall over from exhaustion.

"Can I hold him?" Without waiting for an answer, I lift him out of Tanya's arms.

She says, "I named him Cole, after ..." There's no need for her to finish the sentence. Cole must also be the baby's father's name.

I perch in the rocking chair and set it in motion, replacing the pacifier Cole spits onto my chest. Tanya plops onto one end of the sofa, her whole body wilting. The furniture's familiar—castoffs from her parents' house. There isn't much of it, but she's added accessories—inexpensive pillows, framed photos, and dollar store vases holding fresh-picked flowers. She's created a cozy, inviting home; the kind I hope to have someday. Not lavish and expensive, but comfortable and warm.

"Can I get you anything?" she asks, her energy drooping, along with her eyelids. "Herbal tea? Water bottles? Did you have lunch?"

It's late afternoon—I would guess naptime for the baby, and from the way Tanya fights to keep her eyes open, she could use one too.

"We had a late breakfast." Kye assures her, claiming the other end of the sofa and relaxing against the cushions.

Tanya's head falls back and her eyes drift closed.

"You look tired." I keep my voice low.

"Single parent," she responds. "I'll be tired for the next eighteen years, from what I'm told. Feels like the longest part of eternity."

"Why don't you take a nap?" I suggest, absorbing the infant warmth, the smell of baby powder. "Let Kye and me get to know this guy."

Her eyes pop open. "I'd be a terrible hostess, and the poorest kind of friend to run off and take a nap only minutes after you've arrived. We haven't seen each other in years. So much ..." She yawns, her eyes drifting closed again. "To catch up on."

"We'll catch up," I promise. "Go lie down and rest so the four of us can have dinner together and you can tell me all about what's been going on since I left."

When Tanya doesn't move, Kye stands, hovering like he wants to help, but doesn't want to overstep. "Tanya," I say. "Kye's going to help you find your bed. You need to take a power nap."

By now, she's so far gone that she has no protests left. "Okay." Kye pulls her up by the arm and leads her into a bedroom down the hall.

Cole fusses as if sensing that his mother has left the room. I rock the chair harder, fascinated by the little arm sticking out from the blankets. I stroke his chubby hand and let his fingers curl around one of mine. His forehead wrinkles with expression as his eyes drift closed, and he lets out a content little sigh. I'm in love.

Kye returns to sit quietly, watching me rock Tanya's baby. "Full disclosure. There's a new man in my life," I tell him.

He reaches out and tucks the blanket over a tiny foot that has escaped the bundle. "You'll make a good mom someday."

"You think so?"

"I know so. Look at him." He gestures at the baby. "He's not fussing anymore."

"He was exhausted." I continue rocking, afraid to slow down.

"Not everyone can rock a fussy baby to sleep. It takes patience and love and a strong maternal instinct."

I pull Cole more tightly into my chest. "How do you know what it takes?"

He kicks his shoes off and lies sideways on the couch, fully relaxing. "I don't remember, but I'm sure it's true."

"Thanks." While I love talking motherhood and babies with Kye, I don't want to edge into uncomfortable territory while we're here. I need to change the subject. We're both more relaxed than we have been in days, and the place is quiet, and I'm holding the most perfect little miracle in my arms. I can't think of a better time to bring up Kiersten's accusations. "Kye, do you feel like we're in over our heads?"

His eyes flicker from my face to the ground. "If I did, I would tell you, and we'd figure it out together. Why would you ask me that?"

I nudge his knee with my foot to keep the tension from forming. "Kiersten mentioned something that bothered me. And hauling an ill woman across the country can't be easy."

He curses. "That's what this is about? Something Kiersten said? She's being a jealous snot. Of course this isn't easy, but I knew it wouldn't be—I promise I have no regrets."

"She seemed so ... smug. I felt like she was insinuating that you'd confided in her."

Kye reaches over to rest his hand on my leg. "Babe. I would never talk about you with Kiersten except to make sure she knows how much I love you." The way he looks at me screams that he's telling the truth. If he did confide in her, it wasn't about that. I hope. I need to get past this overwhelming paranoia that woman planted.

The baby sighs, content. I don't want to put him down. Holding him is the sweetest sensation. It's no wonder Tanya chose to give parenthood a whirl. I'm not ready for anything like this. Not yet. Especially not with everything else riding on my shoulders. But someday. I can see myself someday sitting in a similar chair with my own child, and right now, the idea isn't quite as frightening as it once was.

"You're not going to put him in his bed at all, are you?" Kye's fingers draw circles on my knee.

I shake my head. "Nope. Not for now. If we have research to do, I'm doing it from this exact spot, with my arms full."

Everything in his expression softens. "I can definitely work with that."

By the time Tanya wakes up, Kye and I have talked through everything that happened in the days leading up to my family leaving here in such a hurry. "They never explained what was happening," I tell him. "Just that we had to go, and then in a matter of hours, we did."

"We need to decide what events became the catalyst for you leaving each time you moved. There must be a pattern, and if we can find it, maybe we can figure out what happened to your father."

"What happened to your father?" Tanya asks, yawning from the doorway. She nods at the baby in my arms. "You didn't have to do that. He would have stayed asleep in his crib."

I adjust his weight and tuck his blankets more tightly. "Yes, I did. I don't know how you ever put him down."

"Trust me, when you've gone without sleep for three days and counting, you'd hand him over to a stranger on the street for the possibility of a twenty minute power nap." She settles onto the couch next to Kye. "So what are we talking about? I thought your father died when you were six?"

Kye stands on the guise of stretching, but the look he shoots me burns with questions.

"I always believed he had," I respond. "But we never knew for sure. He wasn't the type to pick up and leave his family. He was protective, and paranoid like Gram. All I remember is that he left one night and didn't come home for over a month, and Gram and Mom told me that he had died trying to protect us. I believed them. Had no reason not to. We never had a funeral or a memorial service for him. No one I loved had ever died before, so when Mom and Gram packed up everything we owned and moved us to Colorado, I was too young to wonder if he would come looking for us."

Tanya's eyes bore into me, laden with sadness and grief. "Abby. You understand that he might have left voluntarily, right? It happens all the time. To good people who love their families, who have built good things and are living comfortable lives. Some people snap, and then they go."

"I do. I get that. But I don't think that's what happened with my dad."

Kye bites his thumbnail—a new habit he's picked up. "He wouldn't be the first like us to do such a thing. Rhys and Isleen disappeared, and no one ever knew what happened to them. So did Theron and Raina, and we know that they had at least one kid while they were in hiding."

"Who?" Tanya straightens, tucking a foot under the opposite thigh as her eyes dart between me and Kye.

My cheeks warm with embarrassment. We're getting careless. "It's a legend, an old one, about my ancestors, and Kye's. It's a puzzle we're piecing through, and sort of the purpose of this trip."

She makes a noise that sounds suspiciously like ah-ha, and stands, heading for the kitchen. "I'm starving. Would you two like anything? Baby food perhaps?"

Kye moves closer to grip the back of my rocking chair. "We'll pass on the baby food," he says, "but you don't need to cook. Let's go out. My treat."

She turns away from her mostly empty refrigerator, blinking with disbelief. "I'd turn you down, but you have no idea how long it's been since I ate something I didn't prepare myself."

"Better make it somewhere nice then," Kye says.

A surge of love crashes over me. Kye's sweet side will always be the chink in my proverbial armor.

Tanya returns from the kitchen with three glasses of water. "It's a deal, but only if you agree to start from the beginning of this legend—let me help you with your puzzle. I could use some adventure in my life."

Kye clears his throat to make known his concern, but I raise my brows in challenge. We can trust Tanya. "Okay."

She sets a water glass on the table near my elbow. "You should start with the part where you explain why you never told me about your Gift?"

The bottom drops out of my courage. "What do you mean? I ... I don't know what you're talking about." I can feel Kye's gaze cutting into me like razor blades, so I avoid looking at him.

"Abby. I know." She stops near my chair to stroke the baby's downy head. "I've always known. I don't know how your grandmother supposed she could keep you hidden when everywhere you went, peace followed." She leans down and scoops Cole from my arms. When he stirs, she bounces to calm him. "My parents were always straight with me. They told me what I do, and that it's something no one will ever be able control, least of all me, so I should be extra careful about who I spend time with. They educated me about my ability and my heritage, which has been my biggest protector in life. I don't know the whole story about Theron and Raina, but I do know about Rhys and Isleen, and if you'll be patient while I get dressed and bundle up the baby, I'll tell you everything that's been passed down through my family. We can compare notes."

I have a sneaking suspicion that our dinner out will be worth way more than the money Kye will spend to pay for it. It's about time.

FOURTEEN

Rom-Coms and Doritos

ROSE

Three days later, Gabe shows up at my house again. My mom isn't home, so I answer the door myself. This time I'm wearing leggings with Alex's T-shirt. It's a step up from the cut off sweats, as it looks semi-outfit-ish. Sort of, anyway.

Gabe grins, either because he thinks I'm doing better, or he's glad that I answered the door. I'm not sure which. "What are you doing?" he asks, his voice casual.

"Watching sappy rom-coms and eating Doritos. What are you doing?"

He shrugs. "I got bored. I'm not invited to the Dragons' meetings since Abby left, and they're always in meetings. Since I don't have an assignment, I literally have nothing to do, and no one to look after. I figured maybe you're bored, too."

I open the door wider, indicating that he should come in. I'm glad that I moved my movie session downstairs this morning, because now Gabe can see exactly what I'm watching and where I paused it when I got up to answer the door, and there will be no arguing over movies until this one is over. He nods at the tub of dip on the end table. "French onion-ranch combo?"

"It was all we had left." I snatch the tub and the bag of chips off the table and take them to the kitchen. "I told you I'm always eating. It's all I've done since Mexico. Eat and watch TV."

"But you're still exercising? Still training with your Voice?"

"Nope." At his single raised brow, I elaborate. "Been there, done that. I trained my ass off in Mexico. I worked hard to be strong and healthy, to be at the top of my game, and then when the battle happened, I was—as always—left watching from the sidelines. So what's the point?"

"That's not true," he says. "A lot of stuff happened on the surface while we were down that hole. Landon told me about how the shadows converged on you once Abby disappeared. He told me how you convinced them to chase you away from the cenote, how you—all by yourself—got them to follow you like the Pied Piper. He told me how you saw Alejandro plummet to his death, and still held it together well enough to save others from suffering the same fate. So don't try to convince me that you watched from the sidelines, because I know better."

His words stab a wound I didn't know existed, and my emotions bubble like blood getting ready to spill. I remember watching Abby rocket into the water, and Kye and Gabe drop down after her. I remember Alex saying goodbye to me as he dove from the cliff and glided to the water to save Abby, and Victor next. I remember intending to follow, but then that ... that thing, the shadow, chased them, and lots more shadows emerged until they were everywhere. So many that I couldn't see the cenote to follow my friends. I was the lone person left behind—as always, and all I could think was that I needed to be down in that water with the others.

I never made it. The moment he dove off the edge was the last time I saw Alex alive. That's what I remember. The rest of what Gabe says doesn't sound familiar. At all. "I don't remember leading the shadows away." I pause to swallow a huge, painful lump. "I only remember hearing Alex yell for me, and then a loud crunch, and screaming. That's it. Then no one would let me go after him. I was left behind again. Same as always."

"We didn't leave you behind on purpose," he insists. "We waited for you until we couldn't anymore."

I wonder if my being there would have changed anything. If I had been able to rappel down the way we planned, or if I dove in the way Alex did—I wonder if he would still be alive. I've revisited the night thousands of times, and no matter how often I go through it, in the end, nothing has changed. Alex is still dead and Abby and Kye are still gone, and Gabe and I are sitting side-by-side on my living room couch being unimportant losers. "Well. It's over. I need a snack. Do you want a cookie or something?"

"Sure. And how about you bring back those chips, too." He plops on the couch and kicks off his shoes like he intends to stay a while.

I grab the cookies, the chips and dip, and two water bottles and set them on the coffee table in reachable distance, reclaiming my spot on the other end of the couch. "I'm going to turn this back on. I'm all about mind-numbing fictional teen drama these days." I pick up the remote, my finger hovering over the play button. "Unless you were here to discuss something important?"

He kicks his shoes off and props his feet on the coffee table next to the water. "I came to watch TV. I don't care what. I'm sick of my silent, empty apartment."

I don't know where Gabe lives, or what he's doing with his spare time these days. I don't know if he has family, or where they might live in the world. Literally the only thing I truly know about Gabe is that he was once obsessed, maybe in love, with Abby, and since she left, he's been nicer to me. Because we're both left here to pick up pieces of the lives we never expected to have broken.

Not wanting to think too hard about hows and whys, I start the movie again to numb the cascading thoughts and allow Gabe and me to watch the end in companionable silence.

FIFTEEN

Unexpected Ally

ABBY

Tanya picks a local place that serves a bit of everything. It's clean, I suppose, but nowhere near the league of restaurants where we ate when Kye had free reign to use the credit card that was funded by Val. I wouldn't even call this a middle ground establishment. More like a dive.

If this is Tanya's idea of a nice place to eat, she's got to be stone broke. although our lives have gone different directions, her circumstances have been every bit as rough as mine since I saw her last.

As I helped her strap Cole into our car back at her apartment, I recognized that Tanya's priorities remain similar to mine.

We protect the people we love, at any and all costs.

On the way here, she'd pointed out a gym. "See that place? In the mornings, I work in their daycare, and then in the evenings, they let me leave Cole for a couple of hours while I cross the street to that office building and clean the company headquarters in there."

"You have two jobs?" I wondered what I would be doing in her circumstances.

"Three," she'd quipped. "On the weekends I make sales calls for a security company. It's extra money, and I do it from home."

No wonder she's so tired. "Tanya, three jobs is more than anyone should have to handle, let alone a young single mother." I'd reached back and she took my hand.

"I could go on welfare and let the government help us out, but I wouldn't be any better off, money-wise, and this way I'm building my skills and experience to give us an outlook for a better future. Cole's future, and mine, are decided by the choices I make now. I have to do everything I can to make a—not a good life, but a great one for us. I don't ever want to give Cole reason to think he was anything less than a blessing to me." She squeezed my hand, adopting a matter-of-fact tone. "None of these jobs constitutes a career in the making, but one of them could lead to an opportunity that could be. In the meantime, I don't have to send Cole to daycare. Three times a week, I leave him with my friends at the gym for about three hours, and other than those nine hours, he's always with me. I get the best of both worlds."

I'd been in complete and total awe of my friend and her ability for logic. "Sounds exhausting."

"It is." She'd let go of my hand to stroke Cole's hair. "But worth it. I love our life. Wouldn't change it for anything. Except, you know, if someone were to anonymously deposit a million dollars into my bank account, I'd happily find something to do with that, but aside from unexpected financial windfalls, not a single thing."

I wished I'd accepted the "budget" Val once offered me so I could sign the whole thing over to Tanya and give her room to breathe.

Inside the restaurant, Kye uses his killer smile to get us seated in a back corner booth where there's less noise and fewer people. Kye orders drinks and appetizers, assuring the concerned Tanya that she's welcome to order whatever she wants.

By the time the waitress leaves, my curiosity has reached a toxic level. "Okay, I'm dying of suspense. You have to tell us what happened to Isleen and Rhys."

She stares at us for a long moment, lips pressed together. I recognize the same caution that was drilled into me since the day I was born.

"This is so weird," she says, her eyes fluttering toward Kye. "I'm not used to talking about this part of my life with anyone who is not my parents."

"Believe me," I assure her. "It's weird for me too. I've been talking about my Gifts with lots of people this year, and it's still hard to let go of that caution." Under the table, Kye slides his hand into mine. "It gets easier when you see how many of us have been forced to hide in plain sight as a means of survival."

"It will always be survival for me," she says. "My Gift isn't a power that can change things or protect others. I can't use it by myself. I can only amplify others' Gifts, which makes me dangerous. But amplifying is how I knew about Abby's Gifts when we first met."

I lean closer to her, confused. "You knew about my Gifts all along?"

"Well, not the whole time." She swirls the straw in her water, fixing her eyes on me. "Do you remember that night when I snuck out at, like, four a.m.? I took my parents' car to go see Dennis, and on the way home, I hit a curb and popped a tire?"

"How could I forget?" I help myself to chips and salsa the waitress has set on our table. "Your frantic early-morning phone call forced *me* to sneak out too, and to borrow my mother's car, though I didn't have my license yet." I turn to Kye to explain, "Both things which I had never done before, nor have I since."

Tanya crunches a chip with satisfaction and raised eyebrows.

"That poor car," I prod. "Wasn't the axle bent?"

"It was." She sips her drink. "But more importantly, I'd hit my head on the steering wheel, and it was bleeding."

I search my memory of that night, but can't recall blood. "Are you sure? I don't remember you bleeding."

Her smile blooms as she dunks another chip. "Of course you don't. You wouldn't." She chews, swallows, sips. "Remember how I was still sitting in the driver's seat when you got there?"

I have to dig deep to remember. There was a smudge on the window that could have been blood, but my fifteen-year-old brain mistook for dirt, or oil.

"You parked across the street and ran to me, still sitting in my wrecked car in the middle of the road, and what was the first thing you did?"

I recall Tanya's parents' expensive car, half-stuck on the median, with smoke pouring out from under the hood. "Didn't I run up to you, asking if you were okay?"

"You did. And then you pressed your hands against my forehead to check my neck for whiplash."

"I did?" I don't remember that part. If Tanya's an amplifier, and I'm a Healer, then ... "I healed your head wound, without even realizing it was there."

She nods. "Yes. I never dared ask you about it, because it would mean admitting my own ... stuff. Anyway, I figured you're a Healer. Which is why I understood when you left, that your mom was doing what she believed was best for you, even when having you gone hurt. A lot."

"If we had known about you and your parents, things might have been different. Maybe we wouldn't have left so fast. Or at all."

"Your grandmother knew."

This shocks me, and Kye and Tanya both see it in the way I stiffen. "What do you mean, Gram knew? How could she know?" And why didn't she tell me about Tanya? Tell me about the other people in the world who were like me in some way? I imagine how exponentially better my childhood might have been had the adults in my life told me the full truth.

"I didn't know she knew until after you left, or I would have told you everything. Apparently, Isabelle recognized that my mother is Gifted—same ability as mine—and they kept in touch while you lived here. Isabelle was worried that by spending time with me, you would be at greater risk for being discovered. She wasn't wrong. You have such attractive energy that spending time with me could make you look like that red blinking dot on a radar map."

Kye squirms, and I can tell he's thinking that the last thing we need right now is to be a blinking dot. I'm not ready to leave Tanya yet, but I can't put us all at risk either. We should get a hotel.

The baby stirs in his car seat. I'm about to bring up an alternate plan when Tanya silences me with a look, simultaneously replacing Cole's pacifier in his mouth. He sucks on it greedily as if he's expecting milk from it. "Look, I know you're about to warn me about the dangers following you. Believe me, when you called last night, I gave this a great deal of contemplation, but here's the upside, Abby. I may make you easier to find, but I also make you stronger." Her eyes fall on Kye. "And you. Obviously the two of you are pretty damn important, or, you wouldn't be running from allies as well as enemies."

Even with someone to amplify my power, I can't guarantee Cole's continued safety, and I won't put him at risk. It's not fair.

"You're right," Kye tells Tanya, and I'm surprised. "It sounds like you have a different story to tell, and obviously our separate stories intersect at some point. We would be foolish to leave without fully exploring how and where these pieces fit together, because while it's true that Abby's a Healer, her power's fading. She's been cut by the Arawn dagger, and nothing we've tried has made any progress toward Healing her."

His hands shake as he cuts into his steak. "I definitely don't want to be found, but Abby's health is important too. I'm willing to risk staying if you're willing to risk having us here."

"I'm not." I chime in. "Obviously it was my idea to come in the first place, but Tanya, you don't know what you're agreeing to. We don't have one or two scary people after us. We have an army of demons. Shadow demons. And Dragons. They're looking for us too, although not nearly as scary as the demons. And what's left of the Dark Elen—the ones who killed King Eamon and sent Isleen and Rhys into hiding. That's a lot of enemies. I don't want to bring all that down on you."

Tanya has to cover her mouth when she laughs. "You've always been something of a martyr, haven't you? Don't worry about us. Cole and I will be fine. To be honest, I could use some excitement. It'll be good for me."

I do worry. How can she protect her son if she only amplifies her enemy's power? Kye squeezes my knee, silencing my objection. We'll get to those questions. It's time to get back to the subject at hand. "Speaking of King Eamon and Isleen and Rhys, I believe you were going to tell us a story."

SIXTEEN

Absentee

ROSE

I've been home for a month, and after spending several mundane but comfortable afternoons with Gabe, have to visit Jen. I've been waiting for her to show up on my doorstep to find out what happened and where Abby is and why none of us have come to see her, but about the fifth time Gabe turns up unannounced, I decide that it's possible Jen's waiting for me to show up on *her* doorstep for the same reasons.

I don't know why either of us would wait for the other. We've been best friends for as long as I can remember—until Abby moved here, and then we were still besties, with a plus one. Something's changed, and I'm not sure what or how or why. I don't know if it's only me who has changed, or her too, or if maybe our relationship has shifted.

I just know *something* is different. As miserable as I've been about being left on the sidelines of the fight at the cenote, maybe Jen's angry at being left here while I was in Mexico.

One afternoon I take a walk and end up on Jen's porch. I knock, and wait, and knock and wait, and then plant myself on the swing to wait some more. I've been there for a solid hour when icy fingers of air prickle my arms and run up the back of my neck. Dark clouds creep out of nowhere, and the world dims, muting everything as if the sun has dropped from the sky—but sunset is still an hour away. Fear tightens my throat and squeezes into my chest as I stand and start down the driveway, suddenly desperate for the safety of home. From the corner of my eye, I catch a patch of dark gray and whirl, only to find the shadow of a tree waving in the breeze.

My heart whaps against my ribs. I'm an easy target by myself on the streets of Jackson. My memory flashes to the cenote, to how the shadows converged on us, how they screamed and wailed and gnashed. How they pushed physical things and people with the forces of wind and energy and with bursts of singing fire, and how excruciating it was for me to know that the person controlling those forces might never die. That maybe no one could kill him—ever, because he's immortal.

My feet slap on the pavement, flip-flops banging against my heels like shots from an automatic weapon as I cram a scream of fear down my throat, determined that rather than panic, I will keep breathing as I run.

I careen across our lawn at the same time my mom pulls into the driveway. She meets me at the door, carrying a large paper bag filled with groceries. "Oh hey, honey," she says, voice chipper and sandy hair blowing in her face as the breeze from behind me catches up to us. "Did you go for a walk? Did you visit Jen?"

I nod, then shake my head, and grab her arm to drag her inside.

"What's wrong?" She drops her sack on the counter and urges me into a kitchen chair. "What's happened?"

My breath hitches. "I just ... I was sitting on Jen's porch, and out of the blue it got cold, and dark like night, and ... I got so scared. There must have been shadows, because I ran home with the wind propelling me from behind. I think one followed me."

Mom pulls in a concerned breath; her eyes flick toward the door. "I didn't see any shadows, but I'll check again. You're not hurt?"

I shake my head, but when she takes my hands, they're trembling.

"Sweetie, do you want me to call the Dragons to check our house?"

"No," I tell her, feeling stupid as my sense of safety returns. "It's probably nothing to worry about." But as I speak the words, my fear lingers. "Abby took care of our shadow problem here, right?"

"That's what the Dragons claim." Her expression smooths into a carefully neutral mask, and then I know. The Dragons are wrong. There are still shadows in Jackson. There will always be shadows in Jackson. In the world. Shadows are the most common source of evil, and evil will always lurk in the dark corners of human existence. Always. There is no getting rid of them, of it. The Gifted are the peacemakers, and we're destined to fight a never-ending battle. Forever. What I lived through in Mexico, those things that killed Alex? They're coming back. It will all be back someday. Over and over again. The realization makes me want to hurl.

Yet, the Dragons want us to believe that we're safe. They want us to trust that Abby sealed the tomb and rid the town of demons, that she and Kye are meant to die saving us, and that someday the ancient kingdom will be restored. They want us to believe that there are no longer shadows in Jackson. And it's a lie.

Maybe Abby is who they say she is. Maybe she's not. But we're *not* saved. No one person can save us. No one individual can lead every Gifted being in the world. It's up to all of us, as a community, to keep these awful, evil shadows from taking hold and crushing us.

Mom pats my hand and stands. "I'm going to check outside. If there's anything suspicious, I'll call your father and have him come home early. Baby, I don't want you to feel like you have to spend the rest of your life looking over your shoulder. You need to understand that the shadows can't come into our home uninvited. In order for them to pass through these doors, one of us would have to invite them."

I don't know if what she's telling me is true or not, but my mother has never lied to me, so I nod and thank her for checking. While I'm waiting, calming down and feeling crazy stupid, I text Jen.

Came by your house. Waited as long as I could. I miss you. Come see me!

I don't expect her to reply immediately. This isn't the first text I've sent her since I got back. During random moments of loneliness, I've texted her. Moments when I was thinking of Alex and considering crawling into a deep, dark hole. The first time, I fully expected her to show up in my room with chocolate and alcohol and tissues, the way I always have when her heart has been broken. But she didn't. She didn't respond until two days later, and it was short and curt.

I remind myself that she might be angry at me for leaving her behind when I went to see Abby, but to be fair, Jen *was* invited. Abby's mom couldn't afford to send us both, but Landon offered to get a second ticket, because two friends would have made Abby twice as happy. Jen didn't want it. Or claimed she didn't. More like she wouldn't take it. She had the desire in spades, and I still haven't figured out why she wouldn't come with me. Even if she had too much pride to let someone else buy her ticket, Jen's parents can afford to send her. She gets more allowance in a month than I do all year, so I'm pretty sure she could have bought her own ticket if she wanted to go. Spending money would have been a non-issue as well.

What I can't figure out is why she chose not to go with me, and is now acting like she's angry for being left behind. Did she not want me to see Abby and visit my aunt?

Admittedly, Jen and I had a fight before I left, but it was stupid and the same thing we always do. A simple disagreement that sometimes happens, and then we get over it. It's how we work.

I told her I didn't like her boyfriend, and she told me to shove it and mind my own business. I told her I love her and he's making her act weird, and she told me I'm the one who's acting weird and if I don't like how she acts, I shouldn't spend time with her, and blah blah. We have this type of argument all. The. Time.

Weekly, if not daily. This was no different. Except, maybe it was. I don't know what I've missed. Maybe it's time I found out.

Mom returns from outside, massaging warmth into her arms, and clenching her chattering teeth—both actions warning me that the chill is still there. A shiver works up my spine in preparation for being told that there's a demon camped in our yard, but instead, mom's all, "That storm's coming in fast. It's already hitting the higher elevations. There's snow on the tips of the Tetons."

At first I think she's making it up. "There isn't really a storm coming in, is there?"

Rather than argue the point, she takes out her phone and clicks on the weather app, jabbing her finger on the snowflake icon. "It's supposed to reach the valley tonight."

I groan. "Ugh. It was summer. Like, two days ago."

My mom chuckles. "It's always summer in Mexico. Here, summer ended in September. We're heading into holiday season, baby."

The sad part about this conversation is that I've been so out of it that I don't know what day of the week it is, let alone what month. I take Mom's phone and check her calendar to prove that, indeed, Halloween is less than a month away. It's not unusual for us to get dustings of snow in October. Summer is gone, and autumn has been here for quite some time.

I move closer to the window, noticing for the first time the crisp, colorful leaves still sprinkled on the trees, joined by those littering the ground. Our grass has turned a shade of lime green that is closing toward yellow. I've been back for weeks, outside and clearly not seen what's right in front of me. It's been five months since we graduated. Where has the time gone?

I have lost so much more than Alex.

My fingers are numb with the realization that since I've been home I haven't done anything besides hide. It's no wonder Jen wants nothing to do with me. I wouldn't want to hang out with myself. I'm a sorry excuse for a friend. I send her another text.

Text me when you're home. I want to come over.

And then I decide that if she never replies, I'm going back there to see what the hell is really going on with her.

SEVENTEEN

Another Side to the Story

ABBY

Tanya starts her story with, "This is one of those legends that's been passed down over generations, so some details are likely exaggerated or added or changed or whatever. To my knowledge, the only actual documentation we have is a box of old journals written by people on my ancestral line and passed down to my parents. I have them now. They mostly cover mundane daily life details—which are interesting, but give no glimpse into the history of our 'people' as my mother calls them. There's one journal, though, that reads differently than the others. That's where the skeleton of this story comes from. The rest, I assume, is speculation that has filled in the gaps over time. I'm sharing this story the way my grandmother told it to my mother, and my mother to me. Because that's how I remember it best."

Tanya takes a bite of her juicy steak, allowing a second to savor, chew, and swallow, then begins. "The castle was bursting with a celebration the likes of which Dryden had never seen before. A wedding celebration that lasted three days and three nights in honor of the prince and his peasant bride. The celebrations were well underway, and Queen Isleen hadn't seen her son for hours. They'd been receiving threats of war from all angles, and the party had grown so large, Isleen worried that the royal couple's safety would be compromised."

Tanya's words bring to mind Christine, and the possibility that the two have a familial connection.

"She knew there was only one other person in the world who loved her son as much as she did, and that person was not the king—who had planned the opulent party—but Rhys, who was the boy's biological sire, and who had taken the bulk of responsibility in raising him while the king was busy being, well, a king. Doing whatever kings do. Like hunting and ruling and stuff, I guess."

Kye laughs, pausing to choke down another chip. "Well, we know that of King Eamon, so our stories are consistent in this aspect."

Tanya's eyes light with encouragement. "Isleen assigned Rhys the task of guarding the newlyweds, though he was technically *her* bodyguard." She takes another bite, gesturing with her fork. "I assume you know there was an attack on the castle and the king was beheaded, yadda yadda."

"Yes," I tell her. "But that's where the stories diverge." My visions have all been of Theron and Raina, with an occasional glimpse of Isleen and Rhys, and nothing of them after the battle.

"Rhys had personally handled all of Theron's training, so he had every faith that the prince could spirit Raina to safety and then the two of them would survive together. After the king was found dead, Rhys knew he had to get Isleen out of there. He rushed to the Queen's apartment, where she waited with trunks she'd kept packed for such an emergency, and the two of them escaped through secret passageways that wound under the castle for miles, letting out deep in the forest. There, the most trusted of Rhys's guards waited with horses and a modest, unmarked carriage.

"They journeyed through forest and desert until they reached a cottage that had belonged to Rhys's late parents, and there lived out the rest of their days."

As Tanya warned, there are holes in her story, and I need to work through them to make this version fit with what I already

107

know. "Did they ever go back to see if Theron and Raina lived? Why didn't Rhys return to help Theron when the Duke sieged the castle?"

Tanya sips her drink, signaling for the waitress to bring her a refill. "Could be because Isleen had discovered she was pregnant a few days before the wedding, and the stress of what happened to her people, combined with the grueling journey, was devastating enough to threaten the life of her unborn child. Once she and Rhys made it to safety, Rhys employed a Healer, and the two put Isleen on bedrest until she was safe to deliver. It's possible that Rhys never made it back to Theron because Isleen's life was at risk."

"And he was the father of this child as well." Kye swallows a mouthful as his eyes light with ideas.

Tanya strokes Cole's downy head. "Yes. To be honest, and this is just my opinion, but I suspect King Eamon was sterile. He was known to keep a number of mistresses, none of whom ever turned up pregnant, and Isleen only became so after her trysts with Rhys."

The significance of this finally clicks in my brain. "If Isleen had another baby—or more than one—then Theron and Raina weren't the only descendants of the royal lineage. Is that right? Or does that change for all of them because of Rhys being the father?"

"No, it doesn't change." Kye abandons his fork, lost in a puzzle-solving thought. "I read somewhere that Isleen was Dryden's rightful heir. Her marriage to Eamon was one of those arranged deals to form a stronger political alliance with another Gifted kingdom, but it was her lineage that should have inherited the throne. Rhys or Eamon—whoever fathered her children—had nothing to do with that."

"So I'm right to believe that there are more descendants besides me."

Tanya's eyes sparkle with mischief. "Of course there are."

For the first time since I've known Tanya, I'm staring—finding similarities between us. Realization hits. "You're one of them."

Her laugh is rich and full. "We all are. Think about how generations stretch and multiply. The rising of the new generation isn't just on you, Abby, though I can tell you feel like it is. It doesn't matter where we fall on the line, the burden of responsibility belongs to all of us. We all have a role to play. That, my dear, sweet friend, is the real reason why I allowed you come here. Well, that and the fact that I love you."

Cole sleeps through most of dinner, and by the time we get back to Tanya's apartment, he's wide awake, giggling and cooing. Tanya settles him on an activity blanket on the floor while we skim through the journals of Tanya's ancestors.

"What are we looking for, specifically?" she asks, and I'm glad, because I've been skimming this book for twenty minutes, and am wondering the same thing.

"Anything that stands out," Kye says without looking up from his volume. "Indications of a person's Gift, mentions of demons or enemies, anything to do with a curse that was pronounced against Theron and Raina and their offspring, or Rhys and Isleen's offspring. Oh, and most importantly, any hints about what to do for someone who has been cut by a power-draining dagger. We have a lot of topics to cover."

Tanya's eyebrows raise. "A curse?"

I set my book aside. "Yes. We get sick when we're with each other for too long, and even sicker when we're apart."

"That sucks," she says, but her eyes dance with amusement. "And your solution to the problem was to run off together? Makes sense."

"There's more to it than that." Kye's cheeks flush. "We know there's a curse, but we're not sure of the details, because the people who first explained it have been lying to us. We *have* both been sick, but we don't know which symptoms are caused by the curse and which are caused by those trying to drive us apart. Until we know what's what, we're on our own."

"And in the meantime, Abby's life is draining away." She indicates my bandaged arm.

"Not my life," I lie, because while my life is in danger, Kye will remain desperate. I worry it will make him reckless. "My Gifts."

"Abby, I hate to tell you this, but your Gift is an intrinsic part of your life force. Life and Gifts are synonymous for people like us."

"But I can live without my Gifts. I can still go on, once those drain away."

Kye's bleak desperation leaks into his voice. "We all know that's not true." His fingers dance over my bandage and run down my arm to link with my fingers. "So why don't we face what it really is and make our priority Healing you?"

Tanya clears her throat. "Um. Guys. I have an idea." She picks up Cole and bounces him. "You're a Healer, right? And Kye has strong energy—binding energy."

"What's binding energy?" we ask at the same time.

She blinks. "You don't know?"

I shake my head, and Kye does too.

"Well, I don't know your Gift," she says to Kye, "But it must be something to do with communication, because the things you say tend to happen. Even the waitress in the restaurant couldn't serve you fast enough. While I admit that you're incredibly good looking and extremely charming, that's not the only reason why people jump to do what you want. When you speak, things happen. You ask a person to do something, and they become bound to do it. Does that make sense?"

Kye's pulse jumps where our wrists touch. "It does. It makes total and complete sense. How did I not know this before? Why has Val not told me?"

"You have binding energy, Abby has Healing power, and I'm an amplifier, which means that whatever the two of you can do, I can also do while you're with me. Not only that, your Gifts will see a significant boost from being near me. So. What if we combine our efforts to Heal Abby's wound?"

Kye speaks. "We should try it."

"No." My conscience kicks. "I'm full of energy-draining poison. It's in my blood, the same way my Gifts were. I don't think I have enough left to Heal a fly, let alone myself. Even with Tanya's help, and I haven't Seen anything since I was cut. Believe me, I've tried."

Kye takes my hands. "Remember when we were so sick the last two months of school, and Akers would take you in his office and transfer some of his healthy energy into you so you could make it through your classes?"

I nod.

"Doing this would be like that."

I don't want what's inside me to be transferred into Kye or Tanya. "This is a different variety of energy we would be trying to Heal. The curse isn't something that's contagious. It doesn't transfer to other people. This could. This has. It does."

Tanya's hand falls on my arm. "Abby, listen. I never have opportunities like this. I never get to save anyone, or protect anyone or help train Gifted children. I come from a family of amplifiers. We depend on others to help us use our Gifts. This is my chance to make a difference."

I hug Tanya hard. "I understand how badly you want to help, but you have a child who needs you. You can't afford to risk losing your life-force."

"I thought you said it's not your life, just your Gifts?" She sits, forcing me to sit next to her. Cole coos and gurgles as if in agreement with his mother.

"Let us try." Kye sits on my other side, fatigue permeating his voice. "If you die, you know I'm right behind you, and if Tanya gets sick from helping, I'll make sure to deliver her and Cole to Val—or wherever else she wants to go for help—before I do. "

"No."

Tanya and Kye exchange a look. She says, "We may not give you a choice. You don't get to take away our right to use our Gifts, and I choose to help."

Kye grins. "She may be quieter, but she's as feisty as Rose. Tanya, have you ever been to Jackson? You should come for a visit sometime."

The evening blurs by. Kye and Tanya want to help, and I understand that they think Healing me is what's best. Everything about this idea is logical and sound, so why do I feel like darkness hovers? And why are my intestines tied in a thousand tiny knots?

Once Cole has been put to bed, Tanya digs out all the crystals she owns—which I'm surprised to discover is quite a few—and we add them to the ones I brought, and the ones Jonathan loaned me. It's strange to be in the position of patient. We have a short lesson on how to spin chakras and how to find the right Healing tones, and then I lie on Tanya's living room rug, the way I used to lie on the desk in Landon's office.

Kye and Tanya place the crystals along my body, and then each of them spins two of my chakras, the way I've instructed. I dig hard for any remaining traces of Healing, but it's a struggle. My eyes close while I focus, focus, focus. Occasionally, a wisp of power trails along, but it's out of reach, and never enough to grab hold of and draw out. Not enough of a spark to fan a flame. Kye's frustration radiates into me as the minutes drag on, and not a single crystal lifts into the air.

After twenty forever-long minutes, Cole fusses. Tanya's eyes dart between me and the bedroom. "Let's take a break. I'll feed Cole, and then we can try again."

The energy shifts as Tanya leaves the room, and I open my eyes. Kye lets his arms drop and leans against the arm of the couch. "Maybe you need to eat, too."

"I ate at the restaurant, you saw me. That's not the problem. I can't find it." My head spins when I sit up, and emotion breaks my voice. "I'm trying so hard. So hard. I can't find it at all."

He scoots closer and pulls me into his embrace. "Shh. Don't cry. It's there. We know it's there. It's been a long day and you're worn out. Why don't you rest while Tanya takes care of Cole? I'll keep skimming the journals and see what I can find. If this doesn't work tonight, it's okay. We'll try again tomorrow."

He helps me onto the couch and covers me with the throw blanket Tanya has draped over the back. I'm not tired enough to need sleep, necessarily, but I am drained. Mentally. Emotionally. Physically. It feels good to lie here and let my mind be quiet. I want to live. I want to get back home to my mother and Landon. I want to find out what happened to my father—if he's alive, and why he never came back to us. I want to ask Rose to forgive me, and thank Gabe for being such an incredibly dedicated friend. I want to beg his forgiveness too, because I've hurt him, and I didn't want to. I didn't mean to. Part of me wants to kiss him again to be absolutely certain that he and I aren't meant to have a future other than friendship.

I want all these things, but I can't have them unless I find a way to keep going. I probe my wound with my fingertips. Webs of pain shoot out in all directions, up my elbow and into my shoulder, down my forearm into my wrist, tightening the tendons in my neck, followed shortly by searing heat. Alarmed, I pull up my sleeve, and have to stifle a cry of fear in the couch cushion when I see that the angry red lines are turning gray, and have extended past the bandage, spreading up and down the length of my arm.

I don't need to look under the bandage to know that I'm running out of time. I roll down my sleeve to cover the evidence. I've been wearing light-weight flowy blouses over my tank tops. He thinks it's a fashion statement to wear sheer silk tops with denim shorts—which isn't entirely untrue. I've dedicated considerable efforts to hide the severity of my wound from him. Now I'm afraid the days of hiding it are behind me. Another day—two at most— and the gray lines will run across my chest, up my neck, into my fingers. I swallow a lump of fear, wondering how long before this infection reaches my heart. Days, at most.

Maybe I need an actual doctor. Maybe this is something that can be medically treated. Obviously I can't do anything about it by myself. Maybe there's a clinic nearby where we can go. I could tell them I was bitten by a snake. Or a venomous spider. Or stung by a scorpion.

Maybe we should go home and let Valdemar figure out how to help me—at the expense of my relationship with Kye. Maybe it would be worth it. I sit up, ready to open the discussion, when Kye spins in his chair, clutching a book tightly.

"Isleen's power was never restored after Tynan and Theron were born," he says, skimming a passage and mumbling to himself. "Which we knew. That's why the pendant was created. But she had more children once she was free to be with Rhys and live as a peasant. Not one child, multiple. Boys and girls, with an abundance of Gifts, which they suppressed and hid in order to protect their identity. The family, no longer existing as royals, lived out their days in a village set in a valley surrounded by mountains. The Morrigana never bothered them after the king was gone, and even Tynan didn't know they were alive."

"Good for them," I tell him, still wondering how to bring up the idea of us going home. "At least some of them got to have a normal life."

He shakes his head, his eyes glinting. "No, not some of them. All of them, Abby. It says 'the family, no longer existing as royals.' Royals. Plural."

Confused about what he's getting at, I stand and join him in reading from the book.

He continues. "Don't you get it? Rhys was never a royal. None of the new children lived as royals either. The kingdom had already fallen. Isleen would have been the only royal left. Unless ..."

My heart races with hope. "Unless Theron and Raina lived too. Royals. Plural."

He draws me into his lap. "Exactly. Which means that whatever Tynan did to Raina, to Theron, to all of them, they found a way to escape and survive. To beat him and his curse. Rather than going back to fight over the fallen kingdom, they made a life in the mountains."

"Tynan cut Raina with the dagger." Hope soars as I remember one of my visions. "She must have found a way to Heal the wound."

"I agree. There must be a way." He flips through more pages, frowning. "But it's not mentioned here. This is the end."

"What do you mean, the end? How could it be the end? It's a journal. You're only halfway into that volume. That can't be all there is."

Tanya stumbles in, bouncing Cole on her hip. "It is. That's all. I'm sorry."

"There's got to be more," I insist. "They would be crazy to have stopped keeping records of their life."

Tanya's eyes fall on me, sitting on Kye's lap. "Do you keep a journal of your everyday life?"

I shake my head, knowing she's right, and hating it at the same time. "You know I don't."

"They had to make a clean break from the past. If they did keep journals or records after these, they're most likely under whatever new identity the family took when they started over."

My mind spins as piece after piece falls into place and little details start to make sense. This knowledge, these journals, must be what my father was after. This is why we traveled. Not solely to protect me from the demons, but because he knew that there were more of us. He must have believed that if he could find records of the lost royal family, maybe he could begin to find the rest of Rhys and Isleen's descendants.

My father wasn't being chased. He was looking for something. Or someone. A lot of someones. He was looking for our family.

EIGHTEEN

Valuable

ROSE

Seventeen pounds. As I stare at the scale, my brain goes into shutter mode, fluctuating between shock and denial. There's no way I've gained that much. But according to this ridiculous thing, I'm seventeen pounds heavier than I was when I left for Mexico.

Well. I guess that explains why I couldn't get my jeans buttoned this morning. It's the first time I've tried to put on actual pants that aren't leggings or sweats, and I'm chagrined that I didn't see this coming weeks ago. Burning with self-loathing, I storm into my room and snatch the calendar off my desk, wondering exactly how long I've wasted, wallowing in misery as *Poor-Depressed Rose*. What if it's been years, rather than weeks? I don't know.

The calendar has nothing written on it, because I haven't cared to use it. I think we came home on a Tuesday, but it could have been a Monday. Seems like it was September, because the days were still semi-warm. Maybe toward the end? I jab my finger between two possible days and try to count weeks, but then give up. It doesn't matter. It hasn't been long enough for me to forget. And today I wish I could. I don't want to think about Alex anymore, don't want to remember what happened, or what I've lost or what might have been. I want to go back in time to high school and have my friends back, and date lots of boys and not know what it feels like to truly ache.

Frustration builds until I can't hold it in. I pull on a sports bra, yoga pants, and a sweatshirt—because apparently, it's cold out—and lace up my running shoes. Seventeen pounds. Forget that!

My feet hit the pavement at full speed, crunching through fallen leaves and past clusters of pumpkins on vines and houses decorated with spider webs, tombstones and fake skeleton parts. The cool air doesn't feel as scary today as it did last time I was out, and when I pass Jen's house, I'm no longer nervous that there might be shadows under her porch. They're there—the world will always be host to shadow demons, and I'll have nightmares about Mexico for the rest of my life. I'm learning to accept both.

I'm so caught up in my head that I don't recognize how far I've gone until I pass the high school and end up staring into the clearing where Abby was once accosted by shadows. Those days seem like another lifetime. I'm almost into the forest when a voice stops me.

"Really?" Gabe says. "You're really running into the woods alone?"

I stop, breath wheezing. Gabe's also dressed for running, including ridiculous neon green shoes with hot pink laces. I eye him up and down, remembering how Abby used to complain that he was literally everywhere. All. The. Time. "It doesn't appear as if I'll be alone anymore. Besides, the shadow demons aren't chasing *me*. I bet they don't even know who I am."

Gabe stretches his quads, one at a time. "That's the stupidest thing you've ever said. You know better. There are shadows. There will always be shadows, and you, Miss Rose, are also a target on their list."

I snort, rolling my neck and jogging in place to stay warm. "Right. I'm a target. Because clearly, I'm dangerous. My Gift is so desirable that the demon lord wants to steal it. "

"Obviously he does. Just because the energy you emit isn't as strong as Abby's doesn't mean they don't want you as badly as they wanted her. Rose, those demons want all of us. Don't you get that?"

No, I don't. "If that's the case, I feel all kinds of valuable to the rest of you. Abby's had a freaking body guard for the last year, and a whole company of people who have been focused on saving her and Kye. They've had personal training, and a say on the counsel, and their own *spending accounts*. None of you has been even slightly concerned about me. About what I'm going through. About whether or not I'm staying in shape or honing my Gift. Not one of them has come to see me since we got home. I can't even get Jen to answer my texts. How am I supposed to feel like I matter to anyone?"

The way he sucks in his breath, I can tell I've hit a sore spot. "Look, Rose. If you didn't matter, they wouldn't have sent you to Mexico in the first place. If you didn't matter, you wouldn't be back in Jackson."

"What does me being back here have to do with anything? This is my home. I've lived here my whole life. My family's here, and my friends and my history. Of course I came back. Where else would I go? You think I would let them send me away from my home? Why would the Dragons do something so insensitive and stupid? Why would I—or anyone else—deserve that?"

"That's what they did to Abby." His quiet response shuts down my fighting instinct. He continues, "The minute they knew what she could do, she became their puppet. They enlisted Kye to drag her to Las Vegas—where she could have been caught and killed without ever knowing why. And then chasing after the Keys in New York, where Kye did get caught, and then back here begging for help. Rose, this was within weeks of the Dragon counsel finding out what Abby could do. They've been calling the shots and pulling the strings ever since. I mean, come on. You know Abby. Do you really believe she would voluntarily leave us behind without saying goodbye?"

"No." I don't know how to respond to this. Gabe has shot a bazillion holes in the wall of hurt and anger I've built, and now things are at risk of bleeding through. I take off running, knowing Gabe will follow, and am glad when he does so without continuing to talk.

My feet pound the spongy ground in a soothing rhythm, kicking up the pungent scents of pine and oak and freshly sodden earth to further assault my senses. I barrel past thick branches and shrubbery, sloshing through puddles that spread muddy goo up my calves, and burst into the open where I catch a panoramic glimpse of Jackson, spread out below.

I never considered that Abby was a prisoner. I've spent so much time envying her for being important, for being the chosen one. The needed one. The one everyone expected to save our people. I'm her best friend, and yet I've never once stopped to think—after all the things I've seen her endure—that Abby was anything other than lucky to be who she is. She has the right Gifts, the right lineage, the right past lives. I've never had any of that. The only thing I've had— besides my awesome, rocking parents, and my savvy ability to talk people into literally anything and everything I've ever wanted them to do—has been my freedom.

I've never had to beg to stay in one place. I went to the same schools and grew up with the same kids. I've known about my Gifts all along, and have never had to keep them a secret from more than a few strangers. The Dragons have never been able to force me to do anything. I've always had the right to choose. The ability to choose.

Since I've met her, Abby's been doing everything others have told her to do. She did everything she could to please the Dragons. To keep them happy. When they insisted she leave her new home, leave her country, she did it. Partly to protect Kye, but also, because she's their puppet, and didn't know any other way. Maybe Abby ran away because she realized all this. Maybe it was the only way for her and Kye to truly be free.

Gabe doesn't understand how strongly his words have affected me. How could he? I've spent all this time being angry with Abby. In my head, logically, I get that she isn't responsible for Alex's death. I know it. Yet, I'm still angry because she couldn't fix it. She couldn't bring him back. I blame her, while knowing it's not her fault. It's not logical and I can't fix that either.

I stop in a copse of trees, realizing that I no longer hear the rhythmic pounding of Gabe's footsteps as he keeps pace. I turn back, relieved to find him standing fifty yards back, guzzling an entire bottle of water in one gulp. His eyes catch mine, and he grins. "Feeling better yet?"

I want to shoot back a snarky reply of the same variety I've always used with Gabe, but my brain won't cooperate this time. "I'm a horrible person," I croak, surprised to find that my eyes are not only hot, but wet and dripping. "I hate my best friend. I blame her for Alex's death, even though I know it's not her fault. There's no logic in it, but my heart's been full of anger for her, at her. She's been given the world. She's had money and body guards and people bowing to her every whim. That's supposed to be a benefit of *my* Gift. *I'm* the one people used to focus on. But *I* could never be what she is. I resent her and love her at the same time, and I hate myself for feeling that way."

Gabe catches up, offering me a water bottle from the backpack he has strapped to his floating disk, and I brace myself for the criticism that's coming. Gabe will defend Abby until he dies. He loves her, and I get it, but at the moment, my insides are crumbling to bits.

But he doesn't criticize or console. "You can't help how you feel, Rose. Logic and emotion aren't always linked in rational ways, if they're linked at all."

I have to blink to comprehend his quiet acceptance. "I expected you to rip me apart for admitting that."

He swallows more water, but it isn't smooth going down. "I'm sorry I've been so hard on you. You deserve better."

I'm stunned. And confused. And broken-hearted for him, because he must be hurting badly to capitulate so easily. "You deserve better than I've dished to you, too. I'm also sorry."

The ghost of a smile tilts in his lips and eyes. "Truce?"

"For now." I ignore the hand he offers in favor of a hug. "Friends?"

"Absolutely."

As Gabe and I get back to our run, I'm lighter. I'll get back in shape by putting one foot in front of the other, and I'll come back to life this way too.

But I'm going to need Jen. And Abby, though she can't be here right now. I blame her, I'm angry with her, and I need to learn how not to be. In order to do that, I have to find out why they were forced to run.

I'm so deep in thought that I almost don't notice the chill riding my skin, or the shadows creeping along the ground, weaving between our ankles as we track through a murky section of forest.

Gabe stops me when the dark mist is halfway to my thighs.

"Rose, we need to get out of here. Something's not right."

I stop, realizing that this is not your average fog. More along the variety of what we experienced in Mexico. I've seen mists like these overtake Abby time and again. This type of mist is what killed Alex. My muscles seize, forcing me to my knees, unable to breathe. Gabe pulls me up before my knees touch the dirt. "We have to keep moving. I don't know how to defeat these things without Abby's Light."

I can't feel my toes, but somehow push forward. "Abby got rid of the demons in Jackson."

"We all thought so," he says, navigating vegetation we can't see. "But let's be real. No one person can abolish all the world's evils. There will always be demons, shadows. There will always be obstacles blurring the line between good and evil. This is why our generation is rising. It's why we're all here, together for the first time in hundreds of years. This is why we train, and practice using our Gifts for the good of the world."

There's something inspiring in Gabe's words, motivating. For the first time since Abby came to Jackson, I remember what it feels like to be valued for my Gift. My ability to communicate and persuade. I can do things, good things, to help others. To make a difference. I have influence and importance and creativity and I matter. *I matter.*

I turn to face whatever is chasing us, and the thing is so. Much. Bigger. Scarier than any shadows I've seen before. Ten feet tall and twice as wide, and thick like the smoke from a fire. I pull in a breath, two, and center on my vocal chords, the way Val taught me when I was young. "Be gone," I shout, wondering if my exact wording matters. The shadow pulses, but doesn't curl up and vanish the way they've been known to do for Abby.

"Get out of here," I try. "Shoo. Go away. Leave." Every word from me is like a visible punch to the shadow, leaving holes and indentations in the mist, which encourages me to keep trying. "Scram. Skedaddle. Vamoose. Vanish. Withdraw. Get lost." More holes, weaker mist.

"It's working," Gabe says, his voice laced with amazement and admiration.

"I'm out of words," I tell him. "What else means get lost?"

"Banish?" he suggests.

The word hits a note in me. It's the right one. I need to form my sentence in the right way so I don't waste this very important word. Another big breath to center me. "Shadow, I banish you from these woods. From this town. From the state of Wyoming."

My words spark the smoke into flames that jump and lick and burn together until the shadow curls in on itself, sizzling like fireworks until with a last, loud pop, it disappears.

The setting sun reaches through the trees to touch my cheeks, and the birds begin to sing again. As the heaviness lightens in my chest, I turn to Gabe, who is standing there with his mouth agape, and throw myself into his arms. "Did you see that? Do you see what I just did?"

He nods. "I couldn't have predicted *that*. How did you know what to do?"

Energy sings through my veins, rings in my ears, hums under my skin. I'm invincible. "I used my Voice. The thing you've been hounding me to practice all along. I banished a shadow using *my* Gift. Not Abby's, *mine*. Do you know what this means?"

"It means you're an asset to this fight, which is not news—I just got through telling you that."

"It means," I repeat. "We can defeat these demons without Abby's help. It means I'm valuable. I know what to do, and how to do it. I can save us too!"

He swings me around. When he sets me on the ground, both of us breathless and grinning, my eyes find in his something I've never noticed there before. Gabe and I could be friends—good ones—for a long time. If I let it, if we let it, we could be more.

If only my heart wasn't wasted on a dead guy.

NINETEEN

One Tiny Sacrifice

ABBY

"We should try again." Tanya perches Cole on her hip, nodding at the waiting circle of crystals.

"It's getting late," I protest. "We should go to bed. I'll still be wounded tomorrow."

"And weaker," Kye says.

"If this attempt doesn't work, then yes, we'll try again tomorrow." Tanya points a stubborn finger at the circle, determination burning in her eyes. "I brought something to help." She holds up a silver baby rattle, offering it so I can take a look. The silver bulb is embedded with gemstones—green, red, and blue. Gold, purple, orange, and black. The gems have been crushed into tiny flecks and mixed with the silver, leaving the toy with a smooth, glossy finish. I shake it, and the energy aroused by the musical chime surges with power, not unlike when a Healer uses energetic tones. It washes over me, soothing and empowering, and even Cole responds with a slobbery smile.

I hand the rattle to Kye. "No ordinary toy."

Tanya shakes her head. "It's an antique."

A laugh bursts from me. "Of course. Isleen made it, didn't she?"

"Actually, Rhys did. He wasn't Gifted in the way Isleen and the children were, but he was a man of many talents."

Kye taps the rattle against his head, and the chime echoes again. "So what is it supposed to do?"

Cole fusses, his chubby hand reaching for his toy. Tanya says, "Well, it's a rattle. It's intended to entertain a baby."

"And?" Kye prompts.

"And," Tanya continues, "It keeps him safe and masks his aura so he isn't easily found."

Kye hands the rattle to Cole, who immediately attempts to shove it in his mouth.

I watch Cole cover the silver with slobber. "That toy is as powerful as my ring. If anything can give us a boost, this is it." Tanya and Kye follow me to the circle. I lie inside, and Tanya wrestles the rattle away from Cole and places the slobber-covered toy on my chest. This time, they each take one of my hands, and the contact enhances my energy level. "Keep hold of my hands," I instruct them, "and spin my chakras one handed if you can."

Once again, we initiate the Healing process, and I beg my body to release some of the toxins. I won't allow them all to be released. Not into the people I love and who could be harmed. But releasing some of it will prolog my life until Kye is able to restore the order of the Gifted.

I reach deep, stretching, straining, searching to grasp any Healing energy remaining in my body, until the effort steals my breath and forces me to gasp. "I'm sorry. It's useless."

"No." Kye keeps his eyes closed, refusing to release my hand, and squeezing so tightly it might bruise. "We can do this, Abby."

I close my eyes again, absorbing energy as they hum, and adding my voice to theirs as mind to relaxes and lets go.

A little hand touches my leg—Cole is crawling—and a spark of light flickers. My heart pounds with hope. Tanya and Kye are so busy concentrating that neither notices as Cole climbs onto my legs, balancing himself on my knee and thigh, both hands pressed to skin as if he's trying to help. The initial flicker of power turns into a flame. Cole reaches a wobbly hand toward my chest, stretching until he nearly falls, rebalances himself, and then reaches again. I fight a snort of laughter. He wants his rattle! I wish we could stop and let him take it, but Kye and Tanya have a good rhythm going, and some of the crystals are beginning to lift into the air.

Torn between necessity and desire, I watch Cole scoot along my body, never quite able to reach his toy. His face scrunches with frustration, and I brace to feel the crystals drop as soon as he starts to cry, but that cry doesn't come, and his hands press into me as he crawls higher.

My concentration is shot, so at first I don't notice the warm fingers of energy reaching inside me, searching through the mess of infection to find the tiniest flame of Light. It isn't until the Light trails along, burning a line of warmth across my palms and up my neck, that I realize it's being drawn out of me, without help, or consent. As the warmth exits my body, an empty chill creeps in, dull and final, paralyzing me with fear. Something isn't right. I grab for the ribbon of Light, hoping—needing—to keep some of it back—however small a portion—but it slips away fast, and my energy is slo-oow. Peanut-butter-globing along, trying to keep up with runny syrup. Impossible.

When the last of the Light is gone, the crystals fall, cold and lifeless. I lie there, stunned, waiting for my energy to be returned, for the crystals to lift and spin again, but there's nothing.

No warmth. No Healing energy. No Sight. Only cold, cold fear, and the sensation of Cole resting his head on my chest, finally having reached his rattle.

"What happened?" Tanya asks, a note of fear infusing her voice. "It was working. I could feel it working, and then it ... stopped."

Kye's gaze flicks to the baby on my chest, his eyes widening. "Oh no." He licks his lips. "Abby, tell me he hasn't been there the whole time."

"He was reaching for his rattle." I pull my hand free and stroke his downy hair. "He's fine."

He shakes his head, terror riding across his face. "You don't understand. Your energy never reached me." He glances at Tanya, who shakes her head, staring at her son with a gulp.

"Me either."

My heart slams into my feet. "No. We did not transfer my poison into a baby. I refuse to believe that's possible."

In answer, Cole lifts his head, grinning as he shakes his rattle, a tiny red line circling his wrist.

I sit up, clutching Cole to my chest, stunned. Tanya snatches him from me, sobbing as she strips off his clothes to reveal more lines. They come from every direction with no beginning and no end. Random lines that continue to grow, searching for somewhere to settle and thrive. "None of them has touched anything vital yet," I whisper to Kye. "But eventually they will, and it will be fast. He's so small."

Tanya turns to me, holding the baby so tightly he grunts in protest as she kisses his hair. "What do we do? Can we take it back?"

I'm nodding before I have the chance to think that it might not be possible. "Of course. Yes, that's exactly what we'll do. I'll . . . I'll Heal him and take back the bad energy."

She blinks rapidly to hold in the well of tears already forming in her eyes, and we return to the circle, adjusting it for Cole. In the flurry of stripping him down, he dropped his rattle, so I retrieve it and place it in his eager fist, and then run my hands through the space above him, trying to locate his energy.

But it takes an extraordinary amount of time for me to connect with Cole. It's usually so instantaneous that I can run my fingers along the energy plane and get right to work. I've never felt such an absence before.

Kye and Tanya watch in confusion as I drop my hands lower, moving the crystals out of the way so I can rub Cole's soft skin. It doesn't help. It's as if he has no aura, no energy. Kye looks different to me now, too, and so does Tanya. Even my crystals feel cold in my hands, a sensation I've never before experienced.

"I can't," I whisper frantically, still rubbing Cole's skin, desperate to prove that my worst fear has not manifested. "It's not working."

Kye squeezes my shoulder, lending me his energy again as if what worked before might work now, but it's no use, and we both feel it. A tear rolls down Tanya's cheek, but she remains silent, waiting for me to tell her what we can all see for ourselves.

I can't Heal the baby. My Healing power is gone.

TWENTY

Open Wounds

ROSE

Gabe follows me home to make sure I get there safely, and then comes inside, insisting that we plan a new training regimen immediately. It's obvious that I'm out of shape, and though I have a good excuse, it would be foolish for me to continue to wallow. This new discovery has Gabe and I riding an energy high similar to what I felt the night Alex and I took Abby to the club, only to have to rescue her from the demons.

This time we'll be training on our own, without the help of the Dragons. With mutual agreement, we acknowledge that it wouldn't be in our best interest to inform them of our plans. At least not until we find out more about why Kye and Abby left the way they did.

At seven thirty the next morning, Gabe pounds on my door, wearing workout clothes and carrying a full duffle bag. I'm bleary-eyed and bed-headed, wearing my fuzzy Doctor Seuss pajamas when I unlatch the deadbolt. "What the hell, Gabe? The sun's barely awake yet."

He pushes past me into the house. "You were supposed to be ready at dawn. Get dressed. Have you eaten breakfast?"

I raise a brow, unable to find even a hint of the motivation I had yesterday. "I'm going back to bed. Come back in an hour when it's lighter outside."

He continues into my kitchen as if he plans to stay. "Have you changed your mind about training?"

I follow him despite the tempting draw of my warm, soft comforter. "No. But I don't recall agreeing to give up valuable sleep for it either. My days don't start before eight-thirty. Nine if you want me awake and alert."

He turns away from the fridge and rests his hands on my shoulders. "Rose. We have a lot to do, and we need to do it when the Dragons aren't watching. They know your habits, including that you stay up half the night and then sleep late. This is our best chance for optimum privacy. Besides, starting first thing in the morning will make you better. Stronger. Your voice is weakest immediately after sleep, so that's when it's most important to train."

I yawn, knowing he's right, and still longing for my bed. "Fine. I'll get dressed, but just so you know, I'm going to hate you by lunchtime."

"I'm used to it." He opens the fridge and rifles through, frowning at the choices. "You should eat. What do you want?"

"There are breakfast sandwiches in the freezer and juice in the fridge. I'll need a large glass of OJ before we go to keep my throat from hurting. Oh, and you could chop two or three lemons to go in my water bottle. I need the rinds too. It helps strengthen my vocal cords."

He grins as I head upstairs to dress. It seems odd to be friends with Gabe after all the energy we've spent fighting on opposite ends of a personal battle. Right now, he's the only friend I have. There's something healing about being with him, and even I can't deny the necessity in that.

Jen finally replies to a text, six days after I resolve to text her every two hours, all day, every day.

Her:

I'm home, but super sick. Can't hang out, but I miss you too. I want to hear all about Mexico soon.

I immediately text back:

I don't care that you're sick. I'm coming over. What can I bring you?

She replies:

Please don't.

Rather than argue, I lace up my shoes and jog to her house, ignoring the ache of stiffness that comes from mornings spent working out with gung-ho-Gabe. I was in good shape *before*, so it kills me how fast my muscles went to jelly after over a month of inactivity.

My knock on her front door is sharp and loud. Joanna Thomas answers, wearing a starched-white apron and a puzzled frown. "Rose! It's good to see you. How have you been?"

Jen's mom is a piece of work. I would never tell Jen this, but it's like this woman has two personalities. A public one and a private one. The public one is for putting on the show that everyone gets to see. The type where she's the ideal mother whose house is always spotless, who has dinner on the table at five, and whose children were never dirty after playing in the mud. Then there's the private one, where she has a mental breakdown and throws dishes and shoes at her children, and makes up stories about things she thinks they've done, but that are actually memories from her own childhood.

It's the public persona that I am currently facing—which is the only side of Joanna Thomas most people ever see.

"I'm doing better," I tell her honestly. "It's been a hard month, but I'm finally feeling up to going out."

"Oh, good for you," she says, her voice so saccharine sweet that I half expect it to drip down her chin. "I'm glad you're doing well. What brings you visiting today?"

I blink, wondering why I should need to state the obvious. "I'm here to see Jen."

Joanna frowns, and for the first time since I've known her, wrinkles form between her brows, and in the corners of her eyes and lips. She has aged significantly since I saw her last summer.

Jen and I have been friends for as long as I can remember, and her mother has always displayed nuances and oddities, behaviors that are not normal in an adult. I was once in Jen's room during one of her mother's episodes, and witnessed for myself exactly how Jen's great-grandmother's china came to be smashed all over the floor in the hallway near Jen's locked bedroom door. I've seen what my friend has had to live with, and wonder if it has anything to do with why Jen chose not to come to Mexico.

"I'm sorry," Jo says. "Jen's not here. She moved out a month ago. Maybe a month and a half?"

While I was still in Mexico. "What do you mean she moved out? Where would she move and why didn't she tell me?"

Jo opens the door wider, inviting me in, but I remain where I'm standing. "I assumed she had. I can't imagine why she wouldn't have told you, Rose. Are you sure she didn't mention it and you forgot?"

There's something seriously wrong going on, but I can't tell what. "This isn't a small thing, Mrs. Thomas. Moving out is huge. If she told me, or even hinted about it, I would remember."

"Well, no offense, but you've been caught up in your own things lately." Her voice, still sickly sweet, sharpens to a spear point and threatens to puncture the glass ball that's currently protecting my emotions this week. The edge of her point prods a bubble of anger.

"Where did she move?" I redirect the conversation to avoid a messy explosion from me. "Did she go alone? We were planning on getting an apartment together."

"On the other side of town. She moved in with Tommy."

My heart crashes into my chest. How could I not know this? I'm a horrible friend, because a month and a half ago, I was in Mexico having the time of my life with Abby and Gabe and Alejandro, and I was horrible at keeping in touch with Jen. Partly because international cell phone calls are pricey, but partly because I truly was having the best summer ever—even without her. But I don't understand why *she* didn't call *me*. Or text. Why didn't she text?

She could have emailed. I had internet access in the resort café, and went there daily to keep in touch with my parents. I sent her pictures and notes when I could, but she never responded.

Joanna gives me the address to Jen's new apartment before I leave for home. I don't understand why Jen didn't tell me she moved in with Tommy. Unless it's because she knew I wouldn't approve.

I'm not a prude. I mean, hello. I was prepared to move into Alex's room before all the crap hit the fan. But Jen can do better than Tommy. She can. She started seeing him before graduation, and right after that is when she withdrew from me, and from Abby. She was acting weird and resentful and depressed, and I knew something was going on with her. That's one of the reasons I pushed her to go with me to Mexico. She wouldn't do it. She couldn't explain why, because we both knew it wasn't about money.

It only takes me minutes to get home and grab my car keys, but in the process I reconsider. Maybe this is something I shouldn't do alone. Tommy's crazy weird, and quite scary at times, depending on his level of sobriety. So before I leave, I text Gabe.

Jen moved in with crazy Tommy while we were gone. He freaks me out. Want to go with me to visit her?

My finger hovers over the send button for several seconds before I click it. I've been seeing a lot of Gabe lately. He still comes over to hang out sometimes when he's bored, and we usually train for three hours a day, but I've never *invited* him to do anything, social or otherwise. Until now.

He texts back within seconds:

Why does he freak you out?

I don't know how to answer his question, so I tell him:

I can't explain it. A feeling. He acts suspicious whenever I see him. Something about him isn't right.

He replies:

You should trust your gut. Are you going now?

Me:

Yes. She says she's home but not to come over. So I'm going.

Him:

Of course you are. She told you no. Now you have to rebel against that.

Me:

Whatever. I am so not like that.

Him:

No comment.

Me:

Are you coming or not?

Him:

Be there in ten.

Thirty minutes later, we pull up to the shabby building in Gabe's Dragon issued Jeep SUV. The walk is crumbled and pitted, and the grass is green, but tall past my ankles. The chipped stucco appears grungy, as if no one has washed it since last winter. This isn't the best part of town, so I'm glad I brought Gabe. He stays close as we traverse the stairwell to the second floor and find the apartment number.

For a fleeting second, I wonder if coming here was a bad idea. In the months since I last saw Jen a lot of things have changed. Our friendship might be one of those things. I've nearly talked myself into leaving when Gabe knocks, taking away my chance to chicken-out.

There's rustling on the other side of the door, and a man's voice asks, "Who is it?"

"We're here to see Jen," Gabe says.

The door opens with a whoosh, revealing Tommy, wearing boxers and a ripped T-shirt that shows off a horrible blob of a tattoo on his abdomen. "Who are you?"

"Tommy, shut up." I sneer, attempting to push my way into the apartment. He blocks the doorway with a subtle shift of his body. "You know me. We've gone to school together our whole lives."

"Oh, hey, Rose. I didn't recognize you. You look … different."

As if my self-confidence wasn't already at a low. "Thanks a lot."

He glances at Gabe, nodding. "What's up?"

"This is my friend Gabe," I tell him, trying not to sound annoyed. "Can we come in?"

He hesitates, eyeing Gabe up and down multiple times. "Why?"

"I'm here to see Jen. Is she here?"

He blinks. "Why would she be here?"

"You know why," I snap, my patience unraveling. "Joanna told me Jen moved in with you, so stop playing dumb and go get her. Her car's in the parking lot. I know she's here."

"What if she doesn't want to see you?"

"Get her anyway," Gabe pipes up. When he straightens to his full height, muscles ripple in every possible place, making Gabe one of the most intimidating specimens alive. He's not a giant by any means, but he's formidable. A word from him is all it takes for Tommy to drop his arm and wave us into the living room. "Have a seat." He starts down the hall. "I'll go see what she's doing."

The living conditions in this apartment are nothing like Jen's parents' house. It's not a complete disaster, but it's so far from clean, I hesitate to touch *anything*. "This is not like Jen at all. She's a neat freak."

"Dating someone of Tommy's variety isn't like her either," Gabe says. "She's better than this. I don't understand what she's thinking." He pats one of the couch cushions, releasing a puff of dust that leaves us both coughing.

Down the hall, voices raise in anger. Jen's sounds rough, like she's sick. At least she wasn't lying about that. Finally, she comes out.

She's wearing faded yoga pants and a skimpy tank top that shows off her shoulders and chest—which is covered with scabs and open sores. Her hair hangs stringy and lifeless, and her eyes appear sunken into skin that's turned the slightest shade of yellow. Gabe's intake of breath mimics my own reaction. This is not the Jen I've known and loved my whole life. I haven't seen her in months, so the minute she steps into the room, I bound across it and wrap her in my arms. "Oh gosh, I've missed you."

She doesn't respond, except to pat me on the back and then pull away. "I've missed you too. How was Mexico?"

Gabe clears his throat and shakes his head, warning me not to divulge. As much as I want to open the vault and spill everything, I get what he means. The dynamic here has changed. Jen isn't who she was when we left. I don't know this person, and until I do, I should be careful about the details I give away. "It was hard," I tell her, trying to decide what to share. "Lots of training and work. Some horrible things happened while I was there."

She invites me to sit next to her on the couch, so against my better judgment, I do. "Your mom said you were seeing someone there, and that he died or something."

My eyes burn and my throat clogs. I've wanted to talk to Jen about this for so long. She's finally asking, and I'm not comfortable telling her. Now, I'm more concerned about what's going on with Jen. "I was," I croak. "He did. It was a hard summer."

She blinks, showing little emotion, which stabs like a blade into my chest. "I'm sorry to hear that." She pats my hand like I'm a child. "What have you been up to since you got home?"

I'm at a loss. How can she act like Alejandro's death is no big deal? Like I could come home and continue on my merry way as if I'd buried a goldfish instead of a boyfriend? Between the two of us, Jen was always the sensitive one. I'm stunned to see how she has changed in such a short amount of time.

Gabe answers for me. "Rose sustained some serious injuries, too. She's been recovering until this week."

Jen scowls at Gabe. "Shouldn't you be guarding the Queen of Everything?"

He jolts at her hostility. *I* have always been hostile toward Gabe, but Jen has never been anything but nice. He recovers quickly. "I have a new assignment."

Jen raises a brow, snorting at what she must think is irony. Okay, I'll give her that one. It *is* ironic that Gabe and I are spending time together—despite how we hated each other in the past.

"How are you," I ask, desperate to change the subject. "When did you move?"

"Few days ago," she says vaguely, scratching one of the sores on her arm. "I don't know. I've been pretty out of it."

"If you're sick, why wouldn't you stay home where your mom could take care of you?"

She glares like I'm both stupid and ignorant. "She doesn't know. Anyway, she doesn't want anything to do with me. I've been disowned."

"Jen, what's going on?" I blurt. "Please tell me. Let me be your friend. I miss you."

She swallows like I've hit an emotion she hasn't felt in a while, but her face remains emotionally blank. "I miss you too," she says slowly. "But you'd never understand this part of my life. I've chosen a different direction from you. I don't want to always live as a pawn for the Dragons, to go where they say, and live the way they tell me. I have a strong desire to be free, and that's what I choose."

"Free how? To do what?" Gabe asks. "To live in filth?"

She scowls at him and stands, preparing to shoo us away. "This was my only choice. It's only messy because I've been too sick to clean."

"Jen," I say slowly. "Your mom told me you've lived here for over a month. That's a lot longer than a few days. Have you been sick the whole time?"

"I guess," she says. "I haven't kept track."

"Well are you working?" I ask. "Do you have money?"

"I'm waitressing." She waves off her own vague answer. "When I'm well enough."

I don't know what that means. What restaurant manager lets their waitresses make their own schedule? It doesn't make sense. "Have you seen a doctor? Or a Healer? I'm worried you have the Chicken Pox or something."

"Oh sure. Go fetch the queen. I'm sure she'll fix me right up. She fixes everything else."

"Jen, what's wrong with you?" I ask again. I can't take my eyes off the sores. "You can tell me. Let me help you, please."

"I have a doctor," she says. "And I'll be fine, so you can stop worrying."

"I do worry," I tell her. "I love you. I want to make sure you're okay."

She glances down the hall, her eyes darting about as if she's checking to make sure no one's coming. "I'm fine," she says, the strength returning to her voice. Enough strength to sound more convincing. "I am. I'm trying to keep my ... Ahem. Ability in check. It's hard." She holds out her arm and shows us a large red mark where she's burned herself badly. "I've found a way to temper the heat, and it helps with other things too. Slightly unconventional, which is why my parents are so mad at me. But Rose, I want you to know that I'm happy with Tommy. I am. We're going to make a life together, so please don't worry."

That statement alone, is the most worrisome one of all.

"Is there anything we can do to help?" Gabe asks. He's mentally cataloguing the apartment, taking in details and filing them away for future reference. Once again I'm grateful to him for coming with me.

Jen shakes her head. "Let me be." And finally, the first sign of emotion I've seen in her comes out as her eyes glisten. "I need some time to figure out who I am in a way that's separate from my old life. I've spent my childhood being one of the *chosen* children, only ... not. My Gift is useful and so dangerous, and attempting to balance both is exhausting. Please let me have my time away. It doesn't mean I love you less. Just that I need to focus on me for a while."

She leads us to the door. The bones in her shoulders and back stab through her skin when I hug her. She has lost *so* much weight, in such a short amount of time. "I love you," I tell her. "No matter what you decide, no matter who you are. You're my best friend."

She swallows hard. "You shouldn't say that until you know all the things it means."

"Tell me," I beg her. "Let me in."

She shakes her head as sadness descends in the already-gloomy apartment. "I can't. I'm sorry. I'll text you next week when I'm feeling better. We'll get together."

And with that last bit of hope, she shows us out and closes the door.

"That was weird." Gabe leads the way down the stairs. "She's not acting like the Jen we know."

I struggle to find my voice. "Gabe, I'm scared for her."

He reaches out and takes my hand. "Don't worry. Now that we know, we can work on helping her." He leads me to the parking lot, keeping my hand safe and warm in his.

TWENTY-ONE

Haboob

ABBY

Tanya bursts out sobbing, and after what feels like the longest hour of my life, Kye's hand drops from my shoulder. "Take a break, babe. You've been through a lot today and your energy is spent."

I refuse to give up. Not this time. Not on Cole. He's too little to pay a price this high. Eventually, my muscles strain, and Cole kicks his legs and starts to fuss. My hands fall away as Tanya scoops him up, swaddling him in a blanket, cuddling and cooing with a desperate gleam in her frazzled eyes.

"I'm so sorry," I croak, my voice scarcely more than a squeak. "I don't know what happened. I would never have allowed him in the room if I thought this was possible."

She blinks through her tears, nodding as if she understands, but remains speechless. For the next hour, she paces. Cole sleeps in her arms, but she refuses to put him down. Kye holds me close as we watch. I've never felt more helpless. Finally, I can take no more. I stop Tanya from pacing and force her to sit, rest. She does so out of necessity, but refuses to release her possessive grip on the baby.

"My power's gone." Voicing the truth causes a sharp pain to pierce the deepest reaches of my soul. "And Cole needs a Healer. As soon as you can get him to one."

She grits her teeth, finally breaking her silence. "I don't know one."

"My mother," Kye says. "We'll send you to my mother. She can help."

Christine's not as skilled a Healer as me. Before Mexico, I was the most powerful Gifted person alive. Now I'm nothing, and I've left a mess Christine will have to clean up. I hope she can find a way to save Cole's life.

Tanya opens a closet and wrenches out a duffle bag, throwing random things inside. Knowing she's in shock, I take the bag from her and direct her to the couch. While I help her pack—in a suitcase, with clothes and necessities that *aren't* randomly tossed in off a living room shelf—Kye calls his parents and explains the situation in hushed tones. From the look on his face when he joins us in Tanya's bedroom, they're as worried as us. "The good news is they're in the country, so you won't be needing a passport," he tells Tanya, and I'm relieved.

"Good," she says, her voice bright. "Because I don't have one."

I suspect we could get her a fake one in a pinch, but that might take an extra day or two, and it's time Cole can't afford. "Is there a bad news clause to that statement?"

"Yeah." He raises a brow, taking a deeply pained breath. "Looks like she's on her way to Jackson."

We both know what this means. The Dragons have started rounding us up to answer for what went down in Mexico. They'll be stepping up the search for us—if they haven't already. Since we just gave them a solid bead on our location, Kye and I will have to get on the road to somewhere else as soon as Tanya and the baby are taken care of.

"I got you on the six-thirty-a.m. flight," Kye tells her.

It's currently 3:05. Only a matter of hours before they're on their way, and the strongest, most brilliant Gifted beings we know will be working to save Cole.

Within an hour, we're on our way to the airport. "Take the journals," Tanya insists. "And anything else you need. You can stay in my apartment for as long as you need. I doubt *I'll* be back anytime soon." More tears well in her eyes. "I'll lose my jobs. Can't exactly explain why I had to leave the state in the dead of night."

"Can you tell them you had a family emergency?" I suggest.

"Maybe," she says. "But that's not likely to help. Anyway, I can't worry about it now." She tucks Cole's rattle into his blanket—both a protection, and a Healing Key. "When I get back ... I'll find something else." She nods as if to reassure herself.

I know what happens after she shows up in Jackson, and so does Kye, but neither of us has the heart to warn her. It wouldn't change anything. Tanya would go to the ends of the earth to save her son. I'm quite certain it won't bother her at all when the Dragons push her to move to Jackson permanently.

Kye and I return to Tanya's apartment to pack up, debating about whether we should risk a few hours of sleep. I collapse onto her bed, exhaustion soaking through my skin and bones.

"We shouldn't stay here long—especially now," Kye says from the bathroom doorway.

I press my face into the pillow with a groan. "I don't have a visible aura anymore. My Gifts are gone. No one's going to find me, and if they do, I won't be of any use. Especially without sleep."

His footsteps tread across the carpet, and the heat from Kye's skin radiates into me as he crawls over the top of me, starting at my feet and moving up until he can purr in my ear. "Your Gifts are *not* gone. They're just ... suppressed. But you're right that we shouldn't drive while we're this exhausted."

My Gifts *are* gone. I know this as well as I've always known I had a Gift. But I'm not going to argue—not now. "We need to find my dad. None of this will make any sense until we do."

"I agree." He falls onto his side, propping his head on his hand and crossing his ankles. "But I don't feel good about dragging you to Ireland at the moment." He indicates my arm, and the wound that is less than half the size it was yesterday.

Without my Sight, it's hard to know what's right or wrong, or evil or good. I've gone sensationally deaf and blind. "I don't feel right about it either. I can't believe what happened. How could I transfer my powers *and* my poison into an innocent baby? A Gifted baby?"

"Maybe that's why," he says, puzzling it out. "If Cole is Gifted, it would make sense why he loves that rattle, and also why it took him touching you in order for you to release your Light."

"He could be an amplifier, like his mother."

"I don't know. The point is, we can't go to Ireland right now."

"There has to be a way for us to call. Could we somehow get a phone number for that address?"

Kye pushes himself off the bed and returns to the bathroom to pick up his toothbrush. "I'll do some research when my mind is functioning. I'm too beat to think straight right now. Two hours. Four, max, and then we get on the road."

I let my eyes drift shut, still fully clothed and sprawled on Tanya's bed. As I drift into dreamland, my grandmother's voice, faint and distant, floats toward me.

Don't give up. Keep trying. Keep looking.

When the alarm goes off, I wake with a start. Some would argue that sleep is sleep, but mine was not quality. My dreams were riddled with memories of every time I've failed to Heal someone I love, so I drag myself up and into the bathroom, deciding that I truly can function on no sleep if it's the lesser of two evils.

Paper shuffles in the other room, leaving me wondering if Kye slept at all. I find him sitting at Tanya's computer, three separate windows open to different search engines.

"Hey," I croak, surprised at the weakness in my voice.

His head snaps up, a frown indenting his brow. "How did you sleep?"

I shake my head. "At least my body got some rest."

"Are you hungry?" He waves a hand at the kitchen. "We should eat before we go. She doesn't have much, but there are eggs and some bread. We can get your orange juice at the gas station when we leave."

My stomach grumbles uneasily. "Have you found anything?"

"Not enough. Not nearly." He kneads the back of his neck where he carries his frustration. "Abby, the address your mother gave us doesn't lead to a house. It's a post office."

"What does that mean? Why would my mother give us an address to a post office?"

Kye runs his fingers into the hair at the nape of his neck, then smooths it out and lets his hands drop onto the desk. "I don't know." He swivels to face the screen. "Either that's where he receives his mail, or it's the last address he found in his search for more of us. If it's where he receives mail, he has to live somewhere nearby—which would mean he's alive and in Ireland." He blinks and lets that sink in before lowering his voice. "To be honest, I hope it's the latter."

"You don't want my father to be alive?"

"Of course." He lets out a deep breath. "Of course I do. Every girl needs her father. I'd just rather he be alive and in the United States." He doesn't mention that finding him alive would mean he left by choice, and I appreciate that.

"What do you mean by the last address he found? I'm confused."

Kye scrolls back, tapping his finger on the monitor. "I'm not sure what your father was doing. The only consistent evidence I can find is that he was following a trail that led him across the world. If we're working on the theory that he was searching for more of the Gifted, he was either recruiting them to gather together and be trained, or warning them about the dangers of the Elen."

Neither of those ideas seems quite right to me, and I'm about to say so, but hesitate, unsure if my intuition is something we can continue to rely on. Every part of me feels hollowed out, spent. Instead of agreeing or disagreeing, I answer with a noncommittal, "Maybe."

He continues scrolling, then flips to another screen, where he's pulled up a map and pinned stars on each place where I remember living. "If we stick to *that* theory, Isabelle may have known, and once your father ... disappeared, your mother and she continued his legacy by moving on to the next places he had planned to go. Obviously, because you were in school, they had to stay long enough for you to blend in and get an education, but after your father ... the pattern of your moves became less erratic, right?"

"Yes," I agree. When my father was alive, we moved from the east coast to the west coast to the middle of the country, and then back west again. We lived in Phoenix twice, and spent a large amount of time in Las Vegas too.

Kye swivels to face me again. "So where were you living when he ... disappeared?"

"Utah." A tiny town in the foothills of a giant mountain, where roofs sloped like gingerbread and there were more deer crossing signs than traffic lights. "But there had to be more to what he was doing than tracking people. Something that became dangerous enough to scare Gram. They argued the last time he left. It's like she knew he wasn't coming back."

"Do you think he found others here? Obviously *you* didn't know about Tanya—maybe he didn't either."

"Gram knew about Tanya. If he did find others, I never met them." My stomach moans, rolling between stress and hunger, so I head into the kitchen to find the eggs Kye mentioned. The apartment is so small, there's no need to raise my voice. "My father had Sight, so if he was after something else, it was likely something he'd Seen in a vision."

"That doesn't help us, unless we know what the vision was." Kye pushes his chair away from the computer and stands, stretching his arms toward the ceiling. "Unless you could find a way to See the same thing he did ..."

"It doesn't work that way." I turn on a burner and begin my search for a frying pan. "Besides, I can't See anything anymore."

Kye blinks away the sympathy—we both know it won't do us any good. "Have you tried since last night?"

Shaking my head for lack of an explanation, I remove the eggs from the fridge and find a spatula in a mostly empty drawer. "I don't have to. I can feel the absence like a blank space inside me. A folder without any files."

"But the folder still exists." He joins me in the kitchen, searching the cupboards until he finds two glasses and fills them with the last of Tanya's milk.

Maybe. "If so, it's an empty shell." I spray the pan and turn up the burner, anxious to feel the heat warming the bottom. I wonder if this is how Jen feels when she controls fire. There's a degree of power involved in cooking, and I have a moment of gratitude for the small things that are still within my grasp.

"Files can be recovered." Kye sets the glasses on the table, staring again at Tanya's computer.

Not when they've been deleted. I hold the words in my mouth and my hand over the frying pan, waiting for hints of warmth to reach my skin. If only finding my Light was as easy as turning on a switch.

Regardless of our level of exhaustion, we both know we can't stay here, and so we prepare to get on the road again. After gathering our personal things, we straighten the living area, wash our morning dishes, and sweep the floor. There's no knowing when Tanya will be back, so we need to leave this place as clean as possible.

"We should call my parents and make sure Tanya and Cole arrived okay." Kye slams the trunk, and joins me in the car.

"If Christine can't help Cole ..."

"She will." He rests a hand on my knee. "My mom will take care of him."

I swallow, unable to respond with more than a nod.

He pulls out of the parking lot. "I guess we're heading for Utah, so my plan is to keep heading north. Where in Utah?"

"There's a small town next to a lake. It butts up to the slope of a mountain that spends nine out of twelve months blanketed in snow. We lived there when I was young. It's the last place I ever saw my dad."

In the distance, a single brown-tipped peak—which is more of a hill, compared to the Tetons—rises toward the sky like a beacon. The landscape here isn't as flat as Texas. "I'm sorry," Kye says. "It can't be easy to keep revisiting your past this way."

Utah is the one place I've tried to avoid on our journeys, because as much as I want to know what happened to my father, I'm not positive I want to know what *really* happened to him.

I lean against the seat and rest my eyes, remembering. "The town is near ski resorts, so there are rental properties all over. If we want something different from a hotel, we could see if there's a little house or a condo available. Might be more comfortable if we need to stay longer than a few nights, and maybe cheaper than the resorts."

"Good idea. If it's remote enough, maybe the Dragons won't look for us there, and we can stay for a week and rest."

The topic of rest brings to mind the beginning of summer, when I first went to Mexico with Gabe, and how that was the most rest I'd had in what felt like years. In Mexico, I found myself again. Six months ago, I would have done anything, given anything for a week alone in a mountain cabin with Kye. At the time, I was dying for alone time with the man I love, but now I could use a break. We haven't been apart for more than a few minutes at a time since we left Mexico.

"What the ... ?" Kye lets off on the gas, staring out the windshield with his mouth agape.

I follow the direction of his gaze, and feel the blood drain from my face. A tidal wave of dark, red dust blows toward the city at supernatural speed. It's a hundred feet high and three times as wide, barreling across the desert landscape and covering everything in its path.

"Kye, tell me that's not demons. I have no Light. No powers to fight them off. If that's a demon cloud, people are going to die."

He hits the gas again, flipping the car around. "I don't know what it is, but demons or not, it's bad. We need to get inside somewhere."

By now, we're miles from Tanya's apartment, and the red cloud moves faster than we can drive in the city. My hands grip the seat until my knuckles ache. Kye screeches into a restaurant parking lot. "Do you have something to cover your face with?"

The best I have is the sheer top I'm wearing over my tank. Kye whips off his T-shirt and directs me to do the same with my top. I tie the long sleeves around my forehead, backwards so that I have visibility through the fabric.

"On my count, we run inside," Kye says. "Make sure you keep your nose and mouth covered. Whatever that is, it's toxic."

I'm too terrified to do anything but nod. I'm helpless against shadow demons in a way I've never been before. This battle—if there is one—will fall entirely upon Kye to fight, to win. Except he doesn't have Light, which has proven time and again to be our best defense against demons of all varieties. He counts off, and we clutch our door handles in preparation to jump and run.

Debris rains on the windshield, pelting our car and coating it in a layer of fine sand. Kye gives the signal, and I throw my door open, pressing my shirt against my nose and mouth. I try hard not to hold my breath, but as the cloud creeps nearer, it sucks the oxygen from my lungs so fast that spots appear in my eyes while we're still yards away from the door.

Kye grabs my elbow. "Come on."

He wrestles the door open as the wind beats against it, muscles bulging as he wrenches it free long enough for us to crowd inside, then forces it closed again.

My shaky fingers work at the knot holding my shirt to my head so I can uncover my face.

"Smart," says the hostess at the desk. "You shouldn't drive during a haboob. It's good that you came in."

"What's a Haboob?" Kye's nose and mouth appear clean, but the rest of his face and neck are coated with a layer of chalk-like dust, and his hair is thick and red with it.

"It's a desert dust storm. They don't happen often, but when they do, it's an interesting phenomenon."

"This has happened before?" A trickle of relief worms into me. "It's a natural occurrence?"

"Well, not daily, or even yearly. But sometimes." The petite girl steps away from the hostess station, offering us linen napkins. Neither of us can look away from the windows, outside which we can see nothing but glowing red sand. "You're not from here, are you?" she asks.

I shake my head, attempting to wipe the dust out of my eyes with the napkin. Fear has all my senses on alert. "We're passing through."

"Well, I hope you aren't pushing an important deadline, because none of us is going anywhere until this clears up."

"How long will that take?" Kye asks.

"Depends on the storm," she says. "Could be a few hours."

Piles of sand gather in the corners of the window, and mounds form against the door and under the wheels of parked cars. No one seems concerned that this "haboob"—as the waitress called it—is anything other than a dust storm. "How much sand typically piles up?" Kye wonders aloud.

"Once we had almost a foot," the girl says. "It depends on how much rain is up there and where the storm started in the first place."

"It's raining too? How is that possible?" I'm watching for signs that the storm is made of anything more than dust. It feels too big to be coincidence that this once-in-a-long-while storm happens to occur on the day while we're in town. "When's the last time you had one of these here?"

"Three or four years," the girl says, shoving a tablecloth against the bottom of the door to keep the sand from flowing in. "They're common, and yet rare at the same time."

Kye's rests a hand at the small of my back. "It's sand."

I want to believe that. In so many ways, I wish I could comprehend that being true. We've only been here for two days, and storms like this happen once every four years. It's not a coincidence. I clutch the amethyst crystal I've been wearing all day, begging my instincts, if not my third eye, to open, and then I see it. The dark shape, walking calmly through the middle of the wind. I know. It's not just another stranger seeking shelter. It's Boone.

My fingers curl onto Kye's forearm hard enough that he jerks his arm away. "What? What do you see?"

I try to point out the figure to him, but it's already gone. "Boone. I swear I saw him in there."

"If Boone was here," Kye says slowly, "Why didn't he follow us inside? It's not like we're hard to find."

"Maybe we are," I tell him. "Maybe without my Light, he can't tell me from any other female in the world."

Kye squints at the dust, clearly not seeing the same figure that I could see only seconds ago. "Babe, I don't think it's about you this time. It's just a dust storm."

I can't feel anything other than fear, or see anything other than sand and debris flying outside, so I can only hope that Kye's right. When I can no longer watch the hypnotic blank screen screaming past my vision, I head into the bathroom to splash cool water on my face and rinse out my mouth. I'm grateful for the napkin, and use it in place of a washcloth, wishing I had access to a shower.

I take off my tank and shake the sand out over the garbage can, and then do the same with my sheer top. Then I brush my hair vigorously, acutely aware that I'll never get all the sand out until I can wash it, so I braid it to keep it out of my face. When I come out, Kye has also cleaned up, and is back to staring outside, back rigid and eyes narrowed in caution.

"I might as well get you a table," the hostess chirps. "You're going to be here a while."

I'm not a big fan of burgers, but since they're the most dominant menu item, I decide to go with what's popular and order one, because—when in Rome, and if I'm going to die anyway, my taste buds should be happy.

It arrives smothered in a magical blue cheese sauce and topped with fresh lettuce, tomatoes, and avocado, and is accompanied with sweet potato fries and a giant chocolate milkshake.

Kye laughs when I take an enormous bite. "I've never seen you tuck into something with such enthusiasm."

I finish chewing and swallow. "I'm hungry." I swirl a sweet potato fry in the special sauce and savor that too. "And I haven't had a hamburger in months."

His eyes fill with warmth. "Gabe brought you one to the school once. You used it as an excuse to meet up with me."

The reminder of Gabe dampens my enthusiasm. I miss my friend. I miss feeling the security of knowing Gabe is constantly nearby, or behind me, or standing in front of me to keep me from doing something stupid. Not that I don't feel safe with Kye. I do. He has never failed to protect me, and has proven that he loves me enough to die for me. But Gabe and I had a different relationship. Lighter. Less intense. With Gabe, I almost never felt like I was running from something. More like working toward a goal. With Kye—well, we're always on the run. Have been since the moment we met. I have an enormous fear that this will never change.

I suppress a wistful sigh. This is my life now.

"Wanna talk about it?" Kye's shoulders droop as he wolfs down his own burger.

"About what?" I eat another fry and sip my shake, pulling on an air of nonchalance.

"Whatever's on your mind. You're thousands of miles away, and I'd like to know how to get you back."

"I was just thinking about how I hate feeling transient. I'd love to find a safe place where we can hang our clothes in a closet. Unpack our toiletries."

Kye reaches across the table to take my hand. "I'm sorry."

My fingers tangle with his. "I miss my mom. My friends. My dog."

He squeezes my hand. "I'm homesick too. Maybe we should call your mom."

"They'll find us."

Outside, the storm calms. Kye's attention cuts to the window, then back to me. "We're leaving. Maybe now is the best time to call, before we get out of Phoenix. Who knows when we'll have another chance?"

I want to ask Marian about my father, about why she didn't tell me he's alive and how she's dating Landon if she isn't actually widowed. I want to know why no one ever told me about the PO Box. I want to know so many things. Mostly, I need to hear my mother's voice.

"You're right," I agree. "Besides, I shouldn't have to play treasure hunter to find the truth about my family heritage. We deserve every bit of information she has to share. Landon too. And your parents. They all need to start being truthful with us. Forcing them to stop being cryptic could save lives—ours included."

He lets go of my hand to finish his burger. "Maybe we should both make some calls."

I dip one last fry and shove my plate away as the restaurant lights flicker and then go out. The patrons let out a collective groan.

"Everyone stay calm." A middle-aged man stands silhouetted by the small amount of light showing through the window—which now glows more gold than red. The sand is thinning. "Thanks for your patience. Unfortunately, we're going to have to ask you to stay in your seats if you can. Since it wouldn't be safe to open the doors and let you leave, we're going to ask you to please bear with us while we round up emergency candles and flashlights. Make yourselves comfortable. This storm should pass shortly, and if the power's not restored by the time we see blue skies, your meals will be on us, because, well, frankly, we can't ring you up. Thanks for spending your haboob with us!"

He takes a bow to encourage the cheering, and gains some laughter as he dances out of the room.

TWENTY-TWO

Consolation Friend

ROSE

The next morning I pad downstairs for breakfast and find Abby's mother, Marian, at the table having tea with my mom. A fissure of fear zips up my spine. Why would Marian be here unless something horrible has happened? I try to remember the last time Marian came by for social reasons. I think never. "Hey. What's going on?"

"Just a friendly visit." My mom gestures at the vacant chair next to her, and fills a third teacup. There is no such thing as "just a friendly" anything, where Gifted mothers are concerned. Marian and my mom have communicated in the past, but they're both cautious to offer friendship—for obvious reasons, as it's a learned state of mind—and have never been what I would consider *social* with each other.

"Mm hm." I accept the tea, loading it with sugar and cream. "And this friendly visit has to do with Abby." I glance up, skewering Abby's mother with my gaze. "It's good to see you, Marian. How long have you been back?"

She has the decency to look ashamed, which seems about right. They deserted me. All of them. All the talk about being a team and helping each other through things, but when I needed them most, they were too busy focusing on Abby and Kye. Everyone except Gabe.

I intend to make them suffer for it. I'll help them, because it's the right thing to do, but that doesn't mean I have to jump and run the way Abby always has. No. I deserve better and it's time they acknowledged that.

"A couple of weeks," she says. "I should have been here to check on you days ago. I'm sorry. There's no excuse, but I want you to know I've been thinking of you. Often. Landon and I haven't wanted to cause the Dragons to focus their attention on you. You're dealing with quite enough already. I've been overly cautious about keeping you out of the fight."

"What fight?" Her confession surprises me. Abby's mother has always been the type who keeps information in her pocket, and rarely or never shares it.

"As I'm sure you can imagine, the Dragons weren't happy that Abby and Kye left so quickly after everything happened."

I sit back in my chair, sipping the warm, sweet tea. I've tried not to dwell on my lack of knowledge, but it's been hard, and that's partly why I can't reconcile facts with feelings.

Marian continues, "When they discovered the kids were gone, they pulled the four of us—me, Landon, Christine, and Eoin—in for debriefing, and grilled us for every detail. When none of us gave them any, they wouldn't let us leave the country. We were so glad you and Gabe left when you did, or they would have pulled you into it too. With all the complications, it took weeks to clear things up so we could come home, and now we're dealing with the same mess on this end."

My mother stands to retrieve a plate from the counter. She uncovers a strawberry waffle and sets it in front of me, still seaming with warmth. With a grateful sigh, I douse it in syrup and dig in.

"Thanks for warning us," my mother says to Marian. "Rose has only recently been up to accepting visitors. I can't imagine how much harder it would have been on her with extra pressure from the Dragons. Luckily, Gabe has been a big help. He's sent the guards away daily."

Gabe has? This is interesting. Yes, we've been training together, but I haven't realized he's been here so often when I'm not looking. I wonder if he's been taking shifts, guarding me without my knowledge. It's no wonder none of the Dragons has come to question or to check on me. Gabe and my parents have been shielding me this whole time.

"Glad I could help." Marian and my mom exchange a glance. Somewhere along the line, they've become friends, and I've been too oblivious to notice. "Anyway, Rose, how are you doing?"

Her heartfelt question cracks the emotional shell I've spent the last month building. It takes me a moment to find my voice. "Recovering, I guess."

Marian covers my still hand with one of hers. "You have every right to grieve. It's natural, and healthy. What you went through this summer—what you all went through—was more than anyone should have to bear. Honey, I'm so sorry about Alejandro."

The water main in my eyes splits, and tears stream down my cheeks like a river that's lost its blockage. Mom hands me a paper towel, and I mop my face, sobbing without knowing where all this emotion is coming from, but unable to stop the flood. My mother's arms envelop me, and then Marian's there too. They both hug me, crooning about how I'll survive this and everything is going to be okay and I can take as much time as I need to mend. Their loving support only makes me cry harder because it's about time someone remembered me. Eventually, I calm enough to stop blubbering and pick at what's left of the cold waffle, wondering what the Dragons want from me. What they want from any of us. All of us. I could ask Marian. She'd tell me, but Gabe will have more solid information—Marian only gets what Landon tells her, and I suspect he only tells her as much as he has to. Instead, I ask, "Have you heard from Abby?"

Marian's teacup pauses halfway to her lips, giving me the sneaking suspicion that she knows a lot more than anyone gives her credit for. "Actually," she says, "Christine and Eoin heard from Kye for the first time early this morning."

This can't be good. From what I've been told, Kye and Abby are supposed to have cut off all contact with their past lives—including and especially their families. "How are they?"

Her deep intake of breath is a sure sign that things are not at all good. "Sick. Abby's really sick, Rose."

I'm not surprised. I watched Abby grow sicker and sicker from being too near to Kye through the last few months of high school. It's not shocking that running away with him has made her deathly ill. Still, I should feel worry or sadness. She's been my best friend for the past ten months, and we had a strong bond in Mexico. But I'm numb. I don't understand why. "I'm sorry to hear that," I manage, knowing it's not nearly concerned enough, loving enough, or enough of whatever else I'm supposed to be feeling. It's all I can think to say. "We all know that the curse hasn't been broken."

My response doesn't seem to bother Marian. It's like she's not remotely shocked to discover that I no longer have a heart to break. "I'm not sure the *curse* actually exists. There are details, things I don't have time to get into today, that make me question everything we've been told, everything you've all been taught this last few years."

My brows raise involuntarily. "Oh?"

"But that's not why I'm here. Rose, I'd like to keep you informed, and whenever you decide you're ready—or *if* you're ready—I'll tell you everything I know about all of it. Believe it or not, that's quite a bit."

Now my curiosity is piqued. "If not to tell me more about the curse, why are you here?"

"A recent development. Abby and Kye ran into an old friend of Abby's in Phoenix. They went to stay at her place for a few days, and I guess Tanya tried to help Kye Heal Abby of a particularly dangerous wound she got in Mexico."

"She's Gifted?" I ask, not sure what any of this has to do with me.

Marian nods, replacing her now-empty teacup on the saucer in front of her and nudging it toward the center of the table. "Apparently. I'm not sure about the details, but something went wrong, and Abby's highly-dangerous, deeply infected energy was transferred into this woman's nine-month-old son. The kids were unable to reverse the Healing process and remove the energy from the baby, so they're sending Tanya and her son here."

My spine straightens vertebrae by vertebrae. This is bad news. They wouldn't tell our secrets, wouldn't send a stranger here, wouldn't expose themselves unless whatever has happened is catastrophic. "Why? Why would they do that?"

Marian takes a shaky breath. "Kye told Eoin that Abby has lost her Gifts—both of them—completely. If Christine can't help the baby, he may not make it. Kye and Abby can't come back, but Abby is concerned about Tanya having people to support her through this."

Of course she is. And who else but me? The friend who picks up everyone's pieces and forces them to fit in, whether they want to or not. I shake my head before Marian can ask. "No. I'm not up to it. Not right now. I'm sorry."

My mother's eyes go wide with surprise. "Honey, this would be good for you. Get you out of the house, give you someone to talk to about your own trauma—"

"No, Mom. I can't do it right now, okay? As much as I like to help people, I'm not up to this. Not today. Probably not tomorrow, or next week. I can't handle any more than what I'm already dealing with. Maybe they should assign her a Dragon."

There's more though. I can see it in Marian's face. "About that. Listen ... we would like to keep Tanya's presence, and her Gift, a secret from the Dragons until we can make heads or tails of what they've done to Abby and Kye. You and your mother are now two of the six people in town who know Tanya's coming, and why. We need somewhere for her to stay, a place from which the Dragons know to keep their distance. If you can't give her friendship right away, that's okay. I'm sure she's had enough trauma that she'll keep to herself mostly anyway. We need you and Gabe to help us keep her concealed and protected, and to keep her identity confidential."

I don't know how to respond to this, or how to react. I'm stunned, and yet not at all surprised. "You want her to stay here?"

"Oh, no." I'm relieved when Marian grins, and her knuckles loosen their clenching as she wrings her hands together. "She'll stay at my house. In Abby's room. I was hoping that, when you're up to it, you might be willing to come over and meet her. Help her not feel quite so alone, the way you did with Abby."

And look where that's gotten me. "I don't know. Is that necessary?"

She shakes her head, exchanging a glance with my mother. "No. It's not. So no pressure at all. It would just be nice."

I don't need more friends. I don't need something to do, and I don't need the parents taking pity on me for being deserted in my hour of need and offering me a consolation friend. That's what they're trying to do, but it's not what's best for me. Training with Gabe is what's best for me, because I *do* have *my* Gifts, and I'm finally learning how to use them to make a difference. Not that anyone else knows we're training, but still. I don't have time to be the welcome wagon as the vagrant Gifted teens roll into town all broken and needy.

"What are Abby and Kye going to do now?" I wonder aloud. "If Abby has lost her Gifts, doesn't that change everything? Wouldn't the curse be broken?" If she can't fight demons, she can't lead us, and Kye can't lead without her—but I'm Gifted too, and I have the royal blood through the line of Theron—same as Kye—and I can fight demons. Maybe it's time I stepped up.

Marian leans back in her chair, a wrinkle folding between her eyes. "I don't know. I don't know if *they* know yet. I sent her with some information she's looking into, so they might be following leads for that, but health-wise, I'm worried about Abby. I haven't talked to her, but losing her Gifts has to be like losing an arm. I wish they'd come home and let us help them."

160

I wish that too. I wish they'd come back and see the results of what they've left behind. Gabe and I are so miserable, so heartbroken, that we've turned to each other and become friends. Jen has jumped ship altogether, and turned to a life of substance abuse in order to avoid training to use her Gift. The Dragons are divided, as is made obvious by the fact that Landon and Marian are doing things in secret, along with, I assume, Christine and Eoin. From Gabe's and my encounter the other day, it appears that the demons are returning to Jackson. Now an innocent baby may lose his life. This place, these people, we are all a mess, and it started when the two of them left together for the first time. I wish they'd come back and clean up their chaos—fix everything and let us go back to living our lives. At some point, someone will have to.

But I can't say all of that to Abby's mom. That would be like a minister trying to convince his own choir to believe. "Well, since they won't, what do we need to do on this end?"

"Help us take care of Tanya and Cole," she says. "And keep training so you'll be prepared for when Abby and Kye do come back. Because Landon and I suspect that something big is coming, and I can't imagine what will happen if Abby can't summon her Light."

I can. I've seen the other half of a battle without her present. I never dreamed I would have to go through something like that again, but I'm becoming all too aware that the demons that killed Alex will be back. This time, they'll have to face me head-on.

TWENTY-THREE

Desert Bloom

ABBY

A middle-aged man at the next table over grins, eyeing my rings, and catches Kye's attention. "When's the big day?"

"We haven't decided." Flustered, Kye's focus flits around, landing everywhere but on me. "Our engagement is recent."

"Well congratulations, then," He says. "You talked to her father before popping the question, right?"

Kye coughs as if something's caught in his throat. "Her father isn't with us anymore."

The man frowns in sympathy. "Mother?"

Kye sends me a look of desperate discomfort. "I might have brought it up with her mother. She wanted us to wait a year or two, which will probably happen, but her mother loves me, and she knows we're destined to be together, so she's more okay with it than she otherwise might have been." He's watching me, gauging my reaction.

"You talked to my mother? When?"

"Before I left for Mexico. I mean, literally hours before we boarded the plane. "

"What was her response?"

Kye shakes his head. "Do you really want to talk about this now?"

I nod emphatically. "Yes, I do. I want to know what made you think that I'd say yes after you hadn't talked to me in months. How did my mother react?" My mom knew I hadn't heard from Kye, so I'm curious how anxious she was to see me handed off to him.

"Not well." He reaches across the table and takes my hand. "She was furious until I explained the situation. Even then, she was insistent that we're too young. Emphatically insistent."

A sigh of relief shudders in my chest.

"You're not eloping?" The man asks, now bordering on obnoxious in his inquiries. "Running off despite her mother's objections?"

This time my laugh is genuine and rich. "It wouldn't be the first time we've run off together, but no. We've come to visit a friend." My eyes are drawn to the window, where the sky peeks through the sand. In the swirls of red and brown, I see it again. Boone's face. I'd know that puckered scar anywhere. The rest of the conversation is lost on me as the face presses against the glass as if searching for something it can't find. My aura has diminished to that of a regular person, devoid of power, but he might be able to see Kye's. I'm about to bring it up so Kye will be on alert, when the sand wisps away, and then the sky is blue again. The restaurant remains without power, so minutes later, we're ushered out and given a ticket with a zero balance.

Kye leaves a nice tip on the table and we wish our new friend well. "Good luck on starting your family," he says. "In today's world, you're surely going to need it."

"You didn't have to lie to him," Kye says as we head for the car. "If we *were* to get married, it wouldn't happen for a long time."

Kye's mood has soured quickly. His forehead crinkles in the way it always does when he's angry, and his hair spikes as if in anticipation of his habit of running his fingers through it. I rest a comforting hand on his forearm. "It wasn't a lie."

"Don't." He shakes off my touch. "Don't do that. Don't fan my hope or make promises while you don't know what you want, and don't go telling strangers stories about how we're engaged and starting a family when we both know that might never happen. Let's be real, here."

His words hit me like a punch to the gut. "We don't know anything right now, Kye, we—"

"We know that nothing is certain. That's what we know. We know we can't go home. We know you have questions about me, and I have them about you, and we both have them about our families and our Gifts and life. You know what else we know? We're stuck travelling together, whether we want it or not." He stomps away, leaving me at the table, eyes bulging with suppressed emotion while each memory of his words shoves the blade of hurt deeper.

Kye feels like he's stuck with me.

He has questions about me.

Maybe he did tell Kiersten he's in over his head. He seems to be feeling that way today.

A few minutes later, Kye returns to find me still sitting there, staring at his empty chair. "I can't get a signal, thanks to this storm, and I'm not comfortable staying here. Let's get going. We can try calling next time we stop.

Somehow, my feet bring me to the car. It's buried in sand, the hood and top and door handles coated with a thick layer of chalky red dust. Kye opens his door—but not mine, which is unusual for him, and says more about his current state of mind than his words—and starts the car. I open my door to join him, and stop short when I find a cone-shaped saguaro flower on my seat. The tip of the cactus spine and some of the needles are still attached to the bottom. Kye hasn't seen it yet, and part of me wishes I could close the door and walk away, but clearly now is not the time for me to be alone, or to walk away from Kye. Not that I could. I can barely move my fingers to pick up the flower, or my lips to utter, "Kye," so that he'll look.

When he sees what I'm holding, he says, "Where did that come from?"

I nod at the seat, bruising the silky flower petals between my fingers while trying not to stab myself with the needles.

"In the car?"

I can only nod.

He swears, getting out again to come take the flower from me and toss it into the rock landscaping. "We need to go." He nudges me inside and closes my door, then returns to the driver's seat. "How many times do you think you saw Boone in that sand storm?"

I shake my head. "Two or three. Maybe four."

He swallows audibly and puts the car in gear. "I'm glad he couldn't pinpoint you."

Oh sure. The demon leader knows where we are, just not exactly, because Abby doesn't have powers anymore, so of course he can't find me, and if he did, I have no Gifts left to steal. Hooray. Let's have a party.

Not.

It's hours before we stop again. Hard to tell, because the minute we got out of the city, my eyes closed and I dropped off to sleep, having not exchanged more than the most necessary words with Kye. He's chosen a truck stop, for which I'm enormously grateful, because this one has showers, and I'm desperate to clean up. I've gained twenty pounds of sand in my hair and on my skin, not to mention my filthy clothing. I have him open the trunk, informing him of my plan to utilize a shower. He raises a brow, but doesn't object.

"Don't take too long. We need to get more distance today."

Stung by the coolness in his tone, I scoop up my toiletries and a change of clothes and head for the bathroom, fighting the urge to let out the tears that have been building all day. I close myself in a stall, watching the warm mist turn my sandy skin orange, lines of water forming a dirty river that bleeds into the drain. Finally alone for the first time in what feels like weeks, I'm free to let my tears flow.

For all that Kye demanded otherwise, I don't hurry. I need time to get my emotions under control, and I take it. I scrub every last bit of sand from my hair, which takes several washings. The aroma of the specialized herbal blends brings me peace, and by the time I emerge, I'm calm enough to make my calls without falling apart.

I dry off and cover my skin with herbal Healing lotion, trying to avoid staring too long at the gray line where my wound used to be. Once I'm dressed in clean clothes, my damp hair smoothed and my teeth brushed, I step out of the bathroom and accept the phone from an extremely irritated Kye. Clutching his own toiletry bag, he hands me the keys. "I'll go get cleaned up so we can put some miles behind us. Don't go far."

I find a spot of grass outside in the sunshine and sit there to make my call. Mom picks up on the second ring. "Abby? Is it you?"

My chest fills with warmth. "How did you know?"

"Tanya and Cole arrived. She's been filling me in. When an unidentified number popped up on my screen, I imagined it has to be you." I've missed my mother so much, and it's good to hear that she's been missing me too.

"So how are you?" She doesn't wait for me to tell her why I'm calling—she probably knows. "Where are you? Tanya tells me you've been extremely sick. Are you getting enough sleep? Enough to eat? Are you taking your herbs?"

"Mom, I'm fine," I tell her. "It's all been transferred to Cole."

"More reason for you to take extra good care of yourself," she insists. "So that when you get back, you can reverse this thing and Heal him the way only you can."

How can I argue? If I tell her that's not possible and that I've already tried, she'll only worry about me more. If I tell her I'm not coming back, she'll freak out. If I tell her that Cole is going to die as a result of my stupidity—well. That means admitting out loud my worst fear. I have to change the subject.

"Mom," I say, picking a handful of grass and watching the blades fall through my fingers. "Tell me about Dad. Is he still alive? What is this address supposed to mean?"

Her sharp intake of breath tells me I'm not going to like her explanation. "Abby, your father ... He's neither dead nor alive. The last night, when he left our house, things happened. I don't know all the details, but he was badly injured. He should have died, but was instead offered a blossom that took him across the crystal bridge into Tir Na Nog. He accepted. Had no choice, aside from death. He can't come back to us. Ever. In any life."

I don't know what I was expecting to hear, but this was not a *possibility* in my mind. "What do you mean he can't come back to us? How does he have an address in Ireland?"

She lets out a slow breath. "It's not his address anymore. It's mine."

Shock and disbelief go to war in my head. "What do you mean, it's yours? Why do you have an address in Ireland with Dad's name on it? And why would you not tell me about this? I've known about my Gift, about my heritage for a year. Why would you keep this from me?"

"Abby," she says softly. "When your father died, he was on a quest to bring your people together. Not so they're all in one location, but to open a line of communication that would allow you to network, to find each other, to share knowledge and help protect one another."

A half-formed chuckle works its way up my throat. "Clearly, this happened before social media was a thing."

There's a smile in her voice when she replies. "Yes. That convenience would have kept us in one place for longer than we ever stayed. But even with social media, Gifts like yours aren't easy for people to be open about. Not when hundreds of years of secret-keeping have been ingrained in each of you for more lifetimes than you'll ever remember living."

"Doesn't explain the mailbox," I remind her. "In Ireland. Or how you know what happened to Dad?"

"Your father applied for the mailbox before we were married," she says, her voice wistful. "I never understood why, but he told me I should trust him, because someday we would need it."

"The night your father should have died, he was given an opportunity to say goodbye to us. Do you remember that?"

Frantically, I search my brain for a suppressed memory. Something—anything—but it's not there. "No. He never said goodbye to me."

"He did, but you were pretending to sleep."

"That was before he left," I tell her. "I'm sure of it. He argued with Gram. They had a big fight."

"No, sweetie," she says. "It was after he'd come back. Gram argued because she wanted him to give back the flower and stay with us, even if it meant waiting another lifetime to try again—but it was already too late. Your father had accepted his fate on the condition that he could return to his family to say goodbye. That's when he told me about the mailbox."

"What's in it?"

"Letters, I assume," she says, and I can hear rustling on her end of the phone. "He didn't have time to explain. He said that when you came of age, I was to make sure you were able to go to Ireland and pick up the contents."

"And you decided that time was when I was leaving Mexico?"

Her breathing is labored, and I can hear a noise in the background. Baby noise. She must be holding Cole. I smile. My mother adores babies. She continues, "Sort of. That's when I decided I couldn't keep it from you any longer, and that if you were going to be on the run anyway, you should have that location as a potential goal. Or an option, anyway."

"I wish you had told me about it rather than shoving the address in my hand."

"I couldn't," she says. "I didn't want to risk having anyone else hear, and there was no time to write a note. It was a split-second decision. I don't know the purpose of that box, and I didn't know who we could trust. All I knew for certain was that if I gave you the address, you would check into it, and what better time than while no one else is watching?"

"I can't go to Ireland right now, Mom. Even if we could afford it. I can't leave the country while Cole's fighting for his life." Or while I'm fighting for mine.

"Of course not," she tells me. "You shouldn't. Not now. I just wanted you to have it in mind for the future. So what *are* you planning to do?"

"We've been following the path of places we lived when Dad was still with us. Looking for those people who saw him last, who knew him." I wonder if we should change our plans now that I know what the address means, but then I reconsider. "Even knowing Dad isn't somewhere in the world, waiting for me to find him, I still need to go to Utah. I want to know what happened the night he left. I want to know what took him away from us, and who."

"I would like to know that too. But baby, be careful, okay? Your father was experienced and strong. He'd been tracking these people his whole life. You've only been doing it for a year."

"I will, I promise." Kye comes outside, using hand signals to ask if I want a drink. I nod, knowing that my phone time is about up. "Mom, have you seen Rose or Gabe?"

"I've seen them both," she says softly. "Rose is struggling. Starting to come out of her depression, but she's in deep, so it's going to be a while. Gabe too. He wanders over a lot. The Dragons have destroyed him about you leaving. He hasn't had an assignment since."

A flood of guilt crashes down on me. This is not helping. "Tell them I miss them, okay? And that I won't stay gone forever."

"I will, sweetie. I love you."

"Love you too, Mom."

I hang up, averting my eyes to avoid Kye's scrutiny as he joins me at the car. I hate to be a burden on anyone, especially Kye. But I still need to go to Utah. And like it or not, I need him to come too.

TWENTY-FOUR

Clued

ROSE

The next time I train with Gabe, and in all our future sessions, I work twice as hard as I previously have. Physical, mental, vocal. We train under the guise of hanging out, and that prevents people—parents on my end, Dragons on his—from asking too many questions. I suspect my parents are afraid to tip the boat and dump me back into the ocean of depression I lived in after I first came home. It *wouldn't* take much to tip me over, but training with Gabe helps. It redirects my focus, builds my ability and confidence, and releases the endorphins that are critical for overcoming sadness.

Not only am I physically stronger, but my mind stays occupied so I'm not wallowing. I'm happier when I'm sweating and sore, and more emotionally balanced—as in, I'm not holed up in bed pigging out on potato chips and ice cream—because Gabe and I talk. A lot. About everything and anything, except our two taboo subjects. Abby and Alex.

And Vocally—well. The power that zings through me when I tap into my Gift is an intense and unique high I couldn't gain from anywhere else—even if I was a drug user, which I'm not. Using my Gift of Voice is the best therapy of all. Not just because of the high, but because I have this new knowledge of power I can use to help, to fight back. Now I know how to avenge the boy I loved, and this becomes my mission—my ultimate goal.

Working out with me seems to be good for Gabe too. His moods are lighter, his frown lines not as deep as they were a month ago. And I have to admit, the way his muscles ripple when he takes off his shirt, the way his skin gleams with the sheen of hard-earned sweat—calls to my sense of lust in a way I never expected. Rather than seeing Gabe as an enemy, or adversary, attraction is heightened and open and I've become aware of his every move. I can't imagine that there's a female on this planet who wouldn't agree that Gabe's muscles are scorching.

I shouldn't make the comparison, but although Alex was well toned, he could never have been as ripped as Gabe. He just wasn't built that way.

At first, I deny to myself that I'm paying attention, but after Gabe catches me staring for like the eleventh time, I give up the battle with the inevitable, and stare openly. Because muscles. And sexy. Gabe must know the effect he has on women.

We're in my yard doing lunges from the fence to the house, when my mom opens the back door and yells out to us. "Hey, kids, I'm on my way to Marian's to help with the baby. He's been up all night screaming. Poor Tanya needs some rest, and Marian has to work. Do you want to come with me?"

Normally, I wouldn't consider it, but a glance at Gabe tells me he's got a war of emotions happening inside him. Maybe he needs to go to Abby's and see that she's not there, feel her absence. Maybe he has demons to face too.

"Do you want to?" I ask, and the spark of hope that lights his eyes stings, partly because I remember feeling hope like that when Alex looked at me, and partly because I wish Gabe could get over his obsession with Abby—for his own good. She's always on his mind, even when we're together, and I'm surprised by the hurt that gathers in my chest when I think about it. Without waiting for an answer, I tell my mother, "Yeah, we'll come. It's time we met Tanya."

Mom's quick to cover her surprise. "Do you need time to get cleaned up? I hate to keep them waiting too long. She must be exhausted."

The tension radiating off of Gabe is a good indicator that he doesn't want to wait, and I'm ready to give into that—again, for his sake. "If you can give us fifteen minutes, we'll ride with you."

My mother's grin flames to life. "Absolutely. I can wait that long." She bumps the laundry basket she's holding against her hip. "I'll put this away while I wait."

Gabe follows me inside so we can clean up. This week—it's all about personal progress.

We arrive at Marian's house and enter to the sound of a screaming baby and the sight of a harried young mother with deep, dark circles under her eyes, and a severe case of bed-head. It's 2:00 pm, and she's wearing flannel pajama bottoms and a tank top, sitting in Marian's recliner and rocking her baby furiously as if that will calm him. I wonder if she's had a chance to brush her teeth.

Marian ushers us in wearing one boot, and clasping on earrings. "Thanks for doing this." She nods at Tanya. "This momma needs a nap in the worst way, and so does her son. His fever is out of control, so no one in this house has slept. Christine's been here all night as well, but nothing she's tried helps. We're at a loss."

My mother asks, "Has Christine gone home?"

"No, she's asleep in my room. She won't give up until we find Cole some relief, but we're working in shifts at this point." Marian pulls on her second boot and grabs her keys, dancing as she zips the sides of both boots. "I feel horrible deserting you all right now. This is a high-paying client who's a regular at the hotel. I don't feel like I can cancel after taking off so much time last month."

"Of course you can't. And there's no need. There are plenty of us here to help." She dismisses Marian with a pat on the shoulder

172

and marches to Tanya, scooping the screaming little guy into her arms. As he calms momentarily, Mom gestures for Gabe and me to take care of Tanya. Gabe, who is clearly used to following orders, gathers Tanya up, the way my mother did with the baby, and she's so exhausted her only protest is a weak, "Cole."

"Don't worry, sweetheart." Mom takes Tanya's place in the rocker. "We've got your sweet little guy. You rest."

I follow Gabe up to Abby's room where he lays Tanya on the bed and pulls the comforter up to her shoulders. "We'll protect the baby," he says. "You're both safe here."

Tanya nods her silent acceptance. "I'm Tanya. It's nice to meet you. We should talk soon."

"Yes. Later. Sweet dreams." Gabe closes the blinds to block out the sun, and then we tiptoe out.

"Well this is a mess." Pain burns behind Gabe's eyes. I wonder how many times he carried Abby up these stairs and tucked her into that bed. His memories of her must be plastered all over everything in this house.

"Life's messy," I remind him, feeling an urge to defend Abby. "I mean, none of us has any choice but to move forward with all the scary, messy things—we're fighting battles that we didn't start, that should have been fought and ended centuries ago. This isn't our war, but we're all stuck picking up the pieces of it. Some days I'm not even sure we're fighting on the right side. *Look* at what's happening to Abby and Kye. The people they trusted most betrayed them, and they're the ones who've been risking everything to protect the rest of us."

Gabe stops in the hall and turns to face me. "Rose, there's never been a time when people didn't fight. That's what war is. People disagreeing, fighting for different beliefs and rights and thoughts. People scrambling for survival against those who would do them harm, or injustice, or wrong. We're fighting this battle for the ability to live in peace. The Elen want to take our powers, and the demons want to feed on our fear and misery. For every moment you or I—or any of us—hide under the covers and let depression win, we're letting them win too. Every battle we fight without knowing exactly who and what we're fighting for, we risk fighting on the wrong side. That's why Abby and Kye left. They have to find the truth so we all have the opportunity to decide who to fight for, what side to fight on, and why we should continue to fight at all."

There's a light in his eyes, a spark that hasn't been there since before Abby left. It's like he's realizing why she left the way she did. Because she had to. They had to. "Gabe. Do you think they left by choice? Or were they forced to go?"

He shakes his head, glancing down the stairs toward the sound of my mother's humming. "I'm not sure, but I have this fear that it's a little bit of both. I wonder if they chose to leave to protect the rest of us. They were sick. Cursed. Abby was doing better for a while, but maybe that wasn't a good sign. There have to be things they knew that the rest of us didn't—and Rose, that baby down there wouldn't be sick like this if Abby had been able to Heal him. Tanya wouldn't have known to come here to Christine if someone hadn't sent her, and who else but Abby knew that Christine would be here?

"We need to know what happened to cause this. We need to know why they went to Tanya in the first place and where that was. Maybe then we can figure out their next destination. What if they need our help, Rose? What if they're in trouble and they went to Tanya for help, only to make things worse? What if the demons followed them? What happens if the Elen find them while Abby is at her weakest?"

The muscles in my chest squeeze tight. What if he's right and my cousin and my best friend left me behind to protect me? To save us? What if all this time I've been feeling sorry for myself, filled with anger, blaming them, when it was they who were being unselfish? When they left to keep the demons from coming after me?

These thoughts are immediately followed by resentment over their lack of faith, because they didn't know what I can do, never trusted me to take care of myself. No one believes that I can defeat the demons too. That I can save us too. No one has paid close enough attention to grasp that my power is necessary, that *I* am necessary.

I've seen my potential, thanks to Gabe. He's the person who believes in me, who has enough faith in me to drag me out of bed and force me back to life, even on the days when I fought back like a kicking, screaming toddler. I stretch onto my tiptoes and kiss Gabe's cheek.

His look of astonishment brings out a giggle. "What was that for?"

"Thanks," I tell him softly. "For getting it."

He responds with an embarrassed shrug.

"We have to go after them, don't we?"

He nods, leaning against the wall. "I think so. I'm not sure if they can do this on their own. Not if Abby's sick. If she's sick, so is Kye. They're marching into a losing battle—and they probably know it. Always the martyrs."

"Why didn't they tell us?" I ask, my voice cracking. "Why would they go without explaining?"

"Because the Dragons have spent so much time putting all the responsibility on them, that they believe it. They don't know *we* can and should be helping them. So we're going to have to show them."

I swallow a lump that's forming in my throat. "We have to find them first."

His smile grows slowly. "The good news is that we have a huge clue, right here in this house. We don't have tons of time, so this one's on you. As soon as Tanya wakes up. We should be ready to go after them tonight."

TWENTY-FIVE

Destination: Utah

ABBY

Kye opens the trunk so we can put our belongings away, but doesn't immediately unlock the doors. "I know it's a long drive and we've had no sleep, but if we take a minute to decide where we're going, maybe we can power through and get there."

As exhausted as I am, the Utah town is a place where I hope we can settle for a few days. "I'd love that."

He closes the trunk, indicating the building with a nod. "There's an internet café on the other side of the convenience area. They have one of those pay-by-the minute computers. I was thinking we could find a rental and make a reservation."

I follow him back inside. "Did you want to call your parents? Or do you think me calling my mom was enough danger for this stop?"

Kye runs a hand through his hair. "I called while you showered. I had to tell my dad about Tanya's journals so he can pick them up. We have to preserve the Gifted records, and authenticate them. Plus, Dad can research while we travel, and he may be able to find useful information you and I have missed."

I trust Kye. And Eoin, and Christine and Landon and Rose and Gabe. I remind myself this continually. I trust them, and I love them, and I don't believe they would betray me. They're my tribe. My people. The reason I'm fighting to live through this, and to save all of them. To make this better, to give them room to breathe and right the thing that was done to our people so many years ago.

In the internet café, I hijack the chair in front of the computer. Kye raises a brow, but doesn't openly object. I'm not trying to be difficult, but I have a specific idea in mind for accommodations. I pull up a search engine and run a search for houses in Midway, Utah. There are pages and pages of listings to choose from. I scroll the pictures without stopping to click on any, hoping, wondering, wishing and then, halfway down the seventh page I see it. A house that looks like the little cottage where we lived. I click the link, and scroll through pictures of the interior of the house, feeling more and more certain that this is the one. Kye leans closer at my sudden intake of breath.

"I found it. My house. Our house. It's still a rental." I click on the availability dates and details. "It's vacant. I can't believe it. Who buys a house and keeps it as a rental for thirteen years?"

"Smart people," he says, leaning closer to the screen with a hand on the desk. "People with money. It's a tax shelter, a great investment. One of the things the Val dabbled in with Raina's money."

"Or no one is willing to buy it for some reason." I bring up the reservations page, scanning the listed details. Even if we don't stay there, we have to find a way to go inside, check into the nooks and crannies and hiding places that live in my memory. I used to explore every cupboard and crawlspace with the little pink flashlight my father had given me, which, sadly, got lost in one of our moves. There's something about this house, something special. I wish I could See what it is. I wish I could remember what I knew when I was six and lived there with my family intact.

I type in my name to reserve it. "Wait," Kye says. "What if the Dragons own this house? That would make sense, if your family lived there. We can't take that chance. They'll find us for sure."

"We have to go inside. We have to check it thoroughly. The only way to be able to do that is to either rent it or break in. I'd like to avoid getting arrested for burglary."

He tosses his fake driver's license on the table, along with a credit card I've never seen. "Use this."

It pains me to have to point out the obvious. "Kye, if the Dragons helped you get that ID, then they'll know that's you. If Val backs that card, he'll know it's been run."

He turns away. "Val doesn't know about this name. Or that card."

There's something suspicious about his reaction. I pick up the credit card and turn it over in my hand. "It's not stolen, is it?"

He lets out a snort of disgust. "Of course not. You know me better than that."

"Well, I had to ask. How do you have an identity that Val doesn't know about? How do you have a credit card in someone else's name without his help?"

"Kiersten helped me get them." He runs both hands over his face. "I didn't want to tell you, because you were you were already having a hard time with my relationship with her. Didn't need to rub in how much help I asked of her while we were there."

The fact that she helped him doesn't bother me at this point. We need help in a lot of ways, from a lot of people. We're hovering over the pool of desperation, and I'd like to avoid falling into it. What bothers me is that he clearly spent more time with Kiersten than I noticed, enough that they could procure a fake identity and credit account for that identity while I was—probably sleeping. Then he lied about it. Rather than telling me what he was doing, and why—a detail I still don't know for sure—he kept it to himself. After he has promised over and over, profusely, to always tell me the truth. That he would never lie to me again.

His time spent with Kiersten is a lie, even if it is one of omission.

The fiery tears I expect don't come. There is no sadness left in me. Only anger. Pure and unadulterated fury. "Well," I manage in a voice I hope comes across as calm. "Did you think to get one for me, or did Kiersten convince you that you're the only one who needs to hide?"

He jerks back at the implication. But I'm through tiptoeing. I'm through wondering and forcing things and fighting this battle. I love Kye with everything in me, but not enough to let him treat me like this.

"Of course I got you one," he finally says, his voice timid and small. "That was the reason I asked Kiersten to help me in the first place. We needed to look married, and we needed a card that doesn't leave a trail for the world to follow. Our Dragons are phenomenal investigators. By now, I'm certain they know that Tanya's in Jackson, and have most likely sent a team after us. We'll be lucky if we make it to Utah without running into them."

Once again, I glance at the page on the computer screen. "Would we be stupid to rent *this* house? Will they trace us? There are pages of rental houses there. Maybe we should find another one."

He stares at the monitor, scrolling back through the pictures. "I wish you still had Sight."

His words stab swift and true, opening the center of my heart so it gushes. I jump up, gasping for breath, wondering when I stopped being able to breathe. I'm shoving past other patrons to get to the door, and then outside as I beg for tears that won't come. This pain is every bit as deep and true as what I felt the day I believed Kye had left me forever.

That time, I sat on the edge of the bathtub wishing I could throw up and dull this ache, but now I brace a hand on the building trying to breathe. I remember Rose handing me a shot glass, remember pulling back two, and then complying while she dressed me, did my hair, put makeup on me and strapped on shoes, shoving me out the door and into Gabe's arms, where I felt so warm and safe and loved.

I wish I could be there right now.

Kye joins me at the side of the building, keeping a distance of about ten feet—for safety. He swears, in true Kye fashion. "Babe, I'm sorry. Please don't cry. I didn't mean it like that. It's not your fault."

I wonder if this truck stop sells alcohol. If they carry mini-skirts and platform heels. I wonder if there's a cantina nearby where I can drown my sorrows in liquor and music. But none of those things would solve my problems now, any more than they did then. So I pull myself together, and march past Kye and back inside, to the chair I recently vacated. Kye follows, mumbling about how he's sorry, he didn't mean it like that. I block out his voice and focus on making the reservation and getting back on the road. I'm exhausted, and want to sleep the minute we start the car.

Calmly, I print the information for the house where I used to live, and then, without a word, I go back to the page and find another house, a cozy little cottage tucked into the side of the mountain, slightly past the outskirts of town. I fill out the reservation information using the new ID and credit card, and then I print that information too. I map both houses and print the instructions, then I turn and shove the freshly printed papers into Kye's chest. He looks over the map, lips pressed together in concentration, while I use the same card to pay our bill. "We should go."

He nods, eyes still on the printouts as he follows me outside.

And then, once again, as has been the routine since the day we met, Kye and I are on the road. Destination: Utah.

TWENTY-SIX

Screaming and Calming

ROSE

Cole's still screaming when Gabe and I return to the living room. My mother has swaddled him in a blanket and abandoned the rocker in favor of a weird bouncing dance. "Poor little guy," she says, her expression tight. "He'd feel better if he could sleep like his momma."

"Maybe he can't," Gabe says. "Maybe he's so miserable that he needs to tell us all about it, and now that he's going, he can't calm down again."

Gabe's words spark an idea. "Can I try?" I open my arms, inviting her to hand him over. With a deep breath and a tight smile, she presses him into my embrace.

I coddle him close, crooning about how it's okay, and that only makes him scream harder. My mother offers him a beautiful silver rattle. He clutches it in his fist, lowering his volume, but doesn't stop crying.

Since I don't know my mother's bouncing dance, I decide to try my luck in the rocker and settle into the still-warm seat. "Shh," I croon, trying for different tones and wondering exactly what decibel level to use on someone so small. "It's okay little one. Rest. Sleep."

The more he screams, the louder he becomes, until his little voice is hoarse. The sound is heartbreaking for a Vocalist—or, you know. Anyone with a heart. I try again, reaching down through my throat and into the softest part of my chest to find the right spot. "Sleep little guy." I murmur into his hair, letting power vibrate from my lips into his ears. "Rest so you can heal." When his eyelids droop, and his cries become less urgent, hope surges up. It's working. "Rest only. Live until the Healer returns, and suffer no more."

His cries calm to fussing, and then sleep so that his distress can only be heard in his shaky, shuttering breaths.

"What are you doing?" my mother asks. "How is this working?"

"She's using her Voice," Gabe says, careful to keep his quiet. "She's been practicing."

"Be careful," my mother warns. "Choose your words wisely. The things you say using that power can backfire."

"Trust her," Gabe says, scowling at my mother. "She's good at this."

His faith buoys me. I continue. "Sleep only as long as you need and no more. Rest so your body can recover and heal, and then wake happy."

Cole's eyes flutter closed, and his breathing evens out as I rock him. His body relaxes as he settles into sleep, and then he sighs, finally comfortable. My mother shakes her head as she moves toward the kitchen. "I wish I'd had someone like you when you were his age. *That* was nothing short of a miracle."

It's the most rewarding praise I've ever had. Gabe squeezes my shoulder. "Good job, Rose. I wouldn't have thought of that." He follows my mother into the kitchen, where I can hear talk of making tea and the sound of a kettle being filled.

Cole's fist tightens on his rattle, and I stare at his perfect, chubby hands, tracing my fingertips along his arm. He has a smushed little nose, and a wrinkled forehead, and downy, uneven fluffs of hair along his scalp. He's sporting a double chin and his wrists roll like they have elastic bands around them. He is, perhaps, the most perfect thing I've ever seen on this planet, and holding him makes me feel infinitely more powerful than any other thing

I've ever done. He's not my child. I don't even know this boy's mother. But I'll do whatever it takes to make him better. To save him.

That's what Abby was trying to do by sending them here. She's trying to save him too.

Gabe returns from the kitchen, twirling my mom's keys on his finger. "I need to run an errand. Should be an hour, two tops." He glances at the baby asleep in my arms. "Don't suppose you want to come with me?"

I hold Cole tighter, unwilling to slow my rocking. "I'd love to, but this poor guy's had such a rough time. I'm afraid to move and risk waking him. If you don't mind, I'll stay right here until you get back."

He reaches out to touch Cole's head, but stops short of making contact.

My gentle smile blooms. "Don't tell me you're afraid to touch an innocent infant."

His hand jerks away. "I don't want to wake him."

My brows rise as my amusement spreads. "You won't. I've been running my fingers all over his face, and he barely sighs. Go ahead."

"I don't want to break him," he says.

"I didn't say squeeze him," I clarify. "Just touch him. One finger. You're not going to hurt him, promise."

"I don't want to ..." he shakes his head as if he can't think of the words.

"You don't want to what?" I prompt. "Fall in love with him?"

He scowls and creeps closer. "Well look what happened to the last person I fell in love with."

"Pretty sure this one won't run away with another man." I take Gabe's hand and direct his fingers to stroke Cole's smooth, soft forehead. "Just touch him. He won't bite. He doesn't even have teeth yet."

Gabe strokes Cole's hair, tracing the line of his ear with a hand so large that Cole's head could fit in his palm. After a few quiet minutes of baby coddling, Gabe rises from where he's knelt on the floor, brushing himself off as if he's somehow become dusty. "Okay," he says. "I need to get going. When Tanya wakes up, make sure you find out everything she knows. Every. Little. Detail. Where Abby and Kye have been, where they might be going, and why they were visiting her in the first place. I want to know how bad of shape Abby is in, and why Kye hasn't brought her back here to be treated if her life's on the line. If Tanya knows what they were planning next, find that out. Every single thing."

"Yeah," I tell him. "On it."

"Thanks." He nods as if to say good job, and I let out a sigh as the front door snaps closed behind him. It's nice to be getting along, but there are times when I miss the feisty, angry Gabe who was constantly picking a battle. I hope he comes back to fight with me again someday.

TWENTY-SEVEN

Neon Memories

ABBY

Soon after we leave the truck stop, my heavy eyes win the battle and I fall asleep. By the time I wake, dusk has painted the sky bright pink with streaks of orange and blue and the most beautiful white clouds that drift lazily across the horizon.

Kye hasn't seen me stir. He drives in silence, chewing on his bottom lip as he taps his thumbs to the rhythm of a song on the radio.

He didn't mean to hurt me by insinuating that our predicament is somehow my fault, that my loss of Sight was a choice, but I can't help feeling like an absolute failure. I've failed him and everyone else by losing my Gifts.

It's ironic that when I was younger I wished my Gifts away. Back then I was stupid. All I wanted out of life was to be a normal teenager who didn't have anything to hide. It never occurred to me that normal is a myth and that my Gifts made me special, extraordinary. Luckily, we moved to Jackson and I learned. I became an intricate part of a community that needed me, along with my Gifts.

I learned how it felt to matter, and I liked it. I've spent the last year battling demons and shadows—fighting for my life, as well as the lives of the people I love—and in the process, I've become part of a community. Part of a family.

But now ... I'm Gifted no more.

I've never been lonelier. Kye's innocent exclamation has only cemented my new status as outsider.

I should be used to it. This is how I grew up. But back then my aloneness was about me being special in a way no one else could identify. Now it's about me being ordinary in the way I used to wish I could be, but never experienced. I never imagined how badly the loss would ache, or how hollow I'd feel when it came.

Being ordinary sucks rocks.

The car slows, and I blink, realizing that we're still in the middle of nowhere, Arizona. I sit up, worried about more demons or another sandstorm. "What's going on? Why are we stopping?"

"We've crossed into the Navajo reservation. There was a sign back there for a jewelry stand, and I wondered if they might have something that will help you."

The knife stabs deeper. He's desperate for me to regain my powers. But they're gone. I feel it every time I breathe. Rather than argue, I turn away. We pull into a dirt parking lot in front of a long stand made of rough-hewn wood, shaded with a canopy of dried scrub oak. Kye gets out and peruses the goods, peering at every piece and sending me furtive glances every five seconds or so. After a couple of minutes, his scowl deepens enough that I figure I better join him at the stand, or live with his wrath indefinitely.

"You know, you could at least try," he snaps.

I want to scream that it won't do any good because my power is *gone*. End of story. There is no amount of jewelry, natural or otherwise, that will fix that. But we have a long way to travel, and no matter how angry I am, I'd prefer to get to Utah without fighting the whole way, so in the interest of keeping the peace, I pace near the table, examining each piece of genuine turquoise, gaspeite, hematite, citrine, and howlite, all encased and set in a yellow-tinted silver.

I pick them up, hold them in my hands, silently begging for one of them to stir a reaction—any reaction—in my senses. Praying that one will speak to me. Nothing. Finally, a Navajo lady stands, offering me a simple turquoise and hammered-copper pendant. It doesn't appear to be anything special, but as I walk away, she continues to nudge it toward me. "You buy this," she says. "Protection from evil spirits."

"What did you say?" I ask, and Kye, having overheard, joins me near the woman.

"This brings power, luck, protection from enemies. You're looking for it, yes?"

Kye nods, most likely mistaking her demand for something more like a sign. He accepts the piece from her and examines it as if he knows about rocks and metals. "How much?"

The woman names a price that's beyond outrageous, and when Kye reaches for his wallet, I can't not speak up. We have limited funds. "Wait." I snatch the pendant from him and examine it closer. I run my nail along the edge of the turquoise stone, testing the hardness and making sure it isn't a pebble that's been painted blue. I inspect the tiny brown veins, and then the smooth surface before calling the woman on what it is. "This isn't real turquoise, but if you have one that is, we'll consider that."

"It's real," she says, seemingly offended. "You buy that one."

I shake my head, silencing Kye's objection. "No, thank you. I don't want this one." I turn and start for the car.

"Wait." A note of desperation colors her voice. "Maybe you'd like a green one."

I keep walking, turning only to toss over my shoulder, "I'm not looking at anything that's not genuine, real gemstone. I can get the costume crap at the mall for a fraction of the price if I wanted—except I never wear crap jewelry." I stop at the car, which Kye has locked, though we're outside and close by. "There will be more of these jewelry stands further along," I tell him. "Gram and Mom and I stopped at almost every one of them the last time we passed through."

187

Kye grins at the lady. "She's not lying. She knows her stones better than even you do, I promise. So if you truly don't have anything better than what's on this table, we'll keep going."

"Wait," the lady says, and my satisfaction level rises, because I knew she was hiding something great in hopes of selling the imitation stuff instead. She reaches under the table and brings out another pendant, this one not too different from the other one, except lighter blue, and definitely not painted. "This real."

Reluctantly, I stalk back, determined to be sure she recognizes my displeasure at being lied to. I snatch the necklace and run through all my tests again. This is not a painted stone, and when I close it in my fist, the silver on the back feels warm against my palm. I can't See or feel the waves of energy it's emitting, but in an interesting twist, I do feel something, and it gives me a sliver of hope. "Yes, this one is real."

This time, rather than asking how much, Kye looks to me with a brow raised, and I rattle off an amount I'm willing to pay—an amount more reasonable than the one she first told us for the fake stone. "No, no," she insists. "Worth more."

I know my stones, though. While this one is beautiful and I can feel tiny pulses of ... something, coming from it, I'm also ultra-aware that this is a common stone on this reservation, and I can count on easily finding more like it at the next stand, should we decide to stop again. I hand the woman back the pendant. "Let's go," I tell Kye. "I don't have the energy to do this."

He runs a hand through his hair, clearly annoyed, but also relieved. If he had bought this without me here, he would have been swindled.

The lady rattles off another number, and it's still more than we should pay, even if we could—which we can't. We reach the car, and the woman follows, holding out the pendant. "Okay, okay," she finally concedes, and rattles off one last number.

It's still high, but I don't want to haggle anymore, and if I get this piece now, Kye won't stop at every stand we pass. "Okay," I give in. "I guess that's closer to fair."

More relieved than he has a right to be, Kye pays the lady and clasps the pendant around my neck. "It suits you."

"Let's hope it protects us." I climb in my side of the car. "Took her long enough to bring out the real stuff."

Kye shrugs. "I knew it wasn't real. I knew you didn't care. To be honest, I'm relieved you got out of the car and looked with me."

"Why?" I ask, playing with the pendant as it warms against my skin. "I have plenty of Healing crystals already. Why would I need another?"

"You can never have too many," he says. "And you're so down. I thought it would cheer you up."

In reply, I paste on the most genuine grin I can muster. "Thanks."

"It didn't work, did it?" he asks.

Admiring my new jewelry in the reflection from the window, I rest a hand on his forearm. "It helps. Thank you."

As we drive away, there's a sense of respite between us. For once, my love of jewelry and all things pretty has come in handy for something other than Healing.

It's dark by the time we pass over the Hoover dam and approach the neon-lit city of Las Vegas. Memories flit in my mind and longing for familiarity hits me hard. It's most likely travel exhaustion setting in, but I want to plant my feet in one place and stay. As we cruise past the glowing Strip, I wonder if that will ever be possible. If I'll ever be well, have a family, a home where I can hang my clothes and claim a physical space that's bigger than my suitcase. I wonder if Kye and I will ever get past the canyon-sized gulf that has formed between us, and fill it in, or bridge over it, or whatever people do with chasms this huge.

If we can't, neither of us will be able to continue fighting a losing battle for long. Once we break this curse, if we ever do, we'll have some big decisions to make. The most important one being whether or not we have a future together.

The idea of a questionable future is immediately followed by memories of Gabe. His smile, his laugh, the way he carried me inside during a threat like I weighed no more than a beach towel. I miss being doted on, worshiped, and, yes, followed like he was a puppy and I his giving master. Not because I liked having power over him, but because never at any point did Gabe make me feel less than worshiped. I never felt unwanted. Whether I recognized it or not, in Gabe's presence, I always felt loved. Always. That's what I miss the most, because apparently, I'm not feeling it now.

Kye breaks into my train of thought. "What are you thinking about, so serious over there? Wishing we could stop for the night?"

"Last time we spent a night here, we ended up sleeping on a bench in a shopping mall," I remind him. "That doesn't really appeal."

"For the record, I'd love to stop. There are some exceptionally nice hotels in this city. If we felt safe, I'd get us a room in one of the best places and take you to an elegant dinner."

His words evoke the memory of the last time we had a fancy date, that night in New York before he was kidnapped. Maybe Kye's feeling the same nostalgia. "Are you changing your mind about driving straight through? Do you want to stop and try to lay low?"

He shakes his head. "No. I'm wishing for a do-over."

I shift in my seat to face him. "Me too."

He turns down the radio. "What would you do over?"

"A lot of things," I admit, deciding that now is as good a time as any to say it. "I wouldn't have kissed Gabe, for one."

His frown deepens. "I guess I'm glad to hear that. So ... you don't miss him?"

I do. I miss him so much it aches, and I'm afraid that's part of my problem. If I hadn't kissed him, he wouldn't have believed he had a chance, he wouldn't have pursued me, and then I wouldn't be carrying this guilt over deserting him without warning or goodbye. "He's a friend, so of course I miss him," I admit, but then throw in, "I also miss Rose, and would make sure she was okay before we left."

"Yeah, I have heaps of guilt over that too." Regret weighs heavily in his voice.

"I would also like a re-do of my birthday," I add. So many things went wrong that day. My fight with Kye, the call to my mother, my complete rejection of Gabe, sneaking to the club with Rose, being captured and escaping, and the consequential battle that followed us to the cenote before we could deploy into it. So many regrets.

"You and me both." Kye reaches over and takes my hand. I hold on, squeezing his fingers until we're far enough out of town that the lights become a distant blur.

"I would save Alejandro," he says suddenly. "I know we lost other people too, and obviously I would save as many of them that I could, but specifically him, because of what he meant to Rose. I've never seen her as happy as she was with him."

Unfortunately, though I still had my Healing power at the time, saving him was not an option. If it had been, I would have tried, even if it was risky to me. "I wonder how she's doing."

Kye's voice is rough. "She'll never forgive us for leaving the way we did."

"Would you?" I turn away, watching the glow of city lights shrink into the desert background. "If the situation were reversed, once I knew the circumstances behind the story—I'd forgive her for leaving."

He considers my logic. "I would too. It would be hard to understand why we had to do things this way, but I would hear her out and try my best to be empathetic and loving, and hopefully I'd be able to forgive."

"Rose is like us." Hope surfaces inside me for a moment. "She's practical and smart, and she means well. Despite the way she sometimes talks, she's one of the most selfless people I've ever met. Maybe she *will* be able to forgive us someday. If we ever get to go home, I hope Rose and I can rebuild our friendship. I miss it."

Kye squeezes my fingers. "I know you do. I miss my friendship with Landon. And my dad. No offense, but it would be nice to have a guy to talk to."

A laugh bubbles up. "I feel the same way about Rose. She was my go-to for everything."

"What about Jen?" Kye asks. "Before Mexico, the three of you were practically inseparable."

I remove my hand from his, turning it over as if it holds an answer I haven't found. "She got distant while I was sick. She brought my homework and tried to be supportive at first, but then it was like she got bored, moved on. Rose never gave up. She kept coming every day, while Jen ran off and found a boyfriend. Which, you know, is great. It's totally okay—she deserves a guy who makes her happy."

"But?" He prompts.

"But it's weird, because she would never bring him over, never introduced him to Rose and me, or to you, or Gabe, or anyone else. One day, she was determined to learn to control her Gift, and the next she lost all desire to do anything with it. She shut us out."

Kye blows out a breath. "Are you sure you didn't push her out?"

"If we did, we didn't mean to. When Rose first arrived in Mexico, she told me about Jen's boyfriend and how much she hates him because he couldn't or wouldn't look her in the eye—you know how Rose is."

"Do I ever."

"Anyway, there was more. So much has happened that I don't remember what, but Rose and I both felt a high level of concern, and not because she could lose control under stress."

"She has a hot temper, that one." He grins, but I can't return his smile. Jen's Gift of Fire is no laughing matter.

TWENTY-EIGHT

New Adventures

ROSE

Tanya stirs just over two hours after leaving Cole with me. I'm surprised to see her up, since I'm told she didn't sleep at all last night. If that was me, I'd be out until tomorrow, but she stumbles in, with red-eyes and messy bed-hair, hands clutching her breasts as if she's in pain.

My mom's in Marian's garden having tea with Murtagh and some other cute sprites, and I'm still reclined in the rocker with Cole tucked into the bend of my arm while I catch up on TV dramas. "What are you doing awake?" I ask her.

"Cole needs to eat," she says.

My fingers twitch on the blanket, and Cole doesn't move. "He's sleeping pretty solid."

"So am I." She indicates her hands. When I don't readily hand him over, she clarifies, "If he doesn't eat, I'm going to explode from the pressure. I don't usually wake him up to nurse, especially after a bad night, but he's going to wake up starving soon anyway, and I won't be able to sleep until I get some relief."

I stand, shaking the circulation into my legs and feet as I transfer the sleeping baby to his mother and migrate to the couch so she can have the rocker. I watch, fascinated, while Tanya nudges Cole's mouth open and urges him to latch onto her breast. He begins sucking, in his sleep, and Tanya lets out an audible sigh of relief.

I indicate the thick black mark circling Cole's wrist. "Do you think he's hurting?"

"He must be." Her fingers trace his arm as if trying to draw away his discomfort. "He's screamed his head off since this happened—and this is the first he's slept. Must have worn himself out."

"What happened to cause this?" I probe, leaning forward with my elbows on my knees. "Abby's the best Healer in this generation of Gifted. I don't understand how she couldn't Heal him."

Tanya swallows as if she has an enormous lump in her throat. "He didn't need Healing. It was Abby we were trying to help, trying to save, and now my little one's paying the price." Her voice cracks. "I would never have put him at risk if I had known this could happen. Ever. I don't believe for one minute that she did this on purpose—that she could be capable of such a heinous thing—but how could she *not* know this was possible? That it was a risk. I don't get it."

I shake my head, unable to defend Abby, even knowing her as well as I do. She's done plenty of things I don't understand. "Look, Tanya, Abby's a good person, but she's human, and we've lost some good people recently—people I'm told she couldn't save." I scrub my hands over my face, a lot like the way Kye does when he's overly stressed. I probably picked it up from him.

"If she is who she claims to be," Tanya whispers, "She should be here to save us. How can she allow us to *lose* anyone?"

I shake my head, shoving the resentment down as ruthlessly as I'm able. "Gabe has a theory about that," I tell her. "But we need to find Abby and Kye to figure it out. Did they tell you where they were going next?"

She hesitates. "I'm sorry. I think we've been introduced, but I was out of it when you got here. The morning is a complete blur. Who are you?"

"I'm Rose." I explain how long and how well I've known Abby.

"They didn't tell me." Tanya's expression doesn't change, but her eyes bounce with information she is clearly hesitant to share. "We kept getting sidetracked by Abby's inability to function. She was in bad shape. Kye talked about taking her home—which they didn't consider a good option. Then we tried to channel Abby's abilities and Heal her. I didn't understand the cost." Her voice is infused with a desperate level of grief. "If I'd known I was putting Cole at risk, I wouldn't have done it. He's all I have—everything. If I lose him, I'll have no reason to continue living."

I lean closer. "I think there's a way to save Cole. Abby once did something similar to a taxi driver in New York. It was a total accident. That time, it wasn't ..." I catch myself before uttering *fatal*, because Tanya doesn't need to hear that, but I'm looking at this baby, eyes closed in sleep, gulping milk almost faster than he can breathe, his skin a green-ish shade of yellow, and it's clear that this time it could be. He's too little to be able to hold onto that type of bad energy for long without it affecting his organs drastically—and soon. "She knows what to do, but may not recognize it. Tanya, I know Abby. She would never harm someone else on purpose. Especially not a baby. If we can't find her, she'll spend the last days of her life looking for a solution that will include saving Cole. If we do find them, the rest of us will help, and maybe she and Cole will both have a chance. If you know anything, please help me. I can be trusted."

"If she trusted you, why didn't she tell you her plan before she left?"

"She didn't know she could," I reply, hoping, praying that it's the truth. "It happened so fast."

"Abby's looking for her father," she admits. "For signs of what happened to him, where he went, and why. She's tracking things and people he tracked, trying to make heads or tails of the details they've found. They must have reason to think he's still alive."

Abby's father? "He can't be. If he was alive, he would have shown up long before now. He would have found Abby and Marian, or our community here. We're secretive, sure, but the

American contingent of Dragons are based here. He would know that. There has to be something else. I can't believe that they're looking for a dead person."

Tanya adjusts the baby to her other side with a sigh. "If I were to make an educated guess, I'd say it makes sense to look for them in the places where Abby and Marian have lived most recently. That would explain why they ended up in Phoenix."

Our conversation's interrupted when the front door opens. Gabe falters in the process of taking off his jacket when he notices that Tanya has replaced me in the rocker. When he notices that she's nursing, his gaze skitters away, his cheeks flushing. "I thought you'd be asleep."

Tanya gets the chair rocking, not the least bit embarrassed about her exposed breast. "Parenting. Twenty-four-seven. Infants eat when they're hungry, or when their mother is desperate to feed them."

Caught between mortification and mirth, Gabe stutters. "Um. Okay."

"You're back earlier than I expected." I pat the cushion next to me in invitation. He shuffles closer, but hesitates to sit. I grab his arm and pull him down. He's so careful to keep his eyes on me. "I, uh, need a picture of you."

I'm about to ask why he would need such a thing, until I comprehend what he's been off doing. Gabe's getting us the same kind of travel documents that Abby and Kye needed to leave undetected. The thrilling idea sends a surge of excitement through my veins. Finally, I get to have my own adventure. I lean close and keep my voice low. "Will a photo booth picture do? Or you can take my driver's license. I can get a new one later. I mean, if I still need one."

I wonder what my new name will be.

I wonder how old he's making me.

I wonder if my new identity will be old enough to buy alcohol in the States.

Gabe looks confused. "Why would I take your driver's license? You're going to need it. And no, a photo booth picture won't do.

We have to go to the drug store and get one that looks authentic. That's why I'm back now, so we can go and get this done."

Now *I'm* confused. "Why the drug store?"

"Because that's where people get passport pictures."

"I have a passport," I remind him. "It has a Mexico stamp in it."

He clears his throat as if not wanting me to push the issue in front of Tanya. "I'm getting you a ... different one. Just in case. But bring your original too."

I nod eagerly, my excitement level rising. He *is* getting us fake stuff. The passport thing means he thinks there's a possibility we could leave the country. I love this plan.

"I've made some arrangements," he continues, keeping his voice low.

Tanya's not at all discreet about the fact that we're in the same room and she can hear everything. "Look, we're all on the same team. We have similar goals. You don't have to hide your plans from me. I'm all for finding Abby, as long as bringing her here might save Cole."

Gabe frowns.

"What kind of arrangements?" I ask, returning my attention to Gabe's plans.

"Travel money, new accounts, credit cards, that type of thing."

Anticipation burns in my cheeks and eyes, and tingles in my fingertips. "Credit cards?"

He grins, chuckling. "Don't get too excited, Rosie. We're not going to have shopping time."

"But we will have some at some point?"

He shrugs. "We'll see."

"Well," I tell him, rationalizing. "I'm going to need to dress the part, disguise myself as being older than I am, so that will require a change of wardrobe."

"I said we'll see," he insists. "If that need arises, we'll deal with it then."

"As long as it's on the table as being possibly necessary, I'm cool with waiting until we get somewhere."

"Speaking of somewhere," Gabe says, eyeing Tanya as if to question me about what I've found out.

I wave toward her. "She doesn't know. They didn't tell her either."

Gabe sighs. "Those two are getting good at keeping secrets aren't they?"

"Not necessarily," Tanya chimes in, and when I look over, I notice that she has re-adjusted her top to cover herself and now has Cole snuggled with his cheek on her chest, having finished eating. "They didn't tell me where they were going, but before you came in, I was going to tell Rose that they might be headed for Utah. That is, if they've left Phoenix already. They could still be at my apartment. They'd only been there for a few hours before this happened, and they must have had a reason for being there."

I don't like the way Gabe's grinning at Tanya. Especially after I've grilled her and she was far more hesitant with me than with him. "I guess that means we're heading there next. Tanya, can you give me some ideas on what to pack?"

TWENTY-NINE

The Place

ABBY

After the dust storm in Phoenix, we're ultra-aware that the demons are near, which makes us hesitant to stop for long, even to eat. Thank goodness for truck stops with wide varieties of food—I still find whole grain chips and fruit and cheese, and am not forced to resort to living on candy. Yet.

We plunge past the desert landscape, cloaked in the blue film of night, watching the stars glow brighter with each passing hour. When I drift off, Kye wakes me up to point out dancing snow flurries illuminated by our headlights, too light to fall, but too heavy to remain in place, floating lazily toward the ground in crazy, unorganized spirals. Occasionally, we pass desert grass or sagebrush coated in a layer of white, and the desert beyond turns into a fantasy world. "Are we heading into a storm?"

"Looks like it," he says. "But don't worry. As long as the road doesn't ice, we're okay. You can go back to sleep. I wanted you to see how pretty it is."

"Thank you." I'm glad he woke me. It's strange driving through a desert so clear and bright that it appears to be a painting, someone's imaginary creation, and yet, seeing it from the car, it's so real. In the distance, white-tipped mountains rise up, rolling perpendicular to the highway for as far as I can see. They touch the deep blue of the sky, joining forces with the white stars until the earth becomes a character in our story.

There must be faeries out there. Or sprites. I wish I could see them.

In Mexico, I spent many nights on the beach with the sand in my toes, and my nightgown hiked up the way the locals wore sarongs. Those nights, the stars and moon were my allies, they recharged my powers and gave me strength to heal the wounds in my own heart so that I could Heal and See to protect others from the demons.

Despair knocks the wind from my lungs, leaving me gasping for air as I reach up and open the sunroof, begging the moon to heal me again, the stars to give me back my Light. My Sight. My ability to Heal. Anything. Everything I've lost. Something.

"What are you doing?" Kye's hand catches my wrist as the sunroof opens, filling the car with freezing cold that billows with snowflakes.

"I need to touch the moon." I stick my hands out, letting the rush of cold air beat them with icy rockets. "And the stars. They helped make me better in Mexico; maybe they'll rebuild my energy now."

"Babe." Concern coats his voice with sugar. "It's too cold for this. We'll freeze."

I'm not ready to close it yet, so I flip on the heater to full blast, momentarily resting my hand on Kye's arm before returning it to the outside. "Let me know when it's too much," I tell him. "I don't want to make you sick when I can't do anything to fix it."

He lets out a mirthless laugh. "Abby, you're the one who can't afford to get sick. You're already so compromised, so ..." He doesn't say weak, but he thinks it, and he's right. I am.

But I'm not going to stay that way. I refuse to accept the loss of my Gifts as permanent, and in the freezing light of the moon, I vow to not only find what my father was looking for, but to find the Gifts I've lost and restore them.

When my hands are so numb I can no longer feel or move my fingers and my shoulders ache, I close the sunroof and turn away from Kye, feeling no more powerful than I was when we left Phoenix. He drapes a sweatshirt over the top of me, and I curl into it, allowing the lingering scent of his cologne to lull me asleep, and wondering if I'll ever be warm again.

The sun is about to crest the mountaintops when we roll along the road that takes us across the top of the dam. The deep blue lake gleams in the half-light, smooth as glass except for the occasional jumping fish. We follow the lane that takes us over it, with the water on one side and the mountain on the other. At this elevation, there's a layer of frost dusted across the rocks and vegetation, and when we pass a marina, ice has built up on the pillars of the docks. We pass a separated section where an island rises out of the middle, and I'm amazed to see two men in a fishing boat with lines cast into the water. I wonder how they'll catch anything in this cold.

We make the turnoff that takes us into the valley, directed by GPS. Talk isn't required to find our way, but I can't pretend to sleep as we pass through the last place I lived with my family intact. This is the place where he supposedly died. I'm wide-eyed and cautious as we pass quaint stores and a couple of new-ish-looking restaurants. Swiss-style homes that must be a hundred years old are mixed in with newly built neighborhoods that boast a mountain-cabin feel. The road takes us past resorts which have built out and added upon since I saw them last. There are an abundance of horse pastures, and vast, empty land peppered with trees and wild plants and rocky terrain.

This is a wild place, tamed only by those who wish to live in it. That gives me a thrill. The zing of ... something. Maybe it's power, or an echo of power, but even if it's not, my heart throbs as if it knows that there's something here for me. Something important.

Kye pulls into the drive of the office building where we hope they've left us a key in the night drop. "Well," he says, and his hand lands on my shoulder, shocking me with the power radiating off of him. "We're here."

THIRTY

Finding Answers

ROSE

We leave Tanya and Cole sleeping at Marian's and detour to the drug store on our way home. It's surprisingly simple to get a new ID picture, and they give us two for the price. Gabe takes both with a wink and slides them into an envelope, then prepares to leave me at home with my mother while he finishes his clandestine errand.

As I get out of the car, he says, "Packing could be a useful task this afternoon."

The glow of excitement warms my skin, despite the chill in the air. "I'm all about useful tasks today," I assure him. "Will you be back soon? And should I warn my parents or ... is this a secret from them too?"

He flips his keys around his finger, his eyes glinting in the late afternoon sun. "Yes. Tell them. It never hurts to have a support system that's in the know here at home. Besides, maybe they're aware of details that could be useful. I don't think either of us is in danger of being followed immediately, and even the smallest clue could speed up our journey."

I suppress a frown at that. I don't know how fast I want this journey to go, but I don't want to up and leave my parents the way Abby left me, either. "Why don't you plan to eat dinner here tonight? We can talk to my parents together and eat a solid meal before we leave."

"Sure." Hi tips his head flirtatiously, then ducks into his car and revs the engine. "Be back in a couple of hours—with my suitcase. Be ready."

As he takes off down the street, my skin hums with energy. I've been ready for this adventure for a year.

Since my mother caught me dragging a suitcase up the stairs, my parents know I'm leaving before Gabe arrives. Makes for a bit of an awkward beginning, but Gabe handles it like a pro, sticking mostly to details—and I love him for it. My dad saws at his steak and drenches it in sauce. "If you're right, and those kids are following a trail, there must be a pattern to it. Abby's father was never random in his travels, especially when it came to dragging his family along."

"Did you know him?" Gabe asks, shoving a fork full of potatoes into his mouth.

"I knew *of* him," Dad says, shoveling in a bite and chewing. "Seems like I did meet him at some point, though for the life of me I can't remember specifics. Believe me, I've been trying to remember everything I knew about him since Abby and Marian rolled into town. I must be getting old."

"What did you know of him then?" Gabe encourages, keeping the conversation on track.

"Spencer Johnson was a good guy," Dad starts. "Had goals of restoring Dryden, and a plan for how to accomplish that. Not as a royal community the way it once was, but more like an empire of Gifted individuals."

"Empire?" I ask. "An ominous word to use when referring to people with Gifts that are meant for serving others."

"Yeah, that might not be the right term—or maybe it is. I don't know anymore." Dad shoves his plate forward and stands to wander to the window. Outside, the fluttering leaves on the maple tree have turned a bright shade of orange. "Spencer had good intentions. If he had managed to make it happen, the world would have benefited. But there were a lot of people, including some Dragons who were Spencer's close friends, who thought that bringing us all together in that manner was a bad idea."

"Why would Abby's dad do something that our leaders didn't agree with?" I ask.

"Well, consider the Elen. They were basically Gifted people, like us, who gathered together. None of us knows why or how they gathered, or if they had good intentions in doing so. All we know for certain is that once they did gather together, they discovered an undeniable center of power that none of them could contain, and that left them hungering for more."

"Is that why they began stealing Gifts from people?" Gabe asks, his fingers tapping the glass tabletop in a succession like rain on a roof. "When the dagger was created?"

"We can only guess about why they stole Gifts." My father faces us, squaring his shoulders. "But the dagger was originally created as a Healing tool."

"What do you mean a Healing tool?" I can't sit still anymore, so I rise to pace.

"Raina made it."

Gabe's gasp of shock echoes mine. "If this is Raina's thing, how does Abby not already know about this?"

Dad continues, "Before she met Theron, a patient was brought to her in a frenzied state of delirium. He was an empath who had seen a great battle, and who had tried the only way he knew to help those most impacted to survive their losses and move forward. The way he did this was to take their emotional pain, their grief, their mass hysteria upon himself."

"He went crazy." Gabe grips his hands together tightly.

"Raina couldn't Heal that," my father says. "Because the empath's wounds weren't physical, but mental and emotional. So she tended to him the best she could, until he begged her to kill him. Obviously, Raina didn't have that in her. His suffering was the hardest thing she'd ever had to watch, because she was left so helpless."

I can't help but think of Abby. How must she have felt to know she couldn't help Alex? Couldn't save him?

"The empath was determined to die, and tried to harm himself multiple times every day, using whatever household items he could get his hands on. Eventually, Raina had the man's arms and legs tied to the bed to protect him from himself, but he continued to beg her to kill him and put him out of his misery." My father pulls me into his chest.

"But Raina had taken a Healer's oath that she would never harm another, which left her unable to kill the man as he begged, but also unable to leave him in misery. It became apparent that both would be equally harmful, equally cruel. This left her with only one option, and that was to find a way to drain the empath of the power that had besieged him, and leave him as a common, sympathetic human."

"The dagger." Gabe's eyes glaze with the look of someone whose mind is miles away.

"Right," my dad says. "It must have been highly controversial for her to have sought such a weapon, because from what I understand, she commissioned the pieces in secret, individually, and from different sources so that no one would know what she intended to do. And—because she had not yet connected with Theron—she went to great personal expense in order to pay the price for each piece."

"Wait," Gabe asks. "Wasn't she poor?"

My father's lips twitch. "Raina was poor when she met Theron, but only recently. Growing up, she had apprenticed under her mother, and grandmother, who were both well-known, highly respected Healers. At the time when she met the empath, she was making a good living in what would equate as a modern day medical practice that turned out to be the end of her life, as well as the beginning. In order to create the dagger, Raina had to sell everything of value that she owned, including jewels she had inherited from her ancestors. This left her with only her home and the bare minimum of herbs that she needed to treat patients."

"I don't understand." It still doesn't make any sense to me. *Why would Raina create something so dangerous?* "It's a knife made with expensive materials. How did it come to be the thing that drains and transfers Gifted powers?" For that matter, how did the Keys come to be what they are now?

"No one knows for sure," my father says, turning his face away from me so that the setting sun casts his face in shadow. "But the theory is that she had to enhance it with powers of both Darkness and Light."

Gabe lets out a noise of exclamation, waving his hands in enthusiasm. "That's how she became friends with the apprentice to the Prince of Darkness. He supplied the Dark, she supplied the Light, and together they drained the empath of his power and put him out of his misery."

My father beams. "I have considered that the most likely scenario myself."

Eric's face floats through my mind, and his voice, as I heard it that day at the airport when Abby showed up to tell us Kye had been kidnapped. He was so annoyed with everything that had anything to do with Kye, and still so infatuated with Abby. "And in payment," I say, thinking out loud, "Raina must have offered the prince her hand in marriage, which didn't work out so well when she met up with Theron."

"Not exactly," my dad explains. "But close. Raina offered her house as payment, and the apprentice accepted, but then Prince Tynan got word of the weapon that had been forged, and decided he needed to have it for himself, no matter the cost. He didn't want to kill Raina to get it, because the dagger was her creation, thus there was no proof that anyone other than she could use it properly. Instead, he promised his apprentice the only thing that he knew the man truly wanted, and would be willing to betray anyone and everyone to receive."

"Raina." The plot unfolds in my head, leaving me with senses of rage and sorrow for all that our ancestors endured. "Tynan promised Raina to Erim for the price of everything she had ever worked for."

"And he took her house, too," my mother says from the doorway. "That's how the dagger was created. It's how Raina ended up poor, and also why she ran—that's how she came to be in the forest the day she met Theron."

"Full circle," I hum. "Raina sought the dark, lost everything and then clawed her way into the light."

"But the dark came back," Gabe points out. "It always comes back."

I don't know why, but my cheeks plump with a grin I can't stop. "So does the light. As sure as the sun rises every morning. Raina always knew where to look, how to find it under the worst of circumstances."

"Yes," my father says, squeezing my shoulders once more. "Carriers of Light can never lose the ability to see those threads and draw them closer. No matter what happens to them."

"Abby can get her power back, can't she?" Gabe says, standing to join us in front of the window. Now he looks hopeful, too.

My mother joins us as well, taking a deep breath. "It's possible. If she's looking for it. As long as the Dark doesn't overtake her before she can find it."

"What happened to the empath after Raina drained his power?" I have to know. I need to know. The circle must be closed to end this madness.

My father shakes his head. "Obviously, he was no longer effective in the ways of an empath, but because empathy was such an intrinsic part of his true nature, he traveled the land helping others in whatever ways he could."

"Does anyone know what happened to him?" I glance from one parent to the other as they exchange a look.

My mother shakes her head. "No. Of course, there are rumors and stories, but nothing based on fact. There's no record of the empath after he left Raina's care."

"What are the rumors?" Gabe asks, and from the haunted look in his eyes, I wonder if he has heard them himself. I wonder if he knows.

"Well, stories tell of a saintly man, who traveled the world doing good for others, and who was eventually favored by the Morrigana. It's said that the goddesses made him an immortal being, and tasked him with assisting in the restoration of the new order of Gifted."

"You've got to be kidding me." I fit another piece into the puzzle, looking back on everything that has happened since Abby arrived, how desperate the Dragons were to send her away. "Are you talking about Valdemar?"

"I'm not saying that—" she starts, at the same time my father says, "That's not what she meant—"

But Gabe cuts them both off mid-sentence. "Yes. It's Val. It has to be Val."

Ignoring my parents' protests I turn to Gabe. "Do you think Kye knows?"

"I doubt it. If he did, he wouldn't have run off with Abby."

"Why not?"

"Because if Valdemar is the empath Raina Healed before the curse, he's also the only person capable of breaking the curse and helping restore the safety of the descendants of Dryden."

"What do you mean?" I ask, pacing around the furniture. "If Val can break the curse, why hasn't he done it already?"

"He might not know he can." Gabe paces too, steps behind me. "Or how. Think about it. If Raina created the Dagger to save the empath, and then the Dagger was the weapon that was used to build the powers of the Elen, it was also the weapon that brought Raina and Theron together, caused the jealousy of Erim, brought the wrath of Tynan, and took out the entire Royal family."

"The Dagger was the catalyst," I agree.

"Right," Gabe says. "So it makes sense that restoring the empath's Gift would be the only way to bring the cycle full circle."

"And once the cycle ends," I add, "the Dagger can be destroyed forever, and the safety of the descendants of Dryden can be restored."

"Exactly." Gabe takes my hand. "But I'd guess it only works once the empath's power is restored, which might mean the empath has to become mortal again."

"Or cross the crystal bridge." This is a scary thought to me. Maybe this is why Val has been determined to keep Abby far away. Maybe this is why so many life cycles have passed and the curse has never been broken. Maybe Val is a good guy who is doing a bad thing out of fear.

"If this theory is true, we have a lot of work to do," Gabe says.

My slack-jawed parents are watching us with wide, frightened eyes. "This is not your battle," my mother starts.

"Those two need to figure this out for themselves," my father adds.

"Abby's lost her Light," Gabe tells them. "They need us."

My parents object, but I stop them with a hand on each of their arms. "I can help," I tell them. "I know how to defeat the demons now."

THIRTY-ONE

Off Again

ABBY

There's no one in the sales office this early, and the keys aren't in the drop the way we'd hoped. Since we can't check into our rental at the moment, we head to the main part of town hoping to find an open restaurant where we can get breakfast. Neither of us has said anything about my failed attempt to draw in Light from the moon, choosing instead to drive in awkward silence, each drowning in our thoughts.

We pull into the driveway of a coffee shop, and I let out the sigh I've been keeping to myself. It's another two hours before the rental office opens, and we have nothing to do between now and then. I'm dying to get out of this car that's crowded with anguished memories and unspoken questions, and I imagine Kye must be too. I've slept in spurts through the night, but he's been driving for over twelve hours, with few breaks. The last time his traveling got this crazy was when he was trying to get Mexico. To me. I don't know what he went through then, but when he arrived, he was more exhausted than I've ever seen him. This time we have more at stake, more to lose.

I get out of the car and immediately bend into a full-body yoga stretch. "I hope they have eggs. And pancakes. With strawberry sauce."

His eyes glaze over like zombie eyes. He's primed to fall asleep on his feet. "Pancakes would be good."

I drape his arm across my shoulders, to guide him inside. "And tea. Bet you'd love some of that right now."

His only response is to nod. "That sounds good, too."

We sink into a corner booth and order breakfast foods, silent with exhaustion. Kye's lids droop with each minute that we're still. There's a rack of magazines near the door, so I pick one out and flip through it while Kye dozes on the table as we wait out our time. When we've paid and are ready to leave, I take the keys and direct Kye to the passenger seat. "I can find our way back. You go ahead and close your eyes."

"Can't sleep yet," he mumbles. "Have to check the house." But his head falls against the seat, and I have to stifle a laugh. It's not funny, but it's good to be reminded that Kye is not infallible.

By the time I find the rental office again—after three wrong turns and an unintentional tour of the back-roads—there's a car in the lot and the neon open sign is lit. Kye snores softly, so I leave him while I go inside to check in.

The enthusiastic agent takes my new fake ID without really looking at it—not that it would matter if she did, as it looks legit. But it's still a relief, since these rentals have a minimum check-in age, like the New York hotel. "Thank you, Mrs. Akers," she says. It requires more energy than it should for me to not react at hearing the pseudonym. Kye picked our fake last name in honor of Landon, but hearing it directed at me and coupled with the prefix of Mrs. Is jarring. "How long will you be staying?"

I wish I knew. "For a while." My brain scrambles for an acceptable explanation as to why we're showing up last minute to rent a property indefinitely, and not have it be ten shades of obvious that we're on the run. I settle with a line I once heard from a movie. "My husband's writing a novel, and it's not going well. We're hoping that a change of environment—a break from the city—will inspire him. If our experiment works, we'll stay until the novel is finished, which could be anywhere between two weeks and six months."

She shifts from one foot to another. "Um, okay. I'm sorry, but I can't let you stay for six months. This is the off season, and that particular property doesn't have any bookings for a while, but we have reservations in February. So you'll need to be out by then, even if the novel isn't finished."

February is three months away. I hope we don't need to stay here that long. "I'll be sure to let him know."

"Is there anything else I can get you?" Her fingers manically click on her keyboard. "We offer maid service, and grocery delivery if you need. For a small fee, of course."

"Of course," I return, trying hard to keep all traces of annoyance out of my voice. "We'll let you know."

"I stopped there this morning and turned on the heater and made the beds," she meets my gaze with her bright emerald one. "House should be warming up by now, and the driveway is shoveled so you can park close to the door." She hands me keys, along with an envelope with instructions on how to find the house, and owner's manuals that explain how everything works and what amenities are available to property renters. I thank her for her assistance, and join Kye in the car.

The cottage is hidden behind vegetation and set back from the road with a long, tree-lined driveway—perfect for privacy. Early snow covers the rounded roof, reminding me of dwellings I've seen in fantasy movies. Steam rises from a chimney. We're about to enter a house full of warmth.

I park, and then shake Kye awake. "We're here. Should we make sure it's secure before we unload?"

He blinks the grit out of his eyes and follows me to the door. The depth of cold here isn't as bad as the cold in Jackson, but even so, my fingers shake by the time I get the key in the lock and turn the knob. Kye leads, checking all the rooms, and the bathrooms twice, before he declares the house safe. We use what's left of our energy to drag our suitcases inside. Kye heads straight for the master bedroom, a luxurious suite with an in-room hot-tub, and a log canopy bed surrounded with gauze curtains.

Kye lets go of his suitcase halfway in and falls face-first onto the bed.

I hesitate in the doorway, debating, but when he starts to snore, I open another door down the hall and claim the second bedroom as mine. Here, all alone for the first time in what feels like months, I fall sideways onto the bed and close my eyes, finally ready to sleep for real.

My sleep is fitful and crammed with unusual dreams.

Valdemar has taken Cole from Tanya and plans to offer him as a trade to Boone and the demons, but I don't know why. Tanya kneels on the floor, screaming for someone to save her baby.

I try, but can't get to Cole.

I swim for miles in an ocean.

Run for more miles on the shore.

Through a forest.

Then I find Gabe's Dragon disk and ride on it, though I have no idea how to make it go.

I drag complete strangers out of cars and stow away in planes trying to keep up with Val and the baby, but no matter what I do, he finds a way to elude me. Though I'm not sure who is helping me track him, Kye's there with me, and Gabe and Rose and Jen. I feel like Murtagh should be too, like he's always close, but I can't find him. Can't see him, or talk to him, though everyone else can, and has. At least they know where he is. I don't know why he's avoiding me.

Time slips away, and while we search for Val, I continue my personal search for Murtagh, but it's as if he has disappeared from my life completely.

And then I understand why. Murtagh is a magical creature who can only be seen by those who possess Gifts like the ones I've lost. I haven't only lost my ability to Heal or See, but now to communicate and be friends with the one creature who has always had my back. Never again will I see mermaids in the ocean, sprites buzzing, faeries guarding the forest. I may never see Murtagh again. This realization is devastating to me, as I've never considered what it would mean to lose him in the most basic way. I beg Kye to feed me more faerie food, to help me see what is now hidden to me, but he refuses. I don't know why, and he won't tell me.

We continue our search, Kye and me and the others, and when we finally find Val, it's too late. He has already passed innocent Cole to Boone in trade for the dagger.

And we will never be able to get Cole back.

Afternoon sun streams through the blinds, burning a line across my face. Outside, a loud mechanism buzzes and beeps, so I leap up and bolt to the living room window to see if it's Murtagh bringing his sprite friends to find us. Disappointment wells up when I discover it's a snowplow. Missing Murtagh opens another hollow spot in my chest. He's always been the best at keeping me company when I'm feeling lonelier than should be possible. I miss his quirky personality, his glowing forms of communication. He would love this place, with the mountains and the evergreens. There are apple trees along the fence, remnants of a pumpkin vine under the porch, and corn stalks tied with ribbon leaning near a door that's adorned with a pinecone wreath. All around us, mountains rise toward the sky, already coated with a blanket of white that creeps ever closer to the valley.

This quaint little town was my home once, and the energy here must recognize me as someone who belongs, because the place still feels familiar and right.

Kye clears his throat. I turn to find him standing in the hall between the living area and bedrooms looking bleary and confused and still absolutely exhausted. "Did you sleep?" he asks.

"Yes," I hedge, not wanting to argue about the sleeping arrangements before either of us is fully coherent. "You collapsed across the bed, and I didn't want to disturb you, so I slept in the other room."

He frowns, but doesn't remark as he takes in the sunken living room with a rock fireplace dominating one wall. The kitchen is tiny, but the cabinets are made from rich, natural wood, and the countertops warm cut-stone, and the full-size appliances mean we can buy and store plenty of food. "This cabin's cozy. I like it."

"Me too." I indicate the trees in the lush yard. "Looks like there are still apples, if they haven't frozen."

His lips quirk, though not even the ghost of a smile reaches his eyes. "Fresh off the tree."

We share a moment of awkward silence, so I reach for another subject. "We should get groceries. We could run into town soon, or I could call the service if you want to lay low for the night." I point out the TV mounted to the wall above the fireplace mantle. "If you want to stay here and rest, we could find a movie or something."

He takes a deep breath as if zipping in a chest full of words. "Don't you want to go see your old house?"

When I arrived in Mexico I went straight to the beach. Christine gave me time to recover before she dragged me to the ruins, because she knew I needed rest. I wish we had weeks to spare now. "We're both exhausted. I've waited ten years to go back—I can wait another day while we buy groceries and unpack."

He steps closer, the invisible bridge between us growing longer. "There will be no point in buying groceries unless we're positive we're staying. We can't be sure that we're safe here."

I could tell him that we're safe, that I can sense something calming here, but he wouldn't believe me. Not since I've lost my Sight. I'm not sure I believe me. "We'll be here for a few days. As long as we don't feel compromised, I'd like to stay."

"Do you want to unpack first or go into town?" He drops his hand from running through his hair. It stands on end the way it did on the night we spent in New York. So much has happened since then, but that feeling of longing, of need, rushes back fast and hard, stunning me with intensity.

Before I can think it through, I've crossed the room and thrown myself into his arms, pressing my lips to his. My tongue searches his mouth, and my hands grip his shoulders as if he might try to escape. Kye's arms twine around my body and hold on tight as he lifts me off my feet and flips me against the wall, pressing his body against mine, while our mouths scorch each other. My hands slide under his shirt so my fingertips run along his smooth, muscular back. I start to drag the shirt over his head, but he stops me with a firm hand on my wrist. "Babe. Come on. You know we can't."

"Why not?" I nip at his lips, still working on his shirt with my free hand.

"You know why," he says, but there's not a lot of heart behind his objection.

"They lied, Kye," I tell him, pulling the T-shirt up to his underarm and over his shoulder. "They lied about so many things. Maybe they lied about the rest."

"If that was a lie," he says, his tongue darting into my mouth as he presses closer, "you would have known long before now. You knew about the baby before they told us."

"What if I didn't?" I tug harder on the shirt, wishing desperately that he isn't right, and knowing he is. "What if that wasn't Sight at all, but Valdemar's way of making me think I had it?"

He pulls back. "No one can give you power you don't have, Abby. Not even Val."

And with that harsh reminder, the mood dies. I drop my arms and let Kye's shirt fall to his waist. He sets me on my feet, knowing that this isn't going to happen now. "Probably for the best," he says, more to himself than me.

"We'll never overcome this, will we?" I shove away from the wall and head for the kitchen. "This stigma of our broken past, our broken futures. There will always be massive obstacles between us. Keeping us apart. Always. No matter what we do."

"Not after we defeat the demons." He perches on a stool, watching me open every cupboard and drawer as I assess the available supplies.

I slam a cupboard door, and then a drawer, rattling the single spatula inside. "There will always be demons. No matter how many tombs we close or how many Keys we find. No matter how many Gifted children we train or lives we save—you and I will always have opposition. We'll never be able to just be a couple in love."

"You're right." His voice is soft. "We won't."

Unable to face him, I stare at the empty fridge. "I think it's best if I claim that second bedroom. We have the space here, and some privacy might do us both good."

His loud intake of breath tells me I might as well have punched him. After what feels like a million seconds, he says, "Take the master. It has a nicer bathroom." I swallow hard, but can't turn as his footsteps take him into the other room, and then back again. "I put your suitcase inside the door. I'm going to unpack."

And just like that, Kye and me are off again.

The first time we drive by my old house the nostalgia is so overwhelming that I have to make Kye stop the car. This place wasn't home to me for long, but it's the last place I saw my father, and those memories are a treasure I've clung to at times when everything else in life is confusing and wrong. This is the last place where I felt truly whole.

"Do you want to go inside?" Kye asks.

"I'm sure it's locked." My breath fogs the window, and I draw lines through it with my fingers. "We don't have permission. Should wait for the agent to let us in."

Kye shrugs as if he doesn't care one way or another. It's become his fall-back reaction to everything I've done since I told him I wanted my own room. It's like he's trying to be indifferent, but he's not. I understand this hurts him. It's hurting *me*. But if there's one true thing I've learned this last year, it's that no matter how much I love Kye, or how much he loves me, at the end of the day, we'll always make each other miserable. It doesn't matter if we break the curse or not, because there are too many things between us. Gabe and Crystal and Kiersten and Tanya, and Cole, and my lost Gifts, and Val and Zane, and obligation, and Rose. There's death—and not just Alejandro. We lost more Dragons, good men who I didn't know well, but who showed up to fight for me, and died for it. There's fear, and anger, and betrayal, and thousands of miles on a car that doesn't belong to us.

Earlier, as I unpacked—for the first time since we left Mexico—I got thinking about how much emotional baggage we've accumulated. The cargo we carry will never shrink, or go away. Between us, there might be too much to store.

The cherry tree in the front yard of my old house is void of leaves, but that doesn't stop the memory of me climbing to the top-most branches.

The tree is bursting with lush, green leaves accented with dots of sweet purple. I pelt my father's shirt with delicious cherries as I hurl them down. "Sweet pea," he hollers, shielding his head with his arms, "no fair dive-bombing me before I can gather my own ammunition." But I continue pelting him until his paint splattered shirt is pink and damp with sticky cherry juice.

I'm glad the tree is still here.

"You want to go in, I can feel it." Kye turns off the car. "Let's walk the yard. There's no one here to object."

He's right that there's no car in the driveway. Since it's a vacation rental, I doubt anyone will be suspicious about new people in the yard. Still. "I don't feel right wandering freely like that. It's trespassing."

"Who's going to complain?" He gets out, turning briefly to glare at me through the windshield. "Come on."

I follow, worried for reasons I can't name. Maybe I'm afraid to face this part of my past, to finally have my answers. I don't know.

Kye stops at the end of the driveway, waiting for me to catch up, and I pick up my pace, half expecting him to offer his hand, but he doesn't, and that stings. My own fault.

I continue down the drive, but Kye doesn't follow. When I reach the steps leading to the porch, I turn back, squinting against the bright sun. "Are you coming?"

He tries to take a step forward and springs back. "I can't."

Sunlight reflects off of the driveway, pretending to be warmer than it feels, and forcing me to shade my eyes. "You want me do this alone? It's your idea."

"No, I prefer that you not." He tries again to move forward, clearly unable to get any further than where he is. "I'd like to have access to you if you need something, especially under your current circumstances."

I have to take a breath and deliberately ignore the comment about my current circumstances as I backtrack to get a better look at what's holding him up. He's pushing against air. Solid air. "I don't know what's going on, but this house doesn't want me here. I can't go any farther. There's an energetic wall, and it won't let me pass through."

I reach the end of the drive and stand easily at his side without resistance, without feeling the shift in energy that should be present to be holding him back. If I didn't know what I do, I would think he was making up a story, but I've been on the other side of an energetic wall, and they're not something to ignore. "We should leave."

He seizes my shoulders experimentally as his forehead crinkles. "You didn't feel that? How could you not feel that?"

I shrug his hands away. "I just didn't."

"Abby." His deep breath tells me he's running out of patience. If only he knew how low my patience is as well. "Don't pretend you don't know about this. Just because you walked right through the wall doesn't mean there isn't one." He turns away, muttering about me being easier to live with when he was making me sick.

There is a wall, and I'm annoyed that he automatically assumes I'm oblivious to this fact. But to keep the peace, I stay silent while I puzzle through the issues. Maybe I'm able to get through because I'm no longer Gifted. Maybe this is a loophole, and the best way around the problems caused by Gifted people is to walk directly through them. I make a mental note to contemplate this possibility later, and catch up to Kye, who paces like a crazy person. "Stop," I tell him. "You're going to draw attention to us."

"Sorry. I don't understand what's going on. On any level." He eyes me pointedly, and my gaze skitters away.

I take his hand and drag him up the driveway, keeping his hand in mine. "Let's try something." This time when I cross the threshold, I drag him with me. There's some resistance as we step together through the invisible wall, but after two or three long strides that feel heavy and difficult, we make it to the other side, and I'm able to let go of Kye's hand when we get to the front door.

"That was the weirdest thing ever," he says. "I've never heard of an energetic wall letting one person through and not another." He doesn't mention the differences between us and our current abilities, so I don't either, but we're both thinking about them, and the gulf between us grows a foot wider.

I knock on the door, trying to formulate what I should say in the event that someone answers. No one does, but my longing to go in has grown into a hunger that can't be fed. "Let's try the back. I want to see inside."

He raises his brow. "Five minutes ago you wanted to wait."

"I've changed my mind." I stomp across the grass toward the back-yard gate. "I want to go in right now."

"Babe, now might not be the best time. This resistance is strange, and without your help, I don't know what it is or how to read it."

"What you feel is awareness of the energy in this house," I explain. "It might not be resistance so much as knowledge that a great deal of power has been left here."

I struggle to open the gate, so Kye reaches over the top and un-latches it from behind. "Pretty sure I know what fear is, Abby, but thanks. That's not what this is."

"Well, maybe it's—"

"No. It's resistance."

"How do you know?"

He inhales, and then spits his words out like rotten cider. "Because I've been feeling all kinds of strange things since you lost your Gifts," he tells me. "Intuition and feelings, and the weirdest dreams I've ever had. I don't have a good feeling about being here right now. Not at all."

His quiet admission hits me like a load of bricks falling off the roof and onto my head. I'm powerless, and Kye's getting stronger, more powerful. If what he claims is true, he has gained one of the Gifts I lost, and I can't believe how badly it stings. Not wanting to admit that I feel no sense of danger, only determination to push forward, I stomp toward the entrance and twist the knob.

The door flies open, hitting me with the dank smell of must and mold, and the absurd urge to run the other way. Terror claws my throat and leaves my heart pounding in my chest. I cannot see what's in this house, nor hear or feel why I should be afraid. But I am. I turn back to Kye, whose eyes are round and tight with anxiety. "Maybe you're right."

I pull the door closed, and he yanks me off the porch and marches me toward the car. "You need to stop trying so hard to be rebellious and start paying attention to what's happening around you," he lectures as we tromp across the grass. "This is how people die."

"I always pay attention to what's happening around me." It comes out through my grinding teeth. "I've spent my life being hyper-aware of everything."

"Well, if you were still so hyper-aware, you would have seen that there's a portal in that house." He shoves me into the car and slams my door.

He gets into his side before I can find my voice. "No there wasn't. If there was, I would have seen it."

"You should have seen it," he agrees. "But obviously you didn't. If you had, you would have panicked the way I was. We're lucky that room full of demons couldn't feel your energy the way they have in the past. You don't have your Light, and I don't know how to protect you without it. From now on, you listen to me when I tell you something's wrong. Otherwise, I can't promise we'll get back to Jackson alive."

I can't argue with him. I didn't see. I don't know. And he's right. I have no power. I am nothing now but the regular human I used to wish I could be. It sucks rocks.

THIRTY-TWO

Leaving

ROSE

Mom helps me pack while my father books plane tickets. "We should go with you," he says over and over again. "But if your mother and I go, the Dragons will know something's up. They haven't paid attention to what you and Gabe are doing lately. You've both been so despondent, so depressed, that they've let you have your space. This is your biggest advantage at the moment. It means you'll have days, or possibly weeks, before they figure out that you've left. By the time they start looking into where you've gone, you might well have found Abby and Kye and sorted things out."

Gabe and I both understand this, and I acknowledge it as my dad takes his laptop into his office and leaves me and my mother in my room switching from a carryon size to our biggest suitcase and piling in clothes for every possible winter weather occasion. "Listen," my mother says. "I've noticed you and Gabe have been getting along better lately, and that makes me nervous for a totally different, more personal reason. Please ..." she hesitates. "Please don't do something you'll regret. You've already been hurt enough this year. I don't know if I can pick up your pieces a second time in six months."

It takes a lot to make me blush. My mom and I are close—always have been. She knows I'm not the least bit innocent, which is most likely where this is coming from. "Ma, please don't. Gabe's barely a friend, if I dare call him that. Please don't stress over him being able to hurt me in some way. I don't feel that for him."

"He deserves better than a rebound relationship," she says softly. "You both do."

"We're not rebounding," I insist. "We're friends. We've been friends all along." And if I tell myself that enough times, maybe I'll start to believe it. I've always liked Gabe, even when I hated him. She responds with an incredulous raised brow, but says nothing further. I don't know how to take it, but neither do I have time to argue, so I don't.

I've packed my winter coat and boots, sweaters, flannel pajamas, sweat shirts, jeans, under-shirts, a scarf, hat, and gloves, and every other warm thing I own, so I'm surprised when my mother holds up one of my more modest swimsuits with a raised brow. "Ought to throw this in, too."

"Why do I need that?" I snatch it from her with a giggle. It's my least revealing suit, and the only one-piece I own. I bought it two summers ago during a fashion boutique when the lady selling them insisted that this was going to be the new fashion rage. Paid a hefty designer price for the little gold logo on the strap, too. I didn't wear it in Mexico, because it covered too much skin. But in all fairness, the day I bought it, when I took it home and tried it on, I kept it because it looked killer on me. Still does.

"Just in case," she tells me with a smile. "Maybe you'll go somewhere warm. Or maybe there will be a hot tub. It's good planning."

So I figure why not? And toss it into the zipper slot with my fragile undergarments. "Good point." Next she hands me a pair of flip-flops to go with the suit, and rather than argue, I throw them in. "Anything else I'm forgetting?"

She reaches into her pocket, and after a moment of hesitation, draws out a leather cord with a crystal dangling from the end.

"This. It's rose quartz. It's not a communication crystal, which is probably what I should be giving you to help your Voice. It's a heart stone. To help Heal your emotional wounds and strengthen you. To help you find compassion and empathy for others so you can forgive, and to keep you strong." I don't know what to say. She unclasps the silver hook attaches the leather cord so the crystal rests against my collarbone. "Also, it's fitting because of your name."

"Mom." I touch the stone, watching her in the mirror. "Where did you get this? When?"

"It was your grandmother's." My grandmother only died a few years ago, and my mother misses her every day. This is a treasure that's not easy for her to part with.

"But this is yours. Grandma left this for you."

She shakes her head, eyes glistening. "No, sweetie. She left it for us. I'm giving it to you. It's time."

Part of me, the part that loves my mom more than anyone else in the world, wants to refuse to take this treasured piece of her past. But the logical me, the one that has been training and working and using my Gift to fight demons—that part of me knows that this crystal is something I'll need, the way Abby needs her ring. This is my inheritance, my grandmother's legacy, so instead of refusing it and insisting that my mother keep it, I turn in my mother's arms and hug her tight. "Thank you. Thank you for giving this to me when I need it most. Thanks for helping me through the hardest part of this last year, and supporting me in going after Abby, when you'd rather I stayed here hidden."

Her laugh is watery. "Yeah. That's true. I'd love to keep you locked in your room for the next ten years until we're sure this war has blown over, but you'd go crazy, and anyway, that's not where you belong. You were born to be on the front lines, fighting the battle with your cousins. You belong in the fray taking out your anger on the demons who deserve it. More importantly, you deserve to prove to the Dragons how big of a mistake they've made by overlooking your importance for all these years. Because you, baby girl, are the glue."

My cheeks are nearly as warm as my chest. "I know I'm important. I don't need the Dragons to tell me that."

"No, you don't need their acknowledgement," she agrees. "But they need to recognize it all the same. It's about time for that. You're not the squeaky wheel. You don't make huge demands like Jen, and you're not constantly on the verge of dying, like Abby, and you're not off running all over the world at the command of magical creatures like Kye."

"Don't forget Eric," I add. "I'm not the betrayer, either."

She shakes her head, finally backing up from our embrace far enough so she can look at me, while keeping her hands on my shoulders. "You're the fun one," she says. "The one who everyone loves, but no one acknowledges needing. The one who makes everything better, but who never gets credit for saving the day—though you've saved hundreds of days for all of them. You're the glue that holds this crazy community together, and in your time of great pain and loss, they left you to grieve alone."

"If I didn't know better, I'd wonder if I'm detecting resentment in your tone." I push an errant strand of hair behind her ear.

But my mother isn't laughing. She doesn't crack a smile. "Rose, these people aren't perfect. Far from it. None of them is as all-benevolent as they would like you to believe. Not even Abby is selfless all the time—you've already seen that."

I snort, thinking of all the times she snuck off to meet Kye only so Landon could fix her up later. "Yeah. I've seen all of that, and then some."

"You deserve better than the way they've treated you, baby."

"I do." I hug her tightly once again, wondering how deeply my pain has affected her too. "It's not okay, but I want you to know that I don't need their approval to feel good about myself. I don't need them to make me feel included. And I'm not like Jen. I'm not going to run off and rebel to get attention."

She sighs in relief. "Well, I'm glad for that."

"Mom, believe it or not, you've raised me to have bucket-loads of self-confidence. If there's one thing I'm good at—well, besides talking people into things—it's figuring out what I need to do to be happy. I've got this under control." I hug her as tight as I can before letting go and stepping away.

My eyes are wet, and I'm not sure how that happened, but I can't let her see—she can't know how I've lied. She can't know how out of control everything is right now, and how terrified I am for what I'm about to do. She believes in me, and I'm going to have to cling to that faith in all the moments when I have nothing left of my own. I need her faith the way she needs to give it, so I paste on my most confident smile and swallow my fear, then pick up my suitcase and coat. "Well." I scan my room for any last items I've forgotten, and my eyes land once more on the prickly cactus Gabe gave me weeks ago. Maybe he was right—maybe I am made of stronger stuff than I thought. "Guess that's everything."

My mother follows me down the stairs to my dad's office. "You've got about two hours," Dad is telling Gabe. "You already have a stop to make, so it's not enough time to check in on Jen, I'm sorry."

Gabe nods. "Thank you, sir. It's all right. Would you check on her for us? Keep an eye on her while we're gone? There's something off about her situation."

"I agree," Dad says. "And yes, I will. Unfortunately, I'm afraid that I'll have to alert the Dragons about her. Under the circumstances, and with her ability, she's putting a lot of people at risk. I'll keep an eye on her for a few days and won't alert them until the two of you are safely away and as untraceable as possible."

"Yes, sir. I understand. Thanks for that too." Gabe stands from his chair when my mother and I enter the room with my luggage. "Ready to go?"

My eyes ping-pong between the two of them. "Why would the Dragons need to know about Jen?"

"Only if things get out of control," Gabe starts. "A precaution to keep her from burning the city to the ground."

I want to derail this plan, and Gabe along with it. In his eyes is a hint of the controlling Dragon who got so bossy with Abby, and it lights a spark in me. But with distance, and rational thinking, I recognize the wisdom in their thoughts. Someone needs to watch out for Jen while I'm gone, so of course it should be my family. It's with great reluctance that I agree with this plan. "Okay, but don't tell her parents. I don't think they understand how hard things have been for her."

Mom and Dad exchange a glance that speaks volumes. They know more about Jen's family than I do. I want to ask what they know, and how we can help her, but Gabe has our boarding passes in hand and picks up my suitcase. "We should get going. We still have to stop at Marian's and get a key from Tanya."

I nod for him to take my suitcase out while I hug my parents, offering tearful goodbyes and promises to be careful and take care of myself. Then I zip my coat and step onto the porch, closing the door behind me.

"Don't worry," Gabe says as I buckle my seatbelt. "Jen will be okay."

"I hope so." I fiddle with the quartz hanging from my neck. "It stresses me out to leave her, but she wouldn't come with us. She barely talked to us before."

"She hasn't been training, and that would slow us down. Especially if she got angry and lost control and started burning things." He starts the car and pulls out of my driveway. "At the moment, she's pretty volatile, and if she's into drugs, the way it appears she might be, her mood swings could be disastrous. She's dangerous on every level."

I remember the day—only months ago—when Valdemar first tried to force her to use her Fire to help. She was so afraid. As long as I've known her, Jen has been careful, exact, controlled. Now it's like she's become someone else. I hate it. "My parents will watch out for her. When we get back, you and I are going over there and dragging her back to reality using whatever force is necessary, and you're not going to argue with me about her having choices and letting her make them," I add, pointing my finger and then digging it into his shoulder before he can reply. "She may have choices, but her bad choices affect us all, and I'm not going to let her be responsible for something that hurts us. Eric already tried that. One betrayal is more than enough to last a lifetime."

Gabe grabs my finger and shoves it away from him, careful to stay within our driving lane. "I wasn't going to argue. For once, I agree with you. Whatever Jen is doing is bad news, and not only for her. The first time she burns something down, the Dragons will be all over us too."

I don't know if he recognizes that he's referred to himself as part of the rising group of Gifted, but it's true. Somewhere along the line he stopped being "one of them" and became easily, and solidly "one of us." Warmth flutters in my chest.

"That's the last thing we need," I agree. "One more reason we need to find these two and kick some demon ass, fast."

A familiar buzz, accompanied by a tiny blinking glow zooms up to my window. I roll it down enough so the sprite can fly in. "Hey, Murtagh! I haven't seen you since I got home. What have you been up to?"

"Trying find warrior queen," he says, seeming exasperated—though admittedly, it's super hard to tell. Murtagh is so small, and he buzzes faster than a hummingbird, making him appear as if he's an unusually bright firefly. "Left without Murtagh. Very bad danger."

"Abby's in danger?" Gabe asks, and I notice the edge in his voice—the one I remember from Mexico.

"Of course she's in danger," I say. "We all are, which is why we're leaving now."

"All in danger," Murtagh says. "Bad things happening. Faeries angry. Sprites dying. Animals worried. Must find warrior queen."

"You said that." Why do I feel a twinge of envy that even the freaking bug is missing Abby? Worried about Abby? Maybe because, once again, everything comes down to her. "What's happening?"

"Dragons fighting," Murtagh continues, his speedy, backwards talk making everything more confusing than it would be if he'd hurry up and spit it out. "Bad bad demon everywhere. Army in castle."

"What do you mean demons are everywhere?" Gabe asks, concern coloring his voice. "I haven't seen a shadow for quite a while, and nothing like what used to chase Abby and Kye."

Murtagh buzzes again. "Not shadow demon, guy. Spirit demon. Human not see, but feel. Make angry, friends. Hurt and sorrow and hate they spread. Humans become bad."

My chest burns with dread as Gabe asks slowly, "Murtagh, where are these invisible demons? And why can't we see them?"

Murtagh stops buzzing and lands on the dash. For the first time since I've known him, Murtagh has aged. "Demons everywhere. Inside people."

THIRTY-THREE

Fighting

ABBY

This town is both bigger and smaller than I remember it. There are more people, more restaurants and little stores. Main Street has been refreshed, but aside from the businesses there and the resorts tucked into to the mountain, there's not much else. Between breakfast and checking into the house, and now our trip to the store, we've seen the whole town.

If our visit to my old house hadn't left me in a sour mood, I'd be enchanted by the Swiss-style buildings and the sloped hobbit roofs. I could fall in love with this place the way I did with Mexico, but I won't. Not this time. I got comfortable in Mexico, and that's something I won't do here. We can't afford to lose anyone else. I can't allow that to happen.

We return to the cottage with bags of groceries that will last us for a week or two.

Arms loaded, Kye fumbles for the key and unlocks the door, gesturing for me to proceed. I set my groceries on the counter in the kitchen, and turn, stifling a scream. In the corner, near the fireplace hearth, someone has erected a slim Christmas tree, complete with blinking colored lights and a handful of nature-made ornaments. It's beautiful and sweet, but frightens me for obvious reasons.

"Kye," I whisper, pointing at the tree with a shaky finger. "Someone was here."

His eyes go wide as he drops everything on the table and grabs a knife from the block near the oven. "Stay close." We check every room, every corner and closet and under every piece of furniture for signs of demons or Elen, but there's nothing. We approach the tree last, utilizing every ounce of caution we possess. There's a note tucked between the upper branches, secured in place by a pinecone ornament. Kye snags the note and hands it to me to open, keeping the knife in his white-knuckled hand.

Mr. and Mrs. Akers,

Came by to bring over holiday décor, but you were gone. Glad we didn't disturb you while you were working. The rental office will be closed next week for Thanksgiving, so we brought this for you to enjoy a few days early. If you should need anything or have any problems with your rental, please call our after-hours number.

Happy Holidays!
Management

Kye lets out a sigh of relief and his grip on the knife relaxes. "Who puts up a Christmas tree before Thanksgiving?"

"People who are concerned about their renters' festivities and who don't want to have to worry about decorating during a busy season." I take the knife from him, knowing that he's going on very little sleep and could easily hurt himself—or me. "My mom always loved when we felt secure enough in a house that she could decorate Thanksgiving week. She claimed that having it done ahead of time allowed her to fully enjoy the rest of the holiday season."

Kye flexes his fingers and pulls me into his arms in a loose and awkward embrace. "I'll take your word for it. I haven't lived with my mother since I was little. Or any other decorating female, for that matter, so this is new to me. I find it a strange and unsettling practice."

His honest admission startles a laugh from me. "I haven't lived with a father since I was six, or any other protective male, for that matter, until you." And Gabe. But for the sake of peace, I refrain from bringing that up. "There are lots of things I find unsettling about having someone who is not my mother constantly worrying about me."

"And don't forget demons chasing you. That's new too, right?"

"Well, it feels new." I start putting away the food. "But the more we learn about the demons and our history, the surer I am that having them chase us is older than old."

Kye plops onto the couch, flipping through TV channels while I arrange fresh-cut fruit, veggies, and cheese cubes on a plate. It makes me feel normal to make a healthy snack for eating while we zombie out in front of sitcoms.

I haven't relaxed like this with Kye since before we got sick in Jackson, seven months ago. It's been over three months since I enjoyed downtime with Gabe, but this is different. Gabe and I learned how to be comfortable together, as friends. Kye and I are still learning, and it's awkward because we love each other, and yet—we have no hope. Days like today make it hard to keep our balance.

I set the tray on the end table near Kye's elbow. "Here you go."

He frowns. "What's this?"

"I thought you might be hungry," I claim the other end of the L-shaped arrangement, needing to give him his space, but still remain near.

"Oh." He stares at the plate for a long time, but doesn't touch anything on it. After a moment, he stands up and tosses the remote in my lap. "There's nothing on. I'm going for a walk, stretch my legs before it gets dark."

He's out the door, shoes in hand rather than on his feet, before I can think of a reply. It's going to be a long few weeks.

Three days of avoiding eye contact and awkwardly passing each other in the hall with fewer than two words to acknowledge each other have made me stir crazy. Without my Gifts, I'm a wounded bird, afraid to venture out of the nest. This house may be filled with awkward silence, but it feels safe to me—however false that safety may be. Kye takes hours-long walks every morning and evening, leaving me alone to stew. At dusk on the third day, after Kye has been gone for almost two hours with no sign of returning, I seize the car keys and my purse and venture into town.

Though it's spread out, this place is still small. I drive aimlessly, comparing these mountains to the Tetons, taking in the wide fields of recently harvested grain. At the edge of town, I find the lake we passed the day we arrived, and when I come to a place where the shoulder is wide enough, I pull over to snap some pictures.

I haven't taken any since Mexico, and for that I'm sad. We've seen so much of the country, and I should have been better at documenting it. As I emerge from the car, a shadow flies overhead. Fear curls inside me as I whip around, searching the sky for demons. What I find instead has me releasing my breath and staring in wonder. A bald eagle has built a nest on a power pole fifty yards away, and the majestic bird swoops and dives toward the water, pulling up short of splashing in, and then swooping up to land in the nest.

"You beautiful bird." I snap the shutter over and over again. "What are you doing here so late in the winter?"

And then I hear it. Tiny tweets coming from above, downy wings fluttering, the screech of a second, larger eagle as it glides through the air to join its partner in tending to the babies. I'm still snapping pictures when little heads pop up so I can see them. There are four, and all of them have soft, fluttery wings that flap feebly at their parents. This display of natural family is the most beautiful observation I've made in months.

By the time I return to the car, my fingers are numb from the cold, and so are the tips of my ears. The sun has set over the mountain, but the reflection of its light lingers yet, staining the sky a dusky indigo as I traverse the roads to our cozy cabin. Eagles are among the most intuitive of creatures. If there were bad forces here, they wouldn't stay. I purposefully drive by my old house again, hoping, wishing, I could See what might be happening inside. Of course, it's still vacant. I can't imagine that it's an easy place to rent if there is truly a demon portal there. But it looks pristine and beautiful, with nothing out of the ordinary. I don't know what Kye saw, but I wish I could be sure he wasn't mistaken.

A savory aroma wafts from our warm rental house as I walk in, and though Kye is nowhere to be seen, he's obviously back from his walk because the stuffed chicken breasts we bought at the store are in the oven, and there's a sauce mixture cooling on the stove. I replace the keys on the counter where I found them as Kye moseys in, frown-lines creasing his chin and forehead and making him look years older than nineteen. "Thanks for leaving me a note."

His words hit me like a slap. "You never leave me one."

"Because you're here when I leave, so I tell you."

"No you don't," I point out. "You tell me you're going for a walk, and then you stay gone for hours. I wouldn't know which direction to look if you didn't come back. I can't very well use my Sight anymore."

"I never go far," he says on the defense, his voice rising an octave. "And at least you know what I'm doing."

I shake my head, now feeling defensive myself. "How would I know what you're doing? You don't tell me. You don't tell me anything anymore, except that you're leaving. I needed to get out, and you obviously don't want me here, so what else did you expect? That I'm going to sit alone in this house wallowing and waiting for you to come back and close yourself in your room?"

"You could crack open Tanya's journals, get to work on figuring out what we have to do to get out of this mess."

"So could you," I shoot back. It takes everything in me to not throw something at him for being such a jackass. If he'd stayed here long enough, he would know I've already been through all of Tanya's journals again. Twice. "But we've been over them a whole bunch of times. Reading them again is not going to yield any new information, no matter how badly we want them to." And since I'm no longer having visions, I have no clue where to go from here, or what to do next. I'm absolutely stuck.

"While you've been busy moping and pining for ... whatever or whoever you're pining for, I've been out talking to the fae, searching for sprites like Murtagh, and trying to arrange some extra protection for us when we go back to that house. I'm looking for answers in the best way I can. It's not like I'm sneaking off to party at the local bar."

The comment stings, since that's exactly what I did when we fought in Mexico. It's also where I got into trouble with the Elen, and it's how we got forced into fighting a battle we weren't yet ready for.

"I went for a ride," I grind out. "Give me a break."

He shakes his head. "The town's not that big, Abby. You would have had to drive the whole thing about seven times to be gone as long as you were."

I cannot believe we're having this conversation. Gathering my dignity, I dig into my purse and pull out my slim-shot camera so I can shove it into his chest. "I stopped to take pictures of an eagle's nest on the edge of town near the lake. The sun was setting, and the water was spectacular, and you haven't seemed to care what I've been doing with my time, so it didn't occur to me that you would be bothered by that. I'm sorry if I'm not working hard enough for you, but for the record, just because you're not here to see me doing things doesn't delete the fact that I've done them. Maybe the problem is that you're so caught up in your own selfish head that you can't see what's happening to me."

I can't look at him anymore, because if I do, I'll burst into tears, and I won't allow myself to fall apart in front of him. When Kye doesn't take the camera, I shove it in his hand and pivot on my heel, stomp into my room, and close the door.

To avoid having further conversation on the matter, I close myself in the bathroom and run water in the enormous tub. Maybe the best choice is for me to pack up and go home, even if it means going alone.

It isn't until I've taken off my clothes and am setting my jewelry on the bathroom counter that I notice I've lost the quartz crystal pendant I was wearing when I left the house. Today just keeps getting better.

THIRTY-FOUR

Robbed

ROSE

After much hesitation, Gabe and I decide that bringing Murtagh could be to our benefit, so I unzip the top of my carryon and let him crawl in.

Murtagh stays hidden through our first flight, and also when we change planes in Salt Lake City, which leaves Gabe and I to keep each other company. Since the sprite showed up, there's an awkwardness between us that hasn't been present since Abby left. I'm not sure what's changed or why, but we both feel it. The energy between us has shifted, and neither of us knows what to do about it.

As our plane descends toward the runway, the sun sits low in the dusky desert sky, lighting the clay tile rooftops brilliant pink, and setting ablaze the distant rolling expanse of sand so it sparkles like billions of golden gems. This is a place dotted with palm trees and cactus, lively with bright blue swimming pools and breezy ivory sand dunes. Different from Jackson, and nothing even close to Mexico—the Phoenix desert is its own brand of beautiful.

We claim our baggage, and Gabe directs me to the rental car counter, where he deliberately chooses an SUV. I clear my throat, stomping on his foot to let him know I think that's a bad idea. How is he planning to pay for this? But he ignores me, presenting his new driver's license and a platinum credit card. I hold my tongue until we're in the parking garage loading our bags into the back of the silver SUV.

"I thought we were on a budget." Grunting, I shove my carryon between the bigger bags. "We could have survived with a compact."

"We are on a budget." Gabe slams the hatch and opens the passenger door for me. Murtagh rockets out of hiding, and makes a show of inspecting our luggage, and then the rest of the car. "After all my experiences with demons," Gabe continues, "I'd rather be safe than sorry. A compact is lightweight and can be manipulated with strong gusts of wind. I prefer a more solidly built heavy car that can handle rough terrain. Abby and I have almost died way too many times for me to take chances on a tin-can compact."

"Good point."

"Transport good," Murtagh announces, landing lightly on the middle console. "No demon here."

"Glad to hear it." Gabe starts the car and adjusts the mirrors.

I don't want to dwell on how much experience Gabe has dealing with these demons, as opposed to me—who has little to none. Focusing on what I don't know will only freak me out. "I assume you know where we're going?"

"I have Tanya's address, and my phone has GPS, so one way or another we'll find it." He pulls the phone out and taps the screen until a voice tells him which way to exit the garage.

"Are we staying there for the night then? At Tanya's house?"

He pulls out of the stall and heads toward the exit. "That's my plan. Why? Would you rather stay at a hotel?"

"Oh. Um, no, that's fine." I hope Tanya has a couch so one of us doesn't have to sleep on the floor. Gabe's not over Abby, and I'm mourning Alex. Sharing her bed would just be weird at this point, however innocent the circumstances.

Streetlights blink to life as the sky darkens to deep indigo, but the November air is warm, with no trace of impending winter, and I happily toss my jacket in the backseat. "If her complex has a pool, I vote we take a swim break tomorrow."

239

"Or a Jacuzzi one tonight," he adds, "If it's not too late when we get there."

"I like the way you think."

Gabe's phone spouts directions and I roll down the window and let the desert wind pound my face and whip my hair with a freedom I haven't felt since I first arrived in Mexico.

I loved Alejandro. In the short time we had together, we became close in a way that was uniquely ours. We were friends. We talked, and when we weren't talking, we were making out.

The memory of his lips, his hands, nudges in, and I cringe away from the pain until I realize that the blade isn't as sharp as it was a month ago. The air smells like sunshine and desert blooms— though the sun has set and the blooms closed for the night—I tip my head against the seat and allow the memories to flow.

When Alex finally gave me my dance lesson in the bar in Mexico.

And later in the garden, his lips on mine, the lingering tang of tequila and salt. He had an exotic flare that thrilled me at the same time it scared me, and though I had been attracted to him since moment one, that kiss was the instant I knew I was in trouble. I was falling for him, whether I wanted to or not.

A niggle of discomfort worms along my skin. If I truly loved him, why doesn't losing him hurt as badly today as it did when I got home?

"What are you thinking about?" Gabe breaks into my musing.

I turn my head, facing him instead of the window. Of everyone in the world, Gabe will understand, and maybe help me puzzle it out. I trust him. "Honestly?"

He offers a one-shouldered shrug. "Yeah. Why not."

"I'm thinking about Alejandro. It's weird, because I only knew him for a few weeks, but I cared about him. A lot. When I first got home, I thought memories of him would consume me forever."

"And now they're not?"

"No," I admit. "Well, I mean, they are. I still think about him every day. Several times a day. But my heart doesn't ache as badly when those thoughts sneak in. Sometimes it still gouges holes in me, but I've accepted his death well enough to think of him without dissolving into tears every single time."

"I get what you mean," he admits. "I keep thinking I don't *want* to get over Abby. Because what if she comes back and changes her mind? She was so mad at Kye before he showed up, and I'm sure she'll feel that again, eventually. But the longer she stays gone, the less it stings to not have her here. I still want her—like I'm sure you would want Alex if he could come back—" He stutters a bit upon hearing his words. "I mean, um ..." He swears. "Sorry. That came out wrong."

The old Rose would have flipped over this, but I'm not that girl anymore. "To be honest, I'd rather not have a zombie boyfriend. I'd prefer that he hadn't died than to having him come back. For the record."

Gabe lets out a relieved sigh. "I'm sorry," he says. "I didn't mean it to come out that way. I don't want to rub salt in your wounds. I should shut up about Abby. Even though she ran off with another guy, she's still alive ..." He lets out a low groan, once again hearing his words as they fall out of his mouth, rather than before. "Sorry."

Gabe's honest apology does the thing that my memories couldn't and brings my emotions to the surface. A lump forms in my throat and pressure builds behind my eyes. "He died," I admit, unable to keep the grief from spilling from my voice. "Alex died, Gabe. I haven't forgotten. I'll never forget. I don't think I can, and I wouldn't want to. But I need you to do something for me, okay? Something that no one else will do."

He nods, his distress evident as he takes my hand, lacing our fingers together. "First tell me what it is. Don't make me promise to kill you. I won't do that."

Murtagh blinks. "Dragon no anyone kill," he sputters. "Protect warrior queen friend."

A watery laugh bubbles up and past the lump. Gabe has always known how to stir my emotions into a mess. I'm never bored with him. "Don't worry, Murtagh. Gabe couldn't kill me if he tried.

Unlike Abby, I have this indomitable will to live, and no intention of sacrificing myself."

Now it's Gabe's turn to laugh. "Well, I'm glad to hear that. I always used to feel like Abby was looking for new ways to face death."

"Ha. Yeah, that's not me." I shift in my seat, but leave my hand engulfed in his large, protective one. It feels nice, this close contact that is both casual and intimate. Reassuring and safe. "It's nothing like that. I want you to promise not to avoid talking about him. About what happened, and the fact that he died."

He takes his eyes off the road long enough to shoot me a questioning look. "I'm not sure what you mean. Can you clarify?"

A few deep breaths, coupled with our connected hands, help to steady me. "I'm not fragile about it. Not if I take it head-on. It's harder for me to deal with people who refuse to face reality than it is to accept what's happened and move forward. I'm not asking you to bring him up every day, but when the topic comes up naturally, or when I tell you that I'm thinking of him—don't change the subject thinking you can protect me from my pain, okay? Acknowledge it. Allow me to acknowledge it and grieve. Alex died. My boyfriend died a horrible, painful death."

I pause to swallow. "It's possible I'll never get over that. But I won't pretend that it didn't happen, and I don't want the people I love to avoid me because of this thing they're afraid to discuss. It happened, and it sucks." Warm tears drip from my eyes, and I have no choice but to let them fall. "But *I'm* still here. I may never be whole again, but I'm here, and I won't forget him. Alex existed and was a part of my life. I don't want to forget him. So let me talk about him, okay?"

Gabe nods his agreement.

"And when I do talk about Alex, respond, tell me your thoughts, your memories, or anything else. Don't hold back, because I can tell when people do that. It creates distance in the conversation, and then it doesn't feel real, and I need real conversation, Gabe. The same way I need to remember Alex."

"Okay." He squeezes my hand. "Rose, I promise that you can talk about Alex all you want, and I'll never judge you, or chastise you, or be upset over it for any reason, and if I have something to add, I'll share it."

"Thank you." I bring our joined hands to my lips, press them there. "Thanks."

"You're welcome. It's the least you deserve. I can't imagine how strong you have to be that we're having this conversation. I wouldn't be functioning so well if it was Abby who had died that day."

I don't know why, but his broken-hearted comment makes a laugh bubble out of me. "Oh, I'm sure. You'd be a bigger mess than me."

He laughs, too. "I would."

Gabe's GPS directs us to a parking lot, and minutes later we find the correct building and apartment number. Murtagh comes inside with us, hiding in my hair to avoid being seen. Gabe knocks, and after a short wait, he slides the key in the lock. Before he can turn it, the door swings open—not fully latched. His intake of breath sets my nerves on edge as we step inside.

Every cupboard in the kitchen is open, the contents spilled onto the counter and floor. The couch is ripped to shreds and the cushions strewn throughout the living space. Papers, books, and wall hangings have been thrown into a huge pile in the middle of the rug. There's nothing on the walls or along the edges of the room except a computer desk on which rests an old refurbished laptop (obviously refurbished, because it's so huge and thick, there's no way it's newer than seven years). It's open to an email inbox.

"Wow." I crane my neck, searching for a way to make light of the grim situation. "I mean, Kye and Abby are messy, but I lived with them in Mexico. Even they aren't this bad."

Murtagh flutters through the room, occasionally alighting on piles of mess. "Bad, bad, bad. Very bad."

"Tanya's been burglarized." Gabe states the obvious as if he can't believe what he's seeing.

Neither of us moves to step inside, both afraid to disturb the mess. After several long seconds of staring, I tiptoe across the tile, avoiding crunching broken bits of glass. "Who would have done this?"

Gabe follows me, pinching the bridge of his nose. "I don't get the impression that Tanya had valuables that would appeal to robbers, so either someone came looking for *her*, or ..."

"They were here for Kye and Abby." I dig through the pile, searching for traces of clues. "You don't think they've been kidnapped again, do you?"

Gabe's voice cracks. "I hope not."

In a rare moment of clarity, I realize that Abby being alive doesn't lessen Gabe's grief, or make his pain better or worse than mine. Just different. He knows she's out there somewhere, and has an added layer of worry, because for the last year, he's been her protector—and now she's out of reach. Gabe loves Abby the way I loved Alex, and this journey of ours is almost certainly harder for him than me, because he already knows that no matter what happens—whether we're successful or not—he'll lose her anyway. She was never his to keep, any more than I get to keep Alex.

Gabe stares at the chaos, wearing the most helpless, destroyed look I've ever seen on him. This is not the time to discuss feelings. One of us has to do something. One of us has to be the person who can think past the mess and find the clues. "Do you think we should call the police?"

"I don't know." He kicks half of a decorative pillow out of the way, and then starts sifting the edge of the pile with his shoe. "Maybe."

"Maybe we should call the Dragons? I mean, I know we were trying to keep this trip a secret, but maybe we make up a story and get them over here to see what's what. Then they'll know something's wrong and stop fighting with each other long enough to investigate."

He stumbles down the short hallway and pokes his head inside what can only be the bedroom, and then the single bathroom.

"Yeah, the burglars ripped the place apart. The police would be better."

"I wonder what they were looking for." I continue moving Tanya's ruined things, hoping for something, anything. In the kitchen, Murtagh bangs cabinets and drawers, and I assume he's trying to help.

"Either a Key or a weapon," Gabe says from the other room. "We all have amplifying crystals or other tokens. Tanya might have something good. From what I can see, she doesn't own anything else of value."

"If she did own something like that, she'd be stupid not to have taken it with her when they left. How can the Elen not know that?" I stand to move to another section of the pile, and my eyes land on the computer, the open email. Strange that they left while still signed in. I trip across the room for a closer look.

"I agree that none of this makes sense," he says.

A quick scroll tells me that the burglars were looking for clues to Abby—and they found exactly that. The open email is a rental confirmation for a house in small town Utah. My nerves roll. Whoever destroyed this apartment has already seen this. They're probably already on their way there. I forward the email to myself, and then print it.

The only question now is why they picked this particular town, because it's not the kind of place where you go because you're passing through. It's out of the way, high in the mountains. There must be a reason.

Gabe comes out of the bedroom, his olive skin a sickly shade of white. "Whatever the robbers were after, they've either found it and are long gone, or they decided it's not here and moved on."

I stand to retrieve the printout and stop long enough to rest my calming hands on Gabe's muscular shoulders. "There's no sign of a struggle out here. Is there any in there?"

"No," he admits, and I can see the relief trickling in as the tightness in his eyes relaxes a degree. "Abby would have fought back, so if they were here when this happened, there would be something. Whoever did this left nothing uninspected. Nothing. The baby's diapers are shredded."

"No blood? No broken crystals left as a distress sign?"

"Not that I can see."

"Then we have to assume they're safe." I have to help him stay grounded to keep him from losing his cool. "And look." The printout crinkles in my hand as I wave them at him. "They reserved a short-term rental in a resort town in Utah. This must be where they went."

Gabe snatches the printout, his eyes roaming over it. "Do we know why there?"

"No, but we'll figure it out." I nudge him toward the door. "In the meantime, I'm not comfortable staying here tonight. The burglars may be long gone, but they might not be, and I don't want to be present if they decide to come back. Let's get a hotel. If we can't afford it, I'll call my parents and see if they'll let us use their credit card for the night."

Gabe cracks a smile—his first since coming inside the apartment. "That won't be necessary. Landon gave me Kye's platinum card."

"The one issued by the Dragons? We can't use that! They'll swarm us."

"So?"

"So if they swarm us, they'll haul us back to Jackson by morning."

Gabe laughs. "They might show up, but no one hauls me anywhere I don't want to go. We're adults, and despite the fact that Val and Zane think they get to control us—they don't. I'd like to see them try to force me into something I don't want to do. Not going to happen. So the worst thing they can do is cancel the card—and if they do, I have a backup."

"The backup—it's your own?"

He ducks his head. "Obviously."

"Are we going to get in trouble for unauthorized use?"

Gabe shakes his head. "Landon Akers is a signing party on this card." He pulls out his wallet and shows me his new ID, boasting that exact name.

I can't help it. I laugh, hard. "You two are clever. I'll give you that."

"And they can't charge me for fraud if they found out I'm not him, because I have Landon's permission. We need to bring Abby and Valdemar together in order to test the theory about restoring the empath's power. So let them chase us, Rose. What are they going to do? Follow us to Abby? That's exactly the point anyway."

I can think of a lot of things the Dragons could do, but I'm not going to point them out right now. Gabe's coming out of his funk and going into planning mode, and that's exactly where I need him to be.

Before we leave, we go through the apartment once more. When we're sure there's nothing left here that should mean anything to us, we lock the door tight. If Tanya wants us to call the police, we can come back tomorrow. If she wants to notify the Dragons, that's going to have to wait until we're gone. If she wants us to leave everything alone until she can get back here—well, that's her call to make.

THIRTY-FIVE

A Lifetime of Nightmares

ABBY

After a long soak and some detoxifying oils, I calm enough to remember that I can't go home. Not yet. Kye can't get into my old house without me. But the sooner he does—the sooner we resolve whatever happened there—the sooner we can both go home.

I don't want to run anymore. I'd rather face the Dragons and Valdemar and whoever else is trying to keep us apart. If they wanted to drive a wedge between us, they have, and it's not one easily removed—if it can be removed at all. Maybe it's time for us to stop running and stand up to *all* of them. Maybe it's time for me to call my *own* shots, make my *own* decisions. Maybe it's time for Kye to do that too.

Now that I'm no longer Gifted, no longer a Healer or a Seer or the Queen of Light—maybe they'll stop demanding that I do things their way. Maybe they'll leave me alone to live a normal, human existence. Maybe Kye will move on, and Gabe too. And Rose. Maybe I'll move somewhere with my mom and we can start new again. The idea is not the least bit appealing, but if Gram and my mother have taught me one thing, it's that there are always other options.

"Maybe we should move to Ireland," I tell the mirror as I dry my hair and coat my skin with calming herbal cream. Clearly that's where my dad planned to end up.

I'm quite certain that having me move to Ireland—or another country anywhere—is not what my father would have wanted. If everything I've learned is true, then he gave his life trying to bring the Gifted together. He wanted us to lean on each other, to help each other. He wanted me to be with these crazy, kooky people, for better or worse. Not that I want to know what could be worse than what we've already experienced, but I can't live with allowing my father to have died in vain. So Ireland can't be on my list of options yet.

Chills run up and down my arms and back as I pull on my sleep shorts and tank. I'm not packed for winter, and this mountain town is cooler than Phoenix or Texas or Mexico, so I drag on the only sweatshirt I brought. I'm going to have to buy a coat, and shoes that are thicker than the flimsy canvas beachcombers I've been wearing.

I don't have the money to fulfill all my winter-clothing wishes—but I can spring for some inexpensive basics if I shop wisely.

Frozen air seeps through the window glass and presses in on me. I wish I wasn't fighting with Kye. I've become accustomed to relying on his body heat.

As if he's reading my thoughts, Kye knocks. "I'm leaving you an extra blanket. It's going to get cold tonight."

I open the door to accept the offering, and notice that he's wearing flannel pajamas. "Where did you get those?"

"I brought them with me," he says. "It's been too hot to wear them."

"Why did you pack flannel pajamas for Mexico?"

He sighs. "Because I'm used to staying longer than I intend in places I haven't planned to go. I've learned the hard way to pack as if I'm spending a day in every season. Keeps me prepared. Plus, my mother sent them to me last Christmas. I wanted her to see me wearing them once."

"Too bad you never had the chance." I glance at my bare legs, fighting envy for the soft, thick flannel. Kye glimpses too. "Don't you have anything else?"

I shake my head. "You've seen everything I brought with me, a number of times. It's all summer appropriate."

"We're heading into winter," he points out.

I'm not in the mood for sarcasm or irony, and reply with raised eyebrows. "I left Jackson in May, to spend an indefinite amount of time in a tropical paradise. Forgive me if I didn't pack my parka. Right now I'm grateful I packed a sweatshirt, because I almost didn't."

"Tomorrow," he says, "picking up warm clothes for you is top priority. The faeries have warned me that winter is coming, fast. Sheer sleeves and shorts aren't going to be enough anymore."

My lips press together to hold back the impulse to shriek at him about how the faeries predictions would have been nice to know before the big storm was about to hit.

He returns to his room, leaving my door ajar, and comes back a minute later having changed, and hands me the flannel pajamas. "These are the warmest I have. You'll need them more than I do."

I accept, knowing it would be futile to argue. "Thank you. It's very sweet."

He closes his eyes, attempting to hide the pain that's radiating off of him, and failing. "I don't want you to freeze to death." He turns and adjusts the thermostat. "I'm going to crank this up so we get good and toasty. You won't even know a cold front has hit."

The texture of the flannel indulges my fingers in fuzzy warmth as I stroke them, wishing I knew what to say to fix things between us. The awkward silence grows, until he says, "There's chicken in the kitchen if you're hungry. That will help too, because—"

"We burn more calories trying to keep warm," I finish. "I am hungry, and thank you. Did you eat?"

"A little. Wasn't sure if you'd be coming out or not, so I didn't wait. Sorry."

I shake my head. "No big deal."

"I was going to get ready for bed, but if you want company while you eat, I can wait."

This awkwardness is so thick I don't think I can take anymore. "You don't need to wait up for me if you're tired. I'm going to bed soon myself." We both glance in the direction of the clock, knowing it's early.

"Fine." He pivots toward his room. "Goodnight, Abby."

I convince myself it's natural for us to retreat like this. We've been together, nonstop, since Kye showed up in Mexico. It's okay to be anxious for some distance. I love Kye. I've loved him from the minute I first saw him, and I'll love him for the rest of forever. But right now the idea of forcing a conversation with him is exhausting. When I hear the latch on his bedroom door click, I sigh in relief, and head to the kitchen to warm up my dinner, trying not to wonder if this is the beginning of the end.

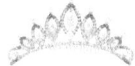

I wake the moment the power goes out, and the silence in the house becomes absolute. The buzz from the fridge, the hum of the furnace, the nearly inaudible electric whir coming from the digital clocks. All of it stops, leaving behind an eerie, frightening muteness that sends my heartrate into overdrive. Minutes later, the wind screeches in like a train that's hit its breaks for an unprepared stop. All of this happens in the blackness of a moonless night.

Fear freezes me in place, wide-eyed and shaking as I fight to convince myself that it's the storm Kye warned me was coming. But no matter how I spread the logic, my brain is convinced that the demons have come for us, and there's nothing I can do to stop them.

I pull the blankets over my head and burrow in, quivering with fear as memories of my recent past crash in, weighing on my chest and shoving me into a full-blown panic attack.

251

Instinct begs me to yell for Kye, or scream, or cry, or move, but I can't. I attempt to summon my Light, reaching into every part of myself where I have ever felt the slightest thread of power, but there's nothing. It feels like hours pass as I lie there listening for the screeching and wailing to bring my nightmares to life, clutching the blankets so tight that my knuckles go numb.

Eventually, the noise calms. I stick my arm out from under the covers and feel on the nightstand for the remote, planning to turn the TV on loud—but the power's still out. Teeth chattering once again, I try to summon the courage to get up and go into Kye's room. I wish I dared look out the window to see the storm, gauge if it's demons, or shadows, or a big winter thing hitting us hard in the lee of the mountains.

Despite my best efforts, fear keeps me immobile, so I remain in position, still and shivering, until I fall into a fitful, restless sleep.

I dream of three glorious and radiant women, tall and statuesque, and more goddess-like than the last time I saw them. This time golden light shines like a halo around them, through them, accentuating their individual shades of hair and giving the appearance of them standing inside a fire.

Morrigan speaks first. "You are afraid, dear one. Fear not. Your mothers have not deserted you."

Macha is next. "To restore balance, you must finish the thing which was begun in the time of Raina."

And last, Badb, "A great battle is coming. Many will die. You cannot save them."

The images flicker, and I fight to keep them steady, because I have so many questions. "How do I get my Gifts back?" I ask, breathless with need. "Who is going to die? How do I restore balance?"

"You and Theron must save the one you love above all others," Morrigan says, her voice waning as the images fade.

"You must restore the powers of the empath," Macha says, her voice distant.

Badb finishes with words that are nearly too quiet for me to hear, "You must destroy the last standing enemy."

When their voices return, they're in unison. "The time has come to face your fate. Delay no longer."

In the next image, Alejandro, still alive, falls into a pool of Acid in Yellowstone and burns to death in front of me. Then he's there again, fighting shadows that somehow cover him with mud from one of the mud pots. He's trampled by a bison, eaten by a wolf—I see Alejandro die in a hundred different ways, all of them equally gruesome and horrid, and never can I find a way to save him.

I jerk awake and peek out from the covers, praying that the storm is over and morning has come, but the night is still black, and the moaning and screeching outside continues. I'm still alone.

Kye pounds on the door. "Abby, are you okay? I need you to answer, because unless you tell me otherwise, I'm coming in."

I'm so traumatized that I can't speak, but as the doorknob turns, I manage a weak, "Kye."

He stops in the doorway, allowing his eyes to adjust. "You're okay?"

I shake my head as well as I can, relief trickling in drop by drop, because I don't have to be alone anymore. "I'm panicking. The demons are here. They're going to kill everyone and there's nothing I can do to stop them."

Kye scoots in next to me and stretches out under the covers, pulling me into his arms and humming a soothing tone. "We're okay. It's just a storm. Just a storm."

"We're going to die," I tell him. "I can't save anyone."

"Sleep, Abby. I'm here." He strokes my hair, my cheek, my neck. "We'll be okay."

I have no energy left to argue, and he's warm and familiar and safe. Never in my life have I slept as well as I do when Kye's with me. It's like my body remembers that we're two halves of a whole. He continues to murmur soothing words, continues stroking my face, continues to hold me tight until I relax against him. Finally the panic subsides and my muscles loosen, and with a last shiver of terror I cling to him and fall asleep.

This time, I don't dream at all.

THIRTY-SIX

Taken

ROSE

We find a reputable chain hotel a few miles from Tanya's house, and decide to stay there for the night until we can call Tanya and ask what she wants us to do about her apartment. We both know there's no point in attempting to get to Utah tonight. It's a long drive, and if we're going to fly, we won't get a flight until morning. Though I can tell Gabe is worried—we both are—neither of us feels like we have reason to rush there in a panic yet.

The hotel isn't the Mexico bungalows, but the lobby's clean and nicely decorated, and their ads claim they have comfortable beds. Gabe checks us in and hands me a key. "You're in 201 and I'm next door in 203."

I shouldn't have worried, but I'm crazy relieved that Gabe didn't get one room with two beds. We're friends, but I still need my space, and he needs his too. Since this expense isn't coming out of our pockets, I appreciate him doing what makes us most comfortable.

Since getting a separate room for Murtagh isn't an option, I offer to let him stay with me. He comes out of hiding as soon as I close the door, fluttering around the room and blinking like a strobe. "Bad, bad things happen, *Agno*. Murtagh must leave, must go. Find warrior queen, bring home."

"Tomorrow, Murtagh." I set my toiletry bag on the bathroom counter and shove my suitcase in the closet . "We can't do anything more tonight. Don't worry. Abby will be okay."

From the way he buzzes between the window and the door, it's clear he doesn't believe me. "Meet there," he squeaks. "Murtagh travel faster than human."

At a loss for words, I hold out my hand so he can land on it. "You're ... leaving? Already?"

He bobs, his wings fluttering so quickly I can barely see them. "Dragon find. Time to end cycle now."

Murtagh's a sprite, and I've never pretended to understand creatures of his ilk, but I know he can take care of himself, and if he decides to go after Abby in the dead of night, he'll likely find her before we do. So I blow him a little kiss and open the door. "Be careful," I beg him, and add, "See you soon," as I watch him zoom off.

I knock on Gabe's door, my stomach complaining loudly. He answers, still wearing shoes, and with his key-card in hand. It's like he read my mind—or my stomach. "Food?"

I blink. "Yep."

"Where?"

"Somewhere close. I'm starving."

He joins me in the hall. "We could see what's on the menu at the hotel bar, or there's a café across the street. If neither of those is acceptable, we might have to drive."

"Let's check the menu at the bar." I lead the way to the elevator, hoping Murtagh managed to find his way out. "I could go for nachos or a sandwich—anything. As long as it's food."

"Did you bring your new ID?" he asks. "They might not let you in without proof that you're legal—which you aren't, because we're in the States now—but we'll ignore that detail in favor of getting food as fast as possible."

255

My defensive side rears. "If you're about to tell me I can't order a drink, you're better off swallowing that statement and choking on it. I haven't gotten drunk since Alex died, and under the circumstances, maybe it's time I did a shot of tequila in his honor." The elevator arrives, and Gabe follows me inside.

"That's a bad idea." He leans against the wall as the doors close behind us. "For a plethora of reasons. Don't you remember what happened last time you and Abby got into the tequila?"

How could I forget? I danced with Alex and fell in love with him on the dancefloor. I drank the good stuff that gave me the pleasant buzz without a stomachache, and then Alex and I strolled in the garden, where he kissed me for the first time.

"I learned to Salsa dance," I tell Gabe, allowing my glare to become an invitation to argue.

"And Abby almost got kidnapped," he points out.

"But she didn't."

"But it started a chain of events that led to ..." he says, prodding the sore spots that I don't feel like testing anymore tonight.

"If you want me to associate Alex's death with us being at the bar, you're going to take me down the path of ultimate guilt—and I'm not going there. Not right now. Thanks anyway."

"I'm not trying to make you feel guilty," he says gently. "The point is that drinking has never done either of us any favors."

The elevator comes to a stop and the doors slide open to reveal the lobby.

"Oh, right." I stomp toward the restaurant, but whirl on him before I get there. "Like you never benefited from Abby being drunk. Are you telling me that her kissing you that night before Kye showed up was a mistake? That it didn't change your world?"

He swallows audibly. "Obviously it didn't change my world, or my outcome, but it wasn't a mistake."

"Are you going to tell me you wish she hadn't figured out how to numb her pain enough to give you the one thing you'd been wanting for months?"

"No. That was ... it was an unforeseen benefit. But look where it got me, Rose. Miserable, and pining for Abby while the two of us hide away in Phoenix. I don't know what we're doing here. We should be on our way to Utah already."

"Yeah, that's going to do us a lot of good. Because clearly, the faster we get there, the faster she can reject you. Again."

His entire being sags like I've let the air out of his balloon. "She's not meant to be mine. I get it. Doesn't stop the want."

I understand that feeling well, and because I do, I tamp down the urge to slap him with more obvious facts. Gabe has gotten my point, and I will get my tequila. We take a seat at the counter and snag a menu from between the salt and pepper shakers. I order a margarita with my nachos, but Gabe sticks with lemon water. I want to give him a hard time about this, find out why he's so on edge, but I'm not in the mood to fight with someone who's too blue to spar.

We eat in relative silence, lost in the sitcom that's playing on a TV in the corner. I'm comfortable in Gabe's company—even though we're not talking. He's like an acquired taste. Kind of grows on a girl.

The watered-down margarita barely relaxes me, but in the spirit of keeping the peace, I decide to leave my alcohol consumption at that for tonight. As much as Gabe benefited from our partying in Mexico, he's also right that Alex paid a high price for not being at the top of his game. I recognize that when I think about it logically, mechanically.

We chat about stupid things that don't matter. Weather patterns between Phoenix and Utah. Whether we should fly or drive. Jewelry stands on the Native American reservations. The Grand Canyon—which I've never seen. If we weren't in such a hurry, I'd vote for the road trip. But we are in a hurry, so the idea of driving is a pipe dream—and we both know it. "By the way," I mention, "Murtagh left."

His brow furrows. "He did? Why?"

I shake my head. "I don't know. Something about ending the cycle. I think he was going to look for Abby, though, so we'll probably run into him when we get there."

"Hope he doesn't warn them to leave before we can catch up."

"I doubt it. I think he wants to drag her home."

Gabe barks a laugh. "Don't we all."

When we're finished with our food, we head back to the rooms and end up standing in the hallway talking for more than ten minutes before I invite him inside.

"Thanks," he says, emotionally and physically backing away a step. "But I shouldn't."

"You know I'm not going to jump you, right?" I tell him, leaning against the door. "I don't want to be alone, but I do want to sit down."

"I don't want to be alone either, but I'm still not coming in your room."

"Why not?"

"It's a bad idea."

"Why?"

"Rose, you lost your first love in the most horrific way possible. You don't need me confusing things further."

The absurdity of his quiet statement hits me, leaves me laughing. "Since when is talking to a woman confusing things?"

He breathes out heavily. "It just is."

I've always been the spontaneous type. I try hard to adapt, go with the flow, and jump on opportunities before they wheel out of town.

Kissing Gabe, in this moment, is a knee-jerk reaction, a totally spontaneous and thoughtless thing that just sort of ... happens. But kiss him, I do. I don't know why either, but he reacts by resting his hands on my hips and dragging me closer so he can get our tongues involved. By the time one of his hands travels up and tangles in my hair, we're both flushed and breathless, and pressed against my door, where Gabe pushes ever closer.

He seems to comprehend this at the same time as me, and gently disentangles himself, starting with his lips. "I'm sorry. Don't know where that came from."

I want to punch him for being so practical, so honorable. Because I'm tired of being lonely. "Yeah, I'm sure you don't. Definitely has nothing to do with attraction."

"That's not what I meant," he stammers. "You're in mourning and—"

"I kissed you, remember? Don't you think it's up to me to decide when I'm ready to kiss someone?"

"Not when you're still grief-stricken," he insists.

I let out a long sigh. This argument will get me nowhere. "Okay, fine. Thanks for going to dinner with me." I slide my key into the slot and open the door to my room. "I'm going to bed. Goodnight."

He stands in the hall, watching me with hooded eyes as I close the door. But he doesn't hear as I'm grabbed from behind, mouth muffled by a large hand, which is then replaced by a hard wad of cloth, and my wrists and ankles bound. Gabe doesn't hear my captors overturn my suitcase to dig through my possessions, or pull apart the beautifully made bed. He's gone into his room already, so he doesn't see as these same men pick me up—fighting as fiercely as I can while bound—and haul me over the big one's shoulders and take me out to the parking lot where they shove me into the trunk of a dark sedan.

Gabe will go to bed thinking I'm pouting. He won't even know I'm gone until morning.

259

THIRTY-SEVEN

Trapped

ABBY

The next morning, I wake up in Kye's arms for the first time in days. My head pounds like a blunt object is beating on my skull, and my scabbed dagger wound throbs in a way it hasn't ached since all my powers were transferred to Cole in Phoenix. Kye's awake, staring at the curtained window, and says nothing as I sit up, groaning with every movement.

"Thanks." I wish I wasn't such a wimp. Wish I didn't need to be held and reassured in the middle of the night to keep the nightmares at bay.

He presses his lips together as if holding in what's on his mind, and I let it be. I'm miserable, achy, and cold, and not up to arguing.

"Have you had a lot of panic attacks lately?" he finally asks. "Intense like that?"

I brush my wild bed-hair away from my eyes and blink to focus in the dim room. "A few," I admit. "They always eventually pass."

"You didn't panic like that in Mexico," he muses. "Or Texas."

I wasn't alone in Mexico or Texas. "I've had nightmares all along. They haven't affected me this way."

He presses his fingers to his eyes. "You're different than you were before. I don't know what to do with that."

When he says *before*, he means before I lost my Gifts. He's right. "I am different. I don't know what to do with it either."

He sits up, letting the blanket fall to rest at his waist while he takes my hand in both of his. "We can get through this. I don't think your loss of Gifts is permanent, but even if it is, this is a bump in the road. We've climbed rockier terrain before."

I don't want to have this discussion right now. I'm hungry and tired and so cold. I withdraw my hand from his and pull the extra blanket tighter. "How about some breakfast?"

He sighs in frustration. "Breakfast would be great, but it'll have to be simple. Power's still out."

No wonder it's so cold. "Good thing we bought fruit and granola."

His breath rushes out in a whoosh as his feet touch the freezing wood floor. "It's a good thing we bought groceries at all. If we'd planned to only eat out, we'd be starving for the rest of today. Maybe longer."

"What do you mean we can't go out?" I stumble to the window and pull up the blinds. The world glistens in blinding white. The top-most layer of it nearly reaches the windowsill, which is higher than my waist. "What are we supposed to do now?"

"First we'll try the fireplace and hope it lights." Kye straightens, a shiver wracking his body as he heads into the living room. "Then we eat our uncooked breakfast and hope the power comes on soon so we can use the toaster. And the TV."

"And lights," I add, remembering too well the eerie feeling of being surrounded by demons. "I'd like lots and lots of lights."

He sits on the edge of the fireplace and turns a silver key at the bottom of the gas insert. Several long seconds later, a golden-blue flame flickers to life, spreading delicious warmth beneath the ceramic logs. "Ah ha. Fire. Should help warm us up."

"Does this mean we also have hot water?"

"Some," he says. "Though until we have power again, I wouldn't advise filling the tub."

Last night I did, so I hope the water heater refilled before the power went out. I turn into the kitchen for fruit and granola, wondering how I'm going to survive in this weather without winter clothes.

As if he can read my mind, Kye says, "You can keep those pajamas. Might need to wear them during the day to stay warm."

"Thanks." No longer hungry, I close myself in my room to crawl back under the covers. This is not how I wanted things to go when we came here.

Five days. We spend five days trapped inside the mountain cabin, and at no point during that time can we see the top of our car, the doors we would need to open to get inside, or the wheels we would have to clear so it could be driven. That's not to mention the mile-long driveway that might as well not exist. There is no shoveling out of this mess.

On the evening of the second day, the power flickers to life. We both cheer because we have a heater again, and lights, and now we can watch TV to keep our boredom at bay.

Each night I go to bed by myself, and by the wee hours of morning Kye comes in to wake me from my nightmares and hold me until I calm. He never asks why I don't give up the idea of keeping separate rooms. He holds me like he always has, but it feels different—*less* somehow. As if he can't stand to see me suffer, but doesn't want to always be the one picking up the pieces as I slowly and surely fall apart.

On the evening of the fifth day, we're in the living room watching an old movie as the wind howls outside and more snow falls, when Kye starts to implode. He bolts upright during a love scene and announces, "I'm hungry," then roots through what's left of our sparse supplies.

We've made a concerted effort to ration the groceries, since we only bought enough for a few days. But with nothing to do besides sleep, watch TV, and read Tanya's family journals—again—it's been tough to fight the instinct to snack.

"Do we have any more apples?" he asks, staring into the fridge.

"I doubt it." He ate the last one yesterday, but if he doesn't remember, I'm not going to remind him. "Try some grapes."

He shakes his head. "They're gone too."

I finished the berries an hour ago. We're indeed at the end of everything. "A sandwich?" I suggest, hoping we still have bread. "I think there's cheese and some lunch meat."

"We're down to crackers and dry granola," He says.

"Do we have eggs?"

He looks, then sighs with relief. "Three. We have three eggs, a sliver of cheese, and two slices of lunch meat."

I join him in the kitchen. "Omelets. That's what's for dinner."

Kye runs both hands through his hair, a sure sign of stress. "We have to get out of here. Go to the store. Get you some clothes. We need to get to your old house and close up shop on those demons so we can leave this depressing town. I hate it here."

I'm not loving it either, but I don't want to facilitate his breakdown—or whatever it is—so I keep my mouth shut and scramble eggs in a bowl, then work on shredding the cheese.

"How are you not going stir crazy right now?" He wanders from room to tiny room. "We have so much to do and we're trapped. Doesn't that bother you?"

"I am stir crazy." I add in the last of the meat. "In case you haven't noticed, I have panic attacks every night since we got here. I can barely stay calm during the day when my brain is functioning, and thinking is only pastime. It takes a lot of effort for me to not lose control. A lot. So forgive me if I don't join you right now, because between the two of us, one person has to remain at least semi-rational."

"I wish we had Jen with us," he says. "She could melt all this snow and get us out of here so we never have to come back."

We're so close to my old house, the last place where I saw my daddy alive, and I hate that I may never get the closure I've come here for. "I'm not ready to leave yet." I pull out a skillet and turn on the gas burner to heat it. "Not until we go to my house."

"Abby, there's a portal there. I hate to point out the obvious, but you can't close it. I don't know how to close it without the help of your Light. We're better off leaving while we're still alive, and sending someone back to clean things up later."

His words send a knife into the softest part of my heart. "Who would you send to clean things up?"

He moves his pacing in front of the breakfast bar, jittering with restless energy. Kye was meant for outdoors. He's not a guy who does well being trapped inside. "I don't know. Landon. Valdemar. Or Zane. Someone who can do what we can't."

What he means is that he wants to send someone who still has a useful Gift. I don't blame him, but after we visited the house the other day, I wonder if my lack of Gifts might be useful in its own way. I did get him through the energetic blockage at the edge of the property. Just because I can't see demons doesn't mean I can't find a way to defeat them. Religious people claim to do it all the time. Why shouldn't I?

The diamond I've worn around my waist since the day I met the Morrigana warms faintly. I press my hand to my belly, hoping, but the stone feels cold against my fingers, and no amount of probing brings forth the slightest hint of warmth. Probably wishful thinking. I pour half of the egg mixture into the hot skillet and swirl it around the bottom. Kye's still pacing, and if his nerves set off mine, panic creeps in, so I focus on the task of cooking, flipping the omelet at precisely the right moment, and then sliding it onto a plate at the perfect level of doneness. Then I start the second one.

I try to hand the plate to Kye, but he's too worked up to see that I've cooked the last of our food and am offering it to him. I set his plate on the counter next to our check-in booklet, and my gaze lands on the list of amenities.

"Remember how the resort has grocery service?" I swirl the pan with the second omelet, and when Kye doesn't reply, continue talking. "The check-in lady said to call if we need anything. Maybe they deliver during snowstorms. They might have ATVs or a snow plow. We could ask them to bring me some sweats or something from whatever store they have in town."

He takes a break from his pacing, momentarily distracted from the cabin fever. "Worth a try. If they can go out, they can get someone to plow our road."

I flip the omelet, hiding my grin as Kye switches gears and leafs through the rental booklet. "I've cooked the last of our food. We literally have nothing left to eat. So we have to do something or risk starving to death, and I don't know about you, but after everything we've been through, it would be the worst type of humiliation to die of starvation after surviving the demons that have been on our heels for the last year."

He barks a laugh and picks up the phone from the cradle. It takes a few minutes, and lots of talking, but when he hangs up, Kye, grinning, swoops over and picks me up. "Have I ever told you you're brilliant?"

"Not recently. What did she say?" My heart races at the spark that's returned to his eyes. I've missed that spark. I've missed the laughter that used to come so easily to him.

"I gave her a list of grocery requests and a budget, and asked her to find you some warm clothes—preferably sweaters, long sleeved T-shirts, and jeans. While she was on the phone, she asked if we needed our roadway plowed, and I told her we've been snowed in for five days. She seemed embarrassed that they haven't made it up here to dig us out for so long. They're sending a plow right now."

My feeling of elation wilts. The funny thing about life is how occasionally, in the moment that you get a thing you've been praying for, you're suddenly disappointed over not getting to see what would have happened if your prayer wasn't summarily answered. We've spent days hoping to somehow be rescued—sprung from our snow-bound prison—but as Kye swings me back and forth, dancing in celebration, dread forms in the pit of my stomach. I don't understand, because obviously this is fantastic news. We won't starve to death, I won't freeze to death, and the road will be plowed enough so we can get out when we need to. It also means that our journey is coming to an end, and we're still far from deciding if we have a future together.

I had hopes of everything working out and being tied up in a neat little bow. But I should have learned by now that my life doesn't work that way. Unfortunately, it never will.

THIRTY-EIGHT

Hostage

ROSE

It's dark in this trunk, and cold, but I'm grateful for the chill because it helps numb the ache throbbing in my shoulders after being bound for so long. It's been hours. We're moving—driving somewhere far from Phoenix. I have no way to gauge how long we've been traveling until pink-ish beams of light smile through the cracks near the hatch. Sunrise. Five hours, maybe six.

The light helps me to see better, but aside from an emergency blanket and empty gas can, there's nothing back here that I can use as a weapon, or to help me escape.

The car slows to a stop. I hear the tell-tale sounds of the gas tank filling, along with a short, mumbled exchange of words. We must be somewhere public, and it's daytime now. Knowing this could be my only chance, I kick the top of the hatch, hard, choking on the gag as I attempt to scream through it. Eventually, the trunk clicks open, and light floods my eyes. Squinting, I scoot as far into the back as possible.

"What do you think you're doing, little girl?"

I blink, squinting to see more than a shadowed halo. My captor stands with one hand on the trunk hatch and the other bouncing the keys on his palm. It's the man from the club in Mexico—the one who tried to kidnap Abby, and then later stabbed her with the dagger. She called him Boone—I'm not so nice as to call him by name—even if it's a dumb one. I mean seriously, last time I checked, America is no longer the wild frontier. But who knows if we're still in America? Maybe we *are* in the wild frontier. I wonder if this guy owns a coonskin hat and if his first name is Daniel?

I attempt to spit the gag out and reply, but Boone shoves it back in and tightens it. "Oh no you don't. If you think I'm going to let you hypnotize us all again, you're not as smart as your counterparts."

I *was* planning to hypnotize them, and I resent being compared to Abby. Fortunately, training with Gabe has taught me to be patient, to wait for the right opportunity.

Without being able to use my voice or my hands, I send begging glances with my eyes, my body rocking with the effort of conveying my message.

My captor shakes his head. "Sick of being in that trunk, are ya?" To my surprise, he and one of his cronies reach in and grab me by the upper arms and drag me out until I'm standing—however precariously—on my bound feet.

This is going to be interesting.

Boone's tall and lanky, with thick chorded muscles that pop out of his neck, and disheveled dark hair that mostly covers his crazy-scary violet eyes. He appraises me like a piece of meat, which makes my skin crawl. It's no wonder Abby's afraid of him. I wish Gabe was here. Not that I want him to be captive too, because if he *was* captive, how could he save me? I don't expect him to come running to my rescue, but I have more confidence when I'm with him. I feel invincible and secure having him near, and less alone. Until this moment, I hadn't realized how much I've come to hate being alone.

But Gabe can't save me now. In all probability, he doesn't realize I'm gone yet, and once he does, he won't have the first clue where to look for me. Maybe he'll think I left because I was sick of him. I've been awful enough to him in the past. I hope our differences are no longer an issue.

"Look girlie, here's how this is going to go," Boone says. "Drake," he nods at the guy who helped drag me out of the car, "is going to free your feet. It's your lucky day, because that's a new car, and I don't want you messing in it, so you're going to use the toilet before we get back on the road."

I'm so relieved I could cry. This could be my chance.

But then he says, "Drake is going to watch you, and that gag will stay in your mouth."

My jaw already aches. I can't imagine how bad I'll hurt if I have to bite this thing much longer. And there's no way I'm letting this weirdo watch me use the toilet. Seriously. Skin crawling everywhere.

"Don't bother trying to escape." Boone's arm sweeps in an arc to encompass the run-down gas station—truly in the middle of nowhere USA. "The people running this fine establishment will do as I say, and there is no one and no place else for miles."

I'll take my chances in the desert rather than get back in this car with demons.

As if he can read my mind, he asks, "You think I'm the scariest thing you've ever met? We're in the land of the Chupacabra. I've left you alive and intact because I need you. On the other hand, that creature might be kind enough to leave you with your life, but he will take all your limbs off first and then lap up your blood while you bleed out." He leaves me behind with Drake while he goes inside the shabby store.

Maybe the demons aren't so bad.

Drake, cuts the ties binding my feet, and I shake the circulation back into them as he leads me to the back of the building—one of those disgusting outdoor gas station toilets that hasn't been cleaned since before I was born—and opens the door. Even before I go in, the smell makes me wretch. I double over, instinctively trying to spit the wadded fabric out of my mouth so I don't have to breathe through my nose, but Drake shakes his head. "No can do, princess. Leave it."

I risk a glance into the restroom, relieved that while it smells horrid, it's only moderately disgusting. As in, there doesn't appear to be feces on the walls, but I wouldn't want to touch them to find out. Glaring at Drake, I shake my arms, whining into my gag.

After a disgusted glance into the restroom, he turns his gaze on Boone. We're out of sight enough that he must feel comfortable disobeying orders, because he cuts the zip-ties from my wrists. "Don't do anything stupid." He pats a gun-shaped bulge in his waistband. "This is the only door, and if you try anything— anything at all—I will not hesitate to shoot you and get this hostage business out of our way."

So I'm to be a hostage. Well. That means these guys will be telling someone they took me. Probably the Dragons. But I'm not valuable to the Dragons, and I'm certain that they won't pay money to save me. Nor will they mount a rescue mission. They don't believe I'm special, or that I have a method of defeating demons. To them, I'm disposable. In Mexico, I was nothing more than an inconvenience with a strong opinion. At home, I've become less relevant than before—if that's possible.

If I'm to be a hostage, I'll have to save myself.

Drake waves me into the restroom and turns, standing square in the doorway with his back to me. He has the courtesy to not watch—that's a bonus. But I'm not feeling like this is the best place for me to try to escape. Anyway, I should see where they're taking me—what they're up to. What if they have also kidnapped someone else? Maybe this is my chance to do something significant—prove my worth. I use the bathroom as carefully and hygienically as possible—meaning I touch nothing—and finish by scrubbing my hands under super-hot water for as long as I can get away with it.

From the corner of my eye, I catch the reflection of a jagged shard of glass that's broken off from the mirror and fallen on the floor. I snatch it and shove it into my back pocket, then tug down the hem of my shirt to make sure it's covered, and return to washing my hands until Drake barks at me to, "Hurry up. We don't have all day."

I go with him, formulating a new survival plan. I can't count on anyone else to save me—but thanks to Gabe's training, I won't give up without a hell of a fight.

There's a split second when I hope that I might not be riding in the trunk again, but then Boone opens it and waves me in, and I have to swallow around the gag, wishing more than anything else that they would let me have some water. I try to ask for it as best I can, but they won't allow my voice to touch their ears, and to be honest, if I were them, I wouldn't either.

"In you go," Boone says. "We got a while yet."

I try again to beg for water, but he narrows his eyes at me, shaking his head. "Sorry. Can't risk freeing your Gift. Going to have to ride back here to keep us all safe."

And in the trunk I go, wishing I had something soft to lie on, or that they'd leave my hands unbound—which they don't. They do leave my feet undone so I can climb in. That's something. My shoulders are sore and bruised, and I let out a muffled yelp as Drake secures my hands again. The bond loosens.

We're on our way again after a short ten minutes, and my body already aches like nothing I've experienced before. My stomach rumbles with hunger, and my head throbs. I can't sleep in such an uncomfortable, claustrophobic space, so I spend my time coming up with clever ways to tell the people I love that I've been kidnapped.

I could send a carrier pigeon. Or a carrier snake from the desert. A rodent might be easier to catch, but a lizard would be faster. I could write a note in the sand, or in the dirt on the hood of this car. I could send them a voice message that would force them to come after me—even if they weren't planning on it. "And what would you say to them, Rose?" I ask myself.

Something like: Help, help! Please help me, I've been kidnapped.

Nah. Too dramatic. Maybe more like: Um, hey so these guys sort of kidnapped me out of my hotel room in Phoenix, and now we're somewhere in a scary desert driving to—I don't know where.

Or perhaps: News alert! Rose has been kidnapped. I repeat, Rose has been kidnapped. Please send all available emergency responders to find her in the trunk of the dirty gold car in the desert far far away.

I'm so caught up in coming up with entertaining ways to announce my kidnapping, that I almost don't hear the distant-sounding voice that responds.

Rose? How are you talking to me? Where are you?

It's Kye's voice, only—not. It's inside me. Like, in my head, and it's weird because it sounds like he's answering a phone call. Without using a phone. Maybe I'm dehydrated and losing my mind.

Kye? How are you talking to me? I'm in the trunk of some scary guy's car in the middle of the desert somewhere.

I adjust my position to muffle the rumble of the engine so I can hear Kye's voice better.

What? How did you end up there? He asks inside my head.

Gabe and I have information for you and Abby. We went to Phoenix looking for you, and were about to head to Utah.

Where are you now?

If I knew, don't you think that's the first thing I'd tell you? Middle of nowhere-ville. Arizona maybe, or one of the surrounding states. Feels like we're going north, maybe? Nevada?

Do you know who you're with?

That guy, Boone. The one who cut Abby with the dagger.

Abby and I are snowed in at a cabin in Utah, but we'll be on our way to help you as soon as we can dig our car out from under three feet of snow.

Dig fast, cousin. About the time this Boone guy figures out that the Dragons won't come after me, he'll get rid of me.

On it. Hang tight, Rose, we'll find you.

272

THIRTY-NINE

Stir-Crazy

ABBY

The resort services version of *right now* turns out to be several hours later, during which I begin to worry that Kye is going mad. He paces every pace-able space in the house, mumbling to himself and glaring out the window every two minutes.

"Kye, stop it," I snap from my spot on the couch. "Sit down. They'll be here."

"Don't tell me to stop it," he snaps back. "What if something happened? What if the demons are keeping us trapped in this house until we starve to death? Or freeze to death? Or worse?"

I'm about to ask what could be worse than starving and freezing, but remember Alejandro and decide that there are lots of things I would categorize as worse. "They're coming," I repeat.

He whirls from staring out the window. "What if they don't? What if we're trapped here indefinitely, with no supplies and no friends and no hope? Maybe it's time to call Val."

Maybe it is. Maybe we've been fooling ourselves all along in thinking that we're meant to break the curse and be together. As much as I love Kye, maybe saving our lives truly is more important than being together. Maybe there's a way for us to each be happy without the other—even if it takes a long time for us to find that happiness. Maybe it's time to discuss alternate possibilities for the future. I rise and go to him, and he meets me in the middle as if sensing that now is the time for the discussion we've been avoiding. "What's this about?" I ask.

"I can't do this anymore, Abby."

And there it is. The bomb I felt coming. Yet, somehow the words—ones I was prepared to say myself—rip open all my wounds, old and new, until I feel like the lifeblood is rushing out of every part of me.

I'm still trying to remember how to breathe when Kye continues, his voice raw and aching. "I love you. I love you more than my own life, more than my own soul. But I don't know how to make you happy. I can't fix all the things that have happened to you, or to me, or to us. I want to—worse than I've ever wanted anything—but I don't see how I'm supposed to try when you won't let me in. You won't talk about your nightmares. You won't let me help you find your Light again. You barely let me hold you when panic takes over, and you only allow that because I'm literally the only option at the moment. I can't stay trapped in this cabin for one more day knowing that you would rather have Gabe here than me."

The anger and resentment I've kept buried since we left Mexico heats up, threatening to explode. "Is that what you think? That I want Gabe? That I wish *he* was here with me instead of *you*? I left Gabe behind, Kye. By choice. I was awake and alert and absolutely capable of making that call. Believe it or not, as much as our parents sent us away, leaving the way we did, in the middle of the night, was still *our* decision."

"I left Gabe behind to go with you because despite everything else, despite my hurt and my anger and my frustrations and all our fights—despite my feelings for Gabe and yours for Crystal, and despite the fact that my best friend lost her boyfriend to a horrible, vicious death—*you*, and my feelings for *you* remained my top priority. I have followed you across countries. Into dark forests, and haunted caves, rabbit holes and crime-ridden alleys. I've cried buckets of tears over things you've said, and done, and things you haven't said or done, and all the expectations I'll never be able to

274

meet. I've changed every single thing about my life since meeting you. Everything. Because since the moment you forced your way into my heart, *you've* been my number one priority. Not Gabe, not Rose, not my mother. You."

"Above and beyond everything else—including my own life. I've left behind everyone else who ever mattered. I've lost my Gifts—my Light—and I don't know if I can ever get it back. Now I'm losing you too." I blink to clear the burning in my eyes. "Because I love you *too* much. You want me to lean on you more than I already do? Knowing that it's only a matter of time before we discover that there's no breaking this curse? That there is no future that involves you and me happy together?"

"That's not why you're shutting me out," he spits. "And we both know it. You left this relationship behind in Mexico. I'm so tired of trying to make up for my mistakes only to have them thrown back in my face. I'm tired of trying to give you your space and protect you at the same time. Abby, I love you. So much I don't know how to breathe when you're not nearby, but being together in this house, with a wedge the size of Canada between us, is killing me. Literally. It's eating me up inside, and you can't even see it. I get that you've lost your Gift, but that's not what created this distance. That's not what this fight is about. It's about you purposefully distancing yourself from me, like you've already decided there is no other side of this mountain."

My fingers clench so tightly into fists that my nails dig into my palms. "Kye. I'm tired of climbing. I don't know if I have anything left. I can't bear the idea of getting to the other side only to have you ride away with Crystal or Kiersten or someone else from your past, and before you object, we know that's what might happen. It might be the only future for us. I want you to live as much as I want to live, and being apart might be the only way. I don't know how to get to the point where we can each move on and be okay with it."

His hand circles my wrist as he draws me nearer, reeling me in the way he did the day we met—the way he always has. "Sweetheart,

I will never, ever be okay with the idea of you moving on with someone else."

The rhythm of my heart shifts and thrums to the beat of a different type of pain—the ache of longing. "Kye, don't."

"Don't what?" He has his other hand on my waist, pulling my body inexorably closer to his.

"Don't tempt fate," I say. "Don't try to distract us from this conversation. This is not what people do when they're breaking up."

His head jerks back as if I've slapped him. "We're breaking up?"

"Aren't we?"

He shakes his head, and the hand gripping my wrist tightens, yanking me closer until he has me trapped in his embrace. "Not in this lifetime."

There's no concentrating with his breath hot on my cheek, in my hair, on my neck. He doesn't kiss any part of me yet, but his nearness, and the possibility that he could easily kiss all of me right now, sends my pulse spiraling out of control. "You just said you can't do this anymore."

When he nods, his lips graze the tip of my ear, and then continue down my shoulder—a light brush along my topmost layer of skin in what feels like the most intimate caress he's ever shared.

"And by that," he breathes, "I meant sleeping in separate rooms. In separate beds. Nothing is right when we're apart like that."

"Kye." I make a weak attempt to pull away, but his grip is firm, his seductive attempts to bring me back to life unrelenting. "We can't ..."

"Because of the non-existent baby," he whispers, his fingers walking up my spine. "I know. Yet, there's this miraculous thing called birth control. In fact, I happened to find an unopened stash of one common, and highly popular method, hidden in the bottom of my suitcase when I went looking for those pajamas you've been wearing for the last five days. A stash I didn't purchase or pack." His eyes flash with confusion and desire, coupled with a sure knowledge that since it wasn't him who bought them, it had to be me.

This discovery explains his most recent bout of frustration. He knows that I planned to seduce him at some point. I have a brief memory flash of sneaking away from Kye at a drugstore with the excuse of needing feminine products, and buying two different types of condoms. This was during the phase of me thinking that extra birth control precaution was going to be our answer. An embarrassed blush rises to my face so fast that my neck feels hot.

"Before you freak out ..." His breath tickles my arm as he leisurely slides toward my wrist. "Let the record show ..." And my palm. "That not only do I still plan to marry you ..." He turns my hand over. "But that you're still wearing my engagement ring, which indicates that you haven't changed your mind either." Finally, finally his lips touch my skin as he kisses the ring I've never once taken off.

Heat flares to life inside me, with a fury I never felt when I called my Light. Every part of me is aware of every part of Kye, as if we're two halves of a whole that's been separated for far too long. Kye gasps as he touches his palm to mine and kisses his way back up my arm. "I love you," he says over and over again. "Abby, I love you, and I don't care what else happens. I'm yours, all yours, body and soul, one hundred and fifty percent—forever. No matter what else happens, what our future holds, I need you to know that, need to prove it to you." His lips burn a trail across my collar bone.

Breathless, I inform him, "You already have."

He shakes his head, hair falling across his forehead as his eyes bore into me. "No. Not in the way I need to. The way you need me to. If we had access to a priest or a judge, I'd beg him to say the words—seal the deal. Right now. I want to know that I own you in a way that no one else ever will, in a way that no one else ever can. I want you to be only mine."

The last time Kye pushed me to elope he had something to hide, but as he lavishes my neck and finds my lips, I decide that it no longer matters if he's hiding something or not.

Things have changed since he proposed in Mexico. Months later, we both know what we're getting into, and though we don't know where we're going, we both know where we've been and what we've experienced. We've seen death, and life, and unspeakable loss, and had our eyes opened to future possibilities. We swore we would never live the way Kye's parents have been forced to live—leading separate lives in countries thousands of miles apart. But after seeing them in Mexico, I wonder if their situation isn't the worst thing ever. When they're together, it's so obvious that they're completely in love, that they want to be together. And they have Kye. Maybe he's the reason they've never fought the madness of their circumstances. Maybe the short slices of time they're allowed are enough to help them survive the long stretches between.

This is what Kye meant that day on the bus when he first told me about his family and how they survive being apart.

It's time I let go of my fear, of my worry and heartache, and give in to fate. This time, this experience with Kye is what I want, what I choose, what will make me happy—make us both happy—for however long that lasts.

"I love you too, Kye." I let go of my resistance to return his kisses, his caresses. "I'm yours. Only yours. Forever."

Without pausing to slow his overworked lips, he lifts me into his arms. "Marry me," he breathes into my mouth. "Please, Abby. Even if it's just for today. I want us to be bound by law, as well as love."

I cling to him as he starts for the bedroom. "Yes," I tell him, giving into the giddy pleasure. "Yes."

A sharp rap at the door brings us to a stop in the hallway. Kye swears, setting me on my feet and planting a last kiss on my nose. "Hold that thought." One more kiss on my forehead. "Don't go anywhere." Outside, an engine rumbles and the sound of the plow scraping asphalt has the metallic ring of a cell door swinging open.

"Perfect timing." Kye opens the door for a burly man, bundled in black and red ski-gear that bears the resort logo.

"Got some supplies for you, Mr. Akers," he says, and I notice that he has already shoveled a path between our door and the driveway, and the driveway to the road. "So sorry we missed your street before. Been a bit overwhelmed with this storm."

"I can imagine." Kye's voice is strained, his every movement leaning toward closing the door again.

The delivery / snow-plow driver hands Kye a clipboard. "Sign here for the charges."

Kye accepts grudgingly, scribbling his name without glancing at the bill. "What about our driveway?"

"Next on my list," he says. "Thought you might need your groceries first, since it took me so long. You wouldn't believe the lines at that place. It's like everyone in town decided to go shopping at the same time."

"Everyone was out of food, like us," I mumble.

The driver glances up and smiles at me. "Hey there. Resort services sent a package with some ladies clothing. I'm supposed to tell you that anything that doesn't fit can be returned at the boutique connected to the resort office."

"Thank you." The euphoria from Kye's kisses begins to fade, leaving reason and practicality space to return. Maybe the driver's timing is a sign. Kye tips the man with cash, and they chit-chat for a moment before the man gathers—far too late—that he has interrupted something.

"Well," he says, his eyes flickering toward the floor. "You two lovebirds enjoy the rest of your week. I hope the supplies are sufficient."

Kye closes the door and whirls back to me. "I'm so sorry," he says, his voice echoing in the silence. "We should have had this talk days ago."

I nod, waiting for him to come to me. He makes it halfway across the room before pausing, with a loud gasp, to clutch the sides of his head.

"What's wrong?" I rush to him, wishing I could See his aura. "Does your head hurt?"

"Gah." He nods, clutching the back of the couch with one hand, and massaging his forehead with the other.

I assist him to the couch and ease him onto the cushions. When he starts to mumble incoherently, I unclasp my necklace and place the crystal on Kye's forehead. I don't have access to my Healing power anymore, but the instincts and knowledge remain. I brush my fingers over his skin, run them along his face and neck, and into his hair, humming as I seek the right tones for this type of Healing. I try to spin Kye's third eye chakra—knowing that, in theory, anyone should be able to balance a chakra~but none of my efforts bring him relief.

After what feels like the longest five minutes of my life, Kye blinks, his eyes clearing, and he sits up. The set of his shoulders and tensing in his jaw indicate that something is wrong, but he's coherent, and that's a marked improvement. "Abby, Rose has been kidnapped."

My chest squeezes. "What do you mean kidnapped? How do you know?"

"I heard her," he says, his voice faint as if he's struggling to believe it. "She talked to me, the same way I talked to you when we were underwater in the cenote."

"Just now?" Kye's arm shakes, and I grab on to keep him steady. He nods. "How is that possible? You and Rose aren't bound by a curse or by fate the way we are."

"I'm not sure," he says, clenching my hand in his. "But Rose and I have related Gifts. We're both communicators. This has never happened before, so we never thought about it being possible."

That something like this could happen has never occurred to me, but Kye's reasoning makes sense. The fact that Rose is in danger sends shivers of fear along my skin. "Tell me what she said to you," I insist. "Tell me everything."

While Kye relays the details of his conversation with Rose, the plow clears the road up to our driveway, and then cuts a space behind the car, scooping the snow away from the bumper. Once the driver is finished, he shovels the rest of the sidewalk, leaving us clear to come and go.

I haven't looked inside the shopping bags he brought. I don't care what my new clothes look like, as long as they fit. It's hard to feel relief over such a trivial thing as food and clothes when my best friend is in serious trouble.

Kye pushes himself off the couch, his eyes boring into me. "About our conversation ..."

I shake my head. "Going to have to wait."

"Yes." He closes the distance between us, and takes my hands. "But babe, I'm not going to change my mind. I meant what I said. I'm yours, body and soul, and I'm ready to take the next step. The next five steps. Whatever. Please let me back in."

Knowing he needs me, but unwilling to make a long-term commitment until this thing with Rose is resolved, I rise onto my tiptoes and press my lips to his. "Okay," I promise. "But let's go slow for now."

He swears under his breath, and I'm not sure if it's because he's relieved or frustrated at being told we're going slow, but it doesn't matter, because he follows up with a smile. "As long as I have you in my arms, in my bed, I can conquer the world."

A shiver runs down my spine, leaving me with the eerie feeling of premonition I've heard the non-Gifted sometimes have. The battles we're facing are against demonic forces that are trying to take over the world, and all I can think is that I hope and pray that Kye truly does have the strength to conquer them.

FORTY

The Dungeon

ROSE

The next time we stop, it's dusk. I haven't eaten in more than twenty-four hours, nor have I had any water. I've slept on and off throughout the day, unable to help it with the heat of the sun warming my trunk like an oven. Luckily, there's a vent that blows air back here and has kept me from suffering a heat stroke.

But I've never been so thirsty.

The driver turns the car off, and it sounds like everyone gets out. Once again, I kick and scream and make noise—as I have every time we've stopped—and am beyond relieved when they open the trunk again. This is only the second time all day, and I've become crazy claustrophobic, which messes with my ability to stay calm and not freak-the-hell-out. I don't know what we're doing at this stop, or where we're going after it, but I do know one thing—they're not getting me back in this trunk without a fight.

Drake, drags me up and out. After the constant darkness, I have to blink hard to force my eyes to adjust to the light of the setting sun. "We're here."

Whatever softness existed in his eyes the first time we stopped is long gone. I'm desperate for food and water, but can't tell him so. Not that my needs should matter to him. Drake is here to do a job, and regardless of any hints of compassion he's shown, he's one of the bad guys who kidnapped me and brought me across state lines as a hostage.

I take a deep breath in the open space, and pick up hints of sweet grapevines, recently turned earth, and pine. The world is cushioned by a soft orange halo, rolling hills speared by tall, pointy trees, and in the distance a large, uneven structure that—as my eyes focus—takes the shape of a castle.

I blink in disbelief. That can't be right. As far as I know, we're still in America, and unless we've transported to an alternate reality, there are no castles here—no royals here. Except Abby, and she doesn't necessarily count. But as Drake drags me along the paved path, the structure continues to look more definitely like a castle. Nearing the entrance, I even catch a scent of dusty tapestries.

What the what?

Drake drags me across a drawbridge that's been permanently extended over a dry creek bed, and we reach an enormous wood door, fitted with iron hinges. I'm worried about where Boone and the others have gone, but can't ask. It's hard enough to breathe, and my raw throat feels blistered from screaming and lack of water.

Using the mammoth iron knocker, Drake raps. The door scrapes open, emitting a puff of dust and fermentation that's not entirely unpleasant. This place has to be a novelty tourist-attraction vineyard, because aside from popular theme park attractions, there isn't a single real-life castle in the United States. If there was, pretty sure I'd know about it. I love castles. I love royal-type things and antiques and quirky tapestries, and aside from a few wanna-be abandoned estates in the East, I have never heard of there being one in the United States.

One of Boone's henchmen, who I recognize from the gas station, waves us in. "Boone wants her in the dungeon where she can scream and yell without us hearing. Going to have to give her water at some point if we want her to live."

Drake seizes my elbow and drags me through the entry and into a courtyard that seems unreal for its absolute authenticity. It feels like the car we arrived in brought us back in time and across an ocean or two. *What is this place?*

In the courtyard, chickens peck at the dirt as if they do this every day, like they're used to finding feed or seeds. The smell of fermented grapes grows richer, stronger, as we continue along the stone walk and into a hallway lined with glassless windows.

As we round a corner, I deliberately scrape my shoulder against the rough stones to be sure I'm fully awake and not having one of Abby's visions, because the realism here is disorienting at best, and terrifying at worst. Drake's taking me to the dungeon, which becomes more frightening with each step.

Voices echo, bouncing off the stones, and I whip my head toward the sound. On the other side of the courtyard, another wooden door stands open, revealing a banquet room decorated in true medieval fashion. Around an enormous rough-hewn table, Boone and some others argue over a sheaf of papers spread from end to end. They appear to be blueprints of some variety, printed on modern paper.

Drake jerks me forward. "Keep walking. Nothing there you need to worry about. Finishing touches and last details before the kingdom can be restored. The royal estate is nearly ready to be occupied—not that you'll be here to witness it. Only portion of this place you need to be concerned about is this one down here." He shoves me into a stairwell so narrow that we can't walk side-by-side. The stairs are small and slippery with grime, and as we continue down it becomes darker, thick with an unusually eerie cold.

My body aches, leaving me shaking from dehydration and lack of nutrients. At the abrupt end of the circular stairway, I stumble and fall to my hands and knees in the dirt. Plumes of dust rise into my face, triggering a coughing fit that I can't hold back—with or without the gag. Drake jerks me to my feet. I'm still coughing so hard that I can barely stand, let alone walk. "Water," I try to croak, and it's obvious that Drake understands.

"Nope. Not going to remove that gag until I've secured you in the deepest, darkest part of the dungeon where you can't make me dance like a chicken or whatever it is you do."

Drake has never seen me in action—he's operating strictly from hearsay. This could be a good boost, because if he doesn't fully understand my capabilities, he's more likely to let his guard down, making him the weak link I should target.

The long hall is lined with musty cells that are guarded with iron doors and lit with dim electric wall sconces—one more sign that we're still in the twenty first century and haven't actually traveled back in time. When we reach the end, Drake shoves me into the last cell. "In you go." He cuts the zip tie off my hands and shoves me away from him. He touches his mouth, then nods at mine. "Go ahead and take that off as soon as I leave."

I start working on the knot, but he stops me with a sharp expletive. "Not yet. I'll be back with food and water." He nods at a camera in the ceiling, indicating that someone is watching and can see my every action. "If you take it off before I get back, I'll leave you to starve. Before you wonder if anyone else ever comes down here, the answer is no. I'm the only one who can stomach this hell hole after being trapped in those caves last year."

He walks out, leaving me staring at the camera and wondering if anyone is truly on the other end, or if it's there to scare me. There's no red light. Shouldn't there be a blinking red light?

What did he mean by being trapped in the caves last year? Drake does seem familiar, but pretty sure I've never seen him in Jackson. I've paid close attention to each and every new person in town—as have my parents, and the Dragons. It's a necessary part of being one of the Gifted few. In order to protect ourselves and our people, we have to be hyper-vigilant. We have to know who is new and where they live and why they've come to town. We have to know how long they plan on staying and if they're aware that they've stumbled into the largest community of Gifted in our part of the world.

Abby and I became friends because I knew. The minute I saw her, I knew she would be either best friend or mortal enemy. Either way, it was in everyone's best interest for one of us to keep her close, to learn more about her, find out what she could do. None of us could have guessed that the timid girl with the haunted eyes is the last carrier of the pure bloodline of the royal family.

Anyway, if Drake had been there when we helped Abby rescue Kye from the caves in Yellowstone, I would have seen him. I would have noticed. By the time we got in, there was no one left besides Abby and Kye and the pieces of the frozen guy, which I luckily didn't have to clean up. It's possible Drake was referring to the caves in Mexico where Alex was killed. I wasn't in those caves, so I don't know. Could he have been party to Alex dying? It's possible. I would never know.

A spark of rage ignites.

I rip off my gag, gasping for air. My jaw aches like never before, but is nothing like the throbbing hole in my heart. I'm done waiting to see what happens next. It's time for me to take control and get the hell out of here. I need a plan. I need a weapon. I need to take these people down—all of them.

I'm not sure my Voice will work after hours of disuse, lack of water, and having spent so much time trying to scream past my gag every time we stopped.

The camera glares at me, still minus signs of power. Drake claimed that this place—whatever it is—is almost finished, so I have to assume that they've either recently built it, or recently restored it. So the idea that the cameras aren't yet hooked up, even if they work—which I question—seems logical. Regardless, I decide to operate under the assumption that they do, and loosely replace the wad of fabric so it looks like I'm doing as I'm told.

Drake returns to find me cowering in the corner, wide-eyed with fear and rubbing my raw, aching wrists. "Here." He tosses a water bottle at my feet and hands me a sandwich made of grocery store bread, a slice of cheese, and a thin slice of commercial lunch meat. Under normal circumstances, I would turn up my nose and ask him what-the-crap he's trying to do to me by feeding me nutritionless junk, but I'm so hungry all I can do is snatch the sandwich and hold it close. "Don't want you to go getting confident on me," he says. "Boss wants you kept alive for the time being, so I'll feed you until he decides otherwise."

My stomach growls as if it's already worried that I'll lose this precious bit of food. It is so hollow already. I hold the sandwich tight against my chest, flattening the bread between my fingers, as Drake steps out and slams my cell door shut.

"Sleep well, my lady. Let's hope your queen cares enough to come find you." The click that follows tells me that I've missed my chance to escape. Drake has locked me in, and I have no idea when to expect him to come back.

But he will be back—of that I'm sure. I'm here and alive for a reason. They need me. I just need to figure out why.

.

FORTY-ONE

Useless Human

ABBY

By the time I change into the basic jeans and hooded sweatshirt the shopping service provided, Kye's suitcase is packed, and he's chomping at the bit for me to finish mine as well. Luckily, after years of experience with Mom and Gram, I'm an expert at quick packing. My belongings are gathered and stowed, my suitcase zipped, and ready to go in a matter of minutes.

Kye nods in appreciation as I wheel my luggage into the main living area. "Impressive."

"I'm a pro." I turn into the kitchen to double check that we aren't leaving behind important herbs or crystals. There's no time to use our newly acquired groceries, which means we'll take the sacks as they came and hope what's in them is usable on the go. I meet Kye outside with the last of our belongings, and together we load them into the car. Neither of us can find words to calm the horrifying panic, but when his hand brushes mine, a spark fizzles along my skin. If nothing else, I finally know where we stand. It helps.

I turn to steal a kiss before we get on the road, but Kye's eyes are wide and round, his jaw tight, as he stares at the sky over the top of the car. Waves of black clouds hurl toward us, unrolling a blanket of darkness to cover everything in their path. "Um, I think the portal broke open."

The wind howls, churning like it did the night of the storm that knocked out the power in our little house. "How does a portal break open?" I shout. "I don't understand."

"I don't know. What happened to the last ones we dealt with? Didn't they break too?" He opens my door and shoves me into the car. "Time to go."

I buckle up as he dives in and yanks his door closed, simultaneously turning the key in the ignition. "What now?" I crane my neck to keep an eye on the shadows barreling ever closer.

"We've already closed two portals. Guess there's one more waiting for us." He throws the car in gear and guns the engine. For precious seconds that feel like an eternity, our wheels slide on ice that has built up beneath the car, but Kye continues to spin until the friction from our tires melts the ice to slush and we gain traction, throwing us down the driveway and into the street.

We screech toward the source of the demons. My old house.

Dread ties heavy sailor's knots inside me. Without my Light, I don't know how to fight off a single demon, let alone an army of this caliber. How can we even try to close this portal? As Raina's heir, I have a responsibility to finish what she started and continue ridding the world of shadow demons. But without power, it's a miracle I can even see them. I can't see Murtagh anymore, and he's one of my best friends.

"Don't start," Kye says. "I can already feel your doubt, your fear, and you know the demons feed on negative energy."

"I can't help it," I grumble. "Last time we did this, I was useful."

"You're still useful. Look, babe, just because you don't have your Light doesn't mean you can't fulfill your destiny. We'll find another way."

"Oh yeah. Great. We'll do *more* research and figure it out in a month. Or a year. In the meantime, we're about to crash a demon party and I have *no* weapons."

"You have weapons, Abby. Everyone in the world has weapons. Your brain, your heart, your compassion. Your positive energy. Your spirit—all the things I love about you—they're weapons to be used against the demons. All you have to do is use them wisely."

I don't know what he's talking about. At the moment, I'm a useless human, and we both know it. As we jerk to a stop at the curb in front of the driveway of my old house, I vow that I will do everything I can to protect Kye. Even if I die, as long as Kye lives, he can save Rose. The two people who matter most to me in the world can continue with the thing at which I failed. They can destroy the shadows, restore Light to the world. They will carry on my legacy.

Thinking of Rose renews my courage and cements my resolve. Light or no, I'll find a way to close this portal and destroy it. Permanently. Kye's more worried about me than himself, so with my fingers on the door handle, I remind him. "We have to get to Rose, or die trying. We're the only ones who know about her— she's counting on us."

"We can't let her down," he agrees. He leans across the seat and crushes me in his embrace, his lips finding mine for what could be his last real chance at tasting me. His fingers thread into my hair, and his chest, warm against mine, heaves with the effort of holding back a mixture of fear and desire. His tongue traces my teeth, finds my tongue, learning the inside of my mouth all over again as he holds on tight. "I love you, Abby. Whatever happens to us, I hope you never forget that, ever again."

"I love you too, Kye. Forever."

He drags in a deep breath. "Are you ready for this?"

I shake my head. "Nope. Never will be."

Kye reaches behind the seat to retrieve my handbag and dumps it on my lap. "Don't forget your extra crystals."

I fill my pockets, and his, with every protective stone we've got, including the rose quartz I've had for as long as I can remember. I gulp, resting my hand on the latch. "Ready?"

"As ready as we'll ever be," he says, sighing. "Let's do this thing."

LEGACY

Thick black shadows roll over the car as we exit, pushing against the doors, insisting that we go away. I meet Kye at the hood and take his hand, determined to stay together as we traverse the driveway in virtual darkness. When I was young, I dreamed about playing games in the dark, though I was always afraid. I was the child who needed a nightlight. When Gram noticed my fear, she marched to the kitchen and brought back a copper cooking lid, which she hung on the wall with a plain, black nail. I wish I had that copper lid now. I wish I had Gram now, too. If I could have that nightlight to guide me right now, I'd love that as well.

"I really hate the dark." It's hard not to remember the true dark of the caves in Mexico where we were trapped for so many hours.

"Me too." Kye tugs on my arm to keep me moving. "From now on, we may have to sleep with the lights on."

"Deal." My toes meet the edge of the curb with a force that sends spasms of pain into my ankle, but when I look down, all I see is the blackness of shadows. "Watch your step," I warn, moving onto the driveway. The demons pulse and throb, squeezing in, trapping us between walls that don't exist, and stealing the air from my lungs.

Utilizing the techniques I learned after the incident on the pyramid, I make a concerted effort to breathe in through my nose, out through my mouth, shallow breaths, but deep enough to reach my lungs in the way I need. This time, there is no voice drawing me toward danger, and Kye's hand is still in mine as we cross what must have been the protective barrier around the house. Nothing about this situation feels right, but I can't tell why.

Are you okay? Kye asks in my mind. I don't have power anymore, so I'm shocked to discover that this part I haven't lost.

I hate the dark. I remind him a second time.

I hate the demons. He replies.

I hate that we should be on our way to find Rose and have to close a portal, first. I continue.

I hate that Raina and Theron didn't finish this job the first time. He shoots back.

I'll second that hate. I grope with my hand in front of me to avoid smacking into the brick walls of the house, and my fingers brush wood—the front porch stair railing. *Front door or back?* I ask, still inside Kye's mind.

We should go in through the front, he thinks to me. *The portal is nearer to the back.*

Maybe we shouldn't use a door at all. Won't they be expecting us?

Kye squeezes my hand and pulls me to a stop. *It's too dark to try looking for another way in. Besides, they already know we're here. Why else would it be necessary to communicate this way rather than speaking? We're not underwater this time.*

As if they can hear our inner-thought conversation, the shadows pulse again, sucking away more precious oxygen. This is not a new sensation. I tighten my fingers on the rickety wooden railing and join Kye on the first step, then the second. We work our way to the top of the porch, unable to see through the pitch blackness of the shadows, unable to hear over the howling wind. What's left of the breathable air has become musty and dank, thick with dark energy that no light could penetrate—except what's lost to me.

We may as well be underwater, hard as it is to breathe.

Kye laughs out loud at my observation, and in that second, the shadows clear enough that I'm able to fill my lungs.

What just happened?

His fingers tighten in mine. *I laughed.*

I squeeze back, now curious. *Did you feel it? The shift? Try that again.*

What? Laughing?

Yes. Laughing. It's positive energy. That's what powered my Light. Maybe if we get some laughter going, we'll push back these shadows so we can see.

He lets loose with a hard, barking laugh. It's flat, different from the genuine one we experienced a minute ago.

Do it better, I insist. *Lighter. Happier. More real.*

He tries again, and then again, without success. *I can't,* he says. *Too nervous. Let's go inside.*

No Kye, I'm serious. This could be a weapon. Maybe the only one I have.

Abby, if it's your weapon, you should be the one laughing.

He has a point. So I laugh. It's forced at first, like Kye's, and not enough to shift the shadows. We're surrounded by negative forces. Deep down, I'm bone terrified, and the demons know it. They squeeze in, forcing us closer together until I'm touching him and he's touching me and we're practically sharing air. Unable to resist, I rise up and kiss his nose. A shadow curls against my lips, and then burns to fumes. Interesting.

My hand reaches the knob, and I twist, preparing to drag Kye in behind me, but he nudges me aside, withdrawing from his pocket an energy wand I didn't realize he'd brought with us. "I'll go first. They know we're here. If it's a trap, I'll be able to fight back." He starts forward, and the shadows recede; a cacophony of voices barrels into us. They're familiar, and confusing, because I don't want to believe that so many of the people that I love, and who I believed to be at home in Jackson—are here, arguing about … something. I can't tell what.

I slide my hand along the wall looking for a switch, find one, and flip it. The bulb flickers, and then shatters, leaving us, once again, in darkness. In the seconds of illumination, I catch a glimpse of the room. There must be a hundred Gifted people in this tiny house. The split second of vision muddles my mind with confusion. How could my mother be here? And Landon? Jenn and Eric and Val? Also Boone and Juri and the familiar henchmen whose names I have never bothered to learn, but whom I have seen multiple times. Rose. Rose is *not* here. Clearly, she couldn't be, or the conversation with Kye was a trap and a lie, and she would never do that to him. Or to me.

Would she?

Who is friend and which are foe? There is no true way for us to know who is out to hurt us, and who is here to save the kingdom.

Did you see all of them? I think to Kye. *My mother? Our friends?*

No. He seems confused. *Where?*

Right here, all crammed into this house.

Abby, how could our family and friends all be here right now? We know they're in Jackson.

I saw them, Kye. I saw them, and I can hear them. Can't you?

I didn't. I can't. He takes my hand, pulling me into his side. Abby, they're not here. They're really not. It's a trick of your mind. Or of their magic. You're just confused without ...

He's convinced. Maybe if I had my Sight, I'd be able to tell the difference. I saw people. I heard people. Familiar ones. Familiar faces. I don't understand how I can see them, hear them, while Kye cannot. I'm no longer Gifted, but he is. This makes no sense.

We need to do something, he thinks.

I take a hesitant step forward, staying oriented by dragging my fingers along the wall. It's neither darker nor lighter inside the house than it was outside, just different dark. Kye follows close behind, with a hand on my back, allowing me to set the pace. *I hope you remember your way in this house.*

I don't. I haven't lived here in so many years, I can't remember if it has one bathroom or two, but at this point it's not worth mentioning to Kye. We know where the portal is. It's what we've come for, and the quicker we shut it down, the sooner we can rescue Rose.

The temperature drops, and vibrations beat in my chest. I can't hear the moaning and howling coming from the portal, but I can feel it. Kye drags me to a halt as my hand meets the sculpted wooden pillar that separates the main living space from the dining room.

This time, his words are spoken aloud. "What. The hell. Is that?"

FORTY-TWO

Hungry

ROSE

I don't know how much time has passed since Drake left me alone in this place. It feels like weeks, but is perhaps only days. I can't tell the difference between day and night, hour and minute, second or eternity. I'm exhausted and famished and so thirsty that I suspect dehydration will be the thing that kills me—which is terribly sad, considering what I've lived through—but I'm afraid to fall asleep.

I can't risk being caught off guard. What if Drake comes back? I could miss it. Or he could bring someone else, and if I'm sleeping, I'll be unprepared for all the what-if's that could come to pass. I wish I *could* sleep though. Maybe it would distract me from the way my stomach cramps painfully, demanding nourishment I can't provide. Instead, I occupy myself with scratching names in the dirt with a rough-edged stone I found in the corner.

Abby Johnson.
Kye Murphy.
Jennifer Thomas.
Gabe Schafer.
Lynda Westover.
Barry Westover.

Landon Akers.
Marian Johnson.
Murtagh.

These people—this list—are my reasons for staying alive. They need to be saved, and I have the ability to do it. "I can command shadows," I whisper. A personal reminder of reality to keep me sane. "I can command people and demons alike. I can save my loved ones." I repeat the words over and over, reminding myself as I add more names—people I hope don't die, people I hope to help protect.

Tanya Heaton.
Cole Heaton

Valdemar ... ? My stone stalls as I stare at the name. Does Val need saving? Does he truly want the restoration of the kingdom, or does he want the cycle to continue so that he never has to let go and move onto Tir Na Nog? I'm not sure. But I leave him on my list, for now.

As I'm trying to decide whether or not I should add Eric—he did betray us last winter—footsteps echo down the stone stairs, and voices. I can't make out what they're saying, but one of them sounds familiar.

I listen harder, straining.

The footsteps continue, echoing off the cold stone walls. Whoever is coming is moving crazy slow. I don't know what's taking them so long.

In my head, I make up all sorts of reasons for the long trip down the twisty staircase. Maybe Drake is bringing a tray of hot food. Beef stew with chunks of carrots and potatoes and garden-grown herbs, and fresh bread. Bottles of ice cold water. Ice cream for dessert.

My stomach protests such ideas with cramps of agony, and my mouth would water—but I'm dehydrated, so forming saliva is nearly impossible. I'm so hungry. So thirsty. So tired and cold and ready to get out of here and go home.

The footsteps reach the bottom, followed by a loud thud, and what may or may not be something dragging along the ground.

"Sends me down to haul the giant by myself," Drake grumbles, and the dragging continues. "Weighs two hundred pounds, and unconscious, double that. 'Lock him up,' he says. 'Chain his wrists and ankles with copper,' he says. Like copper cuffs are so easy to come by in California wine country."

Okay, so we're in California. Probably near Napa, if the scent of grapes is any indication.

Who is the giant Drake's dragging? I stand and creep to the open square of bars in the iron cell door, blinking hard and hoping for a view. Any view. I want to know who's going to be in here with me, and why they've taken another hostage.

Drake rounds the corner and starts down my aisle, pausing to unlock a door down two cells and across from me. I stand on tiptoes to angle my eyes low enough to see what's happening. The view is obscured, but as Drake pulls, shoves, and grunts, I catch a glimpse of hot pink shoelaces in bright green shoes, and know that there cannot be more than one person in this world who would own a pair of running shoes that gaudy. It's Gabe.

FORTY-THREE

Darkness and Light

ABBY

I blink, seeing nothing but the blackest darkness, so complete that it's as if I've been sucked into nothingness. "What is it? What do you see?" I whisper, hoping he'll tell me. I should know what we're up against.

"I ..." He pauses, seemingly at a loss for words. "It's like ..."

"Shadows?" I ask, attempting to be helpful. In response, his hand finds mine and grips it painfully.

"No, it's not shadows. It's ... it's the opposite of that. It's Light, Abby. A floating ball of Light that fills the entire room and burns my eyes like looking into the sun."

"That can't be right. How can an evil portal be filled with Light?"

"I don't know."

"Well is it still evil? Is it even a portal? Maybe it's something else? Something better?"

He squeezes again. "It's definitely a portal, and definitely still evil. I feel it with everything in me—this is nothing like your Light. True Light, pure Light, can only burn that which is the most dark and evil."

"But it's burning your eyes now?"

"Only because it's so bright."

"Yes, and because we're enveloped by darkness. So, what's happening is something has upset the balance. Dark is Light and bad is good and—there's no way for any of us to know the difference anymore. The universe is a jumbled mess of confusion."

"No. It isn't. That can't be what's happening. I'm sure it's only ..."

"Then how?" I ask, removing my hand from his and inching forward, needing to touch this bright Light that I can't see.

"I don't know," he snaps. "It's like they've stolen your Gift and added it to their arsenal."

This is why Boone took my blood. This could be the key to restoring my Gifts.

Kye maneuvers around to block my way. "Stop right there. We've never dealt with this before. You can't go to battle with a thing we know nothing about, especially when you can't see it."

But he's wrong. I do know something about it. I know a lot about it. Of all the things I know about the demon portals, all I've studied and learned about the way the Dark Elen work, there's one thing I know better, and that's my own Gift. The power of Light is difficult to control on the best day, and it took months and months of training, and years of fighting with Gram for me to learn how to control what I could do.

The Elen may know how to manipulate the dark—but I know how best to manipulate the Light, even when it's not in my grasp. Even when I can't see it. I take a deep breath to calm my fears and help me find what little control I have left, and when I'm centered, I grab Kye's hand, trail my fingers along his arm and up his shoulder to his neck, and then I draw him toward me so I can kiss him one last time.

"What are you doing?" His voice floods with anxiety, I suspect because he has an idea of what I'm about to do. "Abby, we should get out of here."

I shake my head and squeeze his fingers. *I love you, Kye. I really do.* I withdraw my hand and hold both palms in front of me as I stride toward the empty blackness, begging the Light to come into me, return to me, where it belongs.

"Abby ..." Kye says, and I shush him.

"Stay where you are," I murmur. "Let me try this."

"Try what? Abby, you shouldn't be in here. You can't see what you're doing."

"That's the point, isn't it?" I tell him. "I can't see it, so I can't be afraid."

He mutters something I don't understand, and I suspect he's searching for creatures of power. We're in the mountains—so there are tons of powerful creatures outside. Maybe even in here. The room could be full of them. There could be a thousand sprites like Murtagh present, and I wouldn't know, because I can no longer see anything of power—at all.

I take a giant step forward, and Kye gasps. I take another, and warmth crawls up my fingers. By the third, there's no denying that I'm nearing the center of power. It burns like waving my hands over a fire, but I keep going.

"Abby," Kye says aloud. "Stop. You should wait until I can get help here. It might not be your Light—they might have one of the Dragons' energy wands." His voice sounds like it comes from a great distance, disembodied, floating through the deepest, hottest blackness. I can't stop, can't wait, can't take anyone or anything else into this battle with me—it's for me, and me alone.

"Kye if something happens to me, please save Rose."

His hand clasps my arm, startling me. I didn't know he was this close. "Shut up. This is not another of your martyrdoms, Abby. It's not even a battle yet. We just got here."

"I'm sorry." I stretch my one free hand toward the center of the heat. It's about to become a battle, as soon as I pass through another barrier that's been set up to keep the Gifted out. His hand on my wrist trembles as I shake him off and take one last long step into the core of the portal's heat. And then the world explodes.

FORTY-FOUR

In It Together

ROSE

Drake doesn't acknowledge me. He locks Gabe in the cell, shaking his head as he shoves the keys in his pocket, and leaves the same way he came.

When I can no longer hear his footsteps, I call out. "Gabe? Are you okay?"

I don't know why I'm surprised when he doesn't answer. Maybe because aside from being locked in a trunk for hours and hours, and not having been offered food or water in what feels like days and days, Boone and his henchmen haven't seriously harmed me. Yet. They haven't beaten or poisoned or tortured me, and they haven't cut me with the dagger they stole from Abby in Mexico. They haven't tried to steal my powers. The idea that they might not want or need my power flits through my mind, leaving me feeling just this side of worthless.

A little voice in the back of my mind reminds me that if I was truly worthless, I wouldn't be here. Then another, more logical part of my brain rationalizes that maybe I've been taken captive, not because I'm valuable to them, but because I'm best friends with the person they want.

I settle onto the dirty floor and lean against the wall with a sigh. Maybe that's why they've taken Gabe too. To use as bait. We're pawns in a large chess game, the goal of which is to capture the other team's queen.

"Murtagh?" I try, hoping our sprite friend has somehow followed us—but there's no response. What if the Elen hurt him too?

More time passes. I hear nothing, save my own breathing, and in the dark, dank cell, see only what my eyes can make out in the slivers of light that filter down from the stairwell. I write my list over and over again, repeating the names, and then brushing over them with my hand to wipe the slate clean and start again.

Sometimes I doze, but never allow myself to fall into a deep sleep. I don't know how many hours I've sat in this cell, awake, but not awake. How many days of my life have been lost? How many hours? I remember back to Mexico and the time I spent with Alejandro, walking on the beach, in the gardens, at the ruins. Making out behind a curtain of mangrove branches, and salsa dancing lessons in the bar where he took me almost nightly. We were so good at sneaking away unseen.

I wouldn't give up a second of my time with him. Not a touch of his skin on mine, or the rough timbres of his voice, the hearty chuckle of his laugh—I couldn't give up any of it. Our time together was cut off so suddenly, after such a short courtship.

Memories of Alejandro make my limbs go weak, my eyes want to close forever, and my heart cries out in agony of despair. But there's nothing to be done. Alejandro can't be brought back to me, and the best thing I can do for him—the most important thing I can do for the man I once loved—is to live through this and carry on to the next thing.

After I returned home, there were days when I was certain that I would never love again. Never be happy again. Never laugh again. Days when living seemed pointless, futile. If I was still in that space, that stage of depression that kept me locked inside a bubble of numbness, I might lie down and die right here, hoping for a chance to go be with Alex.

But Gabe's across the hall, and he's captive too. Just as we suffered depression together, we'll be forced to suffer captivity together.

Gabe wasn't the one who wooed me in Mexico—he was too busy pining for Abby—but he is the one who picked me up off the ground where depression had left me gutted, and set me on my feet again. He's the one who helped—no, forced—me to keep living. Because of him, I started training again. Because of him, I learned how to use my Gift to defeat the Elen shadows—without having to steal an energy wand from the Dragons. Because of him, I understand why Abby is a target on every level.

Alejandro taught me to love, but Gabe taught me how to move forward and live.

Across the hall, Gabe coughs. Maybe he's coming to. "Gabe?" I call. "Are you okay? It's me, Rose."

He coughs again, and something rasps, but I can't make out his words. He must be badly hurt. "Don't try to talk," I tell him. "Not until you can. I just wanted you to know that you're not alone. I'm here. We're in this together, and we'll get out of it. Somehow."

He rasps again, coughs, rasps, and then I hear the single, faint croak as he says my name. "Rose."

FORTY-FIVE

Remembering

ABBY

"Abby!" Kye screams. "No!"

White light careens across my vision with a thunderous boom as my skin is scorched with the fire of a thousand suns. Kye's hand slips off my arm as I'm dumped onto my hands and knees, choking on energy that feels thick like syrup. I've closed my eyes against the brightness, and it scalds my lids, along with every other part of me. My skin stings, and my hair burns and crackles around my ears and on my neck. If I were to stand inside a fire, be burned alive, this might be what it feels like. Except there's no smoke, only heat, and syrupy energy, and loud, consecutive explosions that deafen my ears and make my heart bound with fear.

At one point, the booming explosions slow, and between them howls the wind that hovered outside our cabin the other night, and by some miracle, failed to get inside. I reach behind me to grab Kye's hand, but find nothing of substance. No ground. No walls. No ceiling. No Kye. Nothing but fire and light and so. Much. Noise.

"Kye? Where are you?" I yell. He doesn't reply.

I'm not sure what I expected upon walking into the portal, but to suddenly be able to see all that Kye's been seeing wasn't necessarily it. I don't know if I've gained back my Gifts, or what's happening exactly, but none of this feels right. It's terrifying.

I push myself up to stand, and stumble backward into the blackest darkness, where Kye catches me in his arms. "What were you trying to do?" He huffs in my ear. "Get trapped in there with the demons?"

I shake my head. "I wasn't trying to do anything. I couldn't see the portal! I was just trying to get to a place where I could find out what we were up against."

He squeezes me tight. "That's why I'm going first from now on. This is new territory; nothing like what Val and Landon have trained me for. Nothing like what we experienced last summer."

I want to point out how none of our experiences have been pre-planned, but now's not the time, so I press my lips together and try to force my eyes to adjust to the absence of light. It's a futile attempt. I never expected to end up in a place that was darker than the underwater caves from last summer, especially not a house where I once lived, and where surely light can seep through the cracks in doors and blinds and the windows.

A memory flashes:

It's dark in the bedroom where my father left me only an hour before, but anxiety about where he's gone and why Gram is so afraid keeps me wide awake. I slide out from under my covers and pad to the bathroom, closing the door with a soft click. There's a nightlight plugged into the wall, and I flip it on rather than the brighter bathroom lights so I can avoid having Gram or Mom see that I'm out of bed.

The long mirror hanging over the vanity is divided into three parts, and I climb up on the counter to stare at it. No one else knows about the secret room I discovered two days after we moved in, because I've never told them. As far as they're concerned, only the right or left portions of the mirror swing open to cosmetic storage shelves. But the middle, when pulled at just the right angle, and with the right amount of force, such as an almost seven-year-old's body weight (which I discovered when I was teetering with one foot on the counter and one on the tub as I tried to kill a spider) the middle also opens. Only rather than cosmetic storage shelves behind it, I found a crawlspace filled with dusty books, mouse droppings, and the dank, moldy musk of leaking water.

The books are in a language other than my own, with stamped leather covers and fragile velum pages that crinkle when I turn them. I've sat in this place and looked through these books twice a week, every week, for all six months of our stay here. They bring me comfort in the moments when I'm sad, lonely, or afraid. Tonight, with my father leaving, I am all those things.

I crawl inside the small space and drag the nearest book onto my lap to stroke the cover and ogle the pages in the light of my pink sparkle flashlight. I don't sleep that night. Or the next. Or the next. This feels like a magic place, where nothing can go wrong and everyone is safe.

My father has been gone for almost two months when Gram and Mom meet me at the door after school and sit me on Gram's lap so they can tell me that my father has passed on. Afterward, I find myself once again standing on the bathroom counter, trying my hardest to pry open the mirror and find my spot. I need to grieve, to find some degree of peace, and it seems this is the only safe place left for me.

But the mirror has been sealed. I cannot get back in, no matter how hard I try. I'm devastated.

The nightlight never works again.

I shake myself back into the present, wondering why such a memory would return to me in this moment. I haven't remembered that crawlspace in years. In fact, I'd completely forgotten it until now. But being in this house again makes it feel relevant. I wonder if that mirror covering the secret room, still exists? I wonder if the books are still behind it? I wonder what they say and who they belonged to, and who stored them there in the first place.

Kye takes my hand. *Abby, we need to go outside or something. Find somewhere to regroup and plan. We can't just stand here.*

He's right. We can't. The demons know we're here. I've just accidentally stepped into their portal, and then back out again. But the memory nags at me. We've searched all the histories and literature of the Gifted since the day Kye and I admitted our Gifts to each other. What if those strange-looking books I cradled as a child are the ones we've been searching for all along? What if they hold the answers? If my past is about to collide with my future, this seems like a fitting discovery to make.

Can you see down the hall? I ask in Kye's mind.

A bit, he answers, and I can feel the wariness in him, even without my intuitive Sight.

There's something we need to check in the bathroom—second door on the right. Will you lead me there? It's important.

Without a word, Kye grabs my wrist and pulls me forward.

FORTY-SIX

Royal Lineage

ROSE

"Gabe, I'm here." My limbs are weak, but I pull myself up so I can see his cell door. "I'm all right. Hungry, thirsty, and stinking like ten dogs locked in a kennel for a month, but not badly hurt."

"Rose," he croaks again, and I strain to hear his words. "You have to run."

Any other time, I would reply with a sarcastic laugh, but I don't have sarcasm in me. "I'm sort of locked up at the moment."

His breathing is labored and his voice weak, but it still carries in the cavernous dungeons. "When he ... next time he comes, when he unlocks your door, run. As hard and as fast as you can. Fight them, get away. Don't wait for me, and don't look back. Get as far away from here—" He's interrupted by a coughing fit, but persists when he's able. "Don't go home. Find Abby. She'll keep you safe."

"Abby can't keep me safe," I remind him. "She's lost her Gifts, remember?"

"Find Abby and Kye," he insists. "I don't want you to be in this alone."

There's a note of finality to his tone that leaves me wondering how seriously Gabe's hurt. Does he think he's going to die? My insides twist into tight knots and my hands quiver with anguish. "What did they do to you?"

"This isn't about me," he says. "I'll find a way out one way or another. Either I'll escape, or they'll kill me. But you—Rose, you have to escape. They've figured out your lineage. You're of the blood of Theron. They can use you as a sacrifice, and then they won't need Abby anymore. If they get you both, sacrifice you at the same time—all the tomb doors will open. The demons will be set free."

Fear has me gripping the bars covering the opening in my cell door. "How do you know all this? How long have I been gone?"

"Days," he rasps. "And I know because Boone told me. He insisted that I tell him where Abby is—and when I couldn't ..."

They beat him. "How badly are you hurt?"

He coughs again, and it sounds liquid, bloody. "Not too bad," he says, and from his tone alone, I can tell he's lying. "It took six of them, and I did plenty of damage before they captured me."

"I can't leave you behind."

"Yes, Rose, you can. You will, because you have no other choice. You have to get out of here as soon as possible. They captured Murtagh too. Don't know what they're doing to him, but he can't help us. They can steal my Gift and kill me, but my blood isn't royal. It can't be used to set the demons free. Yours is, it can. You have to go as far away from here as possible, and you have to stay away—forever."

The idea of staying away from my home and family and everything I love forever ignites a fire in my belly. Unlike Abby, I have never been prone to run, and I don't intend to start now. "I'm not leaving you behind, Gabe. I'm not going anywhere."

"I was afraid you'd say that."

"Then why are you suggesting otherwise?"

"Because it's necessary. Rose, you have to understand. The longer you're here, the bigger the chance that Abby will show up, and that will be a disaster."

I have to consciously force my fingers to loosen on the grimy metal bars. "They won't find Abby. They can't." Except I've already summoned Kye. They should be here any time.

Footsteps sound again. Gabe shushes me and resumes his coughing, and I crawl into the farthest corner, the one shrouded in shadows, and hide.

FORTY-SEVEN

Behind the Mirror

ABBY

Kye flips on the light, and for an instant, I can see again. Then, as with the other switch, the bulb shatters. But in that moment, I notice that my old night light remains plugged into the wall. *Why didn't we take it with us?* I wonder. I feel the counter and wall to find the nightlight and switch it on. The tiny bulb punctures the darkness with a comforting glow that reminds me of six-year-old me, and it stays lit, as it always did before my father left.

If only darkness was the only thing I had to fear.

I'm taller now, and my reflection so changed from the one that stared back at me the last time I fought with this mirror. I never expected to come back here again—this house, or this room—but now that I have, it's crucial that I get into that crawlspace. I haven't been inside it since my father disappeared, and I need to know why. After watching me fight with the brass-gilded monstrosity, Kye offers to try.

He trades me places, tugging and pulling on the frame to no avail. I'm about ready to pull down the shower curtain rod and smash the glass when something clicks in my brain. "When I was little," I tell Kye, "I stood on the counter to open it."

"Which would mean you had weight on the bottom edge." He reaches up and presses down on the frame, while yanking hard at the same time. With a snap and a creek, the mirror moves.

"It's working." I run my fingers along the bottom edge to loosen the seal, and pop it open further.

"There's something back there," Kye says, reminding me that I haven't told him about this part of my past.

"Yes." I drag the mirror open further and lean into the dark space. There, on the concrete floor, my pink sparkle flashlight rests on top of a thick leather book.

"Goddesses. Abby, how long have these been here?"

I crawl inside. "I don't know. I only remembered them today."

"My father's going to want to kiss you," he says, a grin in his voice. "But he'll have to get in line. Those books probably have all the answers and then some."

"Or none." And yet, as I pick up my favorite one—which also happens to be the biggest—I know. This is the thing my dad wanted me to find—and he made sure it stayed here until I was old enough to know what it means. Tears burn my eyes as I turn the spine toward Kye. "Can you read it?"

"Not in this crappy lighting." He shoves the flashlight into my hand. I click the button, surprised when a bright white beam shoots forth, pushing the shadows back. Kye freezes in place. "Has it always been that bright?"

I shake my head, trying to remember. At six, I was too small to know the difference between the brightness from a toy flashlight, and the blinding white Light created by positive energy.

"Do you remember where you got this? I don't think that's an ordinary flashlight."

I recall a birthday party, a Christmas gift, flashes of other moments, but focus on only one. "My father," I mumble, reeling. "He used to bring me presents when he traveled. Seems like he brought it to me after the last trip, before he disappeared."

Kye curls his hand over mine on the smooth plastic. "Seems like there's a trace of true Light in this thing. I wasn't aware that we could store our Gifts in inanimate objects."

"You *can* create power boosters, like my ring. The pendant. The Sunstone. I'm not sure this is any different."

"It could be different," he insists. "This 'toy' has power that no one, besides you, has held for hundreds of years. It's not the same as an ancient piece of jewelry that was created when Dryden fell or when the demons were defeated. It's a flashlight. Modern technology. This is power being stored—and recently. The only logical thing is that you must have somehow created this—deposited part of yourself in it."

"I was only six," I argue. "We weren't sure I had Gifts at that point. It was another two or three years before my Healing ability came out."

He grins, wide. "It makes total sense to me. We're born with our Gifts, but often don't discover them for years. When your dad disappeared, did you keep this flashlight with you, always? Sleep with it? Play with it? Take it to the bathroom at night?"

I hug it to my chest. "Yes. Mostly I crawled into that dark, empty room and held these books—and that light. Until we knew he was gone. Then the mirror was sealed, and we moved away, and apparently I blocked out the memory of the crawlspace, the books, and the light."

"Maybe you stored power in it without realizing it."

He makes a lot of sense. Maybe I left a part of myself in that crawlspace the night Gram told me my father was gone. Maybe it was *my* power that sealed the mirror and protected my books from being found. If that's true, maybe I can reabsorb the threads of power I left behind and conjure Light again someday?

Find your inner Light, it will never leave you.

I haven't heard Gram's voice in so many months, I almost don't recognize it until the second time it whispers to me.

Only you can control your Gifts. No one else. Not ever.

I want to believe her—need to think that Giftless is not my forever future. But as hard as I clutch the flashlight, aim it at myself, try to force the energy back into me—the hollowed out feeling remains. With demons at the door, a stack of ancient texts in my arms, and a desperate need to save my best friend, I must preserve what power is left. I click the flashlight off, plunging Kye and me back into the dimness of the nightlight, aided by ribbons of light stretching around the door.

I edge closer to Kye. "There's light coming from the other room."

"I know." He picks up some of the books. "I don't understand what's happening."

"No, I mean, I can see it."

He hesitates, realizing the significance of that. "That's good news, right?"

"Well, I'm no longer blind, so it's helpful."

"Right. It is. Light is good in battling demons, and better if you can see it, use it to our advantage." As if the mention has summoned them, shadows press in, seeping through the cracks and dimming the tiny nightlight bulb. He squints at the heavy book in my arms, lips moving as his brain searches for the language. "After the Fall: A Continued History of the Unorganized Gifted." His eyes flit to mine, dancing with frustration and relief. "Well. This would be great timing if we had time to read it before dealing with the shadows and the portal and everything."

The answering voice is deep, rough with age, and comes from behind us. "That's true. I'd prefer that you let me take it off your hands instead."

I whirl, heart racing. It's too dim to see his face, but I'd know Boone anywhere from his tall, lanky form, and the way he leans casually, arms folded, tapping his foot on the floor. "You."

"Me." Slowly, he straightens, standing in a motion that isn't as fluid as it was a year ago. His shoulder-length hair is tied back, further showcasing the puckered scar across his cheek. The shadows hide his arresting eyes, bringing deep, jagged wrinkles into sharp relief. Boone has aged significantly since I saw him six months ago. By twenty years, I'd guess. Maybe more.

"I should have known you'd be here," I spit, my arms tightening on the book as I clutch it against my chest.

"Yes," he agrees. "You should have. I expected *you* months ago. Been doing more vacationing?"

Kye inches closer, dividing the distance between me and my worst enemy. "Right. Yes. We've been vacationing. Because Abby and I have always been the ones to shrug off our duties so we can play." No one, not even Boone, could miss the sarcasm in his tone.

"Flitting around the Big Apple? Dancing on the beach? Holing up in a mountain cabin? All sounds like cake to me." As Boone steps closer, parts of him seem slightly transparent. "Gloriously delicious cake. Meanwhile, my army and I have been starving ourselves awaiting your arrival."

Hardly. This version of Boone is an image, a projection he has sent from somewhere else, but Kye and I know too well how dangerous projections can still be. A laugh bubbles out of me. "You're kidding, right? What more could you want? You've already taken my Gift." My vision wavers, and my head spins with the memories of all the horrible things Boone has done. "You and I both know that my life will end because of it. I have nothing left to give you."

"You're wrong," He growls. "Your so-called Gift—your Light—I can't use that until you die. Since you're so damn stubborn, I've paid the price. Five years of aging for every month I've waited. I can't afford to let you continue."

It's no wonder he looks so different. But I've aged too. Not at the same rate as him, but I'm years ahead of nineteen. And tired. So tired of fighting the inevitable. The weight of a five-centuries-long battle presses into me with a force I can scarcely withstand. I squeeze the book—information that may have saved us a year ago, had I only remembered it—against my chest. I'm not sure I have the will to resist anymore. "Then don't. End it now."

My eyes catch Boone's violet gaze in the half-light, possibly the only time I've actually been brave enough to stare back at those creepy things, and in them, I find a measure of respect. "If you want me dead so badly, why am I still alive? I can't Heal myself—or anyone else for that matter. I can't See what you're doing anymore. Or what's happened in the past. I can't See my best friend who is a sprite, because I've lost all traces of magic. That leaves an ordinary human girl who happens to know an extraordinary amount about the Gifted culture. It would be *so easy* to strike me down and put me out of my misery. It would be so easy for the shadows to overtake me. Then you could have my Gift. You could keep it. This battle would be over, again."

He shakes his head, laughing that same evil laugh I first heard in a vision when I was young. "That's the problem. I've decided I don't want you dead. I'm tired of fighting this battle over and over. This time, I'm after a different outcome. I'd rather have you with me—immortal."

"You'll get neither," Kye says, his voice deadly calm.

Boone's evil grin has become as familiar to me as some of Kye's quirks. "Oh, animal boy. If only you knew. See, *your* biggest problem is that you've never had to fight your own battle. Call the fairies. Call the sprites. Call the wind in the trees and blah blah blah—let *them* all come do your dirty work. Why? Because you're not man enough to do it yourself."

Each of Boone's words hit Kye like darts into his eyeballs and arrows to his chest, and he doesn't hide his emotions at all. "He's fought far more battles than you'll ever know," I start, needing to defend Kye, because I understand how it feels to have your Gift questioned, to be made to feel insignificant and inadequate because we're taught that we cannot choose our strengths—they choose us.

Boone steps out of the shadows, his image flickering like a dying movie, and as he does, so many things about him seem familiar in an entirely different way than I expect. Not *I've-seen-him-in-every-scary-nightmare-of-a-battle* familiar. There's something else, something more. He steps closer. "I've been waiting for you to recognize me.

All this time. All these years. I've watched you grow, watched you train. I've watched your grandmother haul you from city to city to keep you out of my reach. Every time, she hoped I wouldn't find you—but I always did. A man will always find what's his. A father will always find his own blood."

FORTY-EIGHT

Paralyzed

ROSE

I cower into the furthest corner of my cell with the gag wadded up in my fist. I don't know how to use it as a weapon yet, but I'll find a way. If nothing else, I could strangle someone with it. Drake flings open my cell door. "Let's go. It's time."

I'm afraid to speak, lest I remind him of my powers, but Drake isn't alone. He's brought two large men with him, and they swoop in, shoving another cloth in my mouth and covering it with tape before I can draw a breath. I scream and fight, but they're wearing earplugs, and seem impervious to the noise. One of the men lifts me by my shoulders, while the other clamps down on my legs, duct-taping my ankles, and then my wrists. I'm dumped in a heap on the ground near the stairs, so I can watch in horror as they do the same to Gabe.

Gabe's face is bloody, bruised, and one of his eyes is swollen. He gasps when they grab him, but doesn't fight. I want to scream at him—he's stronger than anyone here. I don't understand why he's allowing this. But I'm suddenly so tired, it takes all my energy to keep my eyes open.

Then I notice his arm, the blackish-red blood oozing from his inner-elbow, in the same place where Boone sliced Abby with the Arawn Dagger. They've taken his Gift. They've done to him what they did to her, and he, too, must be temporarily paralyzed. No wonder he wanted me to leave him—he can't move, and I couldn't lift him, let alone carry him up a flight of stairs. I try again to scream, but Gabe's eyes pierce me—imploring me not to fight for him.

But someone has to. Not just for him, for me. If we let them take us, they're going to kill us. They've already stolen Gabe's Gift. Mine is surely next. They'll lure Abby here, and Kye, and use us to open the final portal—to set the demons free. They'll put Boone on whatever throne they've replicated upstairs, and then they'll kill us all. The Gifted, the non-Gifted, and all the good of humanity.

One more look at Gabe, though, and realization dawns. I can't carry him up those stairs, but these big guys can. I haven't been able to escape this cell on my own, but am now being removed from it. Maybe this is a blessing in disguise.

Gabe sees me puzzling out the facts, and nods as if to say, "Let them do this." He's right. Of course he's right. He usually is. So I give up, go limp and allow my eyes to close as they take me.

My inner arm aches with the burning of a thousand suns. I slide in and out of consciousness in a way that tells me I've been drugged—I have to wake up. Every part of me aches, from the souls of my frozen, bare feet—that are currently strapped to a hard, damp stone—to the top of my greasy head, which weighs about a hundred times more than usual. My arms are wrenched behind me at the most awkward angle, secured together behind the wooden pole that digs into my back every time I move. But my mouth is surprisingly free of a gag for the first time in days.

My eyelids feel like they've been glued shut, and it takes more strength than I have to pry one open. When I do manage to blink, light stabs through the back of my head, fiery and sharp, forcing me to squeeze my lids closed once more until the pain becomes bearable enough so I can try again.

When I do, I'm immediately struck by disorientation. I'm no longer in my cell, but comprehending my new reality sends a hundred brands of fear shooting into me with razor-tipped arrows.

I'm in the center of a cavernous, circular room, made of stone and lit by spotlights that have been staked into the ground. Opposite me, on a raised dais, rests a golden throne, padded with plush velvet cushions, and embedded with real gemstones. The glorious piece is shrouded in shadows, only catching my eye when the angle of the light sparkles off the gems and gleams over the shiny gold.

To my left, the stone wall arches dramatically, giving way to a black hole, out of which seeps no light, but an immensely creepy, and crazy disturbing howl. Maybe it's the wind blowing through underground tunnels, but I suspect that it's something much worse.

From that same direction, voices echo, bouncing in the resonant space until they're impossible to decipher. To my right, four wooden stakes rise from the floor. At the bottom of each lies a roll of duct tape and a length of chain. One stake is occupied by Gabe. Because he's been paralyzed, they've leaned him against the pole and used what must be two or three rolls of tape to secure him to it. I wonder if they understand that the minute his strength returns he will rip that tape to shreds—but maybe Abby's experience was the exception rather than the rule. Maybe he'll remain paralyzed forever. Or lose his Gift, the way she did.

As I'm pondering how to save a man who is twice my size, and can't stand, a loud crash booms through the tunnel, followed by footsteps. Gabe's head swings toward me and his eyes flutter. The groan that escapes is laced with grief and the disappointment of failure. His eyes drift to my arm, where blood drips along my wrist and onto the floor. No wonder I can't move.

Rough-faced Elen stream out of the tunnel, some wrestling bundles that, in the shadowed lighting, appear to be bodies.

LEGACY

To my horror, the first in line, a wide-shouldered, red-eyed demon with inky black skin and a shiny bald head dumps his bundle against the pole next to Gabe. From this angle, it's nearly impossible to see what's happening, but at one point the body slumps forward, sending a cascade of blonde hair over the demon's arm. My throat closes and my pulse skips with fear.

Jen. They've got Jen. She's unresponsive and far too still to be conscious, but she must be alive. There would be no point in bringing her here if she was dead. This gives me a sliver of hope.

Another body arrives, and another. Eric. Then Landon. I don't want to be relieved to see these people, but the part of me that knows they're here because they're alive keeps the grief from taking over. We may all be without Gifts, but we're not alone, we're not helpless.

It's almost an hour before the last body is brought in, and during that time, my thoughts spin with possibilities of who that last pole is meant for. It can't be for both Abby and Kye. I suspect the demons know they're coming—or were coming. The only explanation is that one of them is dead. Or both. The implication cuts out a part of my heart, leaves me numb in a way that has nothing to do with paralysis. What if Abby succumbed to her injury while she was trying to keep the rest of us safe, far from home and all of us who love her? Or what if Kye did what he has always sworn to do, and sacrificed himself to save her? What if they're both gone and the demons are bringing someone else who matters to me? Who else is left?

Visions of my parents, my childhood friends—real and imagined—even my high school teachers parade through my frenzied thoughts. *No one else. Please let that stake remain empty.* When the last body is finally brought in, I gasp for breath, bracing myself. It will be impossible for me to see the last captive once they're bound. The only way I'll have any view is if the demon slants so I can catch a glimpse first.

Of everything Gabe has taught me, the most important is to know who, what, and where. To comfort myself, I make another

321

list. We're in a replicated castle, somewhere in—I think—California wine country. I'm not sure about our purpose, but it has something to do with Boone needing our powers, and maybe our blood, the way he needed Abby's in Mexico. Now for who: Boone. Drake. That guy Tynan who terrorized Abby and Kye before they closed the first portal. And all of us. Me, Gabe, Jen, Eric, Landon ... and someone else. One last person.

Because I can do nothing else to get their attention, I cough. Then I cough again, and soon I have a convincing coughing fit going. The demon carrying the last body shifts, and my fake coughing falters with surprise when I see that it's not Abby or Kye. The demon is carrying Abby's friend Tanya.

We're the last of the documented Gifted. The last in the line of Theron and Raina—and though there are others in the world, we're the last hope for the restoration of the order of the Gifted in this lifetime. This can only mean one of two things.

Either Abby and Kye are both dead, or we're here to wait for them to arrive, and then the battle is about to get all kinds of real.

FORTY-NINE

Into the Portal

ABBY

A hysteria-riddled laugh bubbles out of my chest. "You're not my father. My father was gentle and kind and good. He spent his life working hard to bring the Gifted population together. He gave his life to protect my mother and grandmother and me."

"Abigail." Boone's voice, absent of malice and evil, stabs a pick into my heart with the eerie familiarity of it. "How much do you remember about your childhood?"

I was so small when my father disappeared. Yet, it wasn't all that long ago. I remember his face—or at least, I think I do—and it looks nothing like Boone. Nothing. "Enough to know you're not him."

I've let my anger carry me forward, but Kye grabs my arm and drags me to the door. "Abby, it's time. We need to go now."

"No, Kye. It's not." I wrench to get free, but Kye keeps a strong grip.

"We can't stay here." His voice shakes, but his fingers dig painfully into the soft skin near my elbow. "We were wrong to come here first. We have to go after Rose. She needs us."

Rose. Rose has been kidnapped, I remind myself. *She's in trouble.* Kye's communicating with her through thoughts, so I should pay attention. Getting to her must be a priority, because Kye wouldn't be pushing for us to leave without closing this portal for any other reason.

He opens the bathroom door and I let him propel me out, feet moving mechanically because I no longer care about the portal, or about Boone. I don't care about saving the kingdom or becoming a powerless queen or restoring my Gifts. In this moment, I care about exactly one thing. Getting to Rose in time to save her. Nothing else will be worth anything to me if I lose Rose in the process.

"You remember my voice," Boone says, and because the malice and hatred has vanished from it, I might. But at this point, it's hard to tell if I recognize it because of my visions and dealings with Boone, or because I've known it since I was young. My childhood memories and my more recent ones blur into a tangled mass, and picking out one sound or another seems an impossible task.

"You look nothing like my father," I insist. "I remember his face. I'll never forget his face."

"People change over a decade," he says. "We age. We have surgeries. Or, like in my case, we steal the Gifts of others, and it changes us enough that our own families wouldn't know us in passing."

I whip around, dragging Kye to a halt as my chest heaves with pressure. "My father didn't have violet eyes. He didn't have wrinkles, and his chin was square, not triangular. His hair was dark, I admit, but he would never have worn it long. My *father* would never have shot at my boyfriend, tried to steal my Gifts and left me to die, or given me over to a maniac who meant to do me harm. You couldn't be my father, because my father was brave and smart and good, and you are none of those things."

"Abby ..." he says. "Darling." And in that instant, he's blown the lie. My dad hated that word. Boone is not my father, but he stole something precious from him—his Gift. The same way he stole mine. Maybe Boone thinks that our connected Gifts link us. They don't. They never will.

It's not the first time I question Boone's sanity—certainly, for him to be so obsessed over power that belongs to others, he would have to be off his rocker—but a new idea takes root in my brain. How must the addition of all the Gifts he has stolen affect his mental capacity? What if he believes that part of him *becomes* these people?

Boone closes the distance between us again, flickering slightly the way Tynan did in the subway in New York, and takes his place in the doorway that divides the living room and kitchen. Opposite him, Kye continues to drag me to the exit, prepared to leave as soon as I'm willing to go.

"Don't call me that. You can't trick me into believing your lies. "

"I can help you get your powers back," he offers. "Stronger than ever. Along with any other powers you wish for. You can bring your boy-toy along," he says. "We'll help him gain more powers too. All you have to do is walk through the portal and come out on the other side."

Kye must sense my internal struggle. "He can't. Abby, we both know that's not the way you want things to happen. We both know he's not your father."

Though it's evil, horrible, and the worst thing I've ever considered doing, I'm tempted. So tempted. Because I miss having power. If I still had my power, I would be able to fight off these demons, Boone, and all his henchmen.

"It's a trap," Kye says, fear inching into his voice. He knows I'm considering it.

"I understand," I tell him. I take his fingers and entwine us together. Whatever's on the other side of this portal is something we need. The thing that will end this fight for good. I rise to my tiptoes and kiss Kye. He keeps his eyes open, surprise and wariness mingling in a pattern that is laced with anxiety.

"I can feel you drifting away," he says, desperation evident in his tone. "Don't do this. Please don't do it. We don't know what could happen to you, but whatever that is, you'd be in Boone's territory. Whatever it is will likely be horrible, and I can't bear that."

"I love you," I tell him, and I wipe my lipstick off Kye's chin. Then I turn toward Boone's flickering image, and against Kye's adamant objections, I walk past him and straight into the enormous black hole surrounded by hot, white light. I hold tight to the old book and my flashlight, and step into the portal. The tiny house disintegrates altogether.

FIFTY

In Trouble

ROSE

By the time the demons have Tanya bound, Gabe stirs again. I can tell that he's struggling to wake up. The pallor of his skin is so white he all but glows in the darkness of the shadows. They must have had to slice him deeply to steal his strength, because he has so many layers of muscle, and the loss of blood shows. I can't see his wound well, but I hope that Drake was kind enough to bind it so Gabe doesn't bleed out in front of us. He doesn't look good.

Tanya is far down the line, so I can't tell what's been done to her, but I do know that she can't be bound holding her baby. I hope they don't have him too, but there's no way for me to know. It's possible that he's dead, and if that's true, Tanya will be more heartbroken over losing Cole than I was after losing Alex; she'll be useless when things start to go down.

I need a plan.

Even if I wasn't the only conscious person in this sad group of once-Gifted individuals, Boone's men wouldn't let us communicate. I wish I could reach inside the brains of the others the way I communicated with Kye—and so I resolve to try.

I close my eyes, focus, pinpoint my last memory of Gabe, his face, his eyes, the way his lips move when he speaks. The cactus he gave me, which refused to give up on life, the way he refused to give up on me.

Gabe, can you hear me? Wake up. Wake up and listen to me.

Nothing. He doesn't stir, let alone answer.

I try again, pushing more energy, what little I have, into my efforts. *Gabe, wake up. We're in danger. We have to make a plan.*

Not a flutter of his eyelids. This is bad. So bad. I try the others—all of them—desperation closing in with each failed attempt. None of them can hear me. Can feel me. Drake is not present, but the large men who brought in Tanya stand as they finish securing her to the pole. I'm not sure if they've noticed I'm awake or not, but I have to do something.

I clear my throat and squeak, "I don't suppose I can have some water?"

Neither acknowledges my question, but one glances my way as he drops the empty tape roll on the ground at Tanya's feet. His eyes meet mine, and in them I see nothing. Emptiness. No recognition, or coherence. It's as if he's a robot, here to do a job, and no more. I've always wondered if I could command a robot. I try again, this time forcing what little power I have left into my Voice. "Bring me water."

They don't, but this time, the second also glances my way. They hear me when I speak. They may not understand, but they either hear that I'm speaking, or feel the low vibrations of my Gift.

Never thought I'd be weaker than I was at eight, when a lunchroom bully tried to steal my brownie, and I was so intimidated that I let him. But I was wrong. No matter what I demand or say to our captors, they're impervious to my words.

Without my Voice, I don't know how to stop the demons. But if I don't come up with something—anything—all my friends, everyone I love is going to die. Even my parents, because if I die, and Jenn and Eric and Landon and Tanya and Abby and Kye—if we all die, my parents are next. And Abby's mom. We'll be wiped out, extinct. The demons win. They'll be free to roam and to terrorize those who don't know what they are. The world will become something else entirely.

Gabe groans in his state of unconsciousness. He may not have his Gift anymore, but Gabe's smart. He's resourceful. He's a Dragon. He'll be able to help save our friends. I hope.

"Gabe," I whisper. "Hurry and wake up. We're in trouble."

His head swivels, but his eyes remain closed. He's trying so hard to fight whatever is happening to him. When one of his eyes does pop open, it's glazed and unfocused, but aimed near or at me. That's something. At least he can hear, where the guards, who have taken up residence near the opening to the next dungeon passage, cannot.

"Gabe, wake up," I insist. "We're all going to die. We have to do something."

He blinks, blinks, blinks, and his lips move as if he wants to speak, but can't.

A great flash of brightness from the hall lights up the cavern like sunlight, and I hear a voice. A distinctly familiar one.

Abby is here. All hell is about to break loose.

FIFTY-ONE

Small, Dark Places

ABBY

Light. Noise. Sound. Everything and nothing at once, so much of both. My skin tingles with numbness and my eyes flash with light and dark, never once having a moment to recover. The scar on my arm explodes with burning pain, consuming me until that pain becomes my sole focus, and then I'm shoved unceremoniously forward.

I land on my hands and knees, dropping the book to the hard ground and sending my flashlight rolling away. My landing echoes against stone walls, as do the shouts that accompany my entrance. Voices—multiple voices—uproar in a foreign language unfamiliar to me. The echo making everything louder, overwhelming as I try to orient myself, begging my muscles to move, while they refuse.

What the hell? Am I in *another* freaking cave? Why does every battle have to be fought underground? Why do I always end up facing hordes of demons in small, dark places?

My palms sting from my landing, and the pain in my arm stabs like hot fire. I have to blink, blink, blink to force my eyes to adjust. As I've been doing for weeks, I reach deep inside myself, wishing I could catch the smallest trace of the Light I once controlled—but as I've come to expect, find nothing. Sighing, I refocus my efforts on assessing my current situation.

The walls here are made of stone, as is the ground, but it's manufactured and laid brick by brick, so ... not a cave, but a building. This fact gives me more relief than I imagined it could. I'm tired of caves. I wish I could fight one of these major battles outside in the sunlight. Or the moonlight. Starlight. Freak, a streetlight would work. But manufactured spotlights like the ones here are better than I've had in the past, and buildings are better than caves. They have doors that lead outside, rather than tunnels that take you deeper into darkness and gloom.

Part of me expects to look up and find Kye, unconscious and injured somewhere nearby, even though I left him on the other side of the portal, whole and unharmed. It's how these battles have always gone, and I can't tell how long I was trapped in the portal—in some ways it felt like months.

This time no one's lying injured on the ground, no broken friend dead in a corner. There *is* blood. Lots of it. A long trail leading through the door and into another room, where I'm sure to find something I don't want to see.

Before I can react, an ink-skinned, red-eyed demon, and a gray-skinned one with thick, white hair close in on me. They yank me off the floor and pin my arms behind me so they can—I assume—parade me to the next location, to see whomever they work for, who will then attempt to force me to open yet *another* tomb of demons. But this time, I have no power to open a tomb, no magic jewelry. No Light. I can't hold up the weight of my body at the moment, so I expect this situation, this battle, to go differently than the last two. For better or worse, this tomb will be my last.

"Where are you taking me?" If I'm going to die, I'd like to know who is behind it this time, and maybe where I am. The demons don't respond—I'm not sure they understand. The black one drags me into the next room. In the contrast between light and dark, it's hard to make out what I'm seeing, but there appear to be trees growing out of the ground. The trunks are oddly shaped, and seem to move, the way faerie trees move in a forest. Slowly, and slightly, and ever so gradually, as if they haven't moved at all.

I'm plunked onto a giant armchair, padded in velvet, but plated in gold and encrusted with gems. It's one of the things I would have admired as a child when I obsessed over TV series' about royalty and fifteenth century foreign government. A throne for a King. Or a Queen. But rather than perching in this one while showcasing a corset and a tiara, I'm forced into it, wearing jeans, unable to move, and my wrists are bound to the armrests with duct tape while the white-haired demon binds my ankles to the chair legs.

I can sense eyes watching, but keep mine averted, afraid of who—or what—I may see. I no longer want to know who is here. I don't want to know what he wants, because I already have a plan. I walked through Boone's portal to get here, and he's sure to follow. As soon as he does, when I'm sure Kye is safe, I'm going to let the demons kill me.

I have no powers with which to fight, nothing left to give but my life, and that's what they're after. I have no disillusions about walking out of here alive. But as long as Kye can hold his own against Boone—and I know he can, he always has—he'll survive, and be able to go after Rose. My friends and family are home in Jackson, safe. This battle is about to end for all of us.

It isn't until I hear a faint voice croak, "Abby" that I squint into the shadows and realize my mistake.

Those aren't trees. They're poles. With people tied to them. Six of them. And my best friend, Rose, is one of them.

FIFTY-TWO

Another Death

ROSE

Abby must be disoriented, or hurt. The demons who brought us in have brought her too, and rather than fight, she sits there with glazed, empty eyes and lets them strap her to that stupid, ugly gold throne. Kye's not with her, and that worries me. If something happened to him, she won't have the will to fight back.

She doesn't seem interested in who's tied to the poles on this side of the enormous room—maybe she can't see us?—but she should be, so once the demons have bound her and backed off, I summon what little is left of my scratchy voice and call out to her. "Abby."

Instantly, she goes on alert. Her eyes find focus and she squints as if struggling to see. "Rose? Is that you?"

I can waste no time—there's no telling how long the demons will allow us to talk. Especially me. It can only be an oversight that they have—until now—left me without a gag for the first time in days. "It's all of us, Abby. Me and Gabe, Jen, Eric and Landon. Your friend Tanya too. We've been sliced by the dagger and tied to poles. We're all being drained."

She stares in our direction, looking confused. "How did you get here?"

"I don't know about the others, but they kidnapped me," I tell her, internally begging her to focus. Something's wrong with my friend, different. "I got here via the trunk of some scary dude's car." Part of me is waiting for her to tell me what's happened to Kye, and another part of me is afraid to know.

"I came through a portal," she says, her voice weak. There's no power behind her words, but a wooden mechanical tenor that makes me worry that Abby—the strongest of the strong—has given up all hope.

Another flash of light blazes bright in the other room, more voices, more shouting. Abby perks up, white-hot fear etched into her every feature.

Kye stumbles in, unbound and clutching a book to his chest. He bypasses the demons and goes straight to Abby. "Babe. What were you thinking? Why would you deliberately go through a portal when you're unable to defend yourself? What purpose do you think this will serve?"

"I'm done, Kye," she says. "I can't fight anymore. I'm tired. I wanted to end the battle for all of us, so you could save Rose."

"How are we supposed to do that now?" he asks. "We don't even know where *we* are, let alone where she is."

I clear my throat. "Rose is right here. Along with all our other friends."

Kye whips around, shock etched in the way he stands, the position of his shoulders and hips. "What's going on? What are you all doing here?"

"It's a freaking reunion or something, except everyone is tied up and our powers are being drained. But hey, maybe they'll serve cake later. Or something." I try to shrug, but with my arms tied, all it does is wrench my shoulder in pain. "My guess is that we're here to act as blood sacrifices, since they told Gabe we're of the blood of Theron, but you should verify with the guy who kidnapped me in the first place. Wherever he is. He seems to have big plans. He has a big enough army to have erected a castle and staffed the dungeons, because I've been stuck in it for days."

Kye shakes his head in disbelief, stepping off the dais and moving toward me, incredulous. "Why haven't you fought your way out? How could you let them keep you hostage for so long? Your mouth isn't even gagged." He glances toward Gabe. "And him, how has he not broken free of his bonds? How are all of you here?"

I meet his judgmental gaze with one of my own. "We've been drained, Kye. Our Gifts are useless. The demons have taken them." My attention slides from his face, down his shoulder to his arm. He's not bruised, let alone cut. "Except, apparently, yours."

Kye leans closer, squinting at the line of blood dripping from my arm onto my toes and the ground beneath them, then he glances down the line at unconscious friends, attempting to process this information. "How are you supposed to help open a tomb without your Gifts?"

If my hands weren't bound, I'd smack my cousin right now. So hard. Across the cheek so his eye feels like exploding. "I don't think that's the goal this time. More like exterminating us, maybe."

Recognition dawns as he looks down the row at how many of us have been captured and drained. We're bound, bleeding, creating a river that flows down the slope of the floor toward the dais, where Abby is perched—her Gifts, having been already drained. As he considers his own Gift, and the fact that he hasn't been bound, hasn't been drained, hasn't been kidnapped or chased. "It's me this time, isn't it? All this, all of you—they knew I'd come for you. All of you. They know I'd do anything to save you. I'm the one they want."

"Very good, Animal Boy." Boone strides in, the bright green emeralds in the Arawn Pendant reflecting lights and bouncing them across the room as it dangles from his wrist, stealing the attention from the dagger in his hand. He signals to the silent, who immediately seize my cousin and hold him in place as if awaiting further instruction. "Astute and all that. No. It's not about you, specifically. I only need one of you with power to create a pool of blood and set the demon army free."

He hops up next to Abby and runs the side of his blade along the tape that's keeping her there, draws it up her arm, the sharp edge threatening to dig in, should he flick the handle one way or another. "I was trying to decide which of you is most important to her, which of you she would most likely die to protect. Who would she jump into hell for? Problem is, I've learned she would do those things for any of you. All of you. That makes you her reasons for living. Her motivation, if you will, for refusing my offer of immortality."

His blade rises up Abby's neck, where he angles it against the tender underside of her chin. "What else can I do, but take you out of the equation? I *need* her. But I don't need the rest of you."

Except me. I am of the blood of Theron, and he knows it. So is Kye. What is this game he's playing?

Abby's voice is small, weak, but carries in the vast room. "If you kill them all, I wouldn't accept. If you take my family from me, I'll die too."

His smirk turns to a sneer as he swipes the dagger across Abby's cheek, and then abruptly removes it from her altogether so he can bounce it in his hand once, twice, three times. Before I can breathe in relief, the dagger rockets across the room, embedding itself Eric's chest. He hasn't stirred since he arrived, but wakes abruptly with the burning pain of having an obsidian blade driven into his flesh. He lets out an animal-like noise—half scream of pain, half rage—before blood bubbles out of his mouth. His eyes lock on Abby until the moment they go blank, and then his head falls forward.

Abby lets out a tormented wail, and Kye wrestles against his demons captors, shouting, screaming. "No! Eric. I'm sorry. I'm so sorry. Boone, please. Why are you doing this? Killing our friends won't change Abby's mind."

Hot rage boils inside me, burning through my eyes, into my throat. I no longer care what they do to me, or to my friends. We're all going to die anyway. All that matters to me in this moment is that this Boone dude dies the same kind of horrific, painful death that Alex had to suffer.

LEGACY

I still have the cloth gag wadded in my hands. While no one is paying attention, I un-fist them and drop the cloth on the ground. Doing so loosens the tape enough so I can pull the shard of glass from my back pocket and work on sawing my tape binding. The glass isn't sharp, having crumbled and cracked in transit, and the tape is thick, and I have to be careful not to draw attention to my movements, but it's all I have, and so I keep my face focused forward, while I work furiously to free my hands.

FIFTY-THREE

Golden Throne, Jeweled Dagger

ABBY

Boone's blade sinks into Eric's chest so quickly, and with such finality, that it takes several long seconds for my brain to compute what's happened. His eyes—my friend's eyes—stare at nothing, cold and empty, and too dead to be Healed, while Rose and I both scream at the sight of the blood pouring from his chest and pooling at his feet. Rose wiggles against her bindings, obviously beginning to regain feeling in her limbs. At least the paralysis wears off eventually.

Caught between the horror of Eric's unexpected murder and the fear of what Boone will do next, I force myself to speak. "Why did you have to kill him? He was unconscious! Did he even know why he was taken?"

"Someone had to go first." With a casual shrug, Boone strolls to Eric. He withdraws the dagger with a sickening slurp, wiping the blade on Eric's shirt to remove some of the blood. "I have no bias toward any particular one of your friends. They're all going to die today. It's simply a matter of who dies when, and what I have to do to them to make you reconsider your options. He felt like the least important, thus, he was the first to go."

"Abby won't reconsider, no matter what you do to us," Kye says. "She knows what it would mean to join you, to become immortal. She knows that we're better off dying."

But as my eyes travel from person to person, I'm not sure if that's true. Tanya has a son to raise. My mother needs Landon in her life, because when I'm gone, he's all she'll have. Jen has a lot of relationships to fix, mistakes she may want to rectify before leaving things undone. Even if she doesn't, I want to make sure she understands that I love her and am grateful for her, that I never meant to hurt her.

Gabe ... I need Gabe to stay alive. I have so many things to say to him, so many more things to experience with him. He can't die because I was stupid and left him behind. And Rose. Rose has been my best friend since I moved to Jackson. She's the reason I am who I've become. She held me up and supported me during the hardest times, introduced me to my true destiny, and how have I repaid her for that? I left her in the moment when she needed me more than ever. In so many ways, I owe my life to her.

Eric saved my life once, because he loved me enough. He refused to kill me, no matter that it cost him his only family tie and left him alone. The fact that he was the reason I almost died became irrelevant when he confessed to having loved Raina for hundreds of years. He didn't deserve to die for being my friend, for loving me.

I can't let Boone kill anyone else, even if I don't have the powers I need to stop him.

He bends to touch the blood at Eric's feet, a feral grin splitting his scarred face as he straightens, playing with a tiny marble of red. Ice. His laugh starts low and gleeful, but takes only seconds to become a huge, power-hungry expression of elation as he tosses the marble at the wall and watches it shatter, then bends down and picks up another one. He presses his hand to Eric's still-warm body, and Kye, Rose and I watch, horrified, as Eric's pale skin turns blue while ice creeps up and over his shoulder, down his arm, across his chest.

Beside Rose, Gabe stirs, blinking. His eyes land on me while the others are focused on Boone, and he starts to move, clumsily, and jerkily, and not at all subtle. My eyes widen in alarm, and I shake my head to warn him to be careful.

"Yes," Boone chortles. "Your friends are all going to die, Abigail. Maybe I'll give your Gifts back when you agree to join me. Hell, maybe I'll give you theirs too!"

There's a lump in my throat the size of Kansas. He's serious.

"Course, that means *you* would have to be the one to wield the knife, but I'm sure that can be arranged."

"I won't. I won't hurt my friends." I shake my head as Boone throws another handful of ice across the room, seemingly amused as the ice melts and leaves red rivers of blood cascading down the wall.

He sighs, rolling one last marble back and forth across his palm. After what feels like a ridiculous amount of time, he rips the tape off one of my wrists so he can turn my hand over and place the marbled blood in it. "Feel that? There's power in Gifted blood. Power you need to survive. It's life, you see. Our Gifts. This is how we become immortal. By taking the lifeblood of others." He nods at the marble. "This one was mine—had to be, as Erim betrayed me for you in the beginning. But the rest—they belong to you. You've cultivated them, given them reason to train. These humans follow you, they worship you, and so you'll take their Gifts, because if you don't, they'll suffer. Everyone they love will suffer. Everyone left in the world who you love will also suffer. Those children in Texas. The villagers in Mexico. The baby in Jackson. Your human mother. If you love these people, if they matter to you at all, be merciful. Take their Gifts yourself so you can keep them close. So they can speak to you. So you will know all that they know. This is how the Immortal Elen will continue."

Gram, lying on the floor of our apartment in Las Vegas, taking her last breaths while I hover over her, trying to Heal her and failing miserably. "It's not your time to go, Gram," I said.

340

"Yes, baby, it is."

I held her, my hands and arms and lap covered in her blood, as her spirit separated from her body, as the energy left her for the last time. It was only after that when I began hearing her voice in my head, knowing ancient chants, what herbs should be used to Heal which ailment, and which crystals should be placed where. Gram wouldn't let me Heal her—maybe because she knew that if she died like that, in my arms, I would receive the remnants of her Healing Gift. Maybe she knew it was the best way. If that's true, she gave her life to strengthen and preserve my Gift of Healing. My Light.

Juri may have killed my Gram, technically, but Juri is dead, obliterated by the power Boone just stole from Eric. What Boone has taken from me is far more lasting than that of a mortal body. Nonetheless, the realization of what happened with Gram gives me hope. Not because of her death itself, but because if Gifts can be transferred, shared, stolen—then what has been taken from me can also be restored. What has been taken from all of us can be returned. I intend to get it back. We only have to bleed.

"If I agree to this, will you promise to not make my friends suffer?" I roll the blood marble until I have it pinched between my thumb and index finger, displaying it next to my face, where Boone can see. "Can you promise their deaths will be as quick and painless as possible?"

Kye gasps in shock and horror, his eyes boring into me as if trying to decide if he truly knows me at all. I level my gaze on him, for only an instant, but in that time he finds what he needs. He knows I have a plan.

"I promise nothing," Boone sneers, his nod indicating Eric. "They have to bleed out. But if we get it right, it won't last long. Like this guy here. Minutes, at most."

Bile rises in my throat, but I shove it ruthlessly down. "That will have to be enough," I agree.

Boone stares at me, calculating.

"If you want me to be the one to do it, you're going to have to cut me free. Unless you'd rather I watch?"

Still, he hesitates.

I squish the marble between my fingers, so Eric's blood runs down my arm. "Is there something I say to make this work, or ... ?"

He opens his fisted palm to reveal a gash. "You accept the power here. Take it from the inner arm, here." He demonstrates by drawing lines with the dagger on his inner arm, but not drawing blood. "Pull the energy in as you would when Healing."

I force myself to nod, to fake an eager enthusiasm I don't feel. "That's it? Then I become immortal?"

"You take what's left of their mortal existence, added onto the end of your own. Immortality must continually be fed. We'll start with these, and when your life force thins to ten or twenty years, you'll need to take more."

I gulp audibly, swallowing my disgust. It's horrible, what these demons have done. Have been doing for centuries. I wonder at what point a being ceases to be human and transitions to demon. After murdering five or six people? Twenty? A hundred? I've seen a lot of shadows in my time, and lots of dark, demonic men. Sly ones, silver foxes, cunning and shallow, and yet ... though Boone has outlived one mortal lifetime, and retains a number of stolen Gifts, I'm certain he's not full demon. He's still partly human, which means he can bleed and die. Kye starts to struggle, and the gray demon threads long, rope-like fingers around his neck, threatening to cut off his air supply.

Don't fight them. I think to him. *If you can hear me, wait, I know what to do.*

I nod at Boone's weapon. "Have you changed your mind, or can I borrow that to get to work? If I'm going to kill my friends, I should do it while they're unconscious and can't talk me out of it." I need to get my hands on that dagger and wound myself, bleed myself. Then I need to wound my friends.

Boone frees my feet first, and then my other arm, moving with deliberate caution. It takes every ounce of willpower I have to not kick him, punch him, or knee him in the groin as he bends over me. I'm still weak, and so fragile as an un-gifted human. I have to choose my actions carefully, strike at the right time. "Will it paralyze me again?"

"No, not this way."

I allow him to take my hand and run the blade across my palm, wincing as the skin separates and a new wound gushes forth, along with something else. Something huge and important that I've missed. I'm bleeding. On myself. Into my own wound. Light-infused energy surrounds me as if waiting for an invitation to return. An invitation I'm not sure how to make, but it's waiting, and that knowledge fills me with confidence.

I stare at my bleeding palm for so long, Juri starts to laugh. "What were you expecting? Power to come rushing in? That's not how it works. You won't get your own power back without one of us dying. You saw how I took Eric's?" I nod. "You will never get back what you had before. Your only chance is to take that which belongs to others."

Thus, how the Dark Elen began.

"I have to use the blade?" I ask, refusing to give up hope, and Boone nods.

"The only power draining source ever invented."

I hold out my palm, waiting. Reluctantly, he places the dagger in my hand. The moment I tighten my fingers on the grip, the energy surrounding us shifts. It rushes at me as if all the good, loving energy has been waiting for someone to tap into it.

The weight of the Arawn dagger is heavy in my hand, as the magic and the darkness pulse in the instrument that has been so often demonically abused. I tighten my grip on the hilt and whirl on Boone, shoving the dagger into his thigh as he lunges at me.

He shrieks a stream of profanity that my father would never use. I recall how in Mexico, Boone disguised himself as Gabe, luring me to the tomb, and the memory cements my certainty. Boone is not my father.

The moment Boone pulls the blade free of his thigh, I reclaim it and shove it deep into his chest, without hesitation. He slides to the floor, seizing, his eyes glazed and unfocused like Eric's.

I stare at the blood pouring from his mouth, afraid to move, because it's not over. Killing a demon couldn't be so easy.

Then he gasps. One large, long breath, his body convulsing as thousands of shadows break free of his body, hurling themselves at all my unconscious friends. Rose's eyes pop open. "Good going, Abby. Way to take down the one bad guy. Now what about the rest?"

"Now!" I shout to Kye. During my struggle with Boone, he has managed to gain an upper hand on the demons holding him back, and breaks free long enough to reach the flashlight I dropped earlier. He flicks it on, battling the hordes of demons converging on us.

I yank the dagger free and stumble toward Rose, wiping the blood on my pant leg so I can use it on her next. "What are you doing? I thought you were bluffing. Abby, don't do this. I'm your best friend." Her eyes glare at the offending weapon. "Get away from me with that thing. Stay back. I'm serious."

Rose has almost broken through the tape binding her, but not quite, which makes it easier for me to ignore her protests and slice open her palm, and then re-probe her arm. When I cut the tape holding her in place, she throws a weak punch, and stumbles into me, the paralysis taking its toll. I take her hand and force her to rub her injured palm to the tender spot where she was stabbed in the first place. Once more, the energies in the room shift. "You can't steal my power, Abby, Boone already did." Her voice is as weak as her muscles, but she tries anyway. "I can't believe you would turn on us after everything. After how hard we have fought to keep you safe, to keep you alive."

"Shut up," I tell her, continuing to move her wounded palm over her bloody inner elbow. "I'm not stealing from you. I'm helping you get your Gift back."

As if it hears and understands, a shadow flies at us, launching with sickening speed. Rose is still slow moving—her strength not yet restored—so I shove her behind me as Kye leaps toward us, aiming my flashlight at the demon while wrenching his energy wand out of a holster on his ankle. The shadow shrinks back, cowering in the corner.

I shove Rose's hand against her arm again. "Keep going." As Rose's Gift returns to her, she reanimates—the Gift accompanied by spirit, by strength. "Thank you," she breathes.

More demons escape from Boone, as if all the Gifted lives he took became dark forces that found their home inside him. I hand Rose the dagger. "Help restore Gifts to the others so they can help wrangle the shadows. I have a prison to destroy, and I want to take down as many shadows as we can in the process."

"Abby," Kye shouts from across the room. "Take this." He tosses me the flashlight. "Don't forget to restore your own."

I hesitate, not wanting to take with me a source of their protection. Rose waves me on, standing like she's about to take on the world and knows exactly how to do it. "Take it. We've got this."

Strangely, I believe that she does. A lot has happened since I went away. I shove the flashlight in my pocket, pick up my book, and grab Boone's arm so I can drag his body into the room with the portal, unsure about what comes next, but certain that it's his blood that will finally finish this fight once and for all.

Inside the tunnel, darkness presses in, pulsing with energy and inverted light to create a black hole of nothingness. My Light has not returned yet, so I flip on the flashlight, allowing the warm glow to keep the shadows at bay. Any that dare close in are immediately burned, so they circle the outskirts of the circle cast by my Light and shriek like castle ghosts, waiting for an opportunity while I thumb through the thick book, praying that the information I need is inside it.

Shrieks and shouts coming from the chamber where my friends are fighting act as the worst sort of distraction, but I continue skimming until my eye lands on a word. Neutralize. I go back over the paragraph, and then the page. It's going to take blood and chanting from all of us, the more the better, and a combination of all of our Gifts, but together we can do it.

I glance at Boone on the floor, his eyes glazed and glassy, but his chest continues to rise and fall with each shallow, labored breath as more shadows pour out of him.

"Kye, Rose!" I holler. "When you get everyone revived, bring them in here. I'm going to need help—from all of you." Neither of them responds, and I'm not sure they can hear me over the noise. From the corner of my eye, I catch sight of a roll of duct tape on the floor and dive for it. It takes all my strength, but I manage to roll Boone onto his front so I can bind his wrists and ankles. As payback for what he did to Rose, I press one last strip over his mouth.

When I return to the other room, Gabe's crumpled in a heap on the floor, still paralyzed, and Kye stands guard over him, wielding the energy wand to keep the demons from overtaking Gabe while he's defenseless. Eric's blood runs across the floor beneath his body, which has been—thankfully—left alone, but Jen has been set free, and so has Landon. Tanya's feet have been unbound, but it appears Rose was interrupted before slicing through the tape at her wrists. She gasps and groans as she squirms, trying to free herself.

Landon has Kye's demon captors cornered, an energy wand in each hand, but Jen has Rose cowering in a corner, surrounded by flames tall enough to lick at the tips of her hair.

I run to Tanya and rip the tape free. "Landon ..." I croak.

She's already moving. "On it."

This time, I will not desert my Rose.

FIFTY-FOUR

Burning

ROSE

"You should have listened to me," Jen shrieks. Her flames ignite, reaching for the tips of my hair and sizzling down the loose threads on my tattered clothes. "But you never do. You never have. You think because you have a vocal Gift that it has more weight, more importance than mine. But you're wrong. You may be able to persuade armies to march on anthills, but I can burn those hills into ash without risk or demand to anyone else. I command the fire. Soon, I will command the ice, and your friend Victor's wind, and when I do, Abby's Light can't touch me, can't stop me from taking charge of my own life. I will be a goddess, and you—all of you—will bemoan the day you left me behind to suffer the burning all alone."

"Jen, I never meant to desert you. I would never intentionally leave you to suffer, I've tried to reach out to you—"

"Shut up, Rose," she screams. There's madness in her eyes, and burning hate I've never seen in my friend before. It frightens me. "Your lies only make it worse. You knew I was struggling. You knew I was afraid that the fire would consume me. You knew Val was pushing me too hard, but the minute Abby got homesick—poor, picked on Abby, who was forced to stay in a Caribbean beach house with a maid and a cook and her own private bodyguard—you hopped a plane without more than a 'see ya later.' No one ever considered that maybe I could help. Maybe I could have fought those demons with you. While you were off partying and meeting boys and getting drunk, I was stuck here, alone, with no one but Valdemar and Eric to taunt me about how I'll never be good enough, no matter how hard I work, because no one can truly control fire. Not even someone Gifted with a knack for it."

Behind Jen, Abby has returned, holding something pink and sparkly. Looks like maybe a toy flashlight. Whatever it is seems to keep the demons away.

"Jen." I'm careful to keep my voice calm, neutral. "I did invite you. I offered to pay for your ticket, remember? I practically begged you to come with me because I didn't *want* to leave you here alone. And when I got back, even at the time when I was more devastated than I ever remember, I came to you. I tracked you down at that guy's house and you blew me off. You sent me away. You didn't want anything to do with me."

"Oh stop with the self-sacrifice crap. You came to find me because you were lonely and sad. Abby did what I always warned you she would do—she left when you needed her most—and you came scurrying back to me like a frightened little mouse because you don't know how to be alone."

"I do," I insist, venturing a step forward, only to be pushed back when Jen's flames rise higher and brighter. "I spent over a month alone, holed up in my house while I let depression and sadness win. You want to know the sad thing, Jen? All I kept thinking was how I had let you down, how I'd let Abby down and everyone else. How no one would ever love me again. And I was right—I let you down, and you may never forgive me. But someone does love me. I'm not talking about you or Abby or Alex—who, by the way, died a horrible death there while you were here cultivating your anger.

"I'm talking about the one person who showed up to support me, and who pulled me out of my massive depression. I knew what he was doing, and resisted, but he was stronger. That's why I survived, because of *him*. I'm so sorry that I wasn't strong enough to help you survive, too. So sorry. I tried, Jen. I did. I'm weak, and I didn't know you needed me in that way. If I had, I would have found the strength—for you. Because you're my best friend and I love you."

"People who love each other don't leave one another behind, suffering." Jen advances on me, and her flames rise toward the ceiling, the heat scorching the hairs on my skin and leaving burn marks on what's left of my clothes. I can't hold in the scream that wrenches out of me—I cannot imagine a more painful death than burning, and that death creeps ever closer.

"You're wrong, Jen." Abby's voice rises above my screams and the roaring of the flames. "Sometimes we do leave people we love behind. Sometimes we have to. If we love them enough, if that's the only way to protect them, to save them, we leave despite the agony of loss. Because real love, that is true and pure, is unselfish. It requires nothing, but gives everything."

"Shut up, Abby," Jen spits, rounding on her. "You know nothing about love. *You* don't run away for love. You run because of it. Because you're afraid of having anyone or anything matter to you. Because when we care about someone else, we give them the power to hurt us. Every one of us has cared about you, and look at where that got us! Gabe's paralyzed, Rose almost lost her power, we've almost died multiple times, and Eric—who has loved you for five hundred years—is dead. This ... all of this started because of you, and now it needs to end—right here, with you."

The flames rise and fall with Jen's voice, and I marvel that she has more control of her Gift than I realized, more than maybe *she* realizes. As she focuses on Abby, the flames surrounding me sputter and leap, and occasionally a gap opens between the columns. At one point, the break opens wide enough that I jump through. The flames singe my arms, and eyebrows, and the ends of my hair, but luckily none of it catches as I hurtle out of the circle and bolt to take down Jen before she can burn Abby for a witch or something else she'll regret someday. I tackle her, rolling across the floor old-school playground style.

She screams—because, obviously none of us has been doing enough of that today—in rage, pummeling me with white-hot fists as she wails for me to let her do what she came here to do.

"What is that?" I growl, my breath heaving out of me. "What did you come here to do? Kill me? Burn down the castle? You're not going to kill Abby. That won't solve anything. We'd all end up having to live through this stupid scenario in another lifetime."

"No, Rose," she wails. "I'm the one who's supposed to die, remember? In every dream, every lesson, every vision any of us has ever had, I'm supposed to die. It took me a while to get past that, accept it as my fate, but I have now. I've accepted it and I'm ready. Let me be the sacrifice you need to restore the kingdom, and put me out of my misery."

The fight goes out of me, leaving me limp like a noodle on the cold stone floor. Jen sits up, sniffling, and Abby sits next to her, cautious, still clutching her flashlight. "Jen?" she says. "None of us came here to die."

"I did," she insists. "I've seen it. When I get high with Tommy, I remember things—past life things, battles with demons, and fires I've started and people I've burned. I'm trying so hard to avoid repeating those mistakes, but I have to remember them. All of them. I'm supposed to die—that's how it always ends. I was hoping that this time I won't take the rest of you with me."

So many things make sense now. Jen's reluctance to accept her Gift. Her distance from me and her family and the council. Her drug use and determination to self-destruct. "What kind of absurd story is that? You think drugs make you better? Give you more control?"

She shakes her head. "No. They don't. They make me crazy. They make me so much worse. But I had to try something, Rose. I had to See. The past, my mistakes, things I've been trying to change for centuries, because I can only prevent repetition with that knowledge. Now I know. This will only end once I die. It's time. Can't you feel it? Don't you know? It's time."

My eyes find Abby's, and I can tell that she's as speechless as me. Neither of us had any idea what Jen's been going through, and both feel an enormous weight of guilt. We've been so wrapped up in our own misery that we missed this huge, important thing that was happening to this person we love, and now neither of us has any idea how to deal with it.

"Jen," I tell her. "I don't know what you've Seen, or what you remember, or what you've been told is supposed to happen, but this time is already different. Yes, people have died. We've experienced loss. So much loss. But while you were off with Tommy forcing visions, I was training with Gabe. I discovered my destiny—something I've never considered before, something I couldn't have predicted. I have an important role to play here, and so do you. Our part in the restoration of the kingdom is as crucial as Abby's."

Tears have welled in Jen's eyes, and a few leak out when she squeezes them shut. "I know my part. I've known it all along. At first I thought maybe I could refuse it, change the course of things, do it differently—but it's not meant to be." She opens her eyes, wide and devastated, standing slowly. "And I'm sorry. I'm so, so sorry."

I stand too, pulling her into a tight embrace. "We control our own destiny, Jen. If you want to change yours, you have that power. I've seen it."

She squeezes me back, so tight I can't breathe, so tight that her plan becomes apparent the moment I try to withdraw and feel that she has somehow frozen me in place. I can't move. "I love you, Rose," she says, still holding onto me as flames begin to lick at our feet. "Please forgive me."

And then the fire engulfs us.

FIFTY-FIVE

Bright Pink Star

ABBY

Jen's flames stretch toward the low ceiling, scorching black marks along the brick walls. Both of my best friends are burning—Jen has decided to take Rose down with her, and I have nothing, no Light, no Ice, no Wind that can withstand Jen's inferno. The two barrel into me. Someone is screaming—I swear in the short time we've been in this castle, its walls have collected more screams than anything else—but I'm not sure if it's Rose, or Jen, or me. Perhaps all three of us.

Our screaming attracts the hovering shadows, and they squeeze closer, absorbing our agony, Rose's, Jen's, and mine, to bolster their strength and grow ever larger. I cannot stop Jen's flame, but the shadows I can deal with. I flick on my flashlight, and bright, glowing Light explodes into the space, my vision, the room. The Light I stored as a child consumes the shadows and the flames, it knocks the breath out of me as I hit the ground, gasping while black spots dance in my vision. I struggle through it, forcing myself to breathe. Now's not the time to pass out. Not the time for Sight. It's time to save my friends, and seconds could mean the difference between life and death.

A hand grabs my arm, the blackened, bloody fingers a stark contrast to everything else that has become nearly invisible in the brightness. I hear Kye's voice, and Gabe's, but I can't see them, or anyone else, save the black hand. I can see nothing besides white, white light. At the center of the light, a pink star blinks, growing bigger with each movement of my eyelids. I sense that there's something horrible about that star—a huge, important reason why I should avoid it—but it draws inexplicably nearer, larger with each passing second. Dread curls in my toes, climbs into my limbs, and still, I fight for breath—a losing battle in this room where people and wooden things burn, and smoke billows like clouds in the small, poorly ventilated space.

Another hand touches me, this one on my shoulder. It's larger, stronger, and unburned, and nearly as white as the rest of everything. The connection tells me without seeing his face that it's Kye. He's here, refusing to let me fight this battle alone. The pink light has grown into the shape of a woman that splits into two. As a third forms, I understand what's happening. It's time to let go of my hopes, my dreams for a long, continued life. The goddesses warned me that if I ever used the diamond to summon them, I would not be given the choice to return to the mortal life I've known these past centuries. Jen may have meant to save me, to restore Dryden and leave me on that jeweled throne to protect the rest of the Gifted, but she truly has ended this battle forever.

Unlike the last time I met the Morrigana, I don't find myself lying in comfort, tempted by promises of everlasting life and unending pleasure. This time is different because I can feel the hands of my friends binding me to my body, but I can see us from a distance, looking down on myself. On Rose whose hair and eyelashes and skin are immeasurably burned—beyond my realm of Healing—and on Kye, who has sustained deep injuries himself, but who keeps my spirit and body connected by resting his hand on my shoulder, and Gabe, whose tears run onto my foot as he crawls to me and lays his cheek against my ankle.

There's a separation of spirit, mind, and body that leaves me spinning with confusion as the goddesses Morrigana hover, close enough to touch, and far enough away that it would take me hours to reach them.

"We meet again, Abigail." Morrigan speaks first. She is the Oracle, the supreme fertility goddess, and the most intimidating of the three.

"I ... I didn't mean to summon you." My lame words are beyond inadequate. The last time I had a visit from the goddesses, I had decided I'm better off dying than summoning them for help—because a true death would allow me to try again in another lifetime, to relive the cycle once more.

"And yet, you have summoned us." Macha, goddess of war and regeneration flicks her mane of straight, blonde hair the way a stallion flicks its tail at a fly. Her chin juts out, bringing her perfect cheekbones into sharp alignment with those burning hazel eyes.

Badb, goddess of death, grins and it is equal parts beautiful and terrifying when that smile reaches the dark eyes that never seem to blink. She glides closer to me, the skirts of her gauzy dress billowing along the scorched, bloodied floor and picking up remnants of the battle we've fought. "Death has come to claim you once again, but because you continue to wear our token, you belong first to us."

Morrigan continues, "You have brushed shoulders with death many times since last we met."

"Yes." I try to swallow, but my throat is lumpy with smoke inhalation and damage from screaming, from lack of oxygen. Panic tries to claw into my system, but Badb flutters over me with gentle hands.

"Your mortal functions cease," she explains. "Abigail Johnson, you shall be mortal no longer."

I blink anyway, staring at her and wondering why I'm still so lucid, so aware. Last time I met these women, I felt drugged, sleepy, and so confused. I died then—sacrificed myself to save Kye—and the goddesses decided to give me another chance. This time I suspect that won't be an option.

"What's going to happen to me? Is there any way I can still save my friends?"

Macha answers first. "Some Gifted will live—the line must always continue."

I want to feel relief at that, but I'm sick inside, because I've failed at my soul's timeless task, and there will be no more chances to right things. "Who?" I'm not sure I want to know who will live or die, because whatever the answer, my heart will shatter with loss.

When none of the goddesses answers immediately, the black hole inside me grows. "Will any of them be invited to join me in Tir Na Nog?" I know it's not possible—people aren't together in that place. At least, not "together" together. Not the way I want to be with Kye, or could be happy with Gabe. Not in the way of family groupings as I would hope to be with my parents, and Gram, and Rose.

Badb replies. "Which of you lives, dies, or continues has yet to be determined."

Which of *us*? "I don't understand."

"We are owed a debt," Morrigan insists, her jaw set in a firm line, while her eyes glow with compassion and love. "One must pay the tithe."

"And two," Macha adds, "Must continue the bloodline."

"Another," Badb chimes in, "will guard the space between the realms of men and those of the gods."

"On this day, a great rift has opened the tides of fate. Purest love decides the final outcome."

Morrigan's last phrase leaves me more confused than ever. I clutch the frayed hem of my ruined sweater, unraveling more threads. "I don't know what that means."

"You will choose one," Macha says, her unblinking eyes glittering in the white light. "One to live. The one you love above all others."

"But, you said two to continue the blood line, and another to guard the space between the realms. That's three. Three of my friends should get to live."

"One," they say together. "Choose."

"Now?" Though I've left my body behind, my chest thumps like a racing heart.

"Now."

It's up to me. I have choose. To decide which of my friends should live, while the rest of us die. One who I love more than the rest. The one person who matters most. It should be Kye. But Kye won't survive for long once I'm gone. Would I willingly sentence him to the agonizing death of heartbreak that is sure to follow my loss? What about Gabe? He could survive without me. He could move on, find another person to guard, to love. Maybe she will be able to dedicate her entire heart to him, to love him above anyone else. But there's no guarantee, and Gabe will never forgive himself for not saving me. For not saving Kye and Rose and Jen. No, to choose him would be to sentence him to a lifetime of guilt.

I could save Jen. I assumed she was doing all right own while I was in Mexico. Sure, she was training with Val, but we all had to endure that. I had no idea—couldn't have guessed—how much harder her training was to master. How heavy was the burden she carried, that she felt the need to end herself *and* Rose? I don't believe she would want to be saved—not now, knowing that she killed us all. She would try to end herself again, and maybe take others down with her.

Landon. My mother needs him. She's been single for way too long, and once I'm gone, she'll be alone. I don't want her to have to start over so completely. Although, I'm not sure he's dead. He and Tanya were wrestling demons far from the fire and smoke. Landon may not need saving.

The hand on my arm, my mortal, flesh and bone arm, flexes. Rose. She doesn't deserve to die. She has given everything to help me, to protect me, and when she knew I was in danger, she risked everything to save me, even after I left her. Even knowing I couldn't do the same to save Alejandro. Because deep down, no matter how angry or hurt she was, Rose loves me. It's as simple as that. Of everyone, Rose is the most capable of moving forward, despite having her heart of hearts ground to dust. Rose then. The minute I decide, warmth fills the black space inside me. It has to be her. She's Kye's cousin, descended from Theron. Rose will carry on the blood line.

"Choose," Morrigan says again. I don't have to think anymore, because I know this is the only way. She is the only one. "I choose Rose. Save Rose."

FIFTY-SIX

The Final Destruction

ABBY

I wake slowly, half-expecting to be in my bed, as that's where I've typically ended up after falling into a Healer's sleep. I'm disoriented and confused, unable to remember who I've tried to Heal or why, and it doesn't help that rather than my bed, I'm lying on a rough stone floor, covered in something sticky and wet, my mouth filled with the burned taste of falling ashes. I move my fingers, one at a time, and then all together, following up with the same action on my toes and feet. My body throbs as if I've been dipped in molten lava and my skin scorched off, leaving my insides exposed.

I blink, relieved to discover that the lighting isn't as bright as I expect. I lift my hand, pressing my fingers together to find them sticky with a reddish substance and covered in soot. I blink again, and try—unsuccessfully—to sit up, as memories come rushing back. My friends. I don't know what's happened to them. I need to know who survived—if anyone—and why I'm not yet gone to cross the crystal bridge. There must be something left for me to do before the Morrigana takes me away.

I try to speak, but dissolve into a coughing fit that leaves my lungs shredded. "Shh," a voice soothes. "Don't try to talk. Let me get you some water." I blink, blink, blink to clear the soot and ash from my vision and focus on Tanya. I'm glad she survived the fire, the battle. Her son won't have to be raised by strangers, and that's good news. She slides a hand under my head and holds a water bottle to my lips.

The cool liquid blisters my insides as it goes down. It's going to be a long recovery.

"Thank you," I croak, coughing up some of the water as my charred throat rejects it. I roll on my side, needing to sit up, so she helps me. My muscles scream in agony, every nerve singing with a sensation I can't quite place. I feel as though I've Healed someone who was gravely injured—except that's not possible, because I'm no longer a Healer.

We're in the room with the throne. The one where Jen burned Rose and Boone stabbed Eric, and then I stabbed him. The wood stakes have been blackened to ash, and the golden throne is covered in soot, its jewels no longer glittering because they're caked with grime. Nearby, hushed voices chatter, and above, shadows sweep and hover. It's strange how they wait.

"Who else made it?" I ask, still confused, because I'm not supposed to be alive. None of us are. Except Rose. "And who have we lost?"

Tanya sets the water bottle aside and tries to wipe my face with her dirty sleeve. "I'm not sure. You were the first one I found. But ..." She hesitates. She has bad news.

"Go on," I tell her.

"Landon fell to the demons." Her voice cracks with emotion as she scrubs more violently at the grime on my forehead.

"Is he still alive? Can he be Healed?" I could get him to Christine—as long as his heart beats and his brain functions.

She gives up wiping my face and takes my hand, squeezes. "There was so much blood. I'm certain he's dead. His skull was crushed when the shadows loosened bricks from the ceiling and dropped them on his head."

"I need to see him."

She squeezes my fingers painfully. "That's not a good idea. He's not looking his best."

"Where is he?" I slide my fingers away from hers and summon the strength to stand.

Her gaze flits toward the shadows at the base of the throne, where a misshapen lump lies, still as stone. She closes her eyes briefly, then pushes herself off the ground, and bends to help me stand. "I promise I would tell you if he could be saved. He can't."

I want to check, to see for myself because my mother loves him, but memories of Alejandro haunt me to this day, and the look in Tanya's eyes reminds me why I shouldn't. Still, I take a step toward the body, knowing that Landon and Eric are only the beginning of our casualties.

A shout echoes from the portal room, where I left Boone. After an exchanged glance of surprise, Tanya and I bolt toward the voice.

Rose, whose skin is black with soot, fingers shriveled and bloody, and hair singed to her ears, has cornered half a dozen demons, using my flashlight. She's talking to them, holding a conversation I can't hear, and they're enraptured by her words. None of them tries to run, or to summon any of the multitude of shadows hovering near the portal. There must be hundreds crowded in that corner, restless, but somehow caged.

"Rose," I breathe, relief pouring through me in buckets.

She glances over her shoulder, acknowledging me with a nod, her eyes glistening with relief, and then continues to speak, to command the demons, the shadows, the room. I've made the right choice. Though I will surely soon be taken to Tir Na Nog, the Morrigana allowed me to choose the person who will carry on the royal bloodline, and they rescued her. Saved her from what would surely have been the most painful death I could imagine. Because of that, when the Morrigana comes for me, I won't fight my fate. I've done my part, and now I can move on.

More voices echo from another hallway. Tanya and I shrink into the shadows as footsteps plod closer. A tapestry on the far wall whips aside—this castle is nothing if not authentic—and a group emerges through a passageway. Kye leads a chain of bound and gagged demons, all with familiar-looking dagger wounds, and shuffles them into the corner with the rest. Rose continues to talk, and the eyes of the new captives glaze over the moment her Voice reaches their ears. Gabe brings up the rear of the group of captives, preventing any potential escape attempts. None of them sees me immediately, as Tanya and I remain hidden. Kye barks an order, and the captives obey. He barks another, and the group falls into organized lines, facing Rose. It's as if they can't move without permission.

Gabe is first to look away from the demons, ever vigilant, always watching. He scans the perimeter until he's looking directly at me, and then he squints as if making sure he's truly seeing *me*. The moment recognition sets in, his shoulders sag with relief. He signals to Kye, who doesn't turn to look, but whose aura bleeds purple. He too is relieved.

The demons begin to shuffle, and Gabe takes position near the portal, standing guard as one by one, they step inside. The three of them have rounded up all the people Boone has employed, and are locking them inside the prison.

When the last demon has entered the shrinking circle, Kye beckons for me to come take his hand, and I obey—not because he has his powers back and is using his Voice, but because I long to touch him, assure myself that he's real and safe and restored. Tanya follows, her Gift intensifying every sound, every scent, every sensation. When my hand rests in Kye's, he says, "I found your place in the book. It said the best way to neutralize a demon army is to destroy the prison with them inside. Once this one is destroyed, others down the line will self-destruct, because each of the tombs depends on the integrity of the others. When one falls, the rest will follow."

I squeeze his hand, memorizing the feel of his palm pressed against mine. "And to destroy it, we all have to work together. Sacrifice together. Did you read that part?"

361

"I did." His eyes drink me in, but his voice is laced with pain. "We need to talk," he whispers. "But after. Immediately after."

Yes, we do. I wonder if he knows about the Morrigana coming for me. Wonder if he knows that we'll soon be saying goodbye— forever. "Yes," I force out, "let's do this."

I level my bloody hands on the edge of the portal. My blood. My most powerful weapon. "I need all of you to do what I do. First, touch your injured hands to your wounds to collect some blood, and then place your hands on the edges of the portal."

No one asks questions, they do as I tell them, and soon there are five of us with five different lines of blood, exposed and fresh, prepared to use that blood to seal the door. The words flow through me without warning. It's as if I'm a vessel through which the Gifts of the goddesses are being used for the good of mankind. I start in a language I know nothing of, but that feels authentic and right, chanting, swaying, but never moving my hands even a fraction.

Eventually, my chants change to English. "On earth one mortal force will reign, our foes to rest and peace restore, no sealing tombs or revolving doors, these prisons dissolved forever more." I repeat the chant over and over, voice rising in power, and the Light I was sure I'd lost flows free, rich and strong and from inside my core as if it never left.

My Gift has returned!

My friends join the chanting, picking up the words by the third repeat. The ground shakes, and the walls crack and move and tremble—the way they did when I closed the first tomb, locking Tynan inside. It's working.

And then, a loud pop, followed by more pops, and an explosion rocks the world like a bomb has gone off within these cold, stone walls. Every light flickers—including mine, and the ground quakes. A warning. I let go, shouting for everyone to take cover, and tackle the two people nearest me to the ground.

The portal explodes into a billion miniscule pieces that rain down on us like glass. A first glance tells me that we're all still alive, though Rose is seriously burned, and each of us has shards of the portal lodged in various parts of our skin.

The obnoxious sound stops, and eerie silence descends. "Is that it then?" Gabe asks. "Is it over? Because, even if it's not, we've earned a really nice dinner."

I laugh. "Can we get cleaned up first? Maybe work on Healing Rose."

"Cleaned up with what?"

"Whatever we can find," I tell Kye. "There's got to be a bathroom somewhere in this place."

He drapes his arm over my shoulders, squeezing. "I thought I'd lost you again."

His happiness puts a damper on my mood, but I shove it into a corner and paste on a smile. I don't know how to tell him that it's coming, and soon, which is why Healing Rose is my next priority. "Not yet."

FIFTY-SEVEN

The Most Loved

ROSE

With my mind no longer focused on the adrenaline-pumping task of collecting demons, my skin burns like I'm still on fire. It's a screaming pain so deep and brutal that I can scarcely breathe.

But I'm grateful to be alive. I'm not sure how much of me is burned, or what my future might look like, but I won't ask Abby to Heal me—not this time. I'll scar, without question. Large, ugly patches of deformed skin that I'll hate every time I look in the mirror, but for which I will never be ashamed. Somehow—though I have no idea why—I managed to escape with my life. Even in this insane amount of pain, I kept my head and helped destroy the demons, and their prison.

It's good to finally be a part of the fighting for a change.

Once Abby has checked to make sure the portal is truly, absolutely destroyed, she blinks at me. "Jen?"

I shake my head. There's nothing more to say. Abby knew Jen *might* die, and I knew she absolutely *would*. This is what she wanted, and I'm not going to question that—not anymore. I will grieve the loss of my friends, and drink a toast in their honor the moment I have the chance. I'd give an arm for a flask of tequila about now.

"What now?" Tanya asks.

Kye answers, his questioning gaze locked on Abby. "Once we clear the castle—make sure we didn't miss any demons, or captive friends—I vote we go home. It's long past time, don't you think?"

"Yes," she says, and despite all that's happened, a grin plays at her lips, reminding me how long Abby has been away. "One hundred percent."

"Before we celebrate, there's one last battle to be fought," I inform them, thinking of the curse, the betrayals, of Valdemar. "We have to send Val to Tir Na Nog. The Morrigana has been waiting for him for a very long time."

Gabe and I explain what we've discovered, how Val is the empath for whom Raina created the dagger, and how that same tool contains the key to his passage over the crystal bridge into the legendary Tir Na Nog. Kye's face scrunches in anger as he pieces together how deep his guardian's betrayal has run. This news rocks the foundation on which he has been raised since boyhood.

I don't blame him for his anger. Now's the time when, if we were still in Mexico, I would offer him a shot of tequila. I wish I had one anyway, to dim my current agony. But we're in California, not Mexico—and actually ... "Hey, there's a vineyard outside. There's got to be a wine cellar here. We could tap it for some liquid courage."

He laughs as he storms out the door, but it's the dry, pained variety. I glance at Abby, hoping she'll go after him so I don't have to. My energy is spent. She shakes her head. "Let him go. Trust me, when Kye's troubled, he does better burning it off on his own." Upon hearing her own words, she pales and rushes to my side. She doesn't touch my black, scabbing fingers, but I can tell she wants to. "Oh, Rose, I'm so sorry. You've endured this for too long already. Lie down, and let's get you Healing."

The adrenaline of battle is wearing off, and the heat scorched into my body intensifies with the slightest hint of a touch, even movement of air. To live like this indefinitely promises to be excruciating, but I won't let Abby Heal me. She couldn't Heal Alex, and I won't allow her to take this on herself either. "No. Thank you, but no. I can't give this burden to you."

She shoves her fisted hand in her pocket. Streaks of soot decorate her face, belying the innocence I've always loved about her features, and making her look both lethal and inherently strong. "I'm not asking you. I'm going to Heal you while I still can—that's not up for debate."

While she still can? I take a step back to put distance between us. "Since when did you become my boss? I haven't seen you in months, and you show up here and think that because I got kidnapped you get to order me around? Newsflash, princess. You're not in charge of me. I came to save you and my cousin. Now that you're both safe, I'm outta here. I have a standing offer to stay at Victor's, and I need to go say my proper goodbyes to Alex. Alone." I try to walk away, but every time I move, the heat of Jen's fire rages through my body, and that's not something I can fake isn't happening, not pain I can pretend doesn't exist.

"You're welcome to go visit Victor," she says, her soft voice rising to my ears. "Rose, you're free to live your life, however you'd like, wherever you want, and with whomever makes you happy. But your injuries are more than serious, they're critical. You may not be able to see it yourself yet, but I can. Please, let me help you. For once, let me Heal you."

Under any other circumstances, I would refuse. Absolutely not. No way, no how. But the pain's setting in, reminding me that if I don't get burn treatment, I'll be joining Alex in heaven, sooner than planned. Burns this severe can and do kill people.

"The last time you Healed someone, you almost died. We were told you could never risk that again," I remind her. "I won't put you through that. I can't. I won't be responsible for taking you from Kye."

Abby's expression is closed off, strangely blank, but she holds out a begging hand. "It's not your responsibility to worry about," she says. "It's mine. I have to do this, Rose. More importantly, I want to do it. You're the reason I'm still here."

Her words seem final, her determination unbreakable, and I'm weary. My pain grows louder, sharper, deeper with each passing second, leaving my muscles too weak to keep me standing. I'm now sitting, without having thought to do so, and sitting is excruciating too. "No," I argue. "I can't ... you can't." But as the words leave my mouth, my whole world spins. I'm not going to survive this after all. "Alex," I whisper.

Abby sits next to me, bending over me as I stare at the ceiling. I continue protesting in my mind, but am no longer able to speak. "Shh, Rose. Stay still. We can argue about this all you want when you wake up."

"Make sure *you* wake up." I can't let her die for me, but Abby hovers, and there's no question in her eyes, no hesitation, no doubt. As the darkness closes in, I see only love, determination, and surety in my best friend. She takes my hand, and though her touch sends pain lancing all the way to my chest, I squeeze back.

Abby and I are connected for eternity.

FIFTY-EIGHT

The Biggest Little Sacrifice

ABBY

It's been so long since I Healed anyone, I'm worried that I won't remember how. I run my hands over Rose's energy field, realizing that her situation is more dire than I imagined. Without immediate Healing, her chances of survival are beyond slim. As if to prove my point, while I'm still assessing her injuries, her heart leaps, skipping first one beat, and then two.

"We're going to lose her," I scream to the others. "Find me supplies. Anything you can get. Vines, herbs, crystals—and if you have no crystals, natural stones. Scour the castle, and hurry. She has minutes at the most."

My friends scramble out of their stunned stupor as I remove my rings with shaking hands. I'm hesitant to place them on Rose's sensitive skin, not knowing if this will cause her more pain than she's already experiencing, but it's necessary that I get the placement exactly right. One over her heart chakra. My necklace on her forehead. Kye empties his pockets and produces more crystals, which I also place. Tanya hands me the dagger. Gabe drops the energy wands at my feet, and then my flashlight, and bolts upstairs, as if desperate to find whatever else I need to save Rose.

I start spinning.

For all that I worried, the Healing tones come naturally to me, as they have since Gram died. I may never know the true meaning of the words and tones I sing, but they come to me, strong and true, infused with the strength of five-hundred years, of the blood of many, many Healers. I spin and sing and call the burned energy until smoke rises out of Rose's body. Until the smell of ash becomes acrid and rotten and leaves the rest of us coughing on the remnants of what has been done to Rose. Of all the Healing I've tried, this task is by far the most difficult.

I've Healed my loved ones after being beaten and bloodied, sick with fever and ill with all manner of afflictions, bruised and drowned, but this is my first time Healing someone who was burned by Gifted Fire. It goes deeper than anything I've seen. If I can save Rose, she'll be scarred. This is not a thing I can take from her, however badly I want to, need to. I hope she can forgive me for not leaving her as the perfect young woman she was when we first met.

I spin and sing and call her energy, feeling it rise for a long time. So much longer than I ever have before. My arms weaken and my muscles cramp, but I refuse to let up, refuse to give up. Kye sees me sagging, and slides behind me, bolstering me as he has in times past, loaning me his energy with his hands on my waist. Tanya sees this, and she joins in, placing her hands on my shoulders, amplifying my Healing power by double or more, and causing the wobbling crystals to spin in neat, perfect circles. Rose's energy rises, funnels, and little by little trickles into me, through me, until her pain, her every agony, becomes mine, leaving it impossible not to yelp with pain. Kye's hands flex on my waist, but he doesn't let go, and neither does Tanya.

Rose's energy knits back together, patching, not perfect, but whole, usable for living. When there's nothing more I can do to mend it, I send it back, slowly, carefully, unwilling to risk letting go of myself before this last task is complete. The Morrigana will come for me, but they allowed me back, and now I know why. Because I choose Rose, and they're allowing me be the one to save her.

When the task is complete, the crystals drop, and so do I. Rose is still out cold, but her chest rises and falls in a steady rhythm, and her heart chakra has cleared significantly. She'll live, and though she'll have some pain and scarring, I've taken the worst of it from her. I collapse into Kye's arms, and he holds me, washing my neck with silent tears. He knows what I've done, though I don't have the words or the energy left to tell him. He won't argue, not this time. Because the words we exchange now will be our last.

"I love you babe," he says. "So much. I hope you know that has never ever changed. Not for one day. Not for one minute. You're my destiny, and I'm yours."

"It's over now," I wheeze. "The demons are gone and so are the shadows. We're free. No longer bound by curse, or fate, or anything else except choice."

He nods. "We are free. The curse is lifted. Dryden will never be restored, but it can be rebuilt, like this castle."

"Build it," I tell him. "Use whatever information you find in the book to make things better than before. Be the king you were meant to be all those centuries ago."

More tears fall on my neck, and he muffles a sob in my hair. "Don't sleep too long. I'm going to need your help."

With the last bits of strength I have left, I lift my hand and trace the side of his face, drawing it forward so he can touch his lips to mine. "I love you." And his eyes, the bright blue sapphires that originally drew me to him, are the last thing I see as the darkness claims me.

They're here.

The goddesses Morrigana, and far more beautiful than I pictured when I was a child and Gram told me stories about how they were known to be both benevolent and vicious, quick to anger, and slow to forgive, but loving when it suits a purpose. Though it's only been hours since I saw them, I'm surprised, because this time, I sense the presence of more. More ... people? Spirits? Gods or goddesses? I'm not sure, but though I can't yet see anything but the bright goddesses, I sense that the four of us are not the only ones present.

We're back in the Healer's resting place, the bed that's soft as a cloud, and I've brought the dagger with me. Again, I'm tempted to linger and stay, to lose myself to the euphoria, but I force myself to sit up and become aware, knowing how easy it could be for me to fall into the haze of the heavens and stay there for eternity. The last time I was here, I barely remembered my own mother, and now I have so many more loved ones to leave behind. I want to remember them for as long as I can, keep them in my heart and mind— remember why I made the choices I did, and how I would give up my mortality again to save them.

Morrigan gets right to the point. "You know why you're here, Abigail."

"Yes," I tell her. "I nearly died, and the diamond summoned you."

"Your choices will not be the same," Macha reminds me.

"I understand." My mind is clear right now, which I find both odd and comforting.

"This time," Badb chimes in, "You will choose a fate for someone other than yourself, and he will choose for you."

The nerve endings along my skin tighten in alarm. This is unexpected. "Who?"

The other presence steps into the circle of light. Valdemar. "Hello, Raina."

I shake my head. "It's Abby now."

"Not here, it isn't." He sits next to me, his fingers patting the silk bedding and smoothing a line in it. "Here, you're the same spirit you've been for centuries. We have history, you and I."

"I remember little about my time as Raina. I'd be more comfortable having you call me Abby." He's still stuck in his past, but that doesn't mean I should be stuck in mine—especially one that happened so long ago.

"Very well," he says, his annoyance clear.

I glance again at Morrigan. "Him? You're going to let him choose my eternal fate?" Valdemar's the one who caused the messes Kye and I have had to endure from the beginning. He's the reason we got so sick from being together in Jackson, and even sicker being apart when I was in Mexico.

"No." Badb is the one who answers. "Not him."

Another presence enters, and seeing her makes my throat squeeze with emotion. "Gram." I jump up and latch onto her, so grateful that I won't have to spend eternity alone.

"Darling." She holds onto me. "I'm so proud of all you've done since I left you. When you were a tot, I hoped you would find the strength to be all the things I knew you would need to be, but I admit—I worried."

"Gram, I'm so glad to see you, so happy you're here. I've missed you. I've needed you badly."

"Baby doll, don't you know I've been with you all along? I've never left you. Not really. And I never will." Gram takes my hand and pulls me back to the bed, which has now become an elaborately cushioned, high-backed bench.

I can't take my eyes off my Gram, her kind, sweet eyes, the way her lips quirk when she smiles. The soft, papery feel of her wrinkled skin. "Are they going to let you choose my fate, Gram? For real?"

She shakes her head, running her palm across my forehead and down my cheek to cup my face. "No, sweetheart. Not me either."

"Then who?"

Another presence, and this time, my shock cannot be measured in earthly words. My father stands before me, his face a mask of humble sadness. "My baby girl."

My chest heaves, and my throat closes so tight that the only word I can force out is a mere whisper. "Daddy?"

"Yes, sweetheart. It's me." He doesn't move immediately; a moment of awkwardness hangs between us until I make the leap and throw my arms around him.

"Daddy, I've missed you. I can't believe you're here."

"Where else would I be?"

Heaven is way better than I expected. I won't be alone here after all. "Daddy, I want to go with you and Gram. I don't want to go to Tir Na Nog. I want to be with the two of you." My gaze flits to Val. I grip the dagger tighter, wondering how he got here. "Are you dead too?"

"This isn't heaven," Gram clarifies. "It's a holding place. Your father and I are only here for a visit."

My hopes for a bright, happy eternity shatter like glass on concrete. "Can't you stay with me? I want to be with you. I don't want to spend forever alone."

"That's why we're here," my dad says. "So that you don't have to be alone for this."

Dread settles over me. "For what?"

"It is time," Macha says. "For the choosing."

I set the dagger aside and my dad and Gram each take one of my hands as the light dies and all goes dark. I squeeze tight as memories flow, centuries of them. Battles and Healings and happiness and sadness and so many lifetimes of details, all with one thing in common. Me. I was there. For all of it. For the destruction of Dryden, for the new life built with a family that was no longer royal. For lifetimes lived many times over since the curse began. In Jackson meeting Kye. Escaping from the hotel in Las Vegas, rappelling down Lady Liberty. The pyramids in Mexico with Gabe. Scuba lessons with Rose. Jen controlling her Fire for the first time, and Eric getting me into the cave using Ice. Losing my Gift as it drained away.

The memories ache like an open wound, throbbing, burning, itching as I'm consumed by fire, and covered by ice. My chest aches with the weight of an anvil, and my throat squeezes with the pressure of hands crushing my airway. My head screams from the stress of a vice.

Another presence enters, and I realize that the one being missing from my memories is here. He has been my champion all along, my biggest supporter, and at times, my best and only friend.

"Murtagh!" I cry, because every time he arrives, things get better. Every. Time.

"*Agno* girl! Why sacrifice you, always?"

I focus on him, and the pain begins to fade. "That's my job. It's what I've been taught to do. It's what I was born for."

He shakes his tiny head, bouncing on invisible waves of air. "No, *Calin*. Not. You born lead."

Of course I was. I can't pretend to smile at that comment. "Not anymore."

"*Calin* sad?" He lands on my shoulder. His light dimming as his wings slow. "You want be Queen? Or you happy be free?"

When I think back on my life, the mistakes I've made, how hard I once fought to find normalcy—a life free of the complications of my Gifts—I wouldn't change it. Except for the part where I couldn't save my friends. If I had known a few years ago what I know now, I would have been both terrified and thrilled with the idea that I, Abigail Johnson, was destined to restore a dying generation of Gifted, to lead them into the next phase, to help them protect the world, and teach it that the Gifted have a place in it, however humanity might fear us.

No, I wouldn't change it. Not a thing.

Murtagh is waiting for an answer. "My friend. I would love to witness for myself what happens next. I'm so happy to know that I did what I was born to do—finally. I'm sad that I won't live to see the results of that, but it's okay. Kye will go on, and Rose will go on, and Tanya will raise Cole and they'll go on too. My people will live. If I have to miss the best parts, that's the most important thing to me."

He asks again, "You happy be free?"

My eyes burn with emotion. I'm overwhelmed by the sadness of knowing that I can't go back to them. Ever. "No. I'm not happy to be free. But I am happy that they are."

"You want be Queen then?"

A sob works up my throat. "Yes. I would love to be the Gifted queen and protect the people until the end of time."

"Okay." He leaps from my shoulder to my lap and takes the dagger to the goddesses. "She want be Queen. Murtagh stay."

Morrigan laughs. "You've spent *five hundred years* watching over and assisting our immortal, Valdemar. We have in our presence two Gifted leaders of Earthly souls. On this day, *one* will cross the crystal bridge to satisfy a debt, and *one* will return to mortal life, tasked with watching over and protecting the Gifted people until the next leader rises. Murtagh, you have witnessed both at their best and their worst. You know better than anyone what's in Valdemar's heart, and what's in Abigail's. Only *you* know who is capable of leading their people. It is you who shall decide who will return to Earthly life, and who will cross the bridge."

Murtagh's face scrunches as he faces Valdemar. "Why you make *Agno* sick? Into danger send her?"

The deep lines etched across Val's ancient face soften. "Raina took my power, saved me from my agony, and I swore on that day that I would do the same for her, protect her from the horrid curse that began because of me. I would not let her live an eternity of the suffering I had experienced until that day. I accepted the flower of immortality and stayed behind to watch over her, finding her in each lifetime and protecting her from a distance. This is the only time she hasn't died right away, the only lifetime in which her love for others her burned stronger than the fear of her fate. I couldn't allow her to fail. I've kept my promise, fulfilled my duty to Raina, and set myself free, as well as her."

"You want go home now?"

Tears sparkle in Val's eyes. "I'd love to go home."

Murtagh buzzes over to land on my shoulder. For the first time ever, his wings stop fluttering and he remains still. "*Agno* go home to family, lead Gifted, be Queen. Valdemar cross bridge for goddesses. Home to Tir Na Nog. Murtagh go with master, price for Queen life. Everyone well. Everyone happy."

My heart leaps with fear. "Murtagh, I don't want to lose you."

He hugs my neck with his tiny arms. "It okay. Calin save kingdom. Murtagh hero warrior, here to save you. *Agno* friends forever."

I nod, swallowing tears. "I'll never forget you, Murtagh."

"Live happy, Calin." He kisses my cheek, then turns to Val. "Ready you, Master?" Val nods, closing his eyes as Murtagh plunges the dagger into his chest. Val's face contorts with the anguish of five centuries of pain, and screaming, he disappears with Murtagh into the bright, pink star of light, taking the dagger with him.

The goddesses glide toward us, their sinuous white gowns shimmering, growing brighter, as they fade from view. Macha, Badb, and Morrigan nod in sync. "So shall it be."

FIFTY-NINE

Alive

ROSE

I'm *on fire. Every part of me screams in agony as the flames burn the fine hairs on my skin, melt through flesh and bone, leaving me screaming.*

I sit up in bed, panicking, only to realize that I'm healing, the pain has already diminished significantly, and I'm not actually on fire a second time.

It's been three weeks since Jen lit me, and I've lived the same nightmare, replayed over and over, several times a day.

Abby isn't awake yet, but we continue to hold onto the hope that she'll rejoin us in the land of the living. For the first week, her heart was unsteady, and every breath seemed questionable— Christine thought we'd lose her. But since then her heartbeat has become strong, her breathing steadier, clearer. I spend most of my awake time in her room, though the moving and walking it takes for me to get there causes intense agony. Luckily, I'm no longer bandaged. Christine insists that Abby took the worst of it from me—I'm forming new skin across my torso, and though the area stings, cool air is a relief. Because of this, I can't stand to wear clothes. I'm covered by only a light, cotton robe when I leave my room to sit with Abby each day.

No one wanted to transport Abby long distance after she Healed me, and Kye was worried about making sure the demons are truly gone, so he and Gabe explored the castle and found a level of luxury suites, which we have taken as our own while we wait out the Healer's sleep and the most painful days of my recovery.

It's like staying in a posh hotel. That crazy madman built a full-scale replica of the castle where Raina and Theron were married, only he improved it with modern-day luxuries. The only thing missing was a full staff of servants—which I suspect he planned to gather from the colony of demons he was about to set free.

As soon as she could, Tanya found a phone and called Marian to check on Cole. Not only was he all right, Marian was baffled and excited about how he had miraculously recovered from the lethargy, irritability, and high fever he'd been suffering. This happened on the night the tomb was destroyed. Tanya asked Marian to bring the baby to her in California, and after that, word spread.

I was pretty out of it that first week, unconscious for the most part, and not at all coherent, but by the second night, people were arriving by carloads. Zane and his Dragons. Marian and my parents. Christine and Eoin. Some people from Texas—a young woman herding a bunch of kids and an older man who reminds me of Val, only more talkative and less intense.

This castle has room for all of us. Every time someone new comes, Kye or Gabe or Tanya finds a place to put them, and my parents have the kitchen up and running. We've all had hot, fabulous meals three times a day since they arrived. I'm told they even have group Thai-chi every morning in the courtyard.

If not for the silent, unmoving girl tucked away in the tower room built for a queen, this wild and unwieldy sleepover could almost classify as a vacation. Or a celebration.

Wiping the sweat from my brow, I throw back my covers and reach for the glass of water on my nightstand. Another hand meets mine and helps me lift it to my lips.

"What are you doing awake?" Gabe's voice is husky with sleep as he unfolds himself from the recliner he's positioned next to my bed. He's starting to recover from his beating, but still boasts a cast on his arm, a boot on one foot, and a number of unhealable scars.

I take long, deep pulls from the glass, slaking my burning throat as the water sloshes sloppily down. "Nightmare. I was on fire again."

"I see." He keeps his voice soft, and I can't decide if it's because of the late hour or because he isn't sure if I'm truly awake or not.

"Why are you still in here?" I adjust the angle of my body to see him better. "Your shift ended hours ago." I think. My days tend to blur together, but I've noticed that I'm never alone when I sleep. Finally, I understand why Abby used to get so frustrated with being kept under constant watch. I drain the rest of the water, dribbling drops that slide down my neck and onto my nightgown.

Gabe says, "Did you know that Kye hasn't left Abby's room all week?"

"No." I didn't, but I suspect that my knowing that isn't the point.

He shifts in his chair. "Why do you think he's still in there, where there's not even a TV to keep him company?"

I blink, feeling the weight of my eyelids wanting to close again. "Because he loves her, and wants to be there when she wakes up."

"Exactly," he says, the usual notes of sarcasm absent from his voice. "He's not the only one who feels that way."

Wait. What? "About Abby? I mean, if you want some alone time with her, I'm sure Kye will understand ..."

"Not about her." His voice stays barely above a whisper. "About you."

Did he just say what I think he said? My well-crafted, highly intelligent response is: "Um. Which part?"

I'm skirting the subject, and I know it, but we're in my room, and my bed is warm and my nightgown thin and low cut, and silk, and I'm vulnerable with pain meds and lack of solid sleep.

"I didn't realize I felt this way until I saw you lying in a heap of ashes on the floor next to Jen. I'm falling in love with you, Rose, and I'm determined to see where this goes."

His quiet admission leaves me dizzy with confusion. Gabe loves Abby. He's loved her all along. He can't love me. "What if it goes nowhere?"

He takes the glass from me and sets it on the nightstand, then sits carefully next to my bare legs on the edge of the bed and brushes the backs of his fingers along the underside of my jaw. "Rose, it's *already* gone somewhere."

I shake my head in denial, but my skin tingles with pleasure everywhere he touches. There are so many things wrong with this scenario. Our lives have been turned upside down and spun in drunken circles. Maybe I don't care. "Yes," I admit, stilling his movements with a hand on his wrist. "Friendship. Mutual respect. A truce to the constant battles."

Relentless, he twists his bandaged fingers into mine, allowing his free hand to flutter in what's left of my hair. "I have to admit, I'm sad to say goodbye to the battles. You've been such a worthy opponent."

I swat his hand away. "You're only admitting that because I'm lying here wounded."

He scoots closer. "I'm wounded too, and I'm admitting it because I want you to know that sparring with you has been among the most stimulating, exhilarating, and jarring experiences of my life. Do you know what I've realized?"

"What?" My brow raises in curiosity as he props my back with a pillow and urges me to relax against it, continuing to hover close.

"I've realized that I want more of it. As much as I can have." His lips graze the tip of my nose. "Every day." And move down to my chin. "For the rest." Along my jaw. "Of forever." He stops, his lips a breath away, hovering there, eyes boring into mine with such intensity, such tenderness that I worry we'll both dissolve.

My voice is breathy, and as weak as my objection as I lift my chin to urge him closer. "You love Abby."

He shakes his head, never breaking eye contact. "No, Rose, I love you." A new fire ignites between us when his lips mold to mine as if we were built to fit together, and his tongue seeks mine in a way no one has ever explored—not even Alejandro. Gabe's hands travel, ever-so-careful of my sensitive skin, the crispy wisps of my hair, and the small amount of fabric covering my body. Mini explosions go off in my head with each new discovery, leaving me reeling with this new reality.

Gabe's not lying. He's in love with me, and he shows it in every careful touch, every gentle movement, and the enormous amount of restraint it must take to not push harder for more—knowing how little I can handle at the moment. He kisses me until we're both out of breath and panting, and my throat burns once again. Then he refills my glass with a bottle of water from near his chair and encourages me to drink it down.

"How are you feeling?" he asks. What he's really asking; is it too soon? Am I too vulnerable? Should he wait to pursue this?

"Tired," I admit, allowing my eyes to fall closed. "But happy."

The sigh he lets out shows no sign of frustration, but it emanates off him in waves. Gabe could never hide his emotions well. He moves to stand, but I grab his casted arm and drag him back. "Stay here." It takes more effort than I want to let on, but I rally my muscles and scoot to one side and make room, then pat the place next to me. "My skin—I can't stand having anything touch it. But will you stay close anyway?"

He takes a shaky breath. "Why?"

"Because I want to feel you next to me." And he knows what I'm really saying. I'm hurt, but I need him. I love him, and I don't want to wait.

He's extra careful as he slides in, his breath tickling my cheek as I close my eyes and fall asleep to the sound of him breathing. Together, we'll find the strength to heal.

SIXTY

Awakening

ABBY

My next awareness is of moaning, whining, and red-hot fire burning through my veins, along my skin, down my throat and intestines and in my eyes. I come awake with a jolt, holding in a scream of agony as the flames boil down to a simmer. Waking from the Healer's sleep has always been excruciating, but after losing my Gifts, and then nearly my life, I welcome the torment, because it means I'm alive. I've been given another chance to be with the people I love, and grace will not allow me to begrudge the Morrigana the pain my Gift causes me.

Kye is near, as he always has been. Before I open my eyes, he strokes my forehead and brushes a damp cloth across my lips. When I manage to lift my lids, he's here, sitting next to me, brushing the hair away from my face as he swipes my chakra field with an energy wand, and my pain diminishes.

"Hey," I croak. "Guess I'm alive after all."

"I guess you are." His smile is pained, but in his eyes, there's knowledge—absolute certainty. He was never worried that I wouldn't live through this one. "Welcome back."

"How long?" I push at the comforter, determined to sit up. When my weak muscles rebel, Kye slides an arm behind my back and boosts me until he can shove pillows behind me for support.

"Long enough," he hedges, offering me a glass of water, which I drain in three gulps, grateful for the cool relief as it runs down my scorched throat. As my eyes adjust to the dim lighting, I take note that this is not my bedroom at home. Nor is it a hotel room, or any of the rooms at the places where we've stayed. These walls are made from lovely, old stone, rich and textured, and the small amount of light is provided by sconces mounted along them. There's an empty fireplace, faded tapestries and rugs, and a rustic side table on which Kye has placed a plethora of Healing herbs and crystals. I'm in a large, four poster bed surrounded by gauzy curtains and piled high with pillows and the most luxurious bedding.

I let my arms drop onto the fabulous comfort. "Where are we?"

His laugh is deep and full. "Boone built a castle."

I straighten from my reclined position, grateful that my ab muscles are still in working order—however shaky. "What? Why would he do that?"

He stands to stretch as if he hasn't done so in hours. "My dad claims he used stones from an archeological dig found near the ruins of Dryden. It's an exact replica to the castle described in the history books. My guess is that he built it for the rising."

"The rising?"

"Of the Gifted generation," he says, grinning.

"Naturally." A giggle bubbles out of my raw throat, sending spasms of pain sheering down it like I've swallowed shards of glass. "Did you call everyone here then?"

He raises an eyebrow. "Of course."

"And I suppose they're waiting for me to wake up?"

He chuckles. "You have no idea."

"How long, Kye?"

He takes a deep breath. "You missed Christmas."

I swallow, though it's a hard one to manage. "And?"

He pushes a button on his phone to check the time. "And the New Year will start in about two hours."

Six weeks? I've been asleep for almost six weeks? It takes an extra moment to catch my breath. I manage by reminding myself that when

I went to sleep, I wasn't expecting to come back at all. "Are we having a party?"

He laughs out loud. "That's not the right word. Babe, you have no idea how I've hoped you would wake up in time to see what's going on in this ... building."

He helps me stand, giving me time to catch my breath and work blood into my atrophied muscles, then leads me to the ensuite bathroom, where I find a long, ice-blue dress hanging from a hook on the wall.

Before I ask, he glances at the dress and says, "Rose."

Once again, I can't complain. Rose is alive, and here, in this replicated castle, planning yet another party. "That's my outfit?"

He nods, turning on the gold faucet to run a bath in the enormous, deep tub. "You don't have to wear it if you hate it. But if that's the case, you're telling Rose yourself."

I shake my head, dropping my robe to climb into the tub as it fills with bubbles. I don't care that Kye's watching and I'm naked. I'm pretty sure he has a good idea of what I look like by now. "Like I'd be that stupid."

"Of course not." He perches on the edge of the tub, twirling his fingers in the frothing bubbles. "How are you feeling? You sure you're up to this tonight?"

I raise a brow, refusing to succumb to my fears or my physical pain ever again. "Kye, I missed Rose's birthday party last year. I'm alive and awake. I may be weak, but there's no way I'm missing her New Year's bash. I'd bet money she's got a stash of tequila somewhere."

"Oh, most definitely. This is going to be good." He stands and starts for the door. "Guess I'll get dressed too. How long do you need?"

"Well, if midnight is in two hours, give me one."

"Do you need me to send anyone to help you?"

I shake my head. "That would ruin the surprise!"

Later, Kye returns to show me to a huge, elaborate hall decorated with glittering chandeliers and fresh flowers and tables laden with fancy foods. There's an open bar in one corner, and that's where I expect to find Rose, but she's on the dance floor with Gabe, sporting a short pixie haircut, and seems to be sober. Considering that she's wearing a slinky red dress that only covers her skin from the tops of her breasts to about mid-thigh, and shows only minimal scarring—it appears that she's recovering well.

My mother finds me first, pulling me into her arms and holding on tight. "I've missed you so much, baby girl," she says, still squeezing. "I'm so glad you're awake."

I cling to her, drawing from her unending well of strength. "Mom. I'm so sorry about Landon."

She sniffles, shaking her head. "Don't be. I survived losing your father, and I'll survive this too. As long as I have you, I will always, always be okay."

Too emotional to find words, I cling tighter until she lets go and urges me to join Rose's "Ode to New Beginnings" party.

Rose's parents find me next, and Linda is holding Cole. I kiss his downy head, reveling in the innocence of his sigh, and stroking his chubby cheek.

Tanya joins us, grinning. "Thank you. Thank you for coming to me in Phoenix. This place ... these people. I can't imagine going back to my old life now. Wouldn't want to for anything. I've finally found where I belong."

"So you're coming home to Jackson with us?" I ask.

She glances at Rose's mother, then mine. "It depends."

I sense Kye approaching, and my insides warm. "On what?"

"On whether you go back, or if you decide to stay here." Her quick shrug is meant to be casual, but it speaks volumes about her devotion. Tanya has joined our ranks.

Laughing, I squeeze her hard. "Hooray! You're going where I go."

"Don't leave me behind." Grinning, Kye offers me a glass of punch. I take a sip, relieved to discover that the only spike in it is sugar.

"Or me," Rose says, joining the circle with Gabe in tow.

"Or me," he adds.

"Well." I drain the punch and set my glass aside as a live cover band begins to play. "For all those hoping to go where I go, here's a tip." I point at the dance floor, where no one is doing anything more than standing. "Right now, I'm going to dance, despite my shaky, weak legs. If you want to follow my lead, meet me in my habitat."

And so they do. All of them. Rose and Gabe. Kye and me. Tanya and Cole, Linda and Barry Westover, Kiersten and Jonathan. Even Zane and the Jackson Dragons take turns dancing with Marian. In this room, no one is alone. We've lost so much this year. So many people we loved. Places and things and relationships. The cost of our battle won't be measured in the money spent on Kye's platinum card, or the lifetimes consumed by war, but in innocence lost and friendships forgotten.

Kye takes my elbow and leads the way, loaning his energy when mine is waning. I don't know if we're going to make it as a couple or not. I don't know if we'll go back to Jackson to live, or stay here and do something spectacular with this castle and its vineyards, lush with grapes. I'd like to think we could create a haven for the Gifted of all ages, a place where their energy wells may be filled at times when the world becomes more evil than good. But I don't know yet. I don't know who owns this place, or where Raina's money is, or what I want to do next. There are a lot of grown-up details to iron out, and Zane has assured me that first thing tomorrow, we've got important things to discuss.

But beyond all shadows of any doubt, I know that this is my last lifetime. After a curse of longer than 500 years, my destiny has been fulfilled. The future is a clean slate, and I can't afford to waste a single minute of it.

So I drag Kye and the rest of my newly extended family to the hardwood ballroom floor. And we ring in the New Year dancing.

EPILOGUE

Two Years Later: Dublin, Ireland

ABBY

A chilly drop of rain works past my trench coat and down my neck, adding a shiver on top of my nervous goosebumps. I glance from beneath my umbrella at the half-hidden face of my companion. "Are you ready for this?"

She shakes her head. "No, but I'm not sure I ever will be, and if we stand here much longer, we'll be soaked through. I don't want to have to answer for that."

"Oh goddesses. I'm a grown woman. I don't need your permission to go inside, and you aren't forcing me to stand here." But the tiny silver key feels exceptionally heavy on the chain around my neck.

She takes a cleansing breath, staring at the bright green door. "Well my feet are about frozen, and you can't afford to get sick. Not in your condition. Let's do this." With a nod of finality, my mother closes her umbrella and opens the door, scurrying inside. I follow close behind, shaking raindrops from my hair and tucking my collar tighter. I follow her along the row of mailboxes, wishing they were more clearly marked. After several minutes—during which I marvel at the ornate, iron fronts that are nothing short of exotic art to my American eye—we find it.

Box 203.

I draw the chain over my head and hand the key to Marian. "You should do the honors."

Panic parades across her face. "What if we're wrong? What if this isn't the right key? Or what if it's the right key, and we open the box, only to find it empty? We've come such a long way. What if—"

"Mom." I cup her frozen hand between both of mine. "It's the right key." The truth is, I don't know for sure. It may not be the one intended to fit this box. It may not be the right size. But it's the only one Gram saved, the only one Marian kept through all our moves, and when I touch it, I feel the past coming full circle. "Whatever happens, whatever's in this box—it's not going to change our lives drastically. The battle my dad was fighting is over."

"Right. You're right." Her hands tremble as she shoves the key into the lock, glancing at me once more. "Here goes." She twists, and we sigh in relief when it clicks and the door pops open.

Letters of all sizes, shapes, and colors slide to the floor, wrinkled and bent as if they've been crammed inside for all this time. I bend to retrieve them, but Marian stops me with a hand on my arm. "I'll get the ones on the floor, you clean out the box. I promised Christine I wouldn't let you overdo it."

"By bending?" I raise an amused brow, sticking my hand in the box to scoop out more letters than I'm going to be able to carry.

"You have three more months. If this wasn't so important, she would never have approved your travel plans." She sweeps the letters off the floor, her arms so full that she drops as many as she picks up. "My grandbaby is not going to be delivered by strangers in a foreign country."

"Mother, I'm a Healer too. If something was wrong, I'd know it. Trust me, I'm doing great, and so is the baby." Another bunch of letters slide out of my arms and onto the floor. "We're going to need a bag."

A postal worker pushing a cart down the aisle hears me and turns. He snags a reusable canvas bag from his cart and offers it to me. "That's a lot of mail, you've got there."

My mother laughs. "Well. It's been a few years since we emptied it."

He does a double take when he sees which box is ours. "I'll be damned. We been taking bets on how long this box would sit unchecked. I'd have to see the records, but it's been at least a decade."

I do the math in my head, and inform him, "Fifteen years."

"Aye," he answers in a lilting, musical accent. "Wonder if anyone guessed that. Would you mind staying here while I check? No one's going to believe this."

Laughing, my mother and I agree. When we've gathered the mail from my father's box, I lean against the wall, rubbing the basketball that was once my flat belly, and marveling at the movement inside. I married Kye on the two year anniversary of the day we met, and we're expecting our little one this spring.

After the last demon battle, we spent a year dating each other, while traveling back and forth between Jackson and the castle in Napa. We've had our ups and downs—and there were days I swore it was over between us, but by nightfall, I changed my mind. I always went back to him, and not only because of the nightmares that will plague me for the rest of my life.

His arms will always be my true home, and mine are his. Once I realized that, once we all realized that, it was only a matter of planning a party fit for royalty. In honor of those we lost in battle, we created a wedding to replicate Theron and Raina's—minus the terrible ending.

We've moved into the castle permanently, along with Marian, and Christine and Eoin—careful to keep our living spaces separate. Rose and Gabe are still in Jackson for now—but I suspect that they'll be married soon too, and then I hope they'll join us. I miss my best friend.

For months, we argued with the Dragons over who Raina's money belongs to now that Val is no longer there to oversee it. We wanted them to keep it—continue to fund their peace keeping—and they insisted that we take it to maintain the property in Napa. As a compromise, we turned the castle into a Royal Retreat where Gifted people can come to train, be Healed, re-energize, or simply be reminded that they're not alone—and asked the Dragons to run security for us. We've added private cottages nestled among the grapevines, and turned the dungeons into suites. We're set to accommodate a small army once we open in a few months.

For Christmas this year, Kye surprised me and my mother with this trip so we could finally uncover the mystery behind my father's secret Irish post office box. The bag of letters sits at my feet, a bright orange envelope glaring at me from the top of the pile.

"I want to open one," I tell my mother. "No use in keeping advertisements or junk."

She glares too, biting her lip the way she always does when she's afraid. "Right here? In public?"

"Yes." I bend to pick up the orange one, sliding my finger under the seal. "These people will never see us again anyway."

I unfold the yellowed paper, noting that the date is only six months old, and read aloud.

> *Dear Mr. Johnson,*
>
> *I hope my letter finds you well. I recently came across some correspondence between you and my father in which you discussed a gathering of Gifted individuals—a place where we could meet, be safe, and learn the ways of one another. I know my father opposed the idea, and though I understand why, I'm forced to disagree. I believe that like minds can gather and create good, and I long to be a part of something bigger than myself, to meet people who consider me normal, rather than different. I am lost, and begging to be found.*
>
> *I understand that many years have passed since your correspondence, but if by chance you've been successful in creating such a place, would you please forward me information on how and where to find it?*
>
> *Yours in common legacy,*
> *Peter O'Hare.*

Mom's eyes have filled, but I haven't seen her grin so large in a while. "He did it. They're letters to him. For so many years, people resisted his ideas, but those people's children are growing—and the shadows are no more." She digs into the bag and opens another letter, and then another. "They're all the same. The new generation, searching for each other, rising to noble heights. This was his dream."

As she continues opening more letters, the postal worker returns, hefting a bag that would rival Santa's red gift bag. "Fifteen years of letters that wouldn't fit into a tiny box. You sure you want to take them all home with ya?"

"Yes," we chorus.

My heart swells. While my mother follows the postal worker to work out a method of forwarding future letters, I slide out my phone and dial Kye—unable to wait until we get back to the hotel so he can see. He answers on the first ring. "You know how we've been searching for a way to spread the word about the Royal Retreat? I don't think that's going to be a problem. My father left us more business than we'll be able to handle."

Turns out, his dreams and my dreams were the same all along.

Nichole Giles, the author of DESCENDANT, BIRTHRIGHT, and WATER SO DEEP, has lived in Nevada, Arizona, Utah, and Texas. She is a huge fan of all things paranormal and magical. Her dreams include owning a garden full of fairies, riding a unicorn, and taming the pet dragon she adopted at a recent local ComiCon. His name is Zane. She also loves to spend time with her husband and four children, travel to tropical and exotic destinations, drive in the rain with the convertible top down, and play music at full volume so she can sing along.

Author's Note

In 2006, I set out to write a book about an extraordinary girl who led a lonely life. At the time, I wasn't sure why I was writing, who I was writing for, or exactly what story this girl was trying to tell. It took me over four years to find her story and get the words right. *Descendant* went through so many drafts that I lost count. The same can be said for rejections. Abby's story had a lot of interest from agents, and a couple of offers from publishers—but the number of rejections accumulated in the process added up to several hundred.

At one point, I decided to give up and move onto something new. My last round of submissions for *Descendant* was the result of a lost bet, so imagine my surprise when three months later I had phone calls scheduled with both agents and publishers to talk about my vision for this series. So much time had passed that I had discontinued my work on the series and was focused full speed on other projects. *Birthright* had been abandoned at the halfway point, and *Legacy*—it wasn't even a thought to me anymore. I knew that signing a publishing contract would mean revisiting a world I had left behind, and to be honest, I hesitated. If writing *Descendant* was cathartic, and *Birthright* was healing, I was absolutely certain that writing *Legacy* would be soul-crushing.

I signed anyway.

This series has brought me through more major-life and career changes than anyone will ever know, and the end result reflects some of that. This story would not be what it is if all three manuscripts had been complete when I first began to query. This story would not be what it has become if I had not evolved as a person in the last ten years.

I honestly don't know if the time span has made this series better or worse. But here I am, at the end, and I can finally look backward and be proud of what I've done, what I've written, and all

I've accomplished. Today I've reached a career milestone I thought would never come, a goal that so many times felt impossible.

The point of this note is this:

Finishing this series was a hard thing. Exhilarating and cathartic and wonderful and healing and terrible and soul-crushing and extremely, ridiculously hard. But I did it. And if I can do hard things, you can too.

YOU CAN DO HARD THINGS.

Wherever life takes you, whatever dreams keep you awake at night and haunt you in your quiet moments, I hope you aim higher than you can see, reach farther than you believe you can, and never, ever give up on the things that make you most happy. Every single person in this world has a unique Gift to share with the rest of us. It is yours, and yours alone. The world needs that part of you. I hope you find your Gift and cultivate it until it blooms into something that you can be proud of.

I believe in you.

Acknowledgements

This might be the shortest acknowledgment section I've ever written. Not because I'm not equally grateful, but because my list is bigger, longer, HUGER. And the people who are important to my life, career, and process will always be so. I hope you know who you are.

I would never have begun this journey, this career, without the unending support of the love of my life, Gary Giles. If I am the moon, you are the sun, whose reflection makes me better, brighter, bigger every single day. I cannot believe how lucky I am to be yours.

As if that isn't enough luck for one girl, I get to be mother to four of the most incredible people on this planet. Brayden, Brittany, Madison, and Mckay—you are the stars in my sky, the sand on my beach, the pebbles in my pond, and the seashells in my ocean. The four of you are the boat that keeps me afloat on the ocean of life. I will never stop being grateful that you left heaven to come and be mine.

Special thanks to Heather Justesen and Michelle Argyle for production assistance that will continue to remain unparalleled, to Elana Johnson for refusing to let me quit, no matter how often I threatened it, and to Tova Heaton for the constant reminders of how important one person's story can be.

Love and kisses to my parents and siblings, grandparents, extended family, the FABs, all my writer friends and industry contacts—none of whom I will list a third time, but who deserve a hailstorm of gratitude. I love you all so much. I could never be where I currently am without any and all of those people. I am so incredibly blessed to have you in my life.

And just in case any of you thinks that the end of this series means I need your support any less, you're wrong. I have a lot more stories to tell, so grab a bowl of popcorn and a drink and find a comfy seat on the train, because this journey isn't even close to finished.

Other Books by Nichole Giles

Water So Deep

The Descendant Series:
Descendant
Birthright
Legacy

www.ingramcontent.com/pod-product-compliance
Lightning Source LLC
Chambersburg PA
CBHW060342260626
47160CB00006B/2176